WHAT THE WOODS KEEP

WHAT THE WOODS KEEP

KATYA DE BECERRA

[Imprint]
MAKE YOUR MARK
NEW YORK

SQUARE
FISH

An imprint of Macmillan Publishing Group, LLC
120 Broadway, New York, NY 10271
fiercereads.com

Square Fish and the Square Fish logo are trademarks of Macmillan and are
used by Imprint under license from Macmillan.

Our books may be purchased in bulk for promotional, educational, or
business use. Please contact your local bookseller or the Macmillan Corporate
and Premium Sales Department at (800) 221-7945 ext. 5442 or
by email at MacmillanSpecialMarkets@macmillan.com.

ISBN 978-1-250-21167-5 (paperback)   ISBN 978-1-250-17063-7 (ebook)

[Imprint]
MAKE YOUR MARK

@ImprintReads
Originally published in the United States by Imprint
First Square Fish edition, 2019
Book designed by Heather Palisi and Natalie C. Sousa
Square Fish logo designed by Filomena Tuosto
Imprint logo designed by Amanda Spielman

10 9 8 7 6 5 4 3 2 1

LEXILE: 860L

To you who steals this book, beware—
Bad luck will trail you everywhere,
You'll be plagued by gruesome forces and far worse,
For unleashing this book's Nibelungen curse.

To Jorge and my parents

What you seek is seeking you.
Rumi

WHAT THE WOODS KEEP

1
MY INHERITANCE

Eyes glued shut with sleep, I scramble around for my techno-pop–blasting cell phone.

WITHHELD NUMBER.

After a short deliberation, I decide to risk it and accept the call.

"Happy birthday, Hayden!" Doreen Arimoff's sweet-and-sour voice is like a bucket of ice, exorcising sleep from my head.

(Doreen is *ancient*. She's been in my family's employ since before Mom went missing. And back then Doreen already looked like an unwrapped mummy, though impeccably made-up, elegantly fake-tanned, and manicured to perfection.)

This is the first time Doreen has called me directly instead of communicating with me via my father. "Now that you've turned eighteen," she says, "I have a stipulation from your mother's will to execute. Come by my office today, and we'll go over the paperwork. No need to make an appointment."

Doreen's straight-to-the-point manner fails to hide her voice's tremble at "paperwork." And Doreen's voice never trembles.

"Paperwork?" I rub my forehead. A spike of headache brings back the half-forgotten dream I had last night. The dream featured me (wearing full-body armor, origin unknown) riding a huge black horse-beast and leading an army through fog-layered swamps and burnt fields and ravaged cities. White birds—ravens?—rained down on me and my army while my warriors' battle cries permeated the night. *We'll rise again!*

I blink my vision clear. *I need coffee. Now.*

"Just come by my office, Hayden," Doreen says. "I'll explain everything. Oh, and, Hayden? It'd be best if your father didn't know about our conversation. At least not until I sign your mother's things over to you."

Doreen hangs up, leaving me with many questions.

A burst of impatient footsteps outside my door reminds me that Del Chauvet—aspiring fashion star, French-Senegalese Brooklynite, and my long-suffering roommate—is waiting for me to wake up. I know she's got questions about what exactly happened yesterday: as in, how I managed to scare off a guy *this time*. Del is the mastermind behind my fiasco of a blind date, who left me stood up and battling the storm of the century in Central Park last night. (If that was Del's idea of a "perfect prebirthday present," I fear what her actual birthday present might be.) Del's impatience is tangible through the door, but she'll have to wait.

I strip off and shuffle into the shower, icy floor tiles unfriendly under my feet. As I stand below the hot stream with my eyes closed, flashbacks, dreams, and memories spin in my head.

Dark trees. Whispers in a foreign tongue, its sound harsh. And then there's Mom, watching me from behind a tree, a sad smile on her lips. Always sad. As if Mom knew what was coming—her disappearance in the woods surrounding my childhood home. Today, my memories of Mom are like photographs rescued from a burning house, the edges darkened, middles smudged with soot. Tainted. Vague. Incomplete.

Do not be angry with the dead, my therapist, Dr. Erich, told me again and again over the years of treatment. *They're long gone, and we remain, tasked with figuring out our lives, which go on.* My response to him? *Technically, my mother is missing, not dead.* (Eventually she was declared dead *in absentia*, but that came much later.) Dr. Erich would shake his head slowly, his disappointment palpable. But it wasn't denial that motivated me. It was a compulsion to call things by their true names.

After finishing the shower and blow-drying my hair, I dance into my skinny jeans and put on a tailored cardigan over one of my Hendrix tees. I grab my old, age-ravaged messenger bag and head for my bedroom door.

I can't help the electricity running over my skin. It's like the last ten years didn't happen, and all the progress I made in Dr. Erich's office means nothing, because the simple mention of my missing-presumed-dead mother shrinks my heart into a peanut-size chunk of muscle and blood while my eyes fog up, threatened by unwanted tears.

A long time ago now, in the name of self-preservation, I chose to put Mom's memory behind me, but Doreen's mysterious phone call promises a change, a revelation, ten years after Mom's unfortunate walk in the woods.

I forget all about Del and my failed date, and even about Del's plans concerning my birthday, as I leave my bedroom and head for the exit, determined to face head-on what Doreen has in store for me.

2
MEET THE FAMILY:
DAD, MOM, AND
THE NIBELUNGS

Everything and everyone on Earth is governed by invisible forces lurking just out of reach. For instance, consider the reasons why we don't drift off into the oxygen-deprived space to our deaths but keep our feet firmly on the ground. Thank you, gravity!

My life's no exception. If anything, the number of forces I'm governed by is somewhat higher than normal.

There's a force called *Dad*.

Even with the uncomfortable distance that descended upon us after Mom's disappearance—a distance that seems to be growing bigger every day—Dad still tries to control what I do, where I go, and who I'm friends with. He does it to protect me, or so he says. To overcome this controlling-from-a-distance thing that he does, I stopped telling him what I'm really up to long ago. If ignorance is bliss, then my father's ignorance in regard to my life post-therapy must be one big bucket of undiluted joy.

And then there's a force called *Mom*.

Long gone but not forgotten and still very much present in my life, even attempting to dominate it by haunting my dreams and, as it turns out, by conspiring with our family lawyer to reach out to me from beyond the grave.

Oh, and there's also a force called *Del*. She's forever seeking to improve me—everything from my hairstyle to my dating situation. I'm like one of her vintage dress projects. Who knows? Maybe one day she'll fix me, at long last.

But for now? I'm stuck in the middle, torn asunder by conflicting forces while trying to make sense of things on my own. And when I struggle to understand things that happen to me, I interpret them by applying physical principles, translating it all into a language I *can* comprehend.

I grew up surrounded by all things physics. My dad, Thomas Holland, is a physicist. Or he *was* a physicist before he let his unhealthy obsession with conspiracy theories and Germanic mythologies overtake his research and his life. Dad's academic career imploded after he decided his students needed to know that a legendary warrior race called the Nibelungs (immortalized by the epic poem *Nibelungenlied*, Wagner's opera *The Ring of the Nibelung*, and referenced throughout Tolkien's books) were going to spill into our world via a muon-enabled portal and conquer us all.

Yeah.

Dad lost his university tenure *and* his PhD students *and* got exiled from his beloved physics labs. Now he relies on my aunt's charity, going on with his otherworldly "science" projects out of her spare bedroom. But despite Dad's academic down-fall, I still rely on physics (the real physics, not the crackpot kind) to keep me sane.

It works. Mostly.

ᚠᚷᚠ

My attempt to leave the apartment unnoticed fails. Del inter-cepts me in what passes for our living room. (We have a der-elict coffee table; old, balding carpet; and an antique fireplace we're not allowed to use because—according to our real estate agent—it's a fire hazard.)

In her Disney pajamas and fluffy slippers, Del is a vision of gold, silver, and pink. She has that enviable talent of rolling out of bed in the morning, already gorgeous. Her hair is a halo of tight black curls, and her hazel eyes are focused, hawklike, on me. A red velvet cupcake, its middle pierced by a tiny, burning candle, is her birthday offering to me as she breaks into an off-key, jazzy version of "Happy Birthday." Her French accent is more prom-inent than usual—the only sign she's still not quite fully awake.

She stops singing abruptly, noticing I'm dressed to go out. "Where do you think you're going?"

"To get us some coffee." It's only a half lie. "The good stuff." In one fluid motion, I approach her and blow out the candle.

Seeing right through me, Del sets the cupcake on the cof-fee table and crosses her arms over her chest. "It's Ross, isn't it? What did he say to you? Is that why you didn't wait up for me last night? *How bad was it?*" The words come out in a rapid stream, her cheeks reddening. She's visibly pissed off that the blind date she orchestrated for me crashed and burned.

"Ross never showed yesterday." I don't sound as ticked off as I probably should. The truth is, my pride is hurt, but I'm also kind of glad this Ross person stood me up. I don't need Del's help to get dates. . . . Okay, maybe I do, but I'm never going to admit it to her.

She doesn't need to know this, but the last time I was on anything resembling a "date" was when I was just over seven and Shannon Reaser, the boy next door, was nine. This was back in Promise, Colorado. We were out in the woods, playing hide-and-seek. We always played in those woods, and it was always silly and innocent. . . . But that one time, it was different. I slipped and fell, and when Shannon helped me up, he didn't let go of my hand. We held hands as we walked back home, and I remember that wild sensation of my heart about to jump out of my chest. . . .

When I think of Shannon now, I get this blurry image: features undefined, all except for clear, soft-gray eyes and dark, windswept hair. I wonder what he looks like now. I wonder if he remembers me.

Oblivious to the unexpected storm of memories raging in my head, Del shrugs. "Perhaps it's better that way. . . . One of my little spies informed me this morning that Ross was asking around about you long before he even approached me to set up this date. Like he was digging into your family or something creepy like that."

"Why would he be digging?" My shoulders get stiff, and I wonder if Del notices. "And if he's so interested in my family, why didn't he show up yesterday and ask me whatever he wanted to know?"

"I guess we'll never know. Whatever. Changing the topic, I thought today we'd eat ice cream for breakfast and have a movie marathon till noon-ish and then I'm taking you out for a surprise field trip. And look what I got you!" Del rushes into her bedroom and returns with a Blu-ray in hand.

I'm about to scoff at her ice cream–eating idea (I'm not going through a breakup, nor have I just lost a loyal canine friend) when I notice the title of the movie she bought me. "You found it!" I take the Blu-ray from her hands and adore the cover image in all its bloody, gory glory: a white-eyed man, his mouth twisted in a silent scream because his head's about to explode. The cinematic masterpiece that is Cronenberg's *Scanners*.

"Have I told you what an awesome friend you are?" I smile at Del.

She grins back. "Not lately. And nowhere near enough."

"I'm totally going to have to rectify that." My smile turns sheepish as I put the Blu-ray on the table, next to my untouched birthday cupcake. "Rain check?"

Del's grin falters. "I have the whole day planned out for us."

"And I'm looking forward to spending my birthday with you. I just have a little chore to do first."

"And that chore is *not* getting us some good coffee, I suspect."

"I'll get our caffeine fix on my way back. Doubleshot for you. My treat." I'm not sure exactly why I'm being secretive with her. It's kind of cruel, really. Del has zero tolerance for any kind of mystery; she reads a book's last chapter first to know what's coming. But the memory of that unsettling tremble in Doreen's voice makes me keep my mouth shut.

Eventually, Del lets me go. But not before she tricks me into a birthday video chat with her parents. Del's good-looking older brother is also there, waving at me from the screen and wishing me a *very* happy birthday.

Ironically, I have more contact with Del's family than I do with my own father. And speaking of Dad, he's keeping his distance this morning, which wouldn't be the first time he's been low-key about my birthday. But with this being the first birthday I'm celebrating while living on my own, I'd expect at least *some* interest on his part. Of course, there's a pretty strong chance he forgot about it altogether. I dig into the dark matter of my brain in an attempt to establish how I feel about it and conclude that it hurts. But I can't allow myself to care about this distance between me and my father, the same way I can't let myself go dark with grief for Mom all over again. Because if I do, the next moment, I'll be neck-deep in self-pity and won't be able to see straight.

So I do what I always do when it hurts. I ignore it and busy myself with the here and now, hoping that I can trick myself into being normal. That is, if *normal* is even a word that can be used to describe anything to do with my family.

PERSONAL AND CONFIDENTIAL

December 17

Dr. Thomas Holland
Professor of Applied Physics
Faculty of Physics and Natural Sciences
Ian Trainor University

Dear Dr. Holland,

It is my solemn duty to inform you that, following due process, the investigation panel has ruled to revoke your tenure, effective immediately.

The revocation is on the grounds of numerous counts of academic misconduct, including several attempts to publish falsified data and inclusion of unauthorized material in your graduate lectures. You are, as such, to cease citing your affiliation with Ian Trainor University in all your future endeavors, specifically in relation to your misguided interests in Germanic mythologies and their alleged links to the field of multidimensional physics and string theory.

The panel has instructed the MacEvans Fund to freeze any remaining funds they have allocated for your research in the field of string theory. We are awaiting a legal decision to be made in regard to the portion of the funds that have already been misappropriated by you in pursuit of your pseudoscientific ideas. Your laboratories are to be repurposed and staff reassigned as seen fit by the dean of the Faculty of Physics and Natural Sciences.

Your graduate students (Ms. Arista Kazan, Ms. Du Yi, Ms. An Bo, and Mr. Oliver Pritchett) will be assigned new research supervisors, who will, in turn, endeavor to review and revise your former students' dissertation topics.

Ms. Arista Kazan, who, in addition to being your student, was also in your employ as a research assistant, will face an independent investigation into her own two counts of academic misconduct, which occurred while under your supervision.

Your access to your office and physics laboratories has been revoked. Your personal belongings will be shipped to your current residential address in due course. Please do not attempt to enter the university premises following the receipt of this letter.

On behalf of the Ian Trainor University administration, I wish you all the best in your future endeavors.

Sincerely,

ERT

Hon. Edmund Rogers-Tanner
Distinguished Professor and Tenure Panel Chair
CC: Professor Alberta Mennard
Provost of Ian Trainor University
Professor Ignacio Gularte
Dean of the Faculty of Physics and Natural Sciences

3

UPON THREE CONDITIONS: PART 1

The building where Doreen keeps her practice is nestled between a Jewish deli and an old-fashioned barbershop. As I enter the reception area, Marcia, Doreen's secretary, sets her dark eyes on me with interest. Her forbidding mouth forms a reluctant smile.

"She's expecting you. Go right in."

Despite her instructions, I knock twice before opening the door.

I haven't been inside Doreen's musty office since that *bad* day. My last day at Stonebrook Academy. The day I smashed Jen Rickman's head against a mirror. (At least, that's what everyone believes happened.) Back then, Doreen negotiated a deal with Jen's parents. This deal landed me in homeschooling purgatory and Dr. Erich's care for years to come. I was eight years old when I first met Dr. Erich and almost seventeen when I said my farewells to him at last. The years of my life in between were one big lump of suffocating, medicated fog. Thinking now of Jen and her bloodied hands hovering protectively over her face—and the long oblivion that followed—I wait for the shivers of meds withdrawal to rattle me, but to my surprise I'm as calm as a Cirque de Soleil acrobat in the middle of a death-defying act. No queasiness in the pit of my stomach. No dark stars clouding my vision. Maybe I'm moving on at last. Maybe I'm putting my past behind me, where it belongs, just as Dr. Erich promised I one day would. Is today that day?

"Hayden, darling, take a seat," Doreen says, bringing me back to Earth.

In her thronelike chair towering over a scratched-up redwood desk, Doreen sits tall, the proud ruler of her kingdom-turning-wasteland. (She's going broke; her once-moderately successful practice's now barely scraping up enough income to pay rent, since most of Doreen's clients are no longer among the living and she's too proud or too cheap to advertise and attract new ones.)

I perch on the edge of the chair facing Doreen, the desk between us.

"Does Tom . . . Does your father know you're here?" she asks.

A subtle tremble of her lips appears and vanishes in a blink. Maybe the reason she's all rattled is *me*—I'm what's making good old Doreen nervous, and she'd rather not have me in her office but has no choice. I feel sorry for her, just like I felt sorry for Dr. Erich every time my presence in his office made him uncomfortable and edgy. I have that effect on people—sometimes even on my own father. Del's the only exception, apparently immune to my uncanny "charm." Well, Shannon was immune, too, but he never got to know the grown-up me.

"Nope," I say. "I haven't talked to him today. Not yet."

Doreen purses her lips, a maze of wrinkles forming around her well-lipsticked mouth. Small talk's not her forte. She studies me, and when I start to grow itchy under her stare, she says, "Tom isn't going to like this. Not one bit. He went out of his way to keep Ella's legacy away from you . . . but I'm legally obligated to execute your mother's will, you see. Did you know your mother made special arrangements with me only weeks before her . . . demise, so I'd approach you on the day of your eighteenth birthday and ensure you come into possession of . . . certain items?"

"No, I wasn't aware of that."

The sound of my mother's name, twisted by Doreen's lips into something brittle and sweet, rings in my ears long after it's spoken. I don't think of Mom as *Ella*. *Ella* is for missing-person reports and obituaries, not for my ears or my private thoughts. Her name doesn't belong among the living.

Doreen clears her throat. "Very well."

She stands up, an effort on her part. I follow Doreen's sagging form as it moves about the room, stopping before a vault, poorly concealed behind a tacky painting of a meadow. That painting was here when I was being kicked out of Stonebrook. Some things never change. I focus on Doreen's back as a combination is entered and the vault door creaks open. Doreen shuffles back to the desk, her gnarled hands gripping two yellowed A4 envelopes. Dust and mothball-scented air tickles my nose, making me want to sneeze.

Without an explanation, Doreen hands me one of the envelopes. I stare at it dumbly. The paper is frail against my fingertips. The envelope is marked with my name, written in a flowing cursive. (Mom's handwriting? I wouldn't remember.) I inspect my emotions: nothing but a twinge of curiosity. There are times I worry that my therapy years have rendered me so cautious that, to an unsuspecting observer, I might come off as a robot. It still takes me a few breaths to figure out an appropriate reaction sometimes, but I'm getting better at it.

Doreen nods at the envelope in my hands. "For your eyes only."

She produces a letter opener from a drawer and rips open the second envelope's belly with a single flick of a wrist. Like gutting a rabbit. The delicate sheet of paper she extracts from the envelope quivers in her hands, and her ancient mouth squeezes out the reality-bending words:

"This is a codicil to the last will and testament of Ella Townsend-Holland. It reads: 'To my only child, my daughter, Hayden Bellatrix Holland, on her eighteenth birthday, I bequeath my family estate, known as the Holland Manor, situated in Promise, Colorado . . .'"

Codicil to the Last Will and Testament of
Ella Townsend-Holland

I, Ella Townsend-Holland, of 33 Glastonberry Grove Lane, Promise, Colorado, declare that this is a codicil to my Last Will and Testament.

To my only child, my daughter, Hayden Bellatrix Holland, on her eighteenth birthday, I bequeath my family estate, known as the Holland Manor, situated in Promise, Colorado, upon three conditions.

My first condition is that Hayden goes to the Manor and looks for the gifts I left her. They'll call to her. She needs to listen with her blood.

My second condition is that Hayden uses my gifts to destroy my darkest secret—my hidden treasure, my heaviest burden.

My third and final condition is that Hayden trusts no one where my treasure is concerned, especially the ravens.

Ella Townsend-Holland

Ella Townsend-Holland

Witnessed by Doreen Arimoff and Marcia Strauss

4

UPON THREE CONDITIONS:
PART 2

The cold grip of an invisible hand squeezes my heart and doesn't let go. The whitewashed walls of Doreen's office waltz around me in a drunken, merry circle while my brain processes what I've just heard.

The Manor? Promise? Mom's darkest secret? Her burden?

"Any questions?" Doreen asks when she finishes reading what must be the most bizarre section of a last will and testament ever created (and I include in this list Houdini's request that his wife conduct a yearly séance to communicate with his spirit).

"Where do I start?"

But Doreen's eyes tell me she's as befuddled as I am. So I push back my questions with a shrug. Doreen deflates, her eyes moving to the second envelope I clutch with both hands. When she leans forward, her interest thick and tangible in the stale air between us, I lean back. Irrationally, I expect her to jump me, to wrestle the envelope and its secrets from my hands. My fingers whiten as they grip the envelope tighter.

Relaxing back into her chair, Doreen produces a plastic folder from a file cabinet to her left. "Well then, here's the deed to Holland Manor. In your name." I gingerly accept the folder. "I presume you'd like me to identify some good real estate agents in Denver? I have some connections there. I could negotiate a nice deal for you."

"A deal?" I ask.

"You'd like to sell the house, yes? Legally, Ella's conditions are nonenforceable, you know, so no one can make you go there and look for her 'deadliest secret' or whatever. Besides, considering how old the estate is, it's best not to wait much longer before getting an expert opinion on the property's value. . . ."

"I don't think I want to . . . sell it." My words take me by surprise. Why wouldn't I want to sell an old manor? I have no interest in moving out of my cozy Fort Greene lair and into the shivery sticks somewhere in the middle of nowhere, right? *Right?* Besides, despite his distance and all, Dad would not be happy to hear that I'm even considering . . . But what is it, exactly, I'm considering?

"Don't be silly, Hayden." Doreen's patronizing tone immediately makes me want to say something biting in response. Instead, I grab the paperwork, stuff it into my messenger bag, and leave Doreen's office in a flurry of dust.

Drunk on the oddness of it all, I hurry home, though not before getting two to-go coffees and some bagels with cream cheese from the deli next to Doreen's office. With the deed to Holland Manor and my mother's mysterious, unopened letter burning holes in my bag, I fly through the streets all the way back to my brownstone haven.

Appendix to Patient Admittance Form

PATIENT'S NAME: Hayden B. Holland

AGE: eight years, eleven months

HAIR: dark blond

HEIGHT: four feet, three inches

WEIGHT: eighty-two pounds

DATE: February 26

EYE COLOR: left eye is green; right eye is light brown

TREATING THERAPIST: Dr. Thorfinn Erich (BS, MD, DO, PhD)

APPENDIX A: TREATING THERAPIST'S NOTES:

Slight dark shadows underneath her eyes; lips badly bitten. According to her father, Hayden's lack of appetite has been an ongoing problem.

Only child of Thomas Holland and late Ella Townsend-Holland. Father: tenured physics professor; currently under investigation ("persecution," in own words) because of unorthodox ideas.

The child was referred to my practice following a court mandate issued as a result of a settlement between the administration of her former school and the parents of another student (one Jennifer Rickman), who suffered injuries as a result of a confrontation with Hayden.

No prior violent episodes on Hayden's record.

Earlier this year: The child experienced a traumatic event (mother went missing in the woods) that led to family's relocation from Colorado to NYC. Police suspected foul play; but the investigation came to a halt due to a lack of credible leads.

For someone who had recently lost a spouse under mysterious circumstances, father appears calm and distant. My research into the Holland family only brought up a small piece of news circulated briefly about a Colorado local going missing. I was intrigued by Hayden and her family even before I met the child in person.

First impression: The child is calm, serious, soft-spoken. Minutes into our meeting, she made a joke about Einstein's theory of relativity. First time in my long practice that an eight-year-old explained Einstein to me, sounding like she knows what she's talking about and not simply repeating what she heard in the house.

Counterbalancing moments of clarity, the child tends to retreat into her own world, sometimes while in the middle of a conversation. Subsequently, she stays quiet for long periods of time, staring off into space. I would generally interpret these moments as a defensive response to a recent trauma, but with this patient, I'm not so sure. I'm not fully convinced that she's really "out of it" during those pauses. Could this be a ploy on her part to evade my questioning when the prodding gets too intense?

When asked why she attacked her classmate, the child kept altering her story. The reasons changed from being bullied to it all being an "accident." In response to my challenge of her shifting narrative, the child proceeded to have one of her quiet episodes.

When discussing my evaluation with her father, I sense an overall unease in him, but he would not elaborate as to the source of his obvious tension. At one point he remarked how, even though it was his child under psychiatric observation, it felt like he was the one under the microscope. I had to let it go.

Suggested treatment plan: Recommendation for regular counseling sessions and cognitive behavior therapy, followed by a review after six months. If no improvement is shown, consider medication.

5
PUZZLE ME THIS

According to Isaac Newton's *third law of motion*, every action of a force produces an equal and opposite reaction. In other words, what goes up must come down. Or: Every force has a doppelgänger that masquerades as its double but really is its opposite. Get it?

My opposing force must be Delphine Chauvet, aka Del.

I didn't like Del very much when we first moved in together half a year ago. Our alliance was one of convenience. I was taking a year off before starting college, and I needed a place to live—a place my tiny allowance could afford. I was months out of therapy by then and deciding what to do next. The possibility of having to spend another day under my father's stifling roof was making me want to scream. (Well, technically it was my aunt's roof, but my father was the one making it stifling for me to live there.) I'd had enough of listening to him mumble about the Nibelungs nonstop, curse his former employer, and conspire over the phone with his devoted research assistant, Arista.

As the gods of good timing had it, while I was looking for a place of my own, Del was being pushed out of her Jersey loft by her roommate, who was eager to move in with her girlfriend. The planets aligned, Del responded to my ROOMMATE WANTED ad, and the next thing I knew the two of us were screaming insults (me in English, Del mostly in French) as we forced our moving boxes up the rustic stairwell like a pair of angry but determined ants.

Our first days of living together were tough. The things I couldn't stand about Del included the following: her collection of ridiculous vintage clothing that wouldn't fit in her bedroom and required additional space in the living room; her on-and-off boyfriend, Bolin, who took an instant dislike of me; and her unceasing aspiration to give me a makeover and get my romantic life going. Her recent attempts at matchmaking (Ross, etc.) are just the tip of the iceberg.

It took me a month to warm up to Del. Her adoration of sci-fi movies (the more outlandish, the better) was what tipped the friendship scales in her favor. She confessed later that it was sisterly love at first sight for her, from the moment she first saw my freckled nose and "witchy eyes." By the fourth week in our dilapidated Fort Greene haven, our spirits high on *Buffy* and cheap tequila, we made a pact: to watch all sci-fi movies ever made; to always have each other's backs; and to grow old together, or at least side by side, in case we ever moved out of our brownstone fortress.

I know that Del's been planning my birthday activities for the past month, if not longer. So I feel doubly bad for not knocking on her bedroom door immediately after I return home from my morning detour to Doreen's office.

Still dazed after Doreen's reading of the codicil to my mother's will, I leave my deli haul on the kitchen island and sneak into my room. There, I skim through the deed to the Manor. My busy mind's already going through the logistics. I have some money in savings but nothing to get excited about and definitely not enough to finance airfare to Colorado. My very modest trust fund is off-limits. That leaves my emergency-only credit card. How long will it take Dad to notice if I dip into my line of credit?

With stiff fingers, I open the sealed envelope containing my mother's letter, intended "for my eyes only." Unlike Doreen, I own no letter openers, so my hasty work on the envelope is far removed from her skillful single cut. My impatient fingers tear the envelope into uneven bits.

Inside I find a flash-card-size piece of hard, glossy paper: a gorgeous medieval print of a girl in a long, midnight-blue gown. A dragonlike creature the size of a porcupine is curled at her bare feet. A string of runic symbols is woven around the girl's shape like a halo, covering her entire silhouette, including the spiky creature below her. The girl's widespread hands hold two objects: a bleeding heart (not a heart symbol, but a real one, like from the biology books) and a transparent cup filled with red liquid. The back of the card is covered with familiar, left-leaning writing:

My Hayden,

The greatest power comes from within you. Dig deep. Your hands can handle the heat. In the house on the edge of the woods, the rotten key lies. Yours to finish what I started. Ravens will watch your every step—hold your cards close, keep the birds of prey at a safe distance, and show them you're one of them.

A sheen of cold sweat coats my palms. Mom's presence in the room is elephant-huge. That forest-saturated scent that permeates my memories of her invades my airways now. I want to (need to) scream.

I don't scream, of course. Instead, I set the card aside.

Sitting prim and collected on the edge of my bed, I challenge my mind to produce a single clear memory of my mother. But there are none. Don't get me wrong: I have a whole mental trove of Mom memories, it's just that none of them is something I can hold on to. My mother remains elusive, in the periphery of my vision—there and not-there, dead and alive, like Schrödinger's theoretical cat, its state altering the moment I focus on it.

It's been a decade since I last heard Mom's voice, spoke to her, looked at her. Having her message addressed to me, right here in my hands *now*, it's like all those years never happened. Like Mom never left at all, just took an extended leave and is now back, terrifyingly alive, an uncanny revenant. Would she like this grown-up version of me? A girl raised on books and wishes, brought up by strangers, shaped and polished in doctors' offices? What would she think of me? Would she be proud? Would she love me?

My pondering is interrupted by the bang of a slamming door. Del's frantic footsteps remind me I have friend duties to attend to. Having no better place to hide stuff, I stick the deed to the Manor, the codicil, and Mom's cryptic message under my pillow. My disheveled thoughts and feelings recede back into the dark crevices of my mind, waiting for my next moment of weakness so they can raise their scaly heads above the surface.

I find Del right outside my door: She's all dolled up, her hair pulled into a chic, loose bun, with a few tight curls escaping to frame her lovely heart-shaped face.

Her mouth full of bagel, she asks, "Done with your chore?"

"You're welcome." I eye the bagel in her hand. "And yeah, all done."

"Secrets are bad for the soul." A headshake of disapproval. "Sharing is easy. Let me show you how it's done. I lost my virginity at the age of seventeen to a dashing barista in the back of his Mustang."

"Doesn't sound very comfortable."

"Memorable, though. And now you know one of my dearest secrets. Your turn."

"I don't have any secrets. My life's boring and so am I." I make my way to the kitchen and start on my bagel. After taking a sip of now-cold coffee and fighting the urge to spit it out, I shove the paper cup into the microwave and count off the seconds it takes to reheat.

Del watches me, then pouts a little. "But I have abandonment issues! And you've been kind of aloof lately. More than usual, that is."

We mirror each other's movements as we sit on the floor on opposite sides of our battered coffee table. Obviously, I'm on fire to tell Del about my morning adventure at Doreen's and desperate to hear Del's opinion on Mom's weird conditions. But that means I'd have to tell her all about Promise and Mom's disappearance, and once I start talking, I won't be able to stop, and then Del will know the real extent of how messed up I am.

Del's eyes plead with me, and I break. A little. "I'm thinking about a spontaneous trip," I say.

Del's eyes grow excited. "Where to?"

"Colorado."

A puzzled look. "What's in Colorado?"

"Promise. It's a town. I used to live there, before . . ." I trail off. "Before New York."

There are times I forget what Del knows and what she doesn't. She knows my mother's been missing for years and is declared dead in absentia. What she doesn't know is that the night Mom went missing, the local woods of Promise, for lack of a better word, *erupted*, forming a new clearing in the process. More of a crater, really. As if a burning giant's foot stepped down into the woods, the trees were stomped to the ground, and the grass was burned off. If I didn't know better, I'd say that the night of Mom's disappearance, Promise became the landing site of a small meteorite. But there were no meteorite sightings recorded anywhere in Colorado that night—I checked. No bangs of explosions heard. No flashes of light seen. The local police and fire departments declared it a freak forest fire that burned itself out. Their main theory was that my mother set it and then skipped town.

"As of this morning, I own my family estate in Promise." I watch Del's lips stretch into a perfect little O. "Dad isn't going to be happy about that. He was very thorough when he cut off all connections I had to Promise after Mom disappeared. But I guess he has no control over what Mom planned for me while she was still around. She stipulated in her will that I get the house the day I turn eighteen."

"So that's what your mystery chore was." Del overcomes her surprise enough to speak. "What are you going to do? I mean, about the house? This is huge!"

"I-I know the logical thing would be to sell it. I don't see myself moving to Colorado, but I want to at least have a look at the old place, maybe spend a week there before I let it go. Is that too bizarre, that I want to go back to a place where nothing good has ever happened to me?"

My question is rhetorical, and I don't expect Del to answer. She doesn't. Also, I'm not being completely honest with her, and, knowing how perceptive she is, it's likely she can hear the deception in my voice. Some good things *did* happen to me in Promise. Lots of good things. Take the woods, their dark calm, their unending welcome, their unwavering acceptance of me. On days when Mom wasn't tormented by her demons, she took me deep into the woods and we'd roam for hours, petting the wet moss, collecting strange flowers that grew in the shadowed corners, and listening to the sounds of birds and animals before returning to the Manor for the simple lunch Dad would make for us.

And then there was Shannon. The boy next door, my first friend—my only friend back then. Would he still be living in the house next to the Manor? When I left Promise as a child, I cried about losing the safe haven of my forest and Mom's beloved Manor, but most of all I was devastated because leaving town meant leaving Shannon. We didn't even have a chance to say good-bye. One morning I woke up to Dad telling me I had an hour to pack; the rest of our stuff would be shipped to our new home. I thought of running away, of going to the woods and staying there, eventually becoming a wild girl reared by animals and nourishing myself with berries and roots, but Dad picked me up, packed me into his car with the luggage, and just took off. And that was it.

After we settled in New York, I wrote to Shannon regularly. At least, I did until the therapy started and I lost days, weeks, and even entire months to Dr. Erich's treatment. Since my father was in complete control of my life back then, there's a good chance that none of my letters actually got mailed. Or maybe Shannon moved away or simply moved on. Whatever the reason, I never heard back, and eventually I stopped writing.

"Can I come with you?" Del asks, sounding uncharacteristically timid.

"Don't you have your group project to work on during the break? And what about Bolin?"

She waves her hand in dismissal. "Bolin and I are through. Done. Never again. And I can work on my project while you do your soul-searching or whatever."

I consider it. I've never traveled by myself before. It'd be nice to have a travel buddy. And Del tagging along to my homecoming trip means I'd have a shoulder to cry on if being bombarded by sad memories gets too tough.

"First let's see how much plane tickets cost, and—"

Del doesn't let me finish. She launches out of her spot on the floor to clasp me in a breath-ending hug. "Let me worry about that! Oh, and happy birthday, Hayden!"

URBAN TERRORS
The Stonebrook Incident: Unveiling the Facts

by Ross Hidalgo

Note: Doreen Arimoff, lawyer for the Holland family, has requested we remove this investigative report under allegations of fraud, defamation, and invasion of privacy. The Urban Terrors blogmasters are reviewing her request.

An episode of horrific violence, which in local urban lore came to be known as the "Stonebrook Incident," took place ten years ago on a gloomy September day in an idyllic corner of Long Island. The ghosts of what happened that day still haunt the halls of Stonebrook Academy and the minds of all involved, including the victim and the perpetrator.

My investigation began in the living room of the Academy's former headmistress, Ms. Belinda O'Reilly. Now retired, Ms. O'Reilly fondly remembers Jennifer Rickman, a kind and popular girl, who at the age of nine suffered severe cuts to her hands, head, and face after being thrust into a bathroom mirror by classmate Hayden Holland.

Fingers wrapped around a steaming cup of coffee, Ms. O'Reilly recalls a school assembly that day. The assembly was called to calm the student body after a young pupil's gruesome discovery: Eight birds had crashed to the ground for no apparent reason, inexplicably dead. The boy who found the dead birds had smeared their blood all over his face and would not stop screaming. He had to be sedated and kept on school premises as unusually stormy weather prevented his parents from picking him up promptly. To make matters worse, the Academy's grounds had been partially flooded by the storm, and an old oak tree that served as the Academy's symbol, its image decorating the school's emblem, was struck by lightning and split in half. All these creepy events added to the foreboding background for an incident that shook the Academy to its core.

"I still get shivers when I think about it," Ms. O'Reilly says, recalling how the atmosphere in the darkening halls of the Academy was growing tense with anxiety. "Those bulging black clouds hanging over our school . . . like a curse in the making. And all those dead birds. Hayden's stone-cold face! And blood flowing from the wounds on Jen's forehead and cheeks, her nose smashed in, her lips a gory mess . . ."

Ms. O'Reilly was called to the scene—a girls' bathroom—after a student named Hayden Holland attacked Rickman. Like most students and staff that day, Ms. O'Reilly only saw the aftermath of the attack. The sole eyewitness to the event was Ms. Aileen Lancaster, a geography teacher. My attempts at locating Ms. Lancaster for an interview hit a dead end; she has no digital presence or accurate records that I can locate.

On the other hand, Rickman agreed to meet with me in a café in eastern Long Island. After undergoing extensive therapy and several plastic surgery procedures to remove the worst of the scarring, Rickman's face still bears a reminder of what Holland did to her.

"It all happened so fast," Rickman remembers. "She cornered me in the bathroom. One moment I was standing next to her and we were talking. Just talking. And the next, I was whooshing through the air, my back hitting the wall. And then I was pulled back by this unseen force, and I was flying, headed for the mirror. I didn't even have a chance to raise my hands to protect my face before the impact. It all happened so fast. . . ."

Whooshing? Flying? Unseen force?

I ask Rickman if she was fully conscious during her ordeal. Yes, she was conscious, and yes, she meant what she said: Holland sent her flying into that

"What would a 'monster' have to say in her own defense?"

mirror. When I ask how that could be possible, Rickman whispers that Holland is "not quite human.

"Take what you will from this," Rickman continues, "but this is what I know happened, and I will stand by it."

Suspended from the Academy following the incident, Holland appears to have never returned to the formal schooling system. No details of her life post-Stonebrook can be found on public record. Holland has no social media profiles and no other digital presence.

Rickman believes her attacker just walked away from the incident unscathed and unpunished. She blames Holland's family lawyer for pulling strings to save Holland from a more drastic intervention. Sometimes, Rickman says, she can't sleep at night thinking that this monster's still out there somewhere.

I keep thinking that there are two sides to every story. What would a "monster" have to say in her own defense? If not for a random connection, I might have never received any answer. But a friend of a friend from college mentioned in passing that he knew a girl whose roommate is named Hayden Holland. I asked to be introduced, and soon I was making arrangements for a "blind date" with the "Stonebrook monster" herself.

I could not believe my luck. . . . And then my luck ran out. An hour before I was supposed to meet Holland, I received a phone call from—you guessed it—the Holland family's lawyer, threatening me with legal action if I didn't drop my investigation. But this is not the end. It'll end when the truth is out.

6

BIRTHDAYS ARE STRANGE: PART 1

We are attracted to mysteries. Our perpetual drive to solve the unsolvable, to know the unknown, makes us human.

The *unknowing* bothers us.

To transform the unknowing into knowing, our brain turns to *pattern-seeking*: the newest set of images from the Mars Rover, the sketchy evidence that the elusive Loch Ness monster is alive and well. The human brain is an expert in finding meaning in these artifacts, because in our book, meaning equals truth. Even the most far-fetched of meanings are better than being left completely in the dark.

Your mother disappears into the small-town night, never to be seen again? Your brain immediately launches into its meaning-making mode, not stopping till it settles on the "simplest" and, therefore most probable, explanation: Mom was not mentally well, and, as a child, I was blind to it, too charmed by

Mom's eccentricities and artful detachment to notice objectively that she needed help. Maybe the night she went missing she had an episode, a bad one, and wandered off into the woods. Maybe she fell and broke her neck. Maybe she drowned and her body, trapped by the tree roots and algae, was destined to never be found by the search efforts. And here's the logical continuation of that thought: Maybe whatever Mom had was genetic and it's only a matter of time before I start to lose it, too.

Or maybe Mom just left us because she was never meant for family life and after years of trying, she gave up.

I could drive myself nuts going through possible scenarios. And now, ten years later, when I'm confronted by the truth that Mom cared just enough about me to leave me the Manor along with her cryptic conditions and some nonsensical clues, all the scenarios I mulled over seem faulty. I have to start from scratch. My father would call this experience paradigm-altering.

So if Mom was lucid enough to organize her will with Doreen, does it mean she knew something was coming for her? Was her disappearance not a tragic accident? Did she have any enemies?

Who was my mother, anyway? What motivated her to do the things she did? Mom was always a mystery to me. And, I suspect, to Dad, too. Maybe Dad was attracted to her in the first place because she was a riddle to be solved and he fancied himself the man for the job.

In this vein, let me tell you a bit more about my father. Despite his very unscientific obsession with the Nibelungs, he holds a conviction that all phenomena, no matter how odd, can be scientifically explained. And what we can't yet put into formulae or a neat graph will be a piece of cake for the next generation of savvy humans.

As an antisocial kid educated outside of the formal schooling system, I started collecting unexplained occurrences. While my peers were into seashells and action figures and stuffed toys, I was into creepy incidents preserved in archives and later digitized by other weirdos like me. Influenced by Dad's scientific aura and his manic journal-keeping, I started a journal of my own, where I wrote up my "findings" and "hypotheses."

My first entry was about the Tunguska event—a powerful blast that hit a remote, uninhabited area in Siberia in 1908. It burned nearly nine hundred square miles of the forest to the ground, turning silica-rich soil into glass. The event left no crater, but an unusual concentration of silicates and magnetites in the earth and trees suggested the blast's extraterrestrial origin. The theories range from a giant meteorite impact to a small black hole passing through Earth to some kind of a geophysical anomaly.

The final entry in my journal of scientific mysteries was about a certain incident that the Promise newspapers referred to as the Black Clearing Event. Even now, I remember the newspaper headlines like it happened yesterday: LOCAL WOMAN DISAPPEARS INTO WOODS . . . GIANT CLEARING FORMS SAME NIGHT AS PROMISE WOMAN PERISHES IN FOREST . . . Before I settled on my two leading hypotheses explaining Mom's disappearance (mental-health incident and abandonment), I had this theory that Mom was abducted. But whether it was aliens or evil fairies, I couldn't decide. In the end, I just tore out those pages from my journal and decided to forget all about it.

They say ignorance is bliss. But so is denial.

We don't do gifts in my family. Aunt Nadia doesn't *believe* in birthdays (whatever that's supposed to mean—birthdays are not like Santa or some deity whose existence is subject to faith and worship) and Dad can't be bothered with life outside his "research."

Though I've made my peace with my aunt's stance on birthdays, Del still expresses her disagreement with my family's unorthodox approach to the matter via an occasional tirade on the importance of Tradition (yes, with the capital *T*) and via gift-giving. This time, in addition to my disastrous blind date, my birthday gift from Del is a framed photo of our apartment's door. (Del's got a soft spot for doorways, arches, and everything else that in her artsy mind passes for a gateway.) I run my fingers over the frame's darkened antique silver. Cool, smooth to the touch. I instantly love it. My mind's already spinning, thinking how I can top this amazing gift come Del's birthday in October.

After we have a cozy lunch at Five Leaves, Del takes me to the New York Aquarium. She knows I love all things sea and water, but I adore fish most of all, because they are quiet and aloof and rarely look me in the eye. But today, something about the Aquarium feels off.

As I approach the reinforced glass—a window into an underwater fairy world—the schools of fish race away, into darker realms. I'm about to comment on this weird behavior to Del when I notice a girl in the thinning crowd. She's about my age, though it's hard to tell for sure, since half her face is hidden underneath a low-sitting baseball cap. But it's the glimmering mass of white scars on the girl's exposed neck that makes me do a double take.

Scars. Uneven. Loud.

Not unlike those caused by shards of broken glass.

Jen's bloodied hands covering her face.

The girl isn't Jen—logically, I know that—but still, I'm drawn to her. My heartbeat speeding up, I take a step toward the girl, but a deafening *bang* hijacks my attention. The crowd around me begins to move, its erratic motion making me seasick. Del grabs my hand, drags me away from the glass. I look over my shoulder and see it—what everyone's running away from: a large seal torpedoing in my direction, going full speed.

It hits the glass.

The water in the tank turns pink.

The kids are wailing as they are picked up, carried, dragged away by their parents while the seal's thrashing and twitching. It goes still.

Somewhere close I hear Del cursing in French. My legs have a mind of their own, so she has to half drag, half push me out of the room.

Once outside, we don't stop moving until we get on our train. "Well, that was something. Can't say I've ever seen *that* before," Del says. I mumble a meaningless response.

I *have* seen this kind of stuff before. More than once actually, and the only constant in the equation, every single time, was one and the same: me.

7

BIRTHDAYS ARE STRANGE: PART 2

We don't talk as we ride the packed train back to Fort Greene. The electrified air tickles the hair at the nape of my neck. The storm's gathering, and I feel it with every inch of my skin, with my every blood cell—something's coming, and it's looking for me. It's as if the simple act of hearing my mother's name spoken out loud in Doreen's office has set off some ancient chain mechanism, its endgame not clear but likely sinister.

In a daze, I follow Del up the stairwell into our lair. The apartment's too silent, too dark for me not to suspect what's about to happen. I imagine I can hear their whisper-thoughts coming from the kitchen: *I wonder if she knows we're here. . . . I haven't seen her for almost a month. . . .*

So when my kid cousin Riley (wearing jeans, a red cape over a Spider-Man hoodie, and a hat made of kitchen foil) jumps out of the kitchen, yelling "Happy birthday," my surprise has to be faked. Riley is followed by Dad and Aunt Nadia. I take a breath, bracing for impact; a comet off its orbit, Riley collides with me, squeezing me in a fierce hug. Thanks to his most recent growth spurt, he's taller than most boys his age, reaching just below my shoulders.

"Love the hat, little man," I say as Riley's hands around my waist loosen enough for me to take a breath. "Did you make it yourself?"

"Riley, release Hayden." Dad attempts to separate Riley from me, but my cousin sticks to me like an exotic vine to its host tree. I free up one hand from Riley's grip and manage to hug Dad while Nadia greets Del.

Dad responds to my embrace in his usual detached way. Ever since I moved out of Nadia's house and came to live with Del in Fort Greene, I see Dad roughly once a month. Usually, I'm the one expected to make a trip to Long Island, where Dad resides in Aunt Nadia's spare bedroom. Our meetings are brief and awkward: We exchange some noncommittal sentences— avoiding the topics of Promise, Mom, Stonebrook Academy, or Dad's career suicide—and then we eat a mostly silent meal together and maybe watch some TV. That's about it. Aunt Nadia calls me every other day to check in and to assure me that my father is so very busy with work that he simply has no time to call me himself. Considering he's been on one long work trip after another ever since we moved to New York, I believe Nadia's assessment, though where Dad is traveling to is a mystery to me, since he's technically unemployed.

Today, like most days, Dad's wearing his lucky-charm orange baseball cap. I rarely see him without it. His hair, curling out from under the cap and around his ears, is in urgent need of a cut. His eyes are lined with shadows, while spiderwebs of wrinkles mar his skin, two tones darker than mine thanks to some Mediterranean DNA in his heritage. My dad's getting older, scruffier; his bedraggled appearance is a reminder of things people my age rarely have to think about. Noticing these things about him makes a prickle of sadness roil under my skin, starting in my toes and traveling all the way to the top of my head.

I meet Dad's eyes, but, in his usual fashion, he avoids making prolonged eye contact with me—something I used to take close to heart when I was a kid but not anymore.

Despite Dad's heavy layer of aftershave, I smell tobacco on him. Dad started smoking again after he lost his job. For as long as I remember, he's been one of those serial tobacco quitters who'd fall back on their old habits the moment life gets too tough.

To distract myself from unhappy thoughts, I give Dad a questioning look as I nod my head to Riley's foil hat. Dad shrugs in response just as Riley lets go of me and proceeds to adjust his odd headpiece, smoothing it down the sides of his head with both hands. "They're watching," he explains. "Trying to read my mind."

"Who's trying to read your mind?" I ask, then see Dad's serious eyes saying, *Do not encourage it*. Whatever Riley's new quirk is, Dad doesn't want me to indulge my precocious cousin's runaway imagination. So, like many other unsettling things about my family, I let it go.

I'm burning to tell Dad about Doreen, and Mom's will, but I know better than to poke that pit of snakes. Instead I ask a slightly less charged question: "So how's the job search going?"

Ever since his dismissal, Dad's been job-hunting. Or so he's been telling me and Aunt Nadia.

Caught off guard by my question, Dad takes off his baseball cap and runs a hand through his hair—more gray than copper. His eyes evade mine. "I'm not really looking anymore, Hayden. You see, I found an independent funding source to continue my research."

"Seriously?" I don't mean to sound so disbelieving, but I can't help it. The prospect of someone in their right mind deciding to fund my father's "research" is not something I'd imagined ever happening. "Which foundation is it?"

"Not a foundation exactly. More like a private endeavor."

"What, like a philanthropist who's into the Nibelungs as much as you are?" The words come off bitter. I just broke one of our unspoken rules and mentioned Dad's crackpot science, but it's too late to back down now, so I stare at him expectantly.

Dejected, Dad looks at me, his eyes tired. I already know from the stern shape his mouth is taking that this conversation is over. Since Mom's disappearance, I've barely had an exchange with my father that lasted long enough to be considered a "proper" conversation. I know he's actually capable of producing long sentences: There are hours-long, amateur videos of unfortunate "lectures" my father has given on the topic of the Nibelungs (the legendary dragon-slaying Siegfried; Siegfried's long-suffering wife, Kriemhild; other figures of Nibelung lore). It's only when he's in the same room with me that he gets all fidgety and talks in non sequiturs. The truth is, I've never been able to understand why Dad, a physicist, even became interested in researching far-fetched rumors of a supposed subspecies of humanity or how he decided they must come from another dimension. Whenever I try to figure out exactly what he's talking about, I get bogged down in the details of Germanic legends and very theoretical physics, and I'm still left confused about what the Nibelungs are even supposed to be.

Dad puts his baseball cap back on. "I just want you to know, Hayden, that everything I do, even if it seems crazy to you, is to protect you."

"Protect me from what?"

But, of course, he doesn't say. He never does. And honestly, I have little interest in pushing the matter further. There's too much troubled water under that bridge already, and the bridge isn't even strong enough to hold two people.

ᚠᚷᚠ

I didn't exactly state my plan of keeping the trip a secret from my family, but Del must've read it off me, because her mouth forms a tight line when Nadia enquires about her spring break plans. If Dad suspects anything, he's not showing it. If only I could break through the barrier of his skin and discern his thoughts. Does he ever think of Mom? Does he wish things were different between us after her disappearance? Does he regret the distance? Every time he catches my not-so-subtle stare, he cracks his knuckles and shifts in his seat, visibly uncomfortable in his own skin.

We're finishing our dessert (Nadia's homemade tiramisu) when a storm drops on Brooklyn with the ferocity of a rabid, hungry beast. Dad and Nadia wrap up their visit and rush to get home before the roads flood and the traffic gets bad. As they gather up their things, thunder cackles and roars, shaking the living-room windows. Del twitches like a petrified bunny.

And then, as if orchestrated by the invisible hand of a puppeteer, all heads turn toward the window, and we watch, mesmerized, as a brown pigeon smashes right into the glass and slides down, leaving a bloody trail in its wake before plummeting to the ground.

Observations Journal 2.0

When I was a child, I started my journal of observations. The move was inspired by my dad, the scientist. I wanted to be like him, to explore the natural world, to see things as they truly are: a series of logical, interconnected events, enslaved by the predictability of cause-and-effect and the inevitability of explanation. But then Dad lost his scientific credibility, and my childhood theories, meant to explain the most bizarre and creepy of occurrences, seemed ridiculous and unnecessary.

The irony is not lost on me that today, my eighteenth birthday, I restart my observations journal, this time inspired by my mom.

My goal is to make a record of my experiences of the natural world around me so that I can look for clues about what really happened to my mother.

Today, two events occurred that, while seemingly unconnected, share enough similarities between themselves and to past events to suggest some kind of common element.

The events in question:

a. A seal in the aquarium lost its sense of direction and crashed into the glass wall, and

b. A bird smashed into a window of the apartment I share with Del.

Similar events in the past: Jen Rickman (?) and the Tiger Incident.

Conclusion: Sometimes animals (and possibly humans) go nuts around me for some bizarre reason I've yet to figure out.

What is actually known about the Nibelungs?

There are three sources of information. Some are more reliable than others.

First, there are historical "facts" (the least reliable source?):

The Nibelungs—also known as the *Nibelungen* (in German) or *Niflung* (in Old Norse)—were *possibly* (note the lack of certainty!) a Burgundian royal dynasty ruling over a city called Worms on the Upper Rhine region of Germany in the early fifth century. Details are scarce.

The second sources are Norse and Germanic myths telling us of the race of the Nibelungs and the notable figures in the Nibelung mythology:

There was once a Burgundian princess called Kriemhild who dreamt of a falcon torn to bits by two eagles in midair. Kriemhild's mother interpreted the dream as a prophecy about Kriemhild's future love, doomed to be brutally killed by his enemies. To stop the prophecy from being fulfilled, Kriemhild vowed to never marry—a classic example of a self-fulfilling prophecy, where the mythic hero/heroine's attempt to alter fate in fact expedites this fate.

And then there was Siegfried, a young warrior credited with all sorts of amazing feats, from slaying a dragon to winning a "hoard" of treasure from two clueless brothers whom he killed so as not to share the said hoard with them. (As the brothers were also Nibelungs, the hoard—or treasure—is referred to as *Nibelungen*, that is, "of the Nibelungs.")

Siegfried fell in love with Kriemhild and the two married, but the courtly intrigues shortly took him far away from home. During his travels, he got involved with the Icelandic princess Brunhield, who was strong and proud, an undefeated warrior.

All this ended badly for everyone, with Siegfried getting betrayed and killed by his closest allies, with Kriemhild vowing to avenge him and gain control over the hoard, and with the hoard being lost in the process, never to be found.

And this brings us to the third source of information about the Nibelungs: the little truths hidden in the metaphors of myths.

This is also where the multidimensional physics come in.

Take the very concept of the hoard, for instance: Why not specify that said hoard was nothing more than a simple treasure—as in jewels and gold?

Why define this hoard by a tribal name—the hoard of the Nibelungs?

When referring to the hoard, the legends indeed speak of a treasure but fail to say what this treasure actually was.

What we do know is that should Kriemhild have succeeded in claiming the hoard following Siegfried's death, she would have amassed a Great Power.

What power is this exactly?

This power could be metaphorical, of course, but what is more likely, as Prof. Holland's research suggests, is that the hoard was, in fact a *horde*, a supernatural army that would serve its master, one standing at the ready, capable of conquering the world the moment it's released.

And so, this horde was taken from Siegfried and Kriemhild by their enemies and hidden away. Since Kriemhild failed to locate the Nibelungen horde, how likely is it that this metaphysical army is still concealed somewhere, waiting for the right moment until it can rise up again?

Another—perhaps the most important—metaphor comes from the story of Siegfried's strength. Like many epic heroes, Siegfried was invincible but for one weakness: When he once slew a dragon, Siegfried bathed in the creature's blood. Unbeknownst to

Siegfried, a leaf from a linden tree was stuck to his skin, blocking the dragon blood properties and rendering this one spot his Achilles' heel.

Multidimensional physicists talk of the multitude of universes, but one cannot travel from one universe to another unless a stable opening occurs naturally or is artificially created. Prof. Holland's research has led him to believe that this unprotected spot on Siegfried's skin is nothing but a metaphor for an opening between two worlds.

Prof. Holland hypothesizes that one such opening exists in the state of Colorado. This area, abound with physical anomalies, presents a fertile ground for testing his theory.

4300 Zephyr Boulevard
Canyon Ridge, CO 81236
970-153-8100

Dear Tom,

My doctoral thesis, as you know, was near completion at the
time of your tenure's revocation. Days after your dismissal, I was
advised my thesis was to be reviewed, pending a decision as to the
future of my academic career.

After learning my thesis was deemed unsuitable for submission,
I was presented with a choice: to start from scratch on a new topic
under new supervision and lose years of data and hypothesis-
testing, or leave.

I decided to leave.

I have no regrets.

Shortly after my departure from Ian Trainor, I was approached
by a representative of Blue Haven Research Institute. Have you
heard of it? I was offered a job, and the offer was too good to
refuse.

With your research funding pulled back, in my capacity as the
Institute representative, I come to you with an offer to finance
your research out of the Institute's funds. The details are enclosed.
I hope you accept this generous offer, and I look forward to
working together once more and moving physics and humankind
into a new era of scientific exploration.

Yours truly in science,

Arista Kazan

Arista Kazan
Senior Research Fellow, Blue Haven Research Institute

8
ON THE MOVE

After Dad, Nadia, and Riley depart into the storm, the rest of my birthday evening passes in a flurry of preparations. Del insists on putting the plane tickets and car rental in Denver on her credit card, working on the optimistic assumption that the freak storm ravaging the city is going to pass by morning.

I protest her generous offer of bankrolling my soul-searching trip, and she concedes that I can take care of feeding us while in Promise. I agree but also assure her that I have the fullest intent of eventually reimbursing her for my share of the travel expenses.

Having done the dishes, I check on Del, but she's still deep in the realm of Internet travel bargains. I leave her to it and get started packing. I dig through my wardrobe, grabbing jeans and hoodies and piling them on my bed. Most of the nicer clothes I own are either gifts or purchases forced upon me by Del when we've gone shopping together. (Or more like when

Del goes shopping and I'm persuaded to tag along.) Whether it's a consequence of my homeschooling, years in therapy, or just the way I'm wired, I'm apathetic to clothes. Mostly I just wear jeans, tees, and sweatshirts. I own three pairs of Doc Martens, one pair of sneakers, and exactly one pair of girly sandals with heels. The latter was—you guessed it—a gift from Del. My most extravagant acquisition to date is a tailored leather jacket I bought when I got my college admission letter. Del calls me a tomboy with girly potential. She also swears that one day she'll change me. After failed makeover number three, I hope she's on the verge of giving up.

Once packed, I retrieve the deed to the Manor and Mom's cryptic message from under my pillow, stuffing both into the side pocket of my trusty messenger bag. The card's warm to my skin, as if Mom's demanding I pay attention. I want to. I really do. But what'll it cost me? What price am I prepared to pay to learn Mom's secrets?

ᚠᚷᚠ

Del gets her miracle. The freak storm passes, leaving behind a drizzle and the wind. A lone willow tree in the neighboring backyard is scratching at our building's wall, like a ghost begging for warmth. By the time I join Del in the living room, the evening's given way to a breezy night.

My roommate's languid form is splayed across the length of the couch. Del's all shining skin and long legs tangled with the duvet cover. I wish I had a talent for the fine arts so I could paint her. But with Del's impatience, I guess I'd never get her to sit still long enough for me to give her beauty its fair due.

My laptop on her stomach, Del grins at me. "Good news: Student discounts rock! And not so good news: As I suspected, we can only fly as far as Denver. Promise has no airport. We'll have to drive there. It's about four hours. Can you tolerate listening to my Manu Chao albums that long?"

ᚠᚷᚠ

That night I fall asleep thinking of my father's tired eyes. He says that whatever it is he's doing, it's to protect me.

As he was leaving the apartment, he embraced me, but there was a slight hesitation. He whispered into my hair that he loved me. Caught in the moment, I forgot all about my childhood pains of isolation, about feeling powerless and alone. For a blissful moment, I forgot about all the rage I felt after we lost Mom and all my disappointment at the pitiful detour Dad's career took once he started penning manifestos about time-traveling warrior hordes and anomalies that serve as portals between dimensions. I forgot all that.

In that rare moment, I was just happy that Dad hugged me. Even if his hands were uncertain, like he was embracing a volatile animal that could not be trusted.

9
SOMEWHERE IN COLORADO:
PART 1

Masses attract one another. When an apple falls from a tree, it's the strength of gravity that makes it happen. The farther objects are from one another, the weaker this gravitational force becomes. But it never completely disappears.

Every day, over two thousand people are reported missing in the United States. When my mother left our family home and walked into the fog-shrouded forest, she contributed to the sad statistics of persons never to be seen again. One missing human in a crowd of many.

Yet I feel her visceral tug, as if she calls me, as if her pull defies space and time to reach me. As if my mother is still pulling me, reaching under my skin, entering my bloodstream, making my blood sing in response, in recognition.

ᚠᚷᚠ

The morning comes. We make it to the airport on time only to learn that our flight is delayed due to low visibility, an after-effect of the storm.

While we marinate in the cramped waiting space by our gate, Del chats up an airline rep at the counter and flirts her way into a business-class upgrade for us both. *Seriously?* I don't know how she does it, but her charm works every time.

I stare out the window, wishing the fog would clear out. Eventually it does and we're allowed to board. The plane's almost empty, which partly explains our upgrade luck. Excited at first, Del's chatter weakens as the seatbelt light goes off. She dozes off on my shoulder. Soon restless sleep claims me, too, dragging me into a familiar land of fog and warriors on horse-back, galloping through the woods.

But this time my recurring dream has a new element: Shannon.

He's grown into a tall, menacing figure, which is further enhanced by his armor. His mouth quirks up in acknowledgment of my presence. I can't zero in on his face. Every time I come close, he shifts just out of focus. But I *know* it's him. Even though I haven't seen him in years.

He rides by my side, the two of us at the head of our terrifying army, which is wearing human skins like ill-fitting costumes.

Even asleep, I'm aware that my hands are slick with sweat. My heart's deranged rhythm is an unholy metronome, making me sick to the bones. Every time I come close to waking up, I get dragged back down into the whirlpool of dreams. I descend deeper and deeper and then I reach the bottom, where there's no light, no air, nothing.

We land in Denver, and it's good to have my feet on the ground again. I keep my disturbing dreams to myself, taking sneaky deep breaths to calm myself down when Del's not looking.

While Del goes over the car-rental paperwork with a cute redheaded guy wearing a TRAINEE tag, I loiter close by. I feel the trainee guy's eyes on me, and then Del turns to look at me, too, her face half illuminated, half hidden by shadow. They're talking about me. Del waves me closer. I oblige. "Hayden, this is Mark. Mark, Hayden." As she makes the introductions, I blink at her in confusion, unsure why my presence is required, since all the paperwork is in her name. Voice sweet, she explains, "Mark's father is from Promise. I thought Mark could give us some pointers on what to do, things to see."

The way Mark becomes visually tense when I approach bothers me. He stays silent for too long after Del stops talking, and when he does speak, the words out of his mouth have nothing in the way of sightseeing advice.

"Your eyes are different colors. Weird but not uncommon in Promise, right? I mean, weird how common it is, not that your eyes are weird. Though . . . they are!"

He's still mumbling when I meet his light-brown eyes and then two things happen at once: His pupils shrink into tiny black dots, and my heart rate goes up, not a lot but enough for me to sense the change. There's a familiar tension in my chest, a precursor of the panic attacks I used to have as a child, and cold sweat forms between my fingers. I break eye contact and Mark shakes his head, as if clearing it. The moment passes. I'm not sure if Del even noticed anything odd.

"It's called *heterochromia*," I say, trying to act normal.

A polite smile forms on Mark's lips. "I was just telling Del," he says, eyes flitting, "that you girls should check out Edmunds' Gorge. Also do lots of hiking. The mountains are the best out there. So are the woods."

"Del's not big on hiking."

"There's also this bookshop that has the most amazing coffee." Mark-the-trainee is starting to sound like a tourist-office brochure now. "The owners are as weird as they come, but if you keep an open mind, you'll have a great time."

Del's cracking up as we leave Mark at the counter. Apparently, watching me stumble while trying to talk to cute guys is funny. I guess she didn't notice anything off, like how I made Mark space out for a second. My pre-panic attack feeling lingers as we walk out of the airport and are greeted by sunshine and the clearest blue skies I've seen in weeks.

Our rental is a tiny yellow Kia that just barely fits our luggage and leaves some space for us, too. Del takes the first shift driving. As we get going, I roll down my window and take off my hoodie, determined to soak up every bit of sunlight available. Some of the earlier tension returns briefly to my chest, accompanied by that knotted-stomach feeling that comes with a sensation of being watched or experiencing déjà vu. In my head, I start to repeat the words of my old calm-down song—a lullaby Mom used to sing to me:

The first one was a warrior, the second a handmaiden; their queen who led the army was third. They'll save their people! The blood of the first three, it'll break down the walls—it'll set their people free, and the new world will emerge. . . .

As I repeat the offbeat, Bob Dylan–esque lines, the

uncomfortable feeling in my gut begins to disappear, but then, just like that, the sunny day morphs into a thunderous, lightning-striking nightmare. I hurry to roll up the window before I get soaked. Del reduces the speed and turns on the headlights. She's a good driver and I feel safe with her at the wheel, though my eyes keep returning to the rearview mirror, watching for something, anything, unusual in the thickening fog. But all I can see are the lights of cars moving carefully through the haze.

Observations Journal 2.0

It happened again today.

Just before hitting the road with Del, bound for Promise, Colorado, I observed some kind of random hypnosis. A guy at the car rental got all hazy, his pupils shrinking in size.

He snapped out of it pretty quickly (the exact moment I broke eye contact with him, to be precise), but the lingering sensation of wrongdoing remained deep in my chest.

I'd write off the occurrence as the guy spacing out, if only it didn't remind me so much of the way Dr. Erich sometimes got around me. Or the way Jen Rickman became right before our infamous encounter that led to my expulsion.

Conclusion: Need to investigate if some people naturally possess some type of innate ability to hypnotize others. This is unlikely but worth looking into.

Research findings: The lion's share of what we know (or, more appropriately, _think we know_) about hypnosis has been shaped by popular culture and media. Hypnosis is _not_ a mindless trance but a natural state in which the conscious (logical) mind becomes relaxed, making it possible for ideas to be communicated directly to the inner mind, which is governed by emotions, perception, and habits.

Hypnosis is a recognized psychology method used to treat addictions.

Hypnosis can occur in our daily lives without us even knowing it's happening, like when you're riding a train and zone out, getting lulled by the motion into a state of quiet.

While some people can develop traits and quirks that make them more "charismatic" and "hypnotic" to others, there's _no such thing_ as hypnosis induced by the mere _physical presence_ of a "hypnotist."

Hence, there has to be some other explanation of my (random?) "ability" to put animals and people into a trance.

P.S. Maybe it's just that I'm that boring?

10
SOMEWHERE IN COLORADO:
PART 2

"What are you typing?" Del asks without looking away from the road. Deep into my Internet research, I lost track of time.

"Nothing. Just something silly."

"Right." She sneaks a quick look at me.

I put my phone away. "Just jotting down some observations. Did you notice anything unusual about that guy at the Denver airport?"

"That Mark guy? Sure. He was totally checking you out. His eyes got all dewy."

"Hmm."

"'*Hmm*'? Just take it for what it is, Hayden. You're finally blossoming into the beautiful young woman you were always meant to be, and men are starting to notice."

I inspect her profile, the twitch of her lips telling me she's playing with me. Her next words confirm my hypothesis.

"If only you'd let me give you a makeover, you'd blossom at long last. . . ."

"Oh, shut it, Del!"

To that she says something so crude, we both break out into raucous, loud laugher. The unexpected release leaves me weightless, calm, and with a sense of grateful affection for Del, who always knows what to say to snap me out of my mood.

It's my turn driving, navigating Route 25 through the wall of rain. The car radio's breaking up. Both our phones are running low on battery. We have to find other, nontechnological entertainment. We burn through twenty questions quickly. Del keeps choosing characters from her favorite fantasy book series, while I stick to Kubrick movies ("*Open the pod bay doors, HAL!*") and the Buffyverse ("*I'm sixteen years old. I don't wanna die.*"). As far as our pop culture tastes go, Del knows me as well as I know her. We're getting bored.

Another hour in and Del takes the wheel again, letting me rest. She proposes a new game. "How about *three things*?"

I chuckle. "We're making up games now? Here's one I just came up with: Guess that song." I start humming "Ride of the Valkyries."

Del shakes her head. "Stop being a weirdo, please. And *my* game is legit. You have to name three things I don't know about you yet."

"Ah . . . sounds promising. Number one: My middle name is Bellatrix."

Del rolls her eyes. "I knew that. It was on the apartment lease. Besides, revealing to me the mystery of your middle name isn't good enough. The stuff you share has got to be personal and not things like *I'm wearing pink underwear today.* By the way, I *am* wearing pink underwear today."

"What, are you hitting on me now?"

"Nope. Definitely not. Not that there's anything wrong with you. You're perfect. Or you *would* be if you straightened your hair once in a while. . . . But even with your hair wavy like that, I'd totally do you . . . if I were into girls."

"Just stop talking, *Delphine.*"

For the record, Del loathes her full name. I would, too: It sounds too much like *dolphin,* which is a great name for a mermaid, but for a human girl . . . not so much. But Del barely notices my jab, that's how fired up she is about playing her totally made-up game.

"So you in?" She cocks her head to the side, like a bird. I nod reluctantly. She drums her fingers against the wheel. "I'll go first. We start with the least shocking thing and work our way up to the most shocking, so we can discuss it at length."

"We're supposed to discuss it, too?"

She snorts. "Perhaps you have a better idea for entertainment while I'm doing all the work driving? Do you?"

"No, I do not."

"Okay, so hear this and learn. Thing number one: I'm a sleepwalker." Del pauses for effect, but all I can think about is this creepy old movie *Sleepwalkers,* based on a Stephen King story, which I think is about vampires feeding on virgins or something equally gross.

I say weakly, "Really?"

Del's eyes do this glare-of-death thing when she's stuck between being annoyed and disappointed. This is so not the reaction she was hoping for.

"In case you want to know"—Del's voice comes off slightly pissed-off—"it's a sleep disorder. I've been suffering from it ever since I was a child. It can be pretty dangerous."

"Dangerous to whom?"

Del enunciates, "To me and to those around me. I take pills to control it, and I have to lock myself in my room at night. Once, when I was seven, I wandered out of my parents' house and onto the road. A car was going by, and the driver had to swerve not to hit me head-on. That's what the driver said happened, anyway. I have no memory of it, because I kind of slept through it all."

"That sounds awful, Del." How come I didn't know any of this after living together for months and exchanging vows of everlasting friendship? Maybe I'm not a very good friend after all. "Is there anything I can do?"

She laughs but not harshly, thawing already. She can't stay mad at me for too long. "Not really. But you have nothing to worry about. I have it all under control. Okay, enough about me. Your turn! Better make it good."

I don't think too long about it. "I'm a virgin."

"Oh, honey, I know." Del's face assumes what I believe is her "poor baby" expression.

"What, you're feeling sorry for me now?"

"If only you'd let me give you a makeover."

"Don't be ridiculous." I stop her before she launches into her makeover nonsense *again*. "There's nothing wrong with me. And there are other things in life, you know, aside from chasing after guys or whatever."

"Now that's just sad. A little boy-chasing never did anyone any wrong—in fact, it gets your heart pumping, keeps you spritely and healthy. And besides, what are you—some bad romance heroine fated to fall in love for the first time at the not-so-tender age of twenty-five?" Del chews on her bottom lip, eating away some of her translucent lip gloss. "Okay, whatever, my turn. I was an army brat growing up. Impressed, Ms. Brooklynite-who-has-never-ever-even-left-the-States?"

"I already knew that you grew up moving around with your family, Del."

Can we be this boring? Is it possible we already know everything there is to know about each other? *Not everything*, a little voice hisses inside my head. *She doesn't know what you did to Jen Rickman, why you were expelled from Stonebrook. She doesn't know how your mother went dark and scary weeks before her disappearance, and how there's suspicion that she burned up part of the woods the night she left you. Or the other weird detail. Del doesn't know the* real *you. If she did, she'd run away screaming. Or lose control and smash her head against a mirror.*

Oblivious to the dark thoughts in my head, Del goes on, "Sure, but did you know I lived in, like, fifty different countries, all before I turned ten?"

"Exaggerate much?"

"Not at all. That's like five countries a year."

"And you can count!"

"I've lived *everywhere*. Just ask! Ask me anything about *any* country."

I rack my brain for something difficult to ask, though I suspect Del's telling the truth. She's not one to brag. "The capital of Zimbabwe?"

"Oh, good one." Del all but squeals in delight. "*Harare*. But it used to be called *Salisbury*."

There's no way to check the validity of her answer. I can't look it up on my phone—the battery's now dead and my charger is unwisely packed somewhere in my luggage.

"Another one," Del demands. I ask again. And again. And every time, she's got an answer. Baku, capital of Azerbaijan. Bratislava, capital of Slovakia. And Malaysia has two: Kuala Lumpur and Putrajaya.

"You're like a rain woman," I note. She glows with pride. Del *loves* the movie *Rain Man* and, I suspect, nurtures a secret crush on Dustin Hoffman circa 1988.

My turn to share. I blurt out, "I was expelled from school when I was eight. After that, I was homeschooled."

"I suspected as much." Del shrugs, feigning casual interest. But I know from her long, sideways glance that she's hooked and wants more.

"But did you also suspect the reason *why* I was expelled?" I tease her, knowing I'm now wandering into dangerous territory.

"Because you bored them all to tears with your jeans and hoodies, and they could no longer look at you without wanting to give you a makeover? Oh, no, no, let me try again . . . because you're an antisocial weirdo?"

She's not that far off.

"I might be a weirdo," I say, "but I'm not exactly antisocial, though some people from my former school most likely think I am." And that's putting it lightly.

"You're not going to kill me and bury my body in the woods, are you?"

"Nah, I only do that to girls who *don't* try to give me a makeover."

That's when our GPS loses its mind. The power is on and

the navigator's screen is lit up, but our path on the map's all jumbled, like a kid's scrawl of crayon on a wall. The GPS's sudden demise saves me from having to elaborate on my impromptu confession. Del parks on the side of the road. We take turns staring at the GPS screen as it goes mad. As of this moment, we are somewhere in Colorado. And we are lost.

11
THE FOREST TAKES NOTICE

So our GPS succumbed to madness. Probably all those quantum mechanics and special relativity formulae that keep it going, connecting with a group of satellites circling Earth and communicating to pin our location in the depths of Colorado, finally drove our GPS into insanity, and it just checked out.

We get out to have a look around. Though it's mostly stopped, the rain's presence is heady in every inhale I take. The air's got that drunk-on-nature quality you can only experience far, far away from big cities. Tall whispering firs frame the road, their heads lost to the high mist.

A flutter of wind sends a pang of recognition through my veins, but there's also unease—the kind you get when you know you're lost in an unfamiliar (and possibly hostile) place, its rules a mystery to you.

To make matters worse, it's getting dark, fast. Through the thin material of my tee I feel every outburst of the wind. I need to get back inside the car, but the air here is borderline addictive. My lungs beg for more. It's only when I notice Del's full-on shivering that we get back into our Kia and shut the doors. I slide into the driver's seat and get the car going. The engine sputters but then roars to life.

Del doesn't stop trembling even when it gets toasty inside the car, goose bumps crawling all over the exposed skin of her arms. To distract her I ask, "Can you look anything up on your phone? My battery's dead."

She does as I ask, but her frown tells me it's bad news. "No reception. No Internet. *Nada*." She lets out a nervous exhale. "Are we officially screwed now? I can already see the news all over the web: 'Two hot girls go missing in Colorado while on spring break from hell.'"

"Why is it important that the girls are hot?"

"Because that's the truth. And news reporters never lie. It's in their professional code to only tell the truth."

That's when I notice that the fuel gauge's showing a dangerously low level of gas. How did we miss that?

Our salvation comes after about twenty minutes of driving semiblind and completely alone on the road. A crooked road sign announces we are approaching the "last gas station until Promise." At least we're on the right track.

I take the exit against Del's protests. "What do you expect me to do?" I exclaim. "Would you rather walk the rest of the way? Through the woods?"

"But this is how horror movies begin," she says, her voice small. "Don't you know the first rule of all horror movies? When stranded in a fog in the middle of nowhere, do *not* stop your car and do *not* get out of your car!"

"That's *two* rules. And I thought the number-one rule of

horror movies was to not ever go inside the house. Or was it the basement? Nope, it's . . . never ever split up!"

"You've got it all wrong," Del murmurs. "Number-one rule of surviving a horror movie scenario is—*do not be a virgin*." I snort at that and she laughs, too.

ᚠᚷᚠ

We find the gas station and park. I'm so happy to stretch my legs again. My jeans have become a second skin by now, and an itchy one at that. Also, I seriously hope there's a working shower in Holland Manor.

Once I'm outside, the drizzle envelops my face like a thin veil. Humidity flattens my hair. The air's so saturated with oxygen, it makes me light-headed.

The "last gas station until Promise" and its adjacent little shop are manned by a totally normal young man and his adorable, peach-haired mother. We pick up a regional map, several bags of chips, pretty much all of the fresh fruit the shop's got, and a lot of bottled water.

No one tries to kill us.

But it does get weird: As we pay up, I sense the peach-haired lady's eyes lingering on me with interest. I meet her stare, half expecting her to zone out like that Mark guy did at the airport, but she keeps my gaze and asks, "Aren't you Ella Holland's little girl? You've got her eyes and that expression, like you have the pressure of the entire world on your little shoulders."

A sweet apple I bit into seconds ago sours in my mouth. What's worse, in addition to the nosy peach-haired woman's interest, I also sense Del's attention. Thankfully, the woman's son has disappeared behind the STAFF ONLY door, so I have one less spectator.

"Correct," I tell the shopkeeper, hoping that if I keep it short and sweet, Del and I can get the hell out of here before the former hears something spooky and freaks out on me. But my curiosity immediately overrules my first instinct and I ask the woman, "How did you know my mom?"

"I used to live in Promise. Ella was in my self-defense class."

I do a double take. The idea of my mother, fragile and willow-looking, fighting off pretend-assailants doesn't quite align with my memory of her. In the dichotomy of lover/fighter, the mother I remember was the former—she roamed the woods barefoot for hours; she stood outside the Manor in the pouring rain, her head thrown back in amazement at something unseen to the rest of us.

Ignoring my disbelieving expression, the peach-haired lady goes on, her tone suspiciously casual, "She spoke of you often. And of your father. So sad what happened to her. Such a bizarre tragedy to hit that poor town. And, you know, the police didn't take me seriously then, but I *know* Ella was scared of something. Something that's been hiding in these woods for decades. Ancient evil that poisons the soul . . ."

"All right, we're in a rush, actually. Thanks!" Del nearly shouts. Through the noise of my pounding blood, I can barely hear her words to the woman. A slight pressure on my arm tells me Del's dragging me out of the shop. I begin to protest, many questions bubbling on the tip of my tongue, but Del's determined to get me out. Dazed, I give in and let her. Once safely back inside the car, I volunteer to drive. My hope is that being in control of the car will bring me some quiet and time to consider what I just heard.

I get the car going. Once Del locates Promise on the map and issues directions, she asks, "Are you all right?"

"I'm fine, I guess." I shrug. "Though I don't enjoy being ambushed by total strangers like that."

"She's a nutcase, clearly. Sorry you had to hear that. 'Ancient evil that poisons the soul'? Cliché!"

"Yeah, right?" I nod, glad I'm not the only one who took the peach-haired lady's words for what they were—nutty mutterings. "It's just what she said about my mother being scared of something. . . ."

"What is it, Hayden?"

"Well, it's more of a feeling rather than an actual memory of something that happened, but there were these times when Mom would become jumpy for no reason at all, like she was being watched, maybe. I don't know."

Del gives me a long look; I can feel it like a weight on the side of my face. After examining me for a few long seconds, she issues her verdict. "You look like you just ran smack into a ghost, Hayden. I don't think I've ever seen you this freaked out. And I've *seen* you freaked out."

"I'm not used to talking about what happened to Mom. But I guess I should be prepared for more of that kind of stuff in Promise."

"She was just one very confused old lady." Del sighs. "If you want my unsolicited advice—don't take her words to heart. Don't mull over it."

"I'll try."

Some twenty minutes in, the fog begins to dissipate. The road takes an edgy turn and, following a semiwild path up the slope, we roll right into the woods. The farther in we get, the tighter the forest becomes around us, rough tree branches scratching the car like talons of wild spirits attempting to prevent us from entering their domain.

"Hayden?" Del asks in a small voice.

"Yeah?"

"Are you ever going to tell me about your mom? Like, what really happened to her?"

"I am. But now may not be the best time."

"Is it that bad? Does it have anything to do with this forest?"

Del is uncannily perceptive today, even more than usual. "I don't want to freak you out." Not after the gas station lady's talk of ancient evil.

"You're just making this worse now, you know that, right? Look!" Del points at something to her right. I slow the car down to a crawl, grateful that Del got distracted and there won't be any more dangerous questions. For now, at least.

What got Del's attention is some kind of paramilitary camp. Not something one would expect to come upon during a drive through the woods.

Through the tightly woven forest, I can only see glimpses of it at first: a cluster of camouflage that's too precise, the ground too smooth.

Not a soul in sight.

I hit the brakes.

"Are you insane?" Del protests. "*No.* Stay in the car. Please!"

But my body's already made the decision for me. I'm getting

out, forcing the car door open amidst low-hanging branches scratching at the metal and at my skin. "I want to check this out. Are you coming?"

Del doesn't look happy and doesn't return my reassuring smile, but she still joins me. Her visceral disapproval is digging into the flesh and bone of my back.

I tear my way through the thick woods until we get to the clearing housing the camp. The space is large enough to hold three pavilion tents. Under my feet, the ground's crisscrossed with car tracks—the kind that scream big vehicles, maybe jeeps or Humvees or some other kind of military machinery. I wish my phone wasn't dead and I could take a few pictures.

A weird kind of animal laugh comes from above, prompting me to jerk my head up. A pair of giant ravens are sitting side by side on a sturdy tree branch. One's black, the other's silver-gray. Both stare at me with their beady black eyes. "And what do you want?" I address the black raven, half expecting it to open its mouth and say something or at least repeat my question in that toneless guttural voice of ravens.

When Del notices the ravens, she's not impressed. "Unless they're going to open their mouths—*beaks*, whatever—and recite Poe, can we get moving?"

Hesitant to leave and feeling like I'm missing some important clue, I take another look around. That's when I pick up on a logo printed on the tent closest to me. I get closer for a better look. An indigo pyramid is encircled with the words BLUE HAVEN RESEARCH INSTITUTE. My hands itch to get the Internet working on my phone so I can look up what kind of research this Institute does and what it has to do with Promise.

"Any theories?" I turn to Del, but she seems lost, hugging

herself tightly and absently rubbing her arms and shoulders. When she looks up at me, a hint of concern makes a little frown appear between her eyebrows. "You never mentioned you came from a place that was used as *The Texas Chainsaw Massacre*'s movie set."

"Wait until you see the Manor." My attempt to lighten the mood only makes Del retreat further into herself.

On our way back to the car, Del keeps giving me these strange looks without holding eye contact for long. Before I get back into the driver's seat, I take a casual look at the trees, seeking out the ravens. I feel like they're watching me, but it's probably just my subconscious regurgitating the wording from Mom's codicil and her flash card note. The longer I stare into the trees, the more ridiculous I feel. The birds are long gone.

Released by the forest, we reenter the world at the top of a hill overlooking the town. Promise is nestled at the bottom of a shallow ravine, surrounded by woods, with Edmunds' Gorge darkening the landscape to the north. Two tall silhouettes—a clock tower and a church's steeple—rise up on the town's south side. The sun's almost down, and twilight paints the landscape with eerie colors. I roll down my window and poke my head out.

Welcome to Promise, I guess.

As we head down the hill, following the shape of the road, I dig into my memories to help me navigate the rest of the way until the Manor comes into view. I seem to be moving on autopilot, without needing directions.

I train my eyes on the Manor, but they keep sliding to this other house across the field from my childhood home. The

Reaser house. Where Shannon grew up. The dream I had on the plane to Denver resurfaces, and I strain once more to see Shannon's face, blurry, shifting out of view.

"We're here," Del announces. "Aren't we?"

Unsure anymore what it is that our arrival's supposed to make me feel, I try to quell my rising panic.

My heart has been shattered so many times that by now it's a restored piece of ancient china preserved in a museum somewhere. Still, an army of untethered images, words, and sensations swarms me.

This swarm is dangerous; I fear what I might see in its depths if I stare there long enough. So I do what I always do in my moments of extreme self-doubt: I focus on the mundane, allowing myself to feel the simple but powerful relief that we've made it here without major incidents and excitement at the prospect of my head meeting a pillow soon.

ᚠᚷᚠ

The house is a restored Victorian Queen Anne in all its glory: a conical shingled roof, a rounded porch with sunburst detailing, a lineup of columns and bay windows. *The House of the Rising Sun*, Dad called it, but it was Mom's Holland Manor that stuck in the end.

The longer I stare, the more I see it: the sure signs of abandonment. Empty flower beds, paint peeling off, windows murky with grime.

"My hopes of getting a pizza delivered are dying a slow death." Del's out of the car, joining me on the driveway facing the Manor's front. Her words register, but I don't say anything. Still too consumed with the riffraff of memories mixed with dreams and childhood fears. It's difficult to tell which memories are real and which aren't; post-therapy, my recollections of my time in Promise are all messed up.

"Earth to Hayden?" Del sounds far, far away.

We return to the car and haul our bags up the porch stairs. Before we go inside the Manor, Del fishes out her cell phone from her purse and snaps a picture of the Manor's door. Another item for her collection of portals, as she calls them.

That's when it occurs to me that I've got no keys to the Manor.

Del must come to the same realization, because her perkiness deflates, turning her eyes feral. "We'll break in if we have to," I comfort her.

I inspect the Manor's entrance. To my surprise, a tight row of runic symbols runs along the doorframe, all the way down, to encase the door completely. Another row appears to go around the entire house. A twinge of a memory scratches my mind but vanishes before I can hold on to it. I file the symbols away for now and reach over the wooden plane that crowns the Manor's entrance, letting my fingers run its length. I squirm at the dust and grime that clings to my fingertips but don't stop. This is where Dad used to hide our house keys—in plain sight, he called it. I doubt I'll find anything, but to my shock, my fingers land on what feels like a ring with several keys on it. I seize my find and pull my hand back, triumphant. Del gawks at me in disbelief.

It's almost too easy—as if someone left the keys here for me to find.

Or like someone's been living in the Manor, an unwelcome idea announces in my mind.

I know I'll dwell on all the possibilities later, but for now I locate the central entrance key on the brass ring and slide it into the keyhole. The rusty lock impatiently gives way.

12
MY HOUSE AT THE EDGE OF THE WOODS

As far as the *second law of thermodynamics* goes, heat spreads from hot bodies to cold ones. This direction is dictated by the fact that atoms in hot bodies are more disordered and random than in cold ones. To hypothetically violate this law, a physicist named James Maxwell dreamt up an imaginary creature that could sort out hot particles from the cold ones and, by doing so, reverse the movement of heat and break the second law.

This hypothetical device is called *Maxwell's Demon*.

Imagine: A demon sits in a box, which is divided into two sections by a wall. The wall has a door that the demon controls. The demon acts as a bouncer of sorts by opening the door to let the faster (hotter) molecules flow to one side of the box while leaving the slower (colder) ones to drift on the other side. Hence, the first side of the box will heat up and the second one will cool down. The natural order of things will be overturned and entropy will decrease.

Hypothetically.

When I first read about Maxwell's thought experiment, I actually believed he meant it was a real demon: sad, long-haired, shy even, like the one from Vrubel's painting, *The Demon Seated*. Also the demon was cursed, for some reason, to dwell forever inside that box.

I also liked to imagine that if colder particles were sad emotions—doubts, regrets—those "unwanted" feelings could be sorted out and thrown away.

Could an emotion-sorting demon open and close my heart's door, letting only the happy, warm particles in? Wouldn't that be nice? But if that meant all my memories of Mom would be gone along with my sadness, would I still want to be rid of those sad particles?

ᚠᚷᚠ

I wave Del into the Manor. I start to go in after her, but I hear a distant whisper and pause at the threshold to listen. The whisper comes from the giant pines, spruces, and Douglas firs guarding the edge of the woods, moving to the rhythm of the wind, hissing my name as if mocking me. The sound is framed by the ringing of a wind chime. It sounds almost like the clattering of medieval armor.

A distant whiff of animal musk tickles my nostrils and makes me think of horses. Sweat coats the insides of my arms and my heart beats a little faster. As if on cue, a flashback from my dream: I'm barging into the woods, my legs tight around the muscled back of a horse. A black horse in the white mist. But I've never ridden a horse in my life!

The wind picks up, licking my skin with its icy tongue. Trying to ignore my shivers, I stay out on the porch and scan the darkening mass of trees ahead and around the Manor. My eyes begin to water as I see nothing but the night and what comes with it.

"Hayden? You coming?" Del calls out from the Manor. "I found the central-heating switch. And there's something here you've got to see. . . ."

Dizzy with the night, I step inside. The second I turn my back to the forest, the trees begin to throw my name around. The sound of it bounces from branch to branch, from the mossy ground to the green giants' heads, until it melts away into the dark.

Hayden . . . Hayden . . . Hayden . . .

ᚠᚷᚠ

The Manor welcomes me with an inaudible sigh. Does it think *a prodigal daughter returns*? Or *an impostor invades*? Its presence all creaks and murmurs, the house acknowledges me with a slight atmospheric pressure change. I suspect all these preter-natural sensations are a testament to how exhausted I am.

"Omelette or scrambled?" Del's voice comes from the kitchen.

"You're making breakfast for dinner? And where did you come across eggs?" I make my way to the kitchen to find Del leaning into the open fridge. The kitchen actually looks . . . lived in? Not at all how I'd imagine the kitchen of a house that's been empty for years. The space is relatively clean, the lights are work-ing, and then there's the matter of the fridge's contents. "Wait.

Don't touch anything!" I grab Del's bare hand. In response, she flinches like I electrocuted her. I pull my hand back.

"But I'm hungry!" Reluctantly, she puts back her find—a carton of eggs—and steps away from the fridge.

I come closer to take a look. The fridge is not exactly packed with food, but it's not empty, either. Actually, even the fact that there *is* a working fridge in the Manor should be a warning sign. My eyebrows rise in surprise when I see a row of wine bottles lining the fridge door.

I scrutinize the rest of the items inside: packaged sliced cheese, eggs, a couple of cartons of milk (still another week to go before the expiration date). But no leftovers or anything suggesting someone's been here very recently. It looks more like someone keeps food around because he or she visits here once in a while.

I shut the fridge with unnecessary force and move around the kitchen, opening the cupboards and drawers.

Several boxes of some generic brand of cereal (all unopened). Some bland saltines. A box of whole wheat spaghetti. Canned soup (chicken noodle).

I grab a soup can from the shelf. "Do you know what this means?" I turn to Del, who watches me in silence from the corner, arms crossed over her chest. She arches one eyebrow but stays silent. I continue, surprised she's not as rattled by this discovery as I am, "Someone's been living here!"

"That much is obvious."

I pick up one of the boxes of cereal and shake it in accusation. "And *this* doesn't bother you?"

"The grocery store's off-brand? I've nothing against off-brands, if that's what you're getting at. Though I myself prefer oatmeal in the morning, I'll settle for a generic cereal if nothing else's available." Her face softening, she adds, "You're overreacting. Maybe there's someone who looks after the house, like a custodian or something, and they keep their food here. Or it's a food fairy who found out about our visit and went on a shopping run for us. Who cares?"

I put the soup and cereal back with too much force. "*Who cares?* Really? Don't you think Doreen would've mentioned something about a custodian when she was giving me the deed? I don't think we can stay here."

"You're kidding." Del gets an alarmed look on her face. She shakes her head for good measure. "Not going anywhere. It's dark out. We don't know the town. We're hungry. And there are *eggs* here!"

"Someone's been *living* in my house, Del!"

"Yeah, but you're here now. And if someone does show up, they'll see you and they'll know the owner's back. We'll call nine-one-one if we hear or see anything suspicious. We can barricade the doors, if that makes you feel calmer. But can we please, *please* stay?"

It's the worn-out notes in her voice that do me in. As I nod in surrender, her posture softens up. "Okay," I say, "but I like your idea of barricading the doors."

She claps her hands in celebration and maneuvers around me to get to the fridge. "So what'll it be?" She fishes out the eggs again, hugging the carton gently into her chest.

"I don't know. Scrambled?"

"Scrambled it is!"

As Del busies herself with cooking, I sit at the table, my mind running through possible scenarios to explain the presence of food supplies in the Manor. (Home invasion? Some kind of misunderstanding? Doreen made a mistake and *I'm* the invader?) Something really fishy is going on here, and the main overarching question I have is whether it all connects somehow: Mom's ghostly plea for me to finish her incomplete business, the military base hidden in the woods, the signs of life in the old Manor . . .

Her back to me, Del says, "By the way, these woods are genuinely creepy. How could you sleep at night here when you were a kid, having that forest for a backyard?"

She still has no idea what actually happened in these woods. Would she feel even more disturbed about being here if I told her? "Are you scared?" I tease. "Want me to tuck you in tonight and stay with you till you fall asleep? Sing you a lullaby?"

"Stay out of my bedroom, witch," she laughs, blissfully unaware of how uncomfortable her words make me.

ᚠᚷᚠ

We settle in the "salon" (a hybrid of a library and a living room), but not before I conscript Del to help me make a pathetic barricade out of a dusty armchair propped against the entrance door's handle. Del keeps rolling her eyes but, being a good friend and all, indulges me. Once done, we sit down to eat our egg feast. Empty bookshelves covering the room's perimeter stare at me—with question or accusation, I can't decide. Even after we remove most of the fabric protecting the furniture from dust and time, the Manor still looks inhospitable, despite the signs of life in the kitchen.

We find a pack of minicupcakes shoved at the back of the

fridge and devour them along with an entire bottle of some god-awful, fortified red wine—another gift from our unexpected benefactor. We toast to the "custodian" of the Manor, adding a half-assed "sorry" for eating all their food.

I just hope there won't be any bears coming in through the Manor's door at midnight, finding two stupid girls in their beds and devouring them.

The salon's dark, reflective windows make Del uneasy—I keep catching her looking sideways at them, her forehead creased with concern. Can't blame her. After Fort Greene, where it never gets completely dark at night thanks to all the light from the city, nighttime Promise is so dark, it feels like it's suspended in a jar of black ink.

I stand up, light-headed from the wine, and walk the salon's perimeter, drawing down the curtains to hide us from the night's penetrating gaze. While I'm at it, I avoid looking at my reflection in the window, irrationally scared of what might look back at me. It's an old fear, one I thought I'd exorcised out of my mind a long time ago. But the act of being here now, in Promise, where the events that shaped my childhood psyche crashed and burned like the woods the night Mom disappeared, is akin to being pulled in all directions at once.

With too much force, I jerk the last curtain closed, its weathered fabric tearing at the seams.

Tomorrow I'll find out who the hell's been maintaining the Manor all these years and, when I do, I'll have words with the mysterious, cheap-wine-loving "custodian."

I fall back into my seat next to Del. She's uncharacteristically quiet, meditating over her (third?) pink-glazed cupcake.

When she notices me staring, she stuffs the entire thing in her mouth. Her lips are stained with wine, her cheeks blushing. I probably don't look much different.

"So this is where mysterious Hayden Holland grew up," she says like a doctor giving a diagnosis, and not a very favorable one at that.

"If you think I'm mysterious, then my mother is the Great Sphinx incarnate." Affected by alcohol and exhaustion, I have little control over what's coming out of my mouth. But I don't regret bringing Mom into our conversation. Dad refuses to talk about her. Dr. Erich believes I'm healed and have moved on. But the truth is, I still think of my mother in present tense.

Del puts down her empty glass and pulls up her long legs. Her ankle boots are off and her belt's unbuckled. "What was she like?"

"Perfect." It's not a lie. To the child-me, Mom was just that: a perfect semidivine creature who all but shone in the dark. A common way for young kids to see their parents, I was told. Anyway, I grew up with this image of Mom stuck in my head. And nothing, not even her erratic behavior in the woods, worsening in the weeks prior to her disappearance, could shake that image.

My body relaxes as wine-fueled heat spreads through my veins. I lower my head on the couch's armrest and hug my knees in. Like the good old days of therapy.

My tongue loosened by alcohol, I blurt out, "She was perfect. Made of light. Her head was always up in the clouds. Sometimes she'd just forget to speak and go silent for days, and I'd be silent, too, because I thought it was a game. . . . It'd drive my father nuts. But . . . there was this streak of darkness to her light. Like she knew our family idyll wasn't going to last. If you believe in premonition, I swear my mother had it."

We plunge into silence. I bet Del's just like me at this moment: wading through the chest-high waters of childhood memories, good *and* bad.

"So what *really* happened to her?" Del asks. "I mean, I know she disappeared, but do you have any idea what happened to her?"

I don't register Del's question straightaway. I must be staring at her for too long, because her face tenses. I suspect she regrets asking. On any other day, I'd evade her questioning and retreat into my protective shell, but tonight . . . "I'd say she left us. Just took off without a good-bye, because she couldn't bother with the family life anymore. But some things about her disappearance just don't add up, so I have my doubts. . . ."

And then the metaphorical levee breaks and the river overflows and I talk, opening up like I've never opened up to anyone before.

13
ABOUT MY MOTHER

Villiam of Ockham was a Franciscan friar and philosopher who lived in England between the eleventh and twelfth centuries. Ever heard the expression *Ockham's* (or *Occam's*) *Razor*? Yeah, it's named after him: a philosophical problem-solving device.

Imagine you've got a mystery on your hands that needs solving. You come up with a number of possible explanations based on evidence, speculations, and observations. You hypothesize what the answer could be. But which of the explanations is closest to the truth? By applying Ockham's Razor to the mystery, you can slice away all unnecessary, long-winded explanations and details, until there's nothing left to slice. That leaves you with the simplest answer and, as Ockham's Razor tells us, the simplest truth. Or as close to the truth as one can get.

But then there's a Rube Goldberg machine—an overengineered device that goes through a whole lot of complicated (and unnecessary) steps to perform a simple task. An alarm clock's arrow pulls down a string; the string lifts a gate, which releases a marble; the marble hits a parrot; and the parrot jumps. It goes and goes until two eggs crack and fall into a sizzling frying pan and—voilà—here's your breakfast!

Back before Dad completely retreated into his crackpot science world of the Nibelungs and muon portals, we used to build Rube Goldberg machines with him while Mom watched on and smiled softly.

I know that, in reality, it's almost always Ockham's Razor, but if I had a choice, I'd take a Rube Goldberg machine over it every time.

ᚠᚷᚠ

Yeah, so the levee breaks and the words tumble out of my mouth. "That night she just took off into the woods. But the thing is, Mom got all weird weeks before that. I mean, weirder than her normal weird. . . . She'd wander the woods for hours. We used to go together, for walks and stuff, but then shortly before her disappearance, she stopped taking me. I knew she was sneaking off alone. She'd talk to herself a lot, too. And she had these cuts and bruises on her arms that never seemed to heal. . . ."

Red stains forming on Mom's silk blouse sleeve. She notices me looking, laughs it off—a glimpse of the old Mom in her warm smile. Says she's a klutz! Says she had a strawberry jam accident! I don't believe her. She knows it.

"Am I freaking you out? Tell me when it's too much,

please?" I study Del, trying to read her, but she's unusually quiet, her expression blank.

"And your dad never noticed anything odd?" she asks.

I shrug. "I guess he really didn't. Or didn't want to. My memories from that time are probably skewed, anyway." I back-pedal, starting to regret that I said so much, but Del pushes on.

"And the cops?" she asks. "They searched the woods after . . . she was gone?"

"Yeah, they searched everywhere but found nothing. I mean, nothing useful . . ." I take a deep breath and tell Del about the new clearing that magically appeared the night of Mom's ordeal. I tell her about the burnt trees and soil turned to glass. And I tell her about Mom's blood found splattered nearby the new clearing. Mom was bleeding heavily, it was concluded, and judging from the amount of blood lost, she couldn't have wandered far from the clearing. And yet she wasn't there, or anywhere near it.

I've never actually seen it with my own eyes. Dad made sure the Black Clearing would remain a mystery to me, taking me out of Promise almost immediately after Mom vanished in these woods.

Would I want to see the site of Mom's demise now?

Maybe. Not really. Possibly.

"There was something else, wasn't there?" Del asks. As if blood spilled in the woods isn't enough, she demands more. But she's right. There *was* something else. The last known piece of the puzzle to the Black Clearing mystery.

"It gets creepy." I meet Del's rapturous eyes. I never thought I had a talent for storytelling, but I have Del totally hooked. If

I proceed bluntly, I'm going to give her nightmares. And she's already slightly freaked out; she just doesn't show it. When I take too long to speak, she hurries me on with an impatient hand gesture and a raised eyebrow. *What are you waiting for?*

"They found a finger," I say. "A pinkie. Not far from where Mom's blood was spilled. The finger wasn't Mom's."

A short, loaded silence. "And what were the cops' theories?" Del serves more wine into her glass and tops up mine as she says, "I mean, it's all weird, obviously, but the police must've been working on something?"

My body is my armor, and right now my armor's growing particularly thick, bringing a certain sense of detachment, like I'm a machine going into safety mode after overheating. I continue talking, but it feels like it all happened to someone else. "They went through it all: foul play, Mom left us, even faked her own death for whatever reason. . . . But it never made much sense to me. Let's say Mom did intend to leave us. She took nothing of hers from the Manor. She walked out into the cold night, barefoot and wearing only her nightgown. My father, on the other hand, had a lot of theories, each one crazier than the last. But he's known for that—crazy theories, I mean."

Del stays quiet for so long, I think maybe I tired her out, or maybe it's her turn to get into safety mode, to distance herself in the name of self-preservation. But then she asks the question I've been dreading.

"But what do *you* think happened to her? What do you *really* think?"

What do I think? My answer to Del's question is twofold. "Have you ever heard of Ockham's Razor?"

"Are you really going to tell me that the simplest explanation is always *the* explanation? What is the simplest explanation in this case, even?"

"Not the supernatural one." There, I said it. "So the next one is—whatever comes to your mind after you rule out the paranormal."

I study Del. Her cheeks are flushed with wine and excitement, but her glow's waning and her eyes are half-closed. But even tired, she's not letting this go. I owe her this, I decide—I brought her here with me, and she needs to know why.

"I grew up listening to Mom's stories. She loved everything with secrets, puzzles, and clues to a riddle. She was fascinated with fairy tales and used to tell me that every one of those stories had a grain of truth in it, even the most gruesome ones. *Especially* the most gruesome ones. So when I was little, I believed Mom was kidnapped by . . . let's call them fairies."

"Fairies are not scary," Del says.

"I think you and I read different fairy tales growing up. But okay, let's call them *monsters*. I thought she was taken by monsters into a monster kingdom, because she was their lost princess. They searched for her for years while she hid in the last place she thought they'd look."

Del looks at me like she's trying to reconcile the author of the aforementioned theory and the Hayden she knows well—the mostly logical creature who can explain almost everything with science and facts. I go on, "For a while, I thought that one day they'd release her or she'd break free and walk out of the woods, come back into the house to take her seat at the dinner table, like nothing happened. But now I think she just had one of her episodes and wandered off too deep into the woods. Maybe she fell into Edmunds' Gorge. And the cops were right that the finger from the woods was something else, something unrelated. I realize that I may never know the truth, and I'm okay with that."

That last bit is a lie.

I will never be okay with not knowing what happened to my mother. But the possibility of knowing the truth has always been a scary prospect for me. What if the truth is that Mom left us? Left me? That somehow her mind got twisted and dark to the point where she decided to orchestrate her own disappearance? This possibility is too heart-wrenching to dwell on, because it means Mom never really loved my father. Or me. Or if she did love us, that love wasn't enough to stop her from leaving us.

I stand up to stretch my tired legs. "Should we go for a run tomorrow?"

"Definitely. Possibly." Del crawls off the couch and helps me gather up our dirty plates and utensils. Before leaving the salon, Del picks up her glass and gulps down the rest of the wine. Normally she doesn't drink much. Promise must be really getting on her nerves already. "Wake me up if you get up first. Don't let me sleep till noon, please. Now let's go check out the bedrooms."

Del goes upstairs, but I linger to check that the front door's still locked and the chair we set to block it is not too flimsy. I'm tempted to go and explore the Manor after Del falls asleep, to see if I can find any more signs of our mysterious benefactor whose food we ate and whose wine we drank this evening, but like Goldilocks, I'm simply about to crash. I find my old room upstairs and enter with trepidation.

Here's my old bed, its mattress bare. My painted wooden

bedside table, an ugly yellow lamp atop it. The used-to-be pink-and-yellow wallpaper isn't peeling, but it's heavily weathered, with the colors too faint to discern. Darker squares indicate where my *Labyrinth* posters used to be. I flick the light switch on. The fact that the Manor's got electricity means someone's been paying bills. I wonder if Doreen knew something but didn't tell me; she was eager to help me sell the Manor, but she did seem as confused as I was by Mom's codicil and everything that went with it.

"I found bed linens and stuff," Del yells out from the corridor. I step outside and find her in the linen closet, its door wide open. When Del emerges from the cramped space, her hands hold a pile of white fabric. "Smells clean. Our benefactor's been doing laundry."

"Maybe we should take turns sleeping," I suggest. "In case our mystery resident returns in the middle of the night and my armchair booby trap fails."

"This bedroom can be locked from the inside," Del says, nodding at the guest room behind her shoulder.

"Mine can't."

"You can stay in the master bedroom, though," she suggests. "There must be a lock there." I eye the heavy, dark wooden door at the end of the corridor. My parents' old bedroom. Even the thought of going in there, let alone sleeping there, makes me very uncomfortable. "Nope, I'm good here."

I walk back into my old room and close the lock-free door behind me. After I make the bed with the linens Del found, I set my eyes on the only other piece of furniture present—my bedside table—and, after a short deliberation and more physical exertion than I'd like to admit, bring it to the door. This will do.

I note that pillows are conspicuously absent in the Manor, which makes sense, because Dad's always had this antipillow thing, saying he likes the feel of blood flowing to his head unstopped by the elevation. There was a period of my childhood when Dad kept trying to instill his ways of life in me; that included an attempt at making me sleep without a pillow.

I wrap my messenger bag in some linen and place the bundle at the head of the bed. I fall asleep as soon as my face touches my makeshift cushion.

ᚠᚷᚠ

How long was I out before, disoriented, I jolt awake? My eyes peer into the pitch-black space. There's not a single source of light, not even the moonlight sneaking through the curtains. As the initial disorientation wears off and I remember that I'm no longer in the safety of my tiny Fort Greene bedroom, I listen to my surroundings for any clue as to what woke me. It takes my groggy brain a few intakes of breath to put two and two together and then I break into an uncomfortable sweat, my hands instantly slick: There's a shuffling noise coming from right outside my door.

I switch into panic mode. Did I lock the door? No, because the door's got no lock! The shuffle comes again. Someone's in the house. The mysterious resident has returned. Nothing good can follow.

I think sadly of Del's baseball bat, left in our Fort Greene lair. How I wish I had it with me now. If I scream loud enough, will anyone hear? I can break out of the house and run to the Reasers' in hopes that someone still lives there. That would be quite an introduction back into Shannon's life. Of course, assuming he's still there.

I slither out of bed. My feet recoil from the freezing floor, my toes curling. All evening balminess is gone from the Manor. I dash for the door and run smack into the hard edge of the bedside table I used to barricade myself in. That sure will leave a nasty bruise on my leg. My clouded brain instructs me to go around the bedside table and press an ear against the door.

I hear it again, that soft patter.

Light steps. Barely there, already tuning out.

My heart's beating so loudly, it becomes the only sound I'm hearing for a long moment. I remain unnaturally still as seconds tick by. Then I shove the bedside table out of my way and open the door a crack.

Nothing.

Then, the unmistakable screech of the basement door—opening, closing—downstairs. Someone broke into the Manor and is now hiding in the basement? Now that doesn't make much sense. Or maybe it makes perfect sense. Where else would you hide in an old house?

I swing my door open and stumble into the black corridor. After checking Del's guest bedroom (empty), I cling to a rabid hope that the noises I heard were Del, that she's just getting a drink in the kitchen downstairs. But then . . . why would I hear the basement door?

My heart's suspiciously calm now, but my hands are still cold with sweat. I'm shivering as I move through the house, my teeth chattering out Morse code. I turn on the lights as I go—down the stairs, through the salon, coming to stand before the basement door.

I listen.

A series of weak noises, muffled but there. I clutch the door handle, turn it, let my hand wander inside until I find the light switch. Flick it on. Remind myself that all those Conjuring movies were written and acted by *people* and aren't *real*. *Though they* were *based on supposedly real stories*, my inflamed mind supplies unhelpfully.

Weak light floods the basement. I take the stairs, thinking about every horror movie trope there is. But what choice do I have? Del's missing, and I'm hearing suspicious noises coming from the basement.

You could've called the police, a rational voice in my mind suggests. *Or at least armed yourself.* Frantic, I look around me: To my right, a bunch of dust-covered boxes line the wall. A collection of gardening tools hang on the wall to my left. Nothing remarkable.

Except for the partition covering what I suspect is a crawl space.

It's moved aside, revealing a dark hole in the basement wall.

No way should you be getting anywhere near that.

That's when I hear a cough, followed by a whimper, coming from within the crawl space. It sounds a lot like Del.

"Oh, damn it." At random I grab one of the rusty gardening tools from the wall and approach the gaping mouth of the crawl space entrance. Lowering my head, I slink inside. The crawl space is wide and high enough to assuage my slight claustrophobic tendencies, so I move forward, hunching my back and clutching my weapon of choice, toward a dim light and some scuttling noises. My breathing becomes so loud that

I have to stop and mentally run through the words of Mom's lullaby a few times to ground myself.

After crawling forward a few more feet, my eyes settle on a view that's definitely B-grade horror-movie worthy.

Del's in a small area on the far side of the crawl space. She's on her knees, her back to me. She's digging up the dirt with her bare hands.

I move closer. Del stops what she's doing and looks at me over her shoulder.

The only light down here is from a chunky candle on the ground next to Del. But even in the candle's weak light, I see that Del's eyes are glazed over, and her lips are moving.

She pushes her hands further into the hard soil. Her mouth releases the words, "Dig deep."

HAYDEN B. HOLLAND MEDICAL NOTES:
THE TIGER INCIDENT

DR. THORFINN ERICH

I was not scheduled to see Hayden for another month, but her father called my office yesterday to ask for an emergency appointment. Something terrible happened, he claimed, and he needed my advice on how to proceed.

My receptionist took the call: Hayden's father was crying on the phone, saying, "Something is wrong with my baby girl." Hayden's pet cat was found dead, and suspicion fell on Hayden. I was alarmed, yet awash with disbelief: Nothing in Hayden's personality so far made me think of her as dangerous. Troubled, yes. Impulsive, yes. But not dangerous in a malicious way, certainly not dangerous enough to harm an animal (or a human being) on purpose.

I cleared my schedule to see Hayden this morning.

Enclosed is a transcript of our conversation, taken down from my recording, with additional notes from memory.

Dr. Erich: Hayden, how have you been doing since we last talked?

Hayden: *[shifts in her seat, not meeting my eyes, hands firm on knees]* Fine.

Dr. Erich: Did you have any unusual dreams?

Hayden: *[Looks up in surprise. I can barely hold her gaze. Her eyes appear darker, especially the right one. A wave of primeval unease—the kind, I'd imagine, a human would feel in the presence of a deadly predator—comes over me.]* I dream of Mommy every night. Sometimes she sits on the floor by the side of my bed and whispers secrets in my ear. Sometimes I sense her hands touching my hair. Her hands are very cold.

Dr. Erich: And when she visits you, what does she talk to you about?

Hayden: Some of it is in a language I don't know. But sometimes, she sings to me. *[starts singing softly]*

Dr. Erich: What does it mean, Hayden? The lyrics, they mean something to you?

Hayden: Mommy used to sing it to me every night before I'd go to bed. And whenever it rained outside, she'd just hum it.

Dr. Erich: Interesting lyrics. Do you think your mom wrote this song?

Hayden: *[When she looks up at me, it takes a good effort on my part to keep her gaze. As if she can sense my inner struggle, she sighs and looks away.]* You want to ask me about Tiger, but you're worried about what I'm going to tell you.

Dr. Erich: Is Tiger your cat?

Hayden: You already know the answer to that, Dr. Erich.

Dr. Erich: What happened to Tiger, Hayden?

Hayden: When we first got him, Daddy said I could name him. So I named him Tiger. After Einstein's cat—he was also called Tiger and he always got depressed when it rained. . . .

Dr. Erich: Hayden, what happened to Tiger?

Hayden: Yesterday was a foggy day. And in my head it was foggy, too.

Dr. Erich: Hayden, we've been through this. It's not helpful when you evade my questions.

Hayden: *[sighs]* I'm sorry. I'm upset because Daddy thinks I did it. He thinks I killed Tiger. He didn't say it to me like that, but I know he was thinking it. Daddy thinks something is wrong with me, doesn't he? His thoughts are like little piranhas; they eat everything. Eat all the good things, like memories of my mom. . . .

Dr. Erich: Hayden, do you know what really happened to Tiger?

Hayden: I didn't plan for it to happen. But, Dr. Erich . . . when Tiger died, I

was thinking about what went down with
Jen at school, and how Jen was mocking
me, and how she made other kids make fun
of me . . . and I got so angry. I felt
these odd feelings come over me, and
Tiger was there, in the room with me.
And the next moment, he was on the floor
and not moving, and he was very silent.
I miss him. I miss Tiger. I'm so sorry.

End of transcript. Dr. Erich's
recommendation: Start on medication. Review
condition in six months.

14
DIG DEEP

Sleepwalking is fascinating. Or at least, the mystery around it is. I'm sure those who suffer from the condition may not find it particularly attractive. I've never seen sleepwalking in action, but I've got all the cultural codes about it burned into my blood. I hear "sleepwalker" and get a stereotypical image: a regular-looking person walking around, eyes open but glazed over, hands outstretched, zombielike. Maybe the sleeper is brushing his teeth, or combing her hair, or doing something else equally mundane. The creep factor kicks in when you— the omnipresent observer—realize something's not quite right with this picture.

Modern science has come a long way in its understanding of sleepwalking, but the olden explanations are so much more interesting. Take the Freudian ideas about sleepwalkers enacting sexual wish fulfillment. Or outright absurd ideas that fall firmly into the domain of pseudoscience, like Baron von

Reichenbach's Odic force—some kind of energy, present in all things, living and not. The force, as the Baron figured, was linked to specific lunar phases, hence the term *lunatic* used by some Slavic languages to denote sleepwalkers, literally meaning "one who walks under the moon."

Sleepwalking may be fascinating, but seeing Del totally under its control puts an extra twist into my already twisted gut.

ᚠᚼᚠ

"Oh my God . . . Del! Stop!" My fingers go slack, releasing my weapon. I rush at Del as fast as the tight quarters of the crawl space allow. But she doesn't stop with the digging. If anything, she forces her already-raw hands even harder into the dirt floor. I can't look away from her nails: filled with grime, cherry-red polish peeling off. Worse, Del's fingertips are blistering—angry welts spiraling on her hands, covering her skin up to the elbows. My stomach turns, barely able to keep its contents down.

Stiffly, awkwardly, I lower to my knees and face Del. I try to capture her attention by grabbing her shoulders and giving her a shake. I say her name. But she's out of it completely. With the determination of a girl possessed, her hands keep digging, their motion spookily robotic.

Unlike her hands, Del's eyes are motionless, trained down, fixated on the dirt floor. She's whispering, and, despite the queasy panic surging through me, I lean in closer to listen. Having forgotten to blink, my eyes are burning, releasing tears that I barely feel. My entire world in this moment is Del. I listen. Some of her mumblings are in English, something about digging, and *digging deep*. The rest's in French, too fast and too low for me to understand. But when Del says clearly what sounds a lot like *vieux sang*, I'm about 75 percent certain I know what it means.

Old blood.

"Okay, that's enough digging for tonight, young lady." I wrap my fingers around Del's elbow (her skin's shockingly cold) and heave her upright. I expect resistance, but she complies, pliant under my touch. My treacherous hands start to shake; I have to tighten my grip on Del's arm. I try not to reveal in my voice how completely terrified I am. "Let's go get you cleaned up."

"You need to dig deep." Her earnest tone tricks me into believing she's back to her nondazed self. But a close look confirms that she's clearly not. A veil of dreaminess is cast over her dark eyes. This Del—the physical shell of my best friend, of the girl who's the epitome of vitality—is giving me the creeps right now. Hard to imagine this is the same girl I was just hanging out with, drinking stolen wine and talking about my mother. The same girl, now *minus* her lively persona and *plus* minor burns on her skin. At least, I hope those are minor burns. Del's not screaming in pain, but she might be resistant to it while she's in this trance.

Then Del says in a ghoulish voice, "Abigail Reaser is thinking of you. She says: Stay away from her son. She says your kind has done enough harm to her family."

My kind? "What did you just say?" I release Del's elbow, and she wobbles on her feet. The confines of the small space are pressing down on me, and I get a spill of dizzy claustrophobia.

Del replies, her voice softer but still creepy, "She's in a keeping place, but she remembers everything. She says she gave your kind everything she had, but you can't have her son. You can't have him."

I wish I could just write off Del's statements as sleepwalker ramblings. I really do. But I can't imagine how Del would know about Abigail Reaser and my history with her son. I have no idea what happened to Abigail after Mom went missing and Dad took me out of Promise. All I know is that Abigail was close to Mom. I also knew their friendship was not about dinner parties and carpools. It was something misunderstood, sinister even, judging from the shadows coating their faces when they were together, their mouths sagging with the weight of unspoken secrets.

Shannon had a sleepover in the Manor whenever his mother was in a "bad mood." At times, he'd show up with little cuts and scratches on his skin, but he dismissed those with an impatient smile, and I was too interested in exploring the woods with him to interrogate him about his home life. I shudder now, angry at my childish obliviousness. It wouldn't take a genius to guess what really went on in that house behind closed doors.

"Del, how do you know about Abigail Reaser? How do you know anything about her at all?"

"Dig deep."

"I will. *I will*," I assure her. I'm about to ask her about Abigail again, but this *dig deep* business reminds me of Mom's card, the one that came with the deed to this house. It pictured a girl with a bleeding heart, and Mom wrote on the back: *Dig deep*. I dismissed it as poetic nonsense, thinking Mom meant it metaphorically, as in soul-searching. But what if I'm wrong? Maybe Mom wanted me to literally dig something up? *Maybe Mom's using Del to communicate her will to me.* The thought gives me the shivers.

I snuff out the candle, plunging us into semidarkness. "Dig deep," Del whispers, her legs weakening as I lead her through the crawl space, into the basement, up the stairs, and into her bedroom's en suite bathroom. Once the water's running cold, I direct Del's burnt hands under the stream. Careful with her damaged skin, I gently clean the burns before focusing on getting all the filth from under her chipped fingernails. The mundane task keeps me busy, distanced from the whirlwind of scary thoughts threatening to take over my mind.

When I turn off the water, the Manor becomes too silent for its muteness to be natural. No creaking wood, no groans coming from the old walls settling as the cold rolls in. The house is listening, watching. A layer of sweat covers my forehead. I'm beginning to think there's a chance I made some kind of horrible mistake by coming here, that this place—the Manor, Promise, the woods—is a lot more than it seems and that maybe I'm messing with something I don't understand. *Ancient evil that poisons the soul. Mom's darkest secret, her hidden treasure, her heaviest burden . . .*

I push these thoughts to the very back of my mind and focus on Del. To my relief, by the time I guide her out of the bathroom and toward the bed, Del has come to her senses. More or less. "Is it time to go out for a run?" she asks. "But it's still dark out . . . and I'm *so* tired."

I lower her onto the bed and sit next to her. Trained at me, Del's eyes pose a silent question. Then she winces and cradles her hands against her chest. "I think I got burned. I don't remember how. Or when. My skin hurts."

I urge her not to move, not that I think she'll be going anywhere right now, and run into my room, returning with a travel first-aid kit I packed for the trip. It's not much, but I did bring a tube of aloe vera, since I'm prone to burning myself when I'm left alone next to stovetops and irons.

I take one of Del's hands and apply the gel, moving my fingers in gentle strokes. "You've been sleepwalking. Gave me a fright. I thought we had a break-in. You're lucky I didn't bash your head in." I let go of her hand and take the other one. Her burns don't look too bad now, already fading. Maybe they weren't burns or blisters at all but some kind of allergic reaction?

"Crap! Sorry." She massages her temples with her free hand, wincing at what I imagine is a monster headache. "I must've had too much to drink last night, must've forgotten to take my pills. Can't remember much."

"So you don't remember what you were saying?"

"Was I talking, too? Oh . . . this is so embarrassing."

Hiding my disappointment that she's got no recollection of her nocturnal adventures, I finish with the second layer of aloe vera and let go of her hand.

"It wasn't too bad," I lie, wrapping an arm around her shoulders and pulling her in for an awkward hug. Her skin is so cold. I pull the blanket up to cover her back. Del still seems out of it and, I suspect, she's barely noticing me fussing over her. When her eyes regain that distant-dream quality, my heart twinges with concern. If she goes into her trance again, I won't know what to do to make her safe. But, I wonder, if she does zone out, would it be totally unethical for me to question her more about Abigail and Shannon Reaser?

"You think you can fall asleep again?" I ask, already feeling guilty for even considering taking advantage of Del's powerless state.

"I'll try." Del relaxes onto her back, stretching out across the bed. Once her eyes close, I leave the room.

Deafening thunder shakes the Manor to its foundation, sending a quiver through my bare feet. The wrongness of it is not apparent at first, but then I realize: I saw no lightning flash preceding the thunder. As a kid, every time lightning would flash, I'd count down till I heard the thunder. The act of counting calmed me—something to do with the inevitability of thunder *always* following the lightning. A memory I didn't know I'd lost comes now, fresh and bright: Shannon, the boy with dark hair and attentive gray eyes, would tease me about my counting compulsion, saying that one day the rules would change and I'd be forever counting, waiting for thunder that would never come. This brings me back to Promise, where the elements follow their own rules, it seems. Did Shannon know what he was talking about then? Would he tell me what all of this means if I marched across the field and banged on his door now, in the middle of the night?

Raindrops drum against the Manor's shingled roof. Rattled and with no sleep left in me, I return to my room and find my cell phone, which I left charging. There's no reception and no Internet. The glowing digits claim it's only half past midnight. Mom would call it the witching hour and wink at me. On my phone, I bring up my observations journal and make a third entry in my latest project. I title it "Promise" and record Del's sleepwalking episode.

Altogether, my three entries point at one common factor in all these strange occurrences: me. But I can't think of what hypothesis to make from that.

I set my phone aside and go through my messenger bag until my fingers land on the plastic folder containing the deed to the Manor and Mom's clue card. I read the back of the card. *The greatest power comes from within you. Dig deep. Your hands can handle the heat. In the house on the edge of the woods, the rotten key lies. Yours to finish what I started. . . .*

Was Mom seriously unwell? Was she seeing omens and warnings everywhere? Paranoid about some paranormal force pursuing her? Did she believe there was some higher purpose to her erratic actions? Did she go from innocent walks through the woods to self-mutilation and bloodletting?

I analyze Mom's message and the deed's conditions, sentence by sentence, but my stubborn brain insists on showing me the memory of Del digging in the crawl space, her burnt hands burrowing into the earth.

The greatest power comes from within me? I don't feel that powerful. And what's with all this inspirational crap anyway? Especially coming from Mom, who cut herself and behaved like nothing was off. Like she didn't need help.

Growing angry, I roll my hands into tight fists, my nails digging into the flesh, breaking the skin. Surprised at the pain, I let go and stare at the bleeding crescent marks on my palms, barely visible in the dim light. To relax, I start humming the lullaby Mom used to sing to me, the one about the warrior, the handmaiden, and the queen with her army. *The blood of the first three, it'll break down the walls . . .* I'd never given it much thought, but now, as I study its weird lyrics, an oddly visceral response starts to build inside me, my blood thumping faster and faster. As if my particles, the building blocks of me, are rearranging, making me into something . . . else.

Dig deep.

Okay, Mom, I'm going to dig. I'm going to find whatever it is you've hidden in this house. And when I find it, you won't be a nagging mystery anymore, just a sad memory I'll revisit when it rains. But for now, I'll go to the basement and finish what my sleepwalking friend started—I'll dig.

Blue Haven Research Institute: Incident report #42A382

Supporting document: Eyewitness statement

Subject: Arista Kazan

Date and time: February 23, 8:34 a.m.

Location of interview: Research Lab 3

Interviewer (I.): Please state your full name, age, and position.

A. K.: Arista Kazan. Twenty-nine years old. Senior research fellow in physics at BHRI.

I.: Ms. Kazan, please describe what happened the night Patient X had an episode that led to the destruction of the Institute's west wing.

A. K.: Patient X . . . We started calling her that because she doesn't like the sound of her real name. Every time someone drops "Abigail" or "Abbie," she panics, pulls at her restraints, and screams. Twice on my watch now, the wound on her left hand, where the little finger's missing, has opened up from exertion and her stitches had to be redone. I'm told she's been here in the Institute's care close to ten years, and her wound hasn't healed; it's been seeping blood on and off all this time. And what makes it so much more dangerous is that Abigail's blood is so augmented because of what happened to her in Promise, it becomes volatile whenever Abigail is agitated, emitting anomalous black-body radiation. And you know what that means. . . .

I can see the evidence on our equipment every time Patient X loses her calm in a bad way. Usually, these moments—the radiation release incidents—are linked to her emotions and can be predicted by our monitors, but this time something was different. It is my belief that Abigail used her blood's radiation-generating ability *deliberately*, so she could attempt an escape. She wanted to warn someone of some imminent danger.

I.: Ms. Kazan, it is not your job to make assumptions or draw conclusions about Patient X's motivation. Tell me what happened during your shift, the night Patient X escaped her room and harmed herself in the west wing.

A. K.: Okay, sure. That night was like any other night for me. I did my first round, then went to my lab to run some tests. It was quiet. When I was on my second round, sometime past midnight, I saw a white bird—a raven—peeking into Patient X's room through the barred window. The patient became visibly animated, started screaming at the bird, warning it to stay away from her and her family. I checked my equipment remotely, but there was no sign of an incident coming, so I went back into my lab. It was during my third round that . . . I don't remember what happened exactly.

I.: What's the last thing you recall?

A. K.: Patient X saying my name. She never called me, or anyone really, by their name, never made eye contact with any of us at the Institute. But that night, she said my name, and I approached her room and opened the little window in the door so I could talk to her. After that . . . I remember waking up on a cot in the Institute's recovery room. What happened? No one will tell me!

I.: Ms. Kazan . . .

A. K.: Please tell me, Dr. ◼◼◼◼◼◼◼◼

I.: We hadn't thought it possible for a human to develop such abilities, but Patient X has proved us wrong. Ms. Kazan, you were compelled by Patient X to release her. She then attempted to find her way out of the compound. When she realized she couldn't leave, she cut herself and caused the biggest radiation leak in our history. This took place in the Institute's west wing. It has now been sealed off. There were no survivors.

A. K.: Oh my God! I . . . How could this happen? I . . . It's my fault. . . .

I.: You shouldn't blame yourself, Ms. Kazan, but since your standing with Patient X has been permanently compromised, you're being reassigned.

A. K.: No! I can't lose this job. Dr. ███████████ you can't get rid of me. What's going to happen to my lab? My samples? My research? I can't go through this again.

I.: You're not losing your job, Ms. Kazan. You're way too valuable to the Institute—you have progressed our understanding of blood anomalies in Promise by leaps and bounds. On the contrary, we're promoting you. It is a special project, of sorts, and you're uniquely positioned to do it. As part of your new role, we ask that you reach out to your former PhD advisor Tom Holland and offer to fund his research into the Promise anomaly. You're to relocate to Promise and lead Tom's research team there. You're to set up a portable research base and launch a blood drive campaign. It is the special kind of proteins that we're after that can only be found in blood samples. Our goal is to identify other individuals like our Patient X—augmented humans . . . as well as the augmenters.

A. K.: The augmenters?

I.: Ms. Kazan, what do you think is causing blood anomalies in Promise?

A. K.: My educated guess is that it's geophysical activity in the woods—the same phenomenon that shuts down all cellular and radio activity and causes it to snow in July. It emits black-body radiation that spikes once in awhile, but it's never reached critical level. Yet.

I.: Yes. But unfortunately, that's only the beginning.

15
FINDERS KEEPERS

Every cell of my body shrieks "Hell no!" so it is a sheer feat of will on my part to make the trek from my room to the basement (again), to take the stairs down (again), and to face the shapeless, muted darkness of the crawl space (again!). Mom's words feed on my brain: *dig deep . . . the rotten key . . . finish what I started . . . the ravens . . . my hidden treasure, my heaviest burden . . .*

What was your heaviest burden, Mom? Is that what killed you in the woods?

It's so quiet down here, I can hear the house breathing. Once I reach the bottom of the stairs, I stand still, breathing slowly to quell my rising panic. The lack of sleep combined with Del's freakish incident combined with the last twenty-four hours of flying and driving makes me jittery and prone to hallucinations. For a moment there, I think I feel cold fingers curling around my ankle, but it's just a draft. There's nothing here but old memories and years' worth of useless junk.

I manage to take control of my rampant imagination just enough to move closer to the gaping mouth of the crawl space. That draft I feel on my legs is definitely coming from there, and the air is heavy with the stench of overturned earth, making me think of open graves and cold crypts. No way am I touching the raw soil on the other side of the crawl space with my bare hands—the thought sends a jolt of revulsion through me. Besides, Del did burn herself somehow during her infernal digging spell. Maybe there's a hidden hot water pipe buried in the ground or, worse, a loose wire giving off sparks.

Delaying my descent into the crawl space, I survey a selection of rusty, sad-looking tools lining one of the basement's walls. One's missing—I must've left it where Del was digging. I need a shovel anyway, but it'd be difficult to move around with something that long in the constricting room beyond the crawl space. Besides, the shovel's wooden core makes me think *splinters*. So I settle on a garden spade.

I do a double take when I notice a couple of flashlights stacked on the crooked shelf next to the tools. How could I have missed them earlier? I grab one flashlight, and, miraculously, it works. *Thank the same mysterious source that stocked the fridge with eggs and wine and had clean bed linens just waiting for you*, a nasty voice whispers in my mind.

I fight an overpowering impulse to hang the spade back on its hook, throw the flashlight into a corner, wash my hands, and crawl back into bed. Tomorrow I'll wake up and pronounce the end of our short-lived trip, and we'll get into our Kia and drive off, the Manor be damned.

But when I continue into the crawl space despite my mind's protests, I know the truth is that I'm not going anywhere until I find out what Mom's heaviest burden was and why it had to be surrounded by such a thick shroud of secrecy.

And so, armed with the garden spade and a flashlight, I enter the crawl space and approach the spot where Del was digging up the floor. I inspect the damage done. For one skinny girl, Del sure managed to overturn a whole load of dirt in record time. Her accomplishment is a hole about fifteen inches deep. Done with her bare hands. Impressive!

I keep the flashlight on, placing it on the ground facing the hole. Fueled by my mystery-solving drive and growing anger at Mom for making me do this, I stick the spade into the predug cavity and push on.

After about ten spadefuls, I hit a hard surface. The excitement of the moment makes me forget all about my earlier squeamishness. Vibrating like a tight guitar string, I roll up my sleeves and attack the dirt with my bare hands, pushing the ripped-up soil to the side. For seconds all I can hear is the racket of my animalistic digging and thunderous breathing.

A faint glint of metal catches my eye as a strange object emerges from the dirt. After removing another fistful of earth, the buried object is revealed: a metal box, darkened with mud and time. While the box is not large, its weight, as I heave it out of the hole, suggests that its walls are reinforced steel or something equally dense.

The box is locked. *Is this Mom's heaviest burden?* Let's find out. Before I climb back out of the crawl space, I point the flashlight into the darkness: The ground of the small crawl space is seriously messed up, like an army of the undead has risen out of it. It's amazing what a girl can do when she puts her mind to it!

Clutching my find close to my chest, I clear out of the crawl space.

I must look filthy. As far as I can see, my knees and my arms up to my elbows are covered with dirt, and there's probably a wild glint in my eyes that gives away exactly how disturbed I am right now.

Cat-silent, I move up the stairs, hoping not to wake Del. Back in my room's attached bathroom, I wash my hands, careful to brush the dirt from under my nails. The water in the sink turns brown, then finally transparent again. One look in the mirror prompts me to stick my face under the running stream as well. Good enough. Now, the box.

A simple storage container, nothing interesting about it, if not for the runic symbols crudely etched all over its lid and sides. I haven't done the necessary comparative work, but I bet the symbols are the same as those encasing the Manor's main door and the rest of the building. My knowledge of runic symbol systems is close to nonexistent, but what I do know of ancient protection symbols points to the intent of warding the Manor (and this metal box specifically) against someone or something. I guess it worked; the box looks like it's been untouched for years.

I run my fingers over the runic writing and a sudden heat comes off the symbols. I jerk my hand back and stare at my fingertips, half expecting the skin to crack and peel. It doesn't, but a slight tingling remains where I touched the runes.

As I fiddle with the lock, a faint scratching sound comes from the window. I hurry to the glass, the absence of curtains or blinds making me feel exposed. I listen, but there's no repeat sound, so I turn my attention back to the box and its lock. The lock is small, of the generic type sold in airports for luggage. A type of lock that wouldn't be hard to cut with pliers. I saw some in the basement, right next to the garden spade I used for digging. That would require going back to the basement, of course.

But then I visualize the ring holding the Manor's keys. I didn't pay it much attention when we entered the house—I was too eager to get in—but there were five, maybe six keys on that ring, and at least one seemed tiny enough to fit into this particular lock. I might as well try that before I start messing with the lock for real. I check my messenger bag for the key ring, and once I lay my eyes on it, I know my observation was spot-on: The miniature key is a perfect fit. The lock clicks open and the lid slides up.

Another glossy card. The image: Three ravens (one black, one gray, and one white) form a triangle around a heart, the same kind the girl from Mom's first card holds in her hand. A bleeding human heart, looking freshly ripped from someone's rib cage. Thanks, Mommy!

I start to read another message from Mom scribbled on the back of the card, but then I see the rest of the stuff in the box and everything else seems unimportant.

Another scratching sound from the window. A raven lets out a caw, but I pay it no attention. As I gawk at the contents of the box, the muscles of my face tense, my mouth twisting into a grimace, first of confusion, then disgust.

If this were a horror movie, this would be the moment when I come across a creepy doll with human eyes watching me or when I find myself locked in a room with a cursed mirror, only a flimsy curtain standing between me and its hex.

In the box, three glass vials filled with red liquid sit snug in slots cut out in a Styrofoam brick. The blood looks fresh, not yet coagulated. It whirls around when I pick up one of the vials. But how can it be? The metal box looks like it's been sitting buried in the basement, undisturbed, for years.

A thump against the window makes me look up. Clutching one of the vials, I flick the lights off and go to the window. Spooked by my sudden movement, something takes off from the windowsill so fast that I only catch a glimpse of it. A splash of white against the inkiness of the night. A white raven?

Shivering, I come back to the box and sit on the floor, facing it. After close inspection, I find that each vial is marked with unique letters. The same elegant writing I've been seeing a lot lately—Mom's writing. The vials are labeled *ET-H*, *GD*, and *ED*.

The first label has Mom's initials. Ella Townsend-Holland. Mom's blood, then. And the others?

Shaking my head in frustration, I set aside the matters of the blood's freshness, origin, the vials' creepy location, and that Del seemed to know *exactly* where to dig for them, and I read Mom's second clue. It's got her signature cryptic style, but it's pretty well spelled out—what Mom wants me to do now becomes alarmingly clear:

Hayden, take these vials into the Promise woods and pour them over the spot where the fog's the thickest, where your skin crawls the most. Then draw your own blood. Your intent must be clear. As your blood is spilled, think of the door closing, of an entrance blocked, of a tomb sealed.

As I read and reread Mom's "instructions," I wish someone like Buffy Summers was around so she could ease this strange situation with a quirky remark. But no one's around—just me (frowning and shivering on the inside), three vials of at least a decade-old, uncoagulated blood, and Mom's plea for me to go cut myself in the woods.

I place the flash card back into the box, lock it, and shove it to the back of my empty closet.

16
THE ENEMY ON OUR PORCH

Even hidden away in the closet, the presence of the blood vials is tangible in the room. Vibrating, enriching the air with their subsonic call. A ghost planet unseen by telescopes but felt because of her gravitational pull, the box and its contents call for me, draining me of sleep and reason. I'm nothing but a small celestial object caught in their orbit.

Can't sleep. Can't get Del's glazed-over eyes out of my mind. Can't stop thinking of Mom, of the nightmare her life must've been—the endless cycle of self-mutilation in the woods, driven by her all-consuming belief in some higher purpose. *I'm meant to think of a door closing when I draw my own blood?* The rational part of me laughs at the idiocy of this idea, while another Hayden—the one who wants to believe in magic, the little girl who thought her mother was an elfish queen in hiding—is ready to go into the woods *now* and do exactly as Mom's instructions say.

But I don't go anywhere. I stay in bed, flat on my back, and listen to the rain and wind gently assaulting the roof's shingles, dislodging bits of wood and stone, sending them ricocheting off the walls before perishing into the mud. I read a story once where a woman lived in an isolated house just like this one; every time she lay sleepless in her bed on a stormy night (and it rained a lot in that story), listening to the way the storm made the house sound possessed, she imagined it was a small child playing with a jar of marbles in the attic. Of course, in the story, the house *was* haunted.

I have to make a conscious choice to stop thinking about hauntings and possessions. Even with my penchant for scientific explanations, I'm not immune to irrational fears and occasional night terrors. When I finally start to fall asleep, a half-forgotten memory of Mom emerges from the depths of my mind. I'm five, and the two of us are walking through the woods, collecting rocks, twigs, and dried-up leaves from the forest bed. The intent is to make a collage, Mom says. I want to help, so I reach out for a low-hanging branch and break its leafy tip off. It's for our dinner table's centerpiece, I try to explain when Mom frowns at me, but she speaks before I can.

"We only take things the forest discards, Hayden." Mom's voice no longer has the playful tone it held a minute ago. She stops and looks at me, and I read some strange conflict in her eyes. The branch I broke falls out of my hand. I feel so sad that I disappointed her, that I did something wrong. Silence. My eyes become wet.

"Oh, don't cry, my love." Mom's expression softens, a swift change. She kneels in front of me and takes my little hands into hers. Her skin is warm—not like in the nightmares I used to have as a child in the year after she disappeared. I take a few rapid breaths, pushing the tears back. Holding my hands, Mom whispers, "It's not important now, but there will come a time when it's very important that you listen to me, to what I have to say to you, even if it's not said with words. Can you promise me that you'll listen carefully when the time comes to listen? When I'm no longer around?"

"'No longer around'?" I repeat, her words a frightening puzzle. Her soft voice fills me with sadness over what's going to happen. I don't know what it is yet or when it's happening, but I know it's going to shatter me.

"One day I'll tell you everything," she says. "I'll find a way to tell you. . . . But today?" She smiles and winks at me as she picks up the branch I broke, handing it back to me. "Let's focus on getting that centerpiece sorted."

It didn't occur to me until we started on our way back to the Manor that I never mentioned to Mom that I wanted the branch for the centerpiece. But I'd experienced so many moments just like this one—moments when Mom just happened to know exactly what I was thinking, what my anxiety was all about or what I was planning to do—that I stopped paying attention. It became my "normal."

When we got closer to the Manor, I saw a young woman standing on our porch. Waiting for us. The moment my eyes landed on her slim frame, I couldn't look away. It was as if the woman was magnetic, shaping the world around her to her liking, a black hole sucking all matter in.

The visitor had cropped short hair and skin as oddly translucent as Mom's. There was tension coming off Mom's body in powerful waves; it made me tear my eyes away from the visitor and look at my mother.

I tensed up, too, though I wasn't sure why, but my skin crawled in that instinctive way it does when you know you must run and run fast, but you do a stupid thing instead and listen to your logical mind, staying still. My logic won out that day; the woman on our porch wasn't threatening—her stature fragile, a lonely willow tree on the riverbank. But she still made me afraid somehow, in the turn of her mouth and in the shape of her eyebrows, twisted into thin arcs of disapproval.

A car—a dinged-up silver Volvo, to be exact—parked next to the Manor's porch had a bumper sticker paraphrasing a Dylan Thomas poem, saying WE WILL NOT GO SILENTLY INTO THE NIGHT, and that's what did it for me: I knew then that the woman was trouble, even before she whispered the words of the language from my dreams right into my ear. The possibility of that sound carrying over space between us defied all kinds of laws of nature. I knew then that I was dreaming—that my memory had turned into a nightmare—but the knowledge did little to assuage my sheer terror.

17
PROMISE NEEDS YOUR BLOOD!

In the past, some cultures saw dreams as portals between worlds, twisted visions of our futures or glimpses of our other—unlived—lives. Dreams form a library of patterns. There are common types most dreamers experience at least once in their lifetime: flying, falling, losing teeth, showing up naked to school, the test sheet filled with the crawling spiders of a foreign alphabet.

Sigmund Freud, the father of psychoanalysis, explained dreams as our unspoken desires, expressions of our longing for the forbidden, while Carl Jung put the primary focus on our collective consciousness and its archetypes—the primal concepts of evil and good that we inherit from our ancestors and they inherited from theirs, going back to time immemorial.

Science today has stepped away from psychoanalysis-centered dream interpretation theories in favor of an understanding that dreams actually don't *mean* anything but rather are random impulses generated by the human brain out of thoughts and images stuck in our memory. What we know now is that everyone dreams, but we tend to forget our dreams shortly after waking up, and we only dream of things we've seen or experienced. Our brains craft dreams to make sense of consumed information.

And then there are *my* dreams, *my* brain's attempt to make sense of things I definitely don't remember experiencing. More fleeting sensations than concrete images, my memories of my dreams can be set off by sounds, scents, a certain play of light. I might detect a familiar cadence in someone's voice, which triggers the vivid sensation of hearing that alien tongue that haunts me, its whispers burning the skin of my ears. A hint of a cold draft sneaks into my room and voilà, I'm riding an unsaddled horse, wind attacking my face. And then the dreams evolve into something else. It's me leading a bloodthirsty army, eager to set the world ablaze. It's me running the tip of a blade against my skin, blood drops disappearing into the thirsty ground. It's me looking at Shannon, who's riding by my side, his features unclear but his presence setting my nerves on fire. It's me reaching for Shannon's face only to see the fast-shifting fog devour his features.

It's me *hearing* my blood boil in my veins in reaction to the presence of a strange woman on the Manor's porch.

I struggle to wake up, but the woman's guttural murmurs cling to me, using me to escape out of the dreamscape Promise and into the waking world, leaving me stuck in limbo where I know I'm dreaming, yet can't bring myself to wake up.

It's not real, I insist, but the dream-me has her eyes glued to the face of the whispering woman. My daytime logic is no help. So I turn to dream logic instead.

I can make the woman disappear. I can silence her.

I wish her gone, but she doesn't let go. If anything, her figure solidifies, her murmurs in my ears turning into the loud buzzing of angry wasps.

I wake up to the drumming of rain.

My weary muscles are fatigued. The night of little sleep and too much action has caught up with me. I leave the bed and go to the window. Outside, all I see is rain. I stretch my limbs before leaving the room to look for Del.

She's downstairs, settled at the kitchen table, eyes buried in her laptop. Fingers race across the keyboard. Lips enunciate silent words as she types.

Last night's sleepwalking has no visible effect on Del's physical appearance; my friend is as glowing as ever.

"How are you feeling?" I ask.

She peels her eyes off the screen, but her fingers don't stop their staccato rhythm. "Great. You?"

Right, she's got no memory of her crawl space misadventures. Uncertain of protocol when it comes to discussing sleepwalking episodes with sleepwalkers, I say, "So you're not suffering from any . . . side effects after, you know, going all creepy on me in the basement?"

That gets her full attention. She stops typing. "What do you mean?"

"I found you in the Manor's basement crawl space . . . must have been sometime around midnight. It looked like you were trying to tunnel through the Manor's foundation, while muttering on and on about *digging deep*." I hold back the part where I took over digging duty and found the blood vials.

Del stares at me before breaking into strained laughter. "Sorry you had to witness that. At least now I know why my nails are all messed up this morning. I must've forgotten to take my meds last night, which is ironic since I just told you yesterday about my condition!"

I listen to her laugh it off—she tries too hard to sound casual, dismissive. "So you're really okay then?"

"I'm fine. Just embarrassed. Again, sorry I got you freaked out."

Del looks away, clearly uncomfortable with this conversation, but I press on, way too spooked by our encounter last night to just let this go. "Yeah, it *was* pretty freaky," I say carefully. "Some things you said . . . they were kind of personal."

"Oh." She looks up at me, crossing her arms over her chest. "I suspect it might've sounded like I was making sense or whatever, but the truth is, when I mumble things during my sleepwalking episodes, it doesn't really mean anything. I just say random garbage, and it's superembarrassing afterward. I'd love it if you could just forget it—and I'll make sure not to forget my medication again."

"You had burns on your arms," I say, feeling like I'm trying to catch Del off guard for some reason. "I put aloe on them."

Del rolls up her sleeves and looks at her arms, giving me a full view of her skin. "They're fine. Are you sure?"

I inspect them myself. Whatever was there is gone. "I-I guess not."

"I'm fine," she says once more. "Maybe you were a little asleep, too."

I don't quite believe her, but I let this sleepwalking business go for now. I'm all queasy myself from what I've found in the basement, and I worry if I start digging into Del's secrets, she might start digging into mine. I change the topic. "How's your group project assignment coming along?"

"It'd be so much easier with Internet access, but I guess I can always find a public computer in a library or something when I'm ready to send this off."

"Fancy taking a break? I'm going for a run now to clear my head. Come with?"

"Nah, I'm on a roll here." Del looks up from the laptop's screen. "What's happening later?"

Before I respond, I recall the instructions Mom left for me in the basement—along with the blood vials. Despite Mom's usual cryptic manner, this time it's pretty clear what she wants me to do: Go into the woods, locate some specific spot there, pour the vials out, and cut myself. Should I do it?

Yeah, right. Because Mom was so trustworthy where her obsession with the woods was concerned. No, I doubt I can justify marching into the woods and doing the cutting and everything.

A different plan forms in my head. I need information first—about my mother, about her activities in the woods, and about that woman on the porch that my murky memory dredged up last night. I have to find out why Mom looked so freaked out by the woman's presence. But I don't have much to go by: the beat-up old car with the menacing bumper sticker;

the strange woman's appearance, which likely has changed over the years; the fact that the woman clearly knew my mother . . . So my best chance at finding her would be to talk to Mom's friends or anyone who knew her at all. Logically speaking, stop number one should be the Reaser house. Whether I'm ready to face Shannon is another story.

To Del, I say vaguely, "Maybe I'll go for a drive instead of the run. Have a look around. Bring us some lunch. I'll let you know if I find a library."

"If you can wait till afternoon, I'd like to go with you."

I know Del's going to give me hell about it, but I want to go on my recon mission alone. "Actually, I have a chore to do."

Now, *that* was a very wrong thing to say. Del's attention is now fully on me again. "Ah, you have a mysterious chore again."

"Fine," I say, feeling cornered by Del. "We'll go for a drive together this afternoon. There's no mystery!" To hide that there *is* in fact a mystery, I wrap up this encounter and head back upstairs. But even as I leave Del alone in the kitchen, I can sense her suspicion, almost palpable in the air.

I return to my room and change into some exercise tights and a Hunter sweatshirt. I slide my feet into my pair of sneakers and lace them up tight. Ready, I step out onto the Manor's porch. A freezing blast of wind slams into my chest.

As I close the Manor's door, I almost don't notice a letter-size printout sticky-taped to it. An advertisement flyer. Well, that was quick. Or coincidental. I peel the paper off and turn my back to the wind to read it.

Promise needs your blood!

A blood drive call. I skim through the text about shortages of blood donations in the region. Everyone's invited to give blood to help those in need. The location is a temporary collection point set up just off Promise's main road. In the woods, judging from the directions given. Hmm.

I've never given blood before. In fact, I can't even remember if I've ever had my blood taken or skin pierced for any reason. But it's not the prospect of donating blood that sounds alarm bells in my head; rather it's the recurring theme of blood that keeps chasing me everywhere I turn in Promise.

A sudden bird cry shatters my concentration. I crumple the blood drive flyer into my sweatshirt pocket and look up. The skies are alive with birds, hundreds and hundreds of black dots, crisscrossing. The longer I watch, the more I see it: an odd pattern to the birds' seemingly chaotic movement. The birds group together to form shapes that are reminiscent of the runic symbols. Thinking I'm going nuts, I look away and then up again, but the messy cloud of birds is just that—a cloud, revealing no hidden meanings or messages. I shake it off and start walking, coming to a halt when I see something else—a white blur on the wet ground at my feet. I step back, consumed by goose bumps. A few shallow breaths calm my upturned stomach. I'm grateful I had nothing to eat this morning.

I dare a closer look at what I realize is a bird. Or what's left of it. Its feathers are tainted with mud, its body twisted and broken, but I still know with certainty it's a raven. A white one with a splash of black shaped like a lopsided heart on its left wing.

The sight of the raven brings up a memory of my pet cat. *Tiger*.

Tiger had a short life, and the way he died—dropping dead one day for no apparent reason—darkened my childhood just a little bit more.

I give myself a hug. Can't stand it. Need to get away.

I break into a light run, soil slippery under my unsteady feet.

I quickly gain speed, eager to run away from the Manor, the dead raven, and Mom's ghost, even though I know I can't outrun Mom's blood in my veins.

I race across the field behind the Manor, holding my breath as I pass by the Reaser house. I stop and study the building, which shows no signs of life. No cars parked outside. Windows dark, shutters closed. The lawn unkempt and the porch sad-looking. If anyone still lives here, they don't care much about maintenance. On impulse, I run to the house, fly up the porch stairs, and knock on the door. "Anyone? Shannon?" I yell for good measure, but the house remains silent, disinterested.

I leave. A cold drizzle pinches at my face and flattens my hair. I increase my pace, eager for much-needed body heat. Without breaking my rhythm, I navigate my way through the field, now overtaken by wild, cold-resistant flowers and weeds. Patches of long grass reach up to my knees. At the field's outer edge, I linger, caught on that amorphous line separating the woods from my family's property. An ankle-high layer of fog blankets the ground, stretching as far as I can see ahead. I tease the moving river of white with the tip of my shoe.

As I'm about to enter the woods, a white blur in my peripheral vision gets my attention. The bird swoops from above and lands on a branch high above my head. *Another* white raven? Could there be a whole murder of them out here? My breath still catching after my mad dash across the field, I stare at the bird. It stares back. Waits for something. A strange guardian of the forest.

I change my mind about going into the woods and, vaguely disappointed in myself, turn around and go back to the Manor.

I search for a shock of white on the ground. The dead raven's body. But the bird's remains are nowhere to be found. I even walk up and down the length of the Manor's porch, searching for it, but the raven's gone.

HAYDEN B. HOLLAND MEDICAL NOTES:
ONE-YEAR REVIEW

Treating therapist: Dr. Thorfinn Erich, BS, MD, DO, PhD

Name: Hayden Holland

Height: four feet, six inches

Weight: ninety-four pounds

Date: March 3

Medications: Currently none. Previously, at start of treatment, 0.5 mg of alprazolam daily for one month, then as needed (semi-weekly) for five months.

The patient: Hayden Holland; nine years, eleven months old.

The child looks well, dark shadows underneath her eyes almost gone, lips not bitten into a bloody pulp. Father reports Hayden's appetite has improved.

As we begin our session, Hayden settles on the couch, pulls her legs up, and rests her chin on her knees.

Hayden: What's up, Doc?

Dr. Erich: Hayden, it's been a year since we started working together. Do you remember why you first came to me?

Hayden: Would you like the long story or the short one?

Dr. Erich: How about the short one first?

Hayden: I was brought here because I hurt a girl. Because I'm *daan-ger-ooous*. According to lawyers, anyway. I'm a danger to myself and to others, Doc.

Dr. Erich: Are you being facetious about your episode in Stonebrook, Hayden?

[She shifts, changing her position and resting her forehead on her knees, so I can no longer see her eyes. She stays like that, breathing in and out slowly, for a minute or so before raising her head to stare at me, not blinking, for another long moment. The girl scares me in moments like this. I've been having nightmares about her and her mother ever since Hayden was first admitted into my practice. In those nightmares, Hayden's mother builds herself a throne made of bone but grows too weak, so her daughter has to take over the task. I'm also plagued by nightmares of a more primitive nature—the kind that wake you up at night in a cold sweat and make you recite the words of a prayer you thought long forgotten. I can't show Hayden my fear, but a part of me suspects she already knows I fear her.]

Dr. Erich: Do you know what *facetious* means, Hayden?

Hayden: Yes. I have five tutors. One of them teaches me English literature. Her name is Irene. She's a poet and knows her way around words. We talk for hours. She's blind from birth. I think that's why she freaks out around me less than the others. Because she can't see me.

Dr. Erich: Hayden, you said earlier that you think you're dangerous. At least

"according to lawyers," as you phrased it.
Do you mean to say you disagree with them?
Perhaps you don't think you should be in
therapy?

Hayden: I didn't say that.

[She retreats further into her space, and we
stay silent for some time. As often happens
in Hayden's presence, I begin to experience
icy shivers. It's like the beginning of
an out-of-body experience. A certain
vibe Hayden has tends to provoke these
sensations in me. Again, I cannot show her
my fear.]

Hayden: You shouldn't be afraid of me, Doc.
I usually feel the fog coming long before
it takes hold. It starts with my toes. [She
stares at the zebra-striped shoes she's
wearing.] Then it spreads up to my knees
and goes like that, higher and higher,
until my whole body's made of fog. Then I'm
dangerous. But you have nothing to fear
now, Doc.

Dr. Erich: I'd like to hear the long story
now, please.

Hayden: As you wish. But maybe this time
I'll make it a little different?

Dr. Erich: What do you mean by that?

Hayden: How about . . . this time I tell
you the truth?

Dr. Erich: You've been lying to me? Why?

Hayden: I wasn't lying. Not exactly.
Sometimes, I think the part of my brain
that should let me tell lies is broken. Or
maybe I just never had it to begin with,
like Irene was born without sight. Before
today, I've been telling you some parts of

my story. Just not the *whole* story.

Dr. Erich: Okay, Hayden, I would like you to tell me the whole story now.

Hayden: *[nods]* When we lived in Colorado, one night my mother went missing in the woods. We had a funeral for her, but the casket was empty. It wasn't long after that, I guess, when my dad and I moved to New York. I was having nightmares, and Daddy wasn't sure if going to school and being around all the other kids was the best idea for me. But I wanted to go to school, *so much*. I cried and begged until I convinced him. I tired him out. You know all about my time at Stonebrook. There was this girl, Jen. I could tell she was afraid of me—most people are—but Jen, she was different. She didn't want to seem scared. She hid it by bullying me. Somehow she found out about my mom, about what happened to her, so she went around saying Mom left me because I was a psycho . . . and lots of other things, like my mother would rather die than be with me. I remember everything she's ever said to me.

Dr. Erich: And what did you do then, Hayden?

Hayden: I went up to Jen. I remember that she had her hair in a ponytail, and she was wearing a sparkly blouse underneath her Stonebrook uniform. I wanted to tell her to stop talking bad about me. But instead of talking to her, I . . . *it all went wrong*. I felt the fog tickling my toes, climbing up my legs, like vines. Blood was rushing into my head. I felt like a rocket getting ready to go off. And I . . . The bathroom was empty, except for the two of us, and then Ms. Lancaster, our geography teacher, walked in. You've met Ms. Lancaster, right? Isn't she your patient, too?

Dr. Erich: I cannot discuss such things with you, Hayden. You know that.

Hayden: Right, right, I forget. . . . Anyway, what happened then is all kind of a blur. But I know for sure—here's the new part I was promising you, Doc—what *really* happened that day is I wished Jen would get hurt, and the next second she was flying. First, she crashed against a wall and then she smashed into a mirror. It took seconds. Ms. Lancaster fainted right in the middle of it.

Dr. Erich: Are you saying, Hayden, that you *telepathically* sent Jennifer off flying, so she would get hurt?

Hayden: That's what I'm saying, I guess. But like I *also* said, it was all a blur.

Dr. Erich: But that's not what you originally told me, Hayden. You told me you *pushed* Jen and then you *dragged* her to the mirror. Why change that story now?

Hayden: I have a better question, Doc. I was only eight years old then. I wasn't strong enough to lift Jen. So how could I do what everyone's saying I did?

Dr. Erich: Regardless of the mode in which Jen was hurt, how does this make you feel, Hayden?

Hayden: Like a freak who hurts people . . . people and animals. Do *you* think I'm a freak? Do you think I'm going to be in therapy for the rest of my life?

Dr. Erich: On the contrary, Hayden, I think we're finally making progress.

18
START LOOKING

Why do some accept paranormal explanations and others don't? Are our brains wired differently? Or is it our upbringing, our learned culture that shapes our psyche, making us more or less likely to believe in ghosts and the afterlife, to believe in the existence of mystical forces lurking just out of reach?

One hypothesis is that there's a gene responsible for our beliefs: *the God gene*. But the hypothesis has attracted so much criticism from both the scientific and religious communities that research into it has been minimal.

Genetics aside, those in favor of supernatural explanations are actually in the majority: Seventy percent of Americans believe in miracles; half of Australia exhibits a wide diversity of paranormal views, ranging from the acceptance of ghosts to aliens to telepathy. The list of countries goes on, but what remains unanswered is whether it is a case of truly believing or *wanting* to believe.

Del once told me that I hated talking about anything supernatural. That I used science as a shield, and it'd take a frigging burning UFO falling out of the skies to crash through it. When I asked Del why she wasn't a skeptic herself, she said that it would be a boring world to live in, prompting me to deliver an extended monologue on the miracles of quantum mechanics. (Del might have dozed off.)

Still, the question of paranormal belief remained salient for me. After all, I did grow up in the household of a physicist and a spiritualist. But I admit: Del was onto something with her UFO-crashing metaphor. The paranormal has to slap me in the face for me to pay attention.

ᚠᚷᚠ

Back at the Manor, I tear off my sweatshirt and throw it over the back of a kitchen chair. The blood drive flyer flutters out of my pocket. I pick up the flyer and leave it on the table before turning my attention to breakfast, while Del hovers at the edge of the kitchen table with her laptop.

"This Blue Haven Research Institute keeps popping up everywhere," Del says. I look over and see her tapping the top-right corner of the flyer. In my all-consuming contemplation of Mom's secrets and the mystery of dead white ravens, I didn't even notice the logo—the familiar indigo pyramid. My suspicion meter spikes as I attempt to connect the dots. But the puzzle pieces don't fit. Not yet. I'm missing something. I can bet it's something obvious. It usually is.

I let my brain run over the possibilities while I grab some eggs from the fridge and get the stovetop going. As a plan half forms in my mind, I say, "Hey, how about we go for a drive and check out this blood donation thing?"

"So now you want my company," Del snorts, looking up at me from the laptop screen. I ignore her, busying myself with brewing coffee and checking up on the frying eggs. She doesn't let up. "Is there something you want to tell me?" I can hear a devious smile in her voice. She closes the laptop and follows me with her eyes, knowing full well I don't like being stared at like that. "Like the *real* reason you wanted to come here?"

"I'm not a puzzle for you to figure out, *Delphine*."

"I can't stand secrets and lies, *Hayden Bellatrix*." She matches my exasperated tone. "Secrets and lies are why my family can't tolerate being in the same room with one another for long—you know they only come together to video chat with me to create an illusion of getting along, for my sake as well as theirs! And it's also the reason I left France and came to study here, so I could build a life for myself where everything and everyone is transparent and logical."

I laugh and then my words come out harsher than planned. "'Transparent and logical'? Life's never that. More like messy and twisted. If you want everyone in your life to be transparent and logical, you've come to the wrong place."

Del is silent following my dramatic outburst, and I count breaths till she nods slowly. That's when some of the old hardened resistance in me breaks and I tell her: "I thought I came here to say good-bye to my mom, to close this case I built up in my mind over the years. But I may have jumped the gun on that, Del. Something's not right with this town, and Mom was involved in . . . I don't know what it was, but in her codicil she asked me to finish what she couldn't."

"And you think you owe it to her?" Del looks at me without blinking, her face telling me everything I need to know—she understands this is important to me. "But do you even have any idea what she wanted you to do?"

"Not really. But I think only *I* can do it—whatever it is. I also think she was afraid of something, of someone. Like maybe she was under someone's control or blackmailed or forced to do stuff she didn't want to. Something bad. Maybe . . ." I don't say the rest, but I know Del can read it in my silence: Maybe that's why Mom had to die. "Del . . . I don't think I can leave Promise behind till I know what happened to her." Saying it out loud only solidifies my determination.

Del nods, her expression changing, her face becoming the physical embodiment of my resolve. She says, "You came here to look for something, so you do whatever it is you need to do, Hayden. You just need to figure out what it is. I'll help you as much as I can."

Pushing back unexpected tears, I go and lean over her. The one-armed hug I give her is superawkward, but, as I bury my face in her curls, my restless brain quiets down a little. Del smells of adventures, but also of home—not a particular place, but a sense of belonging, of comfort.

When I let go, she looks up at me, her smile tainted by uncertainty and maybe sadness. She's right. I came here to look for something. It's about time I start looking.

ᚠᚷᚠ

Later that morning, when we step out on the porch, the skies are clear but for a few dark cloud clusters moving toward

Promise from far north. Thankfully, there are no more birds. Once more, I scan the Manor's grounds, searching for that dead white raven. No sign of it. Probably a wild animal took it. Or it was some elaborate hallucination brought on by the combination of insufficient sleep and rich imagination.

I contemplate telling Del about the white raven but decide against it. Without evidence (namely, the dead bird itself), there's no point. Besides, even if I haven't yet reached Del's weirdness acceptance threshold (okay, I am starting to wonder if she's even got one), now would not be a good time to test it.

I pull my jacket tighter around my small frame and make my way to the car. Pensive in her step, Del follows me. Despite the consensus we've reached, our agreement sealed with a hug, the morning exchange leaves a shadow over our moods.

I volunteer to drive. Del doesn't mind: She's just painted her nails a vivid shade of green and doesn't want to smear her creation. In the car, we take a much-needed break from talking about my mom and her secrets.

The blood drive poster comes with a rudimentary map and directions: The Blue Haven blood collection point is in the woodland area just off Pilger Road, Promise's main street that slices the town into halves before stretching out to merge with a highway. This means we have to go through the town's center before going back into the woods again.

It starts to drizzle just as we exit the forest and, through the flimsy veil of rain and mist, the first signs of the town coalesce into view: the clock tower's spire and its twin, the steeple of Promise's only church. Looking up at its two immobile guardians, the township is nestled in a shallow ravine, surrounded by the forest.

When we enter a civilization of paved roads and clean-swept sidewalks, I cast my eyes over the weathered storefronts: a vintage clothing boutique (that gets Del excited), a two-story shop entirely dedicated to clocks, a beat-up computer repairs establishment, and a teeny-tiny grocer. Also, a restaurant (cuisine indeterminate), a pretentious-looking diner, something called "Tea Salon," a dry cleaners, and Angie's Shop of Curiosities, which has its windows curtained and dark.

What bothers me is that every time we stop at a light, we catch these not-so-subtle glances from passersby. The streets are not completely empty—actually, quite a few cars are out and about—but somehow our modest rental stands out enough to catch looks. While I'm doing my best to pay the staring no attention, the uncomfortable feeling in my gut grows. I know I look like a younger copy of Mom—my encounter at the gas station revealed as much—so if someone knew my mother, it'd be no stretch to identify me as her offspring. And considering my theories about Mom being in some kind of trouble leading up to her disappearance, maybe I should be wary. A ridiculous idea of disguising myself passes through my mind, and I'm already imagining Del's reaction if I at last come crawling to her, begging her to give me a make-over. I supress a grin at the thought.

We're driving by a bookshop called Diamonds & Co. when I see it: that car.

The silver Volvo. The very same one I saw in my dream-memory of the dangerous woman on the Manor's porch.

I slow down as my eyes search for the WE WILL NOT GO SILENTLY INTO THE NIGHT bumper sticker. It's there! Okay, not quite, but if you know where to look, you can see it—

faint, mostly peeled off, but there. The memory, the jagged piece of a riddle, rises from the primordial soup of my Promise childhood recollections. All neurons firing at once, I make a drastic U-turn and park the car by the bookshop, brakes squealing in protest. My rushed move comes off more elegantly than I should be given credit for, but Del's not impressed; her French swearing sounds offensive even if I don't quite grasp the meaning. I don't blame her. I'd be pissed off, too. Can't stand reckless driving. "Sorry! I swear I had a reason to do that," I blurt out, already unfastening my seatbelt. Pulling too fast and too strong, I get trapped in my seat. I go slack, calming my body while my heart's about to jump out of my chest. "I need to ask the people in that shop something."

"Let me guess. It's about your mom." Del smiles faintly, her annoyed expression softening. I nod, release myself from the seatbelt's death grip, and rush for the bookshop.

A gasp of cool wind makes me shiver, and the skin at the back of my neck prickles. I'm starting to learn from these sensations, listening to what they're telling me. I think (I hope) it means I'm on the right track, but I've yet to test that theory properly.

I linger on the shop's threshold. Behind me a car door slams, and I turn to catch Del walking in the direction of the vintage clothing boutique. I pull open the door.

The shop's inner space is small but used smartly, so it doesn't appear crowded with people or clumped with merchandise. Lulled by Susanne Sundfør's hypnotic singing wafting from overhead speakers, a few dazed-looking customers wander rows of books. Somewhere, an espresso machine lets off steam. I take a greedy inhale. After drinking our chintzy homemade coffee, this place smells divine. Paper, ink, caffeine.

But also there's a weird aftertaste, like a concentrated ozone imprinted on the air, thickening as I progress deeper into the shop. It defies logic, but I'm 85 percent certain I'm in the right place.

19
DIAMONDS & CO.

"Anything I can help you with, darling?"

I flinch at the sound, then come face-to-face with a silver-haired, gray-eyed man holding a stack of books. The magnetic nameplate on his blazer says GABRIEL.

He might be in his sixties, but it's difficult to ascertain his exact age: The bookshop's subtle lighting imbues the man's features with mercurial qualities, their shape dependent on slants of light. I blink and his face settles, taking on a kind, almost grandfatherly expression. I can't stop gaping at him, zeroing in on a long, precise scar that runs across the left side of his face, barely touching his lips. It's not a messy, unplanned kind of scar left by an accident but a deliberate one, suggesting the cut was delivered slowly, meeting no resistance. The stranger studies me back, unfazed by my silence. Then he does a double take and for a fleeting second his eyes open a little wider, as if he'd just had a private eureka moment and figured something out.

He puts the books down without taking his eyes off me. His mouth twisting into a smile, Gabriel reminds me of someone, but the connection is short-lived.

"Hi," I say, then point toward the shop's entrance. "Would you please tell me who owns that car? The silver one?"

Gabriel grins, showing a perfect set of teeth, his eyes sparkling like I'm the most delightful thing since indoor plumbing. "If you mean poor old Silverfish—that would be mine."

"You named your car . . . Silverfish? Do you know who had it before you? Was it by any chance a woman with short dark hair? I'm looking for her."

If Gabriel is at all surprised by my impromptu interrogation, he doesn't show it. If anything, he looks genuinely happy to be interacting with me, which, in my book, is not bad, considering I give most people *the Vibe* or whatever it is that makes their pupils shrink in fear and their mouths mutter nonsense.

"That sounds like my daughter, Elspeth. Elspeth Diamond," he offers. "She named that car. Something to do with it being repulsive but resilient. It looks like my Elspeth's the person you're looking for. I'm Gabriel, by the way. I own this shop." He extends a hand toward me and I shake it, the brief contact leaving me with a prickling warmth that lingers in my fingertips—the same sensation I had after touching the box from the basement.

"Elspeth," I repeat, savoring the rare name and finding it somewhat bitter on my tongue. No doubt my earlier menace-filled dream-memory of the strange woman on the Manor's porch is to blame for my reaction. What's peculiar is that, aside from this one random memory resurfacing after ten years of exile in my psyche's darkest corner, I have no recollections of Elspeth. Not a single one. To Gabriel I say, "I'd like to meet her. Is she around?"

He doesn't respond, just gives me that weird contented grin again, like he's proud of me for some reason I can't fathom. It occurs to me that, his eeriness aside, I'm being kind of rude—questioning this man about his old car without having even introduced myself first. "I'm Hayden, by the way. My family used to live here."

"Please forgive an old man's wandering mind! I'm just so excited to finally have you back in Promise, Hayden. We had a bet going with Elspeth for the past ten years about whether you'd return or not, and let me tell you, she's not going to be too thrilled that you're finally here!" He sniggers, then stops abruptly and checks my expression, as if he'd said too much. Two twentysomething girls enter the shop and head toward the bookshelves behind my back. Gabriel tracks their movement with an indirect glance, then turns back to me when they're gone.

Okay, this whole thing is weird. Does he not want anyone to overhear us?

"So you know who I am," I say. I might be imagining it, but I'm starting to see some hidden malice behind Gabriel's overly friendly facade. Besides, it doesn't take a detective to assume that if Mom was uneasy around Gabriel's daughter, Mom wouldn't be the best of buds with Gabriel.

If any of my suspicions show on my face, Gabriel doesn't notice—or he does a great job of hiding it. "Well, of course! You look so much like her. Our dearest Ella . . . You know, she was supposed to name you Eydís—meaning *good fortune*—after your great ancestor, but also because that's what you are, our *good fortune*! She went with Hayden instead, but no matter. Her blood thunders through your veins regardless of what name you respond to. And you know what they say about blood?" He doesn't give me any time to respond. "It runs deep! Like a bottomless well."

"You knew my mother."

"Oh yes! Yes, I knew Ella well. What a tragedy. These woods—" Once again, Gabriel cuts himself off and just stares at me. A different look this time, no longer excited or joyful but simply assessing. I wonder if I failed some kind of test when he sneaks a quick but obvious look at his wristwatch. "I'll tell Elspeth to come look for you later. There's much for you two to talk about. . . . Oh, I almost forgot, there's something I'd like to give you. It belonged to your mother."

"What is it?" I barely suppress my anxious excitement, but all Gabriel does is murmur something incomprehensible and beckon me to follow him.

I make a study of Gabriel's back as I shadow him through the store's interior; he's moving with an ease and grace I'd expect from a much younger, athletic person. There's toughness to the way he holds himself, like his spindly physique is a shell, hiding a hard, strong core underneath. As this thought crosses my mind, a peculiar but not unpleasant rush of energy goes through me, sharpening my vision and filling my head with images of my dreamscape army. Of Shannon riding by my side. The imagery is so real, I catch the heady fragrance of wet grass in the air, my eyes filling with wind-induced tears.

I snap out of it, finding myself back in the coffee-scented bookshop, following Gabriel to some unspecified location.

We don't stop until we reach the back of the store, where

a wall made of high-rising bookshelves blocks the way. I follow Gabriel and find a table and armchairs nestled behind the wall of books—a quiet haven hidden from the rest of the shop. Gabriel gestures for me to take one of the antique, overstuffed chairs. Tense, I sit down, edgy and ready to bolt.

"Wait here, dear child, while I fetch your mother's gift. Listen to your powerful blood sing as her amulet draws nearer." Before I can think of a suitable reaction to his creepy words, Gabriel disappears behind a STAFF ONLY door that seems to have materialized out of thin air.

The second he's gone, I jump out of my chair, the visceral wrongness of this place solidifying in my mind. I want to leave. Del should be done with the vintage shop by now. She's probably looking for me. The idea of her walking in here, of being seen by Gabriel, gives me a severe case of dry mouth.

Nothing bad is going to happen. The bookshop is full of people. Gabriel is harmless.

Thoughts and more thoughts, all very logical, rush through my head while I pace the floor. To distract myself, I study the books held back here, but I come to regret my decision immediately.

These books are shelved here, away from customers' prying eyes, for a reason.

Among the topics covered are arcane rituals, witchcraft, runes, and sacrifice. Also Nibelungs.

I pull a book down at random (or maybe because its spine feels warmer to my skin than the rest) and open it to a spot in the middle. The illustration I'm looking at is of a naked woman suspended from a tree, upside down, one leg tied to a branch, the other bent at the knee. A demonic ballerina doing a twisted pirouette. The longer I stare at her face, the more the hanging woman's features remind me of the girl from Mom's first clue card. The woman's long black hair touches the ground; her hands are spread wide, one holding a cup and the other a bleeding heart. The woman's mouth is smiling, but it's the grin of a person in a trance. *A sleepwalker?*

Cold sweat coating my back, I close the revolting book and try to insert it back into its spot on the shelf, but the book doesn't fit there anymore; the books around it have pressed together, closing the opening. With the book still in my hand, I take one step toward the safety of the bookshop proper, but then the STAFF ONLY door swings open, spitting out Gabriel.

He assesses the situation. I say, voice weak, "I was just looking around. Nice collection you got here."

"Yes. Books Elspeth and Ella amassed over many years, child. They're yours as much as ours, so why don't you keep that one. Seems like it chose you." He nods at the book in my hands. I start saying I don't want it, that the thought of sleeping under the same roof, let alone in the same room, with it makes me sick, but my tongue doesn't turn the right way. So instead of dropping it like my hands want to, I bring the book close to my chest and hold it tight.

When my brain fog dissipates, I notice Gabriel has returned with a small red box, the kind that holds jewelry. Remembering his earlier comment, I listen to my blood. It doesn't sing. The only thing I *can* hear is the trapped-bird drumming of my heart against my rib cage.

Gabriel lowers himself into one of the armchairs, but I remain standing. With a sigh, he offers me the box, and I accept it. It's surprisingly heavy, its surface rough to the touch. I lift the lid and a jolt of electricity travels through my body at the sight of a round, silver pendant. Its stylized design replicates the image from Mom's second clue card—three ravens, one black, one gray, and one white, circling the misshapen dot of a heart.

"What's with all the hearts and blood? Were you and my mother in a cult or something?"

At that, Gabriel laughs so hard, he bends over, hands cradling his stomach. When he calms down enough to speak, his tone is condescending. "Dear Hayden, it pains me that you know nothing of your heritage, it really does! I guess we shouldn't be that surprised at your ignorance, considering our poor Ella perished before she could fully initiate you into her world, but I'm not at liberty to tell you anything just yet. My Elspeth is in charge now, and she'll be in touch, but for now why don't you keep your mother's amulet? Take it into the woods to where the earth was burned black and let it show you its message. Elspeth will explain the rest." Gabriel's unsettling words hover around me as I stare at the amulet in my hands. Had I ever seen Mom wear it? My mind draws a blank. I close my eyes and try again—wading through the murky waters of my childhood memories. No recollection of the amulet. Besides, there was nothing in Mom's codicil or any of her clues about it.

"Why can't you just answer my question? What was my mother really into?" I sound desperate and I know it, but I don't care.

Gabriel looks me in the eye, another one of his assessing stares, before saying, "You strike me as a person who would be extremely skeptical about mere words, no matter how truthful, coming out of an old man's mouth. And I don't know any magic tricks good enough to *make* you believe."

"Try me. With words, I mean, not magic tricks."

He shakes his head, an impatient gesture. I've failed another test, it seems.

I remember the book I'm clutching and open it to the disturbing drawing of a hanging woman, the image already imprinted on my mind. I show the illustration to Gabriel. "Okay, riddle man, if you won't tell me anything useful about my mother, can you at least tell me what this means? Is she being tortured?"

"Au contraire, dear child, she's rather content. Can't you see she's smiling?"

I wait for more, and he delivers. "This is Eydís, the Nibelungen goddess of sacrifice and good fortune. Legend has it, one fateful night, Eydís decided to hang herself from the Tree of Life and Death. Some say she sacrificed her heart and mind for wisdom. If only her descendants were as dedicated as Eydís was."

"You said earlier I was supposed to be named Eydís. After an ancestor? *This* Eydís?" I point at the book again.

Gabriel's smile turns impish. "The real question here is what are *you* willing to sacrifice for wisdom? Or more likely, *who* are you willing to sacrifice?"

I swear I can hear Del calling for me from the depths of the shop. I'm torn between running toward her voice and staying here in the hopes that I can actually extract useful information from Gabriel.

When I take another look at him, something's not right with his face. The mask of a mild-mannered bookshop owner is slipping away, revealing . . . something strange. It occurs to me that maybe this is exactly what people who freak out on me feel—an ungrounded urge to skedaddle. Before I can figure out what I'm looking at, Gabriel stands and disappears behind the STAFF ONLY door, leaving me alone with Mom's amulet, the book, and many unanswered questions.

20
BLOOD DRIVE

I find Del in the bookshop's fashion section, leafing through an album of photographs depicting out-of-this-world elaborate dresses and impractical shoes. Her lips in a tight line, she has worry in her eyes when she sees me.

"Found what you were looking for?" she asks, putting the album back. She eyes the items in my hands and I hastily stuff the box and the book into my messenger bag.

"Just more questions," I say. "Let's get out of here, okay? I'm starting to believe this entire town's been taken over by body snatchers."

"Don't know about that. The woman running the vintage shop seemed nice enough, even though I didn't buy anything. And Angie, the psychic from the magic shop, read my fortune and told me I was going to meet a tall dark stranger. Today. I think I'm starting to like it here."

Back in the car, I analyze my first day in Promise so far. Those weird little things I keep adding to my Promise tally— the blood vials, Mom's clues, my recovered memory of Elspeth, Gabriel's riddles—still refuse to come together in a coherent way. Maybe I'm going about it all wrong. Maybe it's time to abandon logic and go with my heart instead? Or is it my gut I'm meant to listen to?

I do find it peculiar how the Black Clearing keeps popping up. Both Mom and Gabriel want me to go there, although their instructions are different. Does Gabriel somehow know about the blood vials and what my mother wants me to do with them? And if Mom left me the amulet, why didn't she mention it in her codicil or in any of her clues I've found so far? It feels like all the puzzle pieces should be starting to fit by now, but instead they're all too different to match together, leaving me more confused than before. Maybe, like my alleged ancestor Eydís, I should just go into the woods and suspend myself from a tree in hope of gaining wisdom. At the very least, some blood might rush into my head, bringing with it new ideas.

ᚠᚷᚠ

As we drive farther away from Promise's center, quirky small-town storefronts disappear, replaced with decrepit houses, dim and beige, as if all their color got stripped away over the years by the constant rain. There are fewer people here, and those walking the narrow streets move fast, keeping their heads down. The streets are clean yet unkempt, as if the town knows it's on its last breath and those who could leave have packed up and left already; the rest are stuck here because they have no choice.

It's springtime, but Promise seems frozen in an eternal fall, its spirit crushed by rain and wind. It's wet and miserable, and yet this place feels right to me. As if, despite it being inhospitable and damp and glum, it wants me here—and I belong.

ᚠᚢᚠ

Once we enter the forest, Del's first to spot it: a laminated poster marked with Blue Haven's pyramid-in-a-circle logo. An arrow points straight ahead. Shortly after that, our car rolls into a militarized zone.

I reduce speed and gawk at a small army of uniformed women and men swarming a large, cleared-out area of the woods, which is not that different from the abandoned one we saw the day before. A cluster of camouflage-painted pavilion tents lines the outer periphery of the clearing. A convoy of army trucks and jeeps is parked by the trees near the road.

A medical blood collection point?

Hmm . . . Sorry, not buying it.

The road ahead is blocked by a security gate. Before I can decide whether to be concerned (especially since doing a U-turn on this narrow forest road wouldn't be easy to accomplish), a lone male figure in olive khakis and a dark-camo Windbreaker emerges from the human swarm and signals us to pull over.

I stop the car and watch the guy approach. An edgy kind of anticipation tightens its icy paws around my throat. Del is uncharacteristically silent by my side.

I roll down my window, and the Windbreaker guy leans in close enough for me to see the hint of stubble on his chin and catch a scent of him. Woodsy. Unnerving. His eyes are dark gray, one slightly darker than the other—as if that one iris couldn't decide between dark and light gray and got stuck in between.

I've seen these eyes before.

I flinch when he brings himself even closer. Pausing mere inches away from my face, he studies me. His face unreadable, he asks, "Are you here to donate blood?" His voice is friendly enough but also guarded, undecided on my status—*friend or foe?*

The name tag sewn into his Windbreaker reads REASER.

Three (pounding) heartbeats later, I finally say it.

"Shannon?"

"Do I know you?" A little wrinkle appears on his forehead, looking misplaced on his young but serious face. It's clearly formed after years of frowning in surprise, a habit Shannon first acquired as a kid while hanging out with me. Any doubt I had about this guy's identity is erased from my mind now. With the wild blood rushing into my head, I can barely hear myself say, "It's Hayden. Hayden Holland. And here's my friend, Del." I nod in Del's direction. "And yeah, we're here to donate blood. I guess."

I have a lot more awkward words where that came from. Some are shaped like questions, others as apologies for not being in touch for ten years, as well as some excited words full of disbelief. But after one close look at Shannon's stony face, all my words wither before being spoken. He shows no signs of recognizing me, and it hurts. But I was the one to leave Promise

159

(and Shannon) behind, so I guess I don't have much ground to be angry about his blank look, do I?

"Leave your car here and follow me, please," he says. "Don't stray off the path. And don't touch anything." He doesn't take his eyes off me. All the prolonged staring makes me want to squirm. I glance at Del for support, but all she does is grin at me and mouth *hot jerk*. Rather unhelpful.

I consider leaving my bulky messenger bag in the car but can't bring myself to part with it. The slippery ground gurgles under my feet, and I hone my movements, focusing on staying upright and not falling into the mud, face-first, at Shannon's boot-clad feet.

Shannon's got at least a foot and a half on me. A flash from my recent dream sends a wave of heat over my face, my brain struggling to reconcile the scrawny boy I used to chase through the woods with this impressive human specimen towering over me. His mismatched gray eyes are the sole relic of Shannon from my childhood memories.

I only face him directly for a moment. Shannon's quick to turn his back on me, eager to get going. Del keeps close as we head for one of the tents.

With Shannon leading the way, I watch his neck and the line of his straight-cut brown hair. My eyes slide down to take in his wide shoulders and well-formed back, its muscular shape clear under the Windbreaker. I *think* I almost catch him a few times wanting to turn, to look at me. He doesn't do it, but the hesitation is there in his step.

Silent, we approach one of the tents. Like the others, it's forest green and blends with its surroundings. The entrance is guarded by two burly, uniformed guys. They look like they

160

mean business. No weapons on them—at least, none that I can see, but I bet they're hidden, strapped to their waists or whatever.

"What kind of a blood collection needs guards?" I ask. Shannon stops abruptly, and I almost run into his back. Del lets out a snort-giggle hybrid only I can hear.

"The kind that's also a research station, chock-full of expensive, high-tech equipment," Shannon replies, his tone pleasant in a tour guide sort of way. He pulls the tent's thick plastic door to the side and we step in, entering a space jam-packed with hissing, puffing equipment and busy men and women in medical coats.

Del trips over the threshold, and one of the passing white coats catches her midstumble. "Are you all right?" He gives her a long look. Del finds the audacity to give the guy a flirty smile. He's not bad looking—just ten years older than she is, if not more.

"What are you monitoring for? Has an alien mothership finally landed in these woods?" Del asks him before giving me a meaningful look. The white-coat guy produces a polite, tight-lipped smile and mumbles something about being away from his post for too long. I guess even Del's charm has limits.

After passing through the lab area, we reach an improvised observation room separated from the rest of the tent by a hospital curtain. Beyond, simple bare cots line the room's walls.

"Not a very talkative bunch, are you?" Del directs her next intel-gathering attempt at Shannon. But he doesn't even acknowledge her question, indicating instead that the two of us should sit down and wait. Del turns to me. "The stuff we have to go through to donate some blood around here! I bet they won't even give us juice and cookies afterward."

Quiet still, Shannon steps outside the observation room but is quick to return, carrying a large office binder and leaving us no time to snoop around.

He comes to me first and wedges some papers into my hands. I quickly sign the standard-seeming forms, the pen nearly tearing a hole when I apply too much force. The entire time, Shannon keeps his eyes trained on my shoulder, avoiding my face. I look up at him in surprise when he starts talking. "As you're probably aware, Promise is under scientific observation. Here at the base, we double as a blood donation clinic and research facility. The document you just signed is a release form, allowing us to use some of your blood for research purposes."

"Whoa, wait a moment there, *soldier*," Del protests just as I'm about to ask Shannon why he thinks I'm probably aware that Promise is under scientific observation. "It says here that Promise is under some kind of observation." Del points an accusing finger at the form. At least one of us bothered to read it. I feel all idiotic now, having signed a form without knowing what it said. Doreen would be horrified.

"Yes, I believe I just said that." Shannon studies Del, a mix of amusement and annoyance in his eyes. I want to scream in frustration. We've only been reunited for a few minutes and his aloof manner is already driving me mad.

Del ignores his jab and rolls her eyes. "*And* it says there are potential risks to new arrivals who haven't been exposed to Promise's air pathogens *from birth*. . . . Risks like hallucinations and bouts of sleepwalking. Seriously, dude? Is there anything you should've told us about before we came into your creepy little tent? Maybe your people could've put a little warning sign right next to the one that says WELCOME TO PROMISE." Del glares at Shannon before meeting my eyes. "Don't know about you, but—"

"Blood is how we track the pathogens," Shannon says slowly, careful to choose his words. He looks at me directly and adds, "I'm not sure exactly why you're so surprised about this place, but I'll make it quick since your friend's clearly in a hurry to leave."

"Oh, don't worry about me." Del stands up. "I'm most definitely *not* letting you poke me with a needle. I'll even go so far as to say I don't believe for a second that any of the blood collected here ever reaches a hospital. So I'll just wait outside for Hayden to finish. That is, if you're really going through with this?" From her *I-dare-you* pose, which makes her look like an outraged kitten, I know Del's not expecting the words I'm about to say. But I need to ask Shannon some questions, and the only way I see to do it is by staying here a little bit longer. And that means letting him jab me with a needle.

"I'll meet you outside."

She walks out of the tent, shaking her head. With Del gone, I'm about to face up to Shannon's aloofness and ask if he remembers me, but I get distracted when he takes off his Windbreaker, revealing a simple black tee underneath. It's not tight exactly, but it's definitely snug against his chest and arms. When he sits on the cot by my side, a thin scar on the side of his face comes into view: a precise line that runs down his neck, just avoiding his jaw. Noticing me looking, he shifts his head, hiding the scar in the shadow of his chin.

"Why are you here, Hayden?" he asks.

With his hands now gloved in plastic, he pulls up my sleeve and adjusts a tourniquet over my arm. His cold fingers are quick, practiced. Parts of me are tense and parts are relaxed. I just hope I won't blush or blurt out something inappropriate as he prods my skin, looking for a vein.

I take it from his question that (a) he *does* remember me, and (b) he's not too thrilled about me being here. "Because I haven't been here for a while," I snap. "I don't need your or anyone's permission to come back."

He flinches at my outburst, but he's quick to regain his composure as he continues to run his fingers over my exposed skin. I react to his probing with a shiver and goose bumps. "Freezing in here," I say when our shared silence becomes too loaded and heavy.

He drops my hand like it's hot. I watch him grab his discarded Windbreaker and offer it to me. After I stare at Shannon dumbly for long enough, he places the Windbreaker around my shoulders, semihugging me briefly in the process. Done with his chivalrous act, he meticulously changes his gloves, then takes my hand again and disinfects the patch of my skin that he's about to pierce with a needle.

"You looked confused when I mentioned our research here at the facility. So I take it that your sudden return to Promise has nothing to do with your father's work?" Despite his gruff tone, his hands on me are gentle.

"My father's work?"

"It'll only hurt a little." The needle pierces my vein and Shannon quickly attaches a collection tube. A sudden buzzing in my head and my stomach's queasiness have nothing to do with the numbing sensation of warmth in my arm. *Why would Shannon mention Dad's research?*

As Shannon releases the tourniquet and lets my blood flow, my body weakens and I sway in my seat, the room dancing before my eyes. Shannon's at my side, close, his sudden warmth bringing me reassurance. "You're all right?" His eyes roam over my face.

"All good."

"Not going to faint on me, *Hay?*"

Hearing my old childhood nickname makes me giddy and sad. "Nope, *Shan.*"

Shannon's mouth wants to smile, but it doesn't quite happen. "What was that you said about my father's work?" I ask carefully, really hoping I got it all wrong, that I misheard or misinterpreted.

Carefully, Shannon pulls the needle out of my vein and presses a cotton pad to the burning spot. Then he reaches for my other hand and places my fingers over the pad. Gently. "Press it like that," he instructs, and my breath hitches. I watch him as he peels off his plastic gloves and throws them into a medical waste bin.

I repeat my question. I can't say I'm ready for the bomb he drops, but it doesn't exactly come as a surprise when he finally tells me, "I thought maybe you were accompanying Professor Holland on a data-collection trip this month. I thought one day you might, since he's back here so regularly."

What? Dad, back in Promise? What is going on?

21
SOME TRUTHS BUT MOSTLY SPECULATIONS

A new sensation—like the beginning of an earthquake, a rumble—starts in my chest. How much weirdness can I take today? What did my earlier encounter with Gabriel Diamond really mean? Did I actually find three vials of blood in the Manor's basement?

And did Shannon just say my father's been coming to Promise on a regular basis? To collect *data*?

As an afterthought, I note that Shannon's wording also implies he's been thinking about me, wondering when I'd come back to Promise, but I decide not to dwell too much on that one, at least not now.

Pressing the cotton too strongly against my pierced skin, I wince in pain. "'This month'? As in, Dad comes here *once a month*? *Every* month?" The rumble in my chest deepens, and I imagine I can hear the wind outside intensify, as if in response to my inner turmoil. On cue, furious raindrops hit the tent, attacking it from all angles. "My father's been coming to Promise for months? Or is it *years*?"

"Well, yeah." Shannon keeps his eyes down as he puts away the blood collection equipment and then marks the tube containing my sample, his handwriting neat and boy-ish. "Professor Holland comes here once a month. You know, for his research. He's been coming for years. The first time he returned was a few months after you left. I thought you knew."

Am I being unnecessarily dramatic, feeling so betrayed by this news? So what's the big deal—my father's been coming here. For his research, Shannon says. *Research?* Unwilling to show Shannon how shaken up and hurt I really am, I hear myself say, my voice dead, rough, "It's *Doctor* Holland."

"Huh?" Having finished taking my blood and filing it, Shannon looks lost, unsure of what to do with me next.

"It's *Doctor* Holland. Not *professor* anymore—*doctor*. He's been stripped of his tenure. But they couldn't take away the doctor title, because his PhD's still legit. Though I'm sure they'd like to revoke that, too, if they could." I make every *they* sound like I'm talking about a league of devils. But the harsh reality is, it's my father who's to blame for his fall from academic grace.

I have one of those nasty epiphany moments that paints my world black. "He stays in the Manor when he comes here, doesn't he?"

"Well, yeah." Shannon looks at me funny again, oblivious to the fire consuming my world.

I want to go outside, expose my face to the slashing rain and scream, *My mother was in a cult and my father is a crank and a liar. I've got really good genes, don't I?*

To my astonishment, what pisses me off the most about Dad's little secret is that for all these years he's been using the Manor as his own personal retreat—stocking it with eggs and wine—and all the while placating me with his we-must-leave-Promise-behind rhetoric, preventing me from claiming the house Mom owned and willed to me. But who's more pathetic in this scenario? Dad for lying to me, or me for eating it up like some dumb goldfish?

My vision grows cloudy, as if a thick, gray fog has come down like a veil over my eyes. My chest's about to explode. *Crap.* I haven't felt this angry for years. And I remember too well what happened the last time I got all explosive on the inside. Jen Rickman happened, that's what. Outside, the rain and wind are howling in sync, singing an ode to my fury.

"Are you all right?" Concern in Shannon's voice has a soothing effect on me. I take a long breath while he continues, "You just got superpale superquick. You *are* going to faint, aren't you?"

"I'm fine," I cut him off but without much gusto. "I just need to get out of here." I stand up and go stumbling toward where I think the exit is. Shannon follows, keeping close, probably scared to be held liable if I fall and break my head open.

"Your father's research *is* important, Hayden," he says, as if he could read my earlier thoughts.

Without slowing down, I fire back, "My dad's been laughed at and ridiculed by his former colleagues and students for as long as I remember. But that all pales in comparison with the fact that he's been lying to me about coming to Promise for years!"

"You didn't know. That figures."

I want to say something else—something dismissive—but

I look back to catch a glimpse of Shannon's expression, and its unexpected kindness stops me. I pause and turn to face Shannon, my heartbeat slowing down. "Well, thanks for the . . . personal treatment. It was nice to see you and all. But I want to get to the Manor before the weather gets any worse."

The wind is wailing outside and I wonder how Del is holding up out there, especially since I have the car keys. She must be soaked by now. I'm about to walk off when Shannon asks, "Why are you *really* here, Hayden?"

Because my long-gone mother sent me on a creepy treasure hunt from beyond the grave.

Because I want to face my childhood demons.

Because not a day's gone by since I left Promise that I didn't think about you.

"Because Del and I have some time to kill over spring break, and Promise is as good a place as any," I say.

With a nod, Shannon steps back, letting me go. If my dishonest answer has disappointed him, he doesn't show it.

As I leave the tent, I hear the familiar, pompous notes of Wagner's *The Ring of the Nibelung* start to play. Haven't heard that one in awhile. Also, not something you'd expect to hear at a militarized scientific base in the middle of the woods. Despite my determination to leave, I pause. In response, my heart quiets, and that bad kind of fog that was clouding my vision only seconds ago dissipates completely. Wagner's subtle sounds, growing inspired, gain force, bringing Mom to my mind. In the months leading up to her disappearance, she'd listen to Wagner's *Nibelungen* over and over again, enough times for some of her favorite pieces to become recurring earworms for me in the years to come.

"It's Wagner. My mother loved it," Shannon says faintly, so close that I feel his hot breath on my neck. I turn and meet his stormy-sky eyes and experience a brief but all-consuming sensation of falling.

"Mine, too," I say.

22
UNCANNY

Uncanny is used to denote a type of emotional and cognitive dissonance one feels when encountering something that's familiar but also scary and mysterious. Something that looks right but feels wrong.

In psychology, the concept of the uncanny was primarily shaped by Jentsch and Freud. The latter drew heavily on linguistics: In German, *uncanny* (*unheimlich*) denotes the *un*familiar, the awareness of *non*belonging that makes all your senses go haywire. Under the sway of the uncanny, you're discombobulated—not quite at ease, not quite at home.

The bread and butter of horror movies, the uncanny is rooted in that moment when you look at a little boy's face only to find it tainted with the all-black eyes of the possessed; when you watch a hapless protagonist tap her boyfriend's shoulder and, as he turns around, shrink back at the signs of decay on his rotting skin.

Uncanny is how the grown-up, unfamiliar version of Shannon makes me feel. Home and not home, belonging and non-belonging. This Shannon-provoked uncanniness is razor-sharp, rubbing against my heart: I *know* him, this handsome guy who looks at me like he knows me one moment and then the next studies me like I'm an alien-bug-specimen trapped in his net. I know I'm as good as a stranger to him now, and I have no right to expect a warm embrace . . . still, I can't help but feel hurt by his unwelcome.

ᚠᚷᚠ

I come to find Del right outside the tent, hiding under a big black umbrella held by one of those burly, seemingly unarmed guards I noticed earlier. Dark hair cropped short, features wide and bold, the guy definitely qualifies as the tall dark stranger Del was promised earlier. Probably thinking the same thing, Del's standing close to the guard, saying something into his ear, making him smile. Engrossed in the conversation, she doesn't notice me.

Watching Del flirt up a storm, I welcome cold, rain-soaked air into my lungs, holding it in for ten long counts while going through the lyrics of Mom's lullaby in my head. The lyrics normally calm me down, but this time, instead of bringing me peace, they disturb some dark chords of my psyche. The song features three protagonists, and it's their blood that's supposed to break down the walls keeping out a new world. Hmm . . . *The blood of three. Three vials in the basement. Three ravens.*

"Plotting world domination? Earth to Hayden?" Del's finally taken notice of brooding, thinking me. I force a smile.

Before she joins me on the way back to the car, she slips the guard what must be her phone number. But he's shaking his head. "No reception here, Del. Unless you have a satellite phone, I can't reach you."

"And what are we going to do about it, Santiago?" she teases in her *come-closer* voice. Del didn't waste any time while I had my skin poked and prodded by my former childhood friend.

"Around here, we do it the old-fashioned way: We agree on a day and time and I call on you then."

"Call *on* me?" Del chuckles. Santiago looks dead serious. Captivated by the two of them, I ignore raindrops slapping my face.

"We're staying at the Holland Manor." When I speak up, Santiago pins me with his eyes and does a double take before his surprised features rearrange themselves into a pleasant expression. I wonder if I know him from somewhere, because he most definitely seems to have recognized me. Del looks at me funny, too, but I suspect for a different reason. Unperturbed, I continue, "We don't have any plans and will be here all week. You can call on Delphine tomorrow evening."

"Oh, I sure am going to." Santiago winks at Del, managing to make it look cute and not cheesy. From the corner of my eye, I notice Shannon watching me as I observe the exchange between Del and Santiago. When our eyes meet, Shannon busies himself with his wristwatch. I hate that he rattles me so. My face warms up, and I want to leave the tent behind before Shannon can see me blushing.

Once we're in the car, Del takes up the driver's seat and scowls at me. "What is your problem, little Miss Busybody?"

"I thought I was helping!" I protest.

"Sure. . . . Thanks for your *help*." She steps on the gas and twists the wheel. "Nice jacket, by the way."

I must have a blank look on my face before I realize I still have Shannon's Windbreaker around my shoulders. It faintly smells of him—that raw wild scent of the woods.

"Stop the car!" I start to pull the jacket off my shoulders, but Del shakes her head.

"No way! Too late now. Ugh, like we needed another reason for Santiago to visit." Del's grumpy outburst breaks the spell I'm under. The spot where the needle broke my skin prickles. I rub at it gently until the sensation disappears, taking with it a flushed memory of Shannon's deft fingers running over the length of my arm.

As we cruise away from the research camp, Del breaks the silence and says, "Arranging my dates for me, are you?"

"I thought you liked the guy."

"Of course, I liked him," she scoffs, "but no one in their right mind agrees to be *called on* like this, not without running some background checks first. Besides, it's always best to meet in neutral territory for the first time, and you just all but invited this dude we barely know *and* his brooding friend, the hot jerk who gives me the creeps, into our home. Nice move!"

"All right, I'm sorry! But Shannon already knows where we're staying anyway, and if Santiago wanted to know where to find you, I'm sure he would've figured it out, with or without my help. Besides, I don't remember inviting Shannon to come along, so you can relax on that account." I don't comment on the "gives me the creeps" part.

On our way to the Manor, I fill in Del about Dad's betrayal of my trust. But instead of sharing my indignation, Del's just relieved to know the identity of the Manor's secret benefactor. Bothered that she's not feeling my pain, I change the topic and give her the rundown of my bizarre encounter with Gabriel and then, for good measure, show her the drawing of joyful Eydís swinging from her tree. Once again, Del's not impressed. In my last bid to break through Del's apparent Promise-resistant bubble, I show her the amulet that supposedly belonged to my mother. I wait for her to frown in suspicion at the amulet's decoration of ravens circling the human heart, or at least at the fact that the damn thing came from some random dude and not from the lawyer who executed Mom's will, but Del remains unperturbed. She even makes a pointed comment on how people in small towns are bored out of their minds and get megaweird without even noticing it.

In frustration, I decide not to share my grisly discovery of the blood vials in the Manor's basement. Rolling my eyes, instead I ask Del politely if she's being possessed by a body snatcher from the Boring Planet of Logic and Reason. In turn, she inquires whether I finally had my UFO Crash Moment and, if not, what was it that caused this one-eighty in my attitude toward the supernatural. I concede that she makes a good point. Ever since we came to Promise, I started seeing omens and clues everywhere. And I'm not sure what to make of this new me.

23
EYES LIKE YOURS

On our approach to the Manor, I experience a spike of déjà vu when I see Silverfish parked in front and a lone figure clad in a long, slinky red dress standing on the porch.

Once I'm out of the car and walking toward the visitor, my vision becomes blurry in the drizzling rain and some trick of perception makes the woman look like Mom. Long hair hanging around her face and shoulders . . . a faraway look . . . *She came back. The woods have released her.*

As I near her, the stranger's hypnotic, ruby-red lips quirk in a maybe-smile. The exposed skin of her shoulders and arms shines bright, almost translucent, bluish veins showing through. It must be an optical illusion; human beings are not supposed to emit light.

When my eyes regain focus, I realize the woman doesn't look like Mom at all. Her hair is black and cut short (why did I think it was long?), and her eyes are dark blue. She doesn't look that much older than I am, except for her eyes. Del's newly found skeptic self might laugh at me, but I think what's staring at me from beyond the woman's deep-blue irises is ancient. *Beyond time.*

Even aside from her unnerving eyes, she has the strangest face I've ever seen: well-shaped lips; a sharp, long nose; and chiseled elfish cheekbones made even edgier by her pixie-cut, shiny hair. No hint of makeup. But it is her lips—the shape of them—that triggers another weak half memory in me, a hint of recognition. In my vision, the woman is scowling at my mother, and her glower makes my skin crawl. The two of them—Mom and this stranger—are alike and yet the exact opposite of each other, their differences not obvious to the naked eye but visceral. Felt not seen.

Mesmerized by her electric presence, I keep staring at the visitor. And the longer I stare, the more I grow certain that something doesn't make sense. If this is the *same* woman who visited my mother more than ten years ago, how come she looks so young?

Interrupting my thoughts, the woman offers her hand and, without thinking, I shake it. She emits warmth and certainty. Cautious, I let the words out. "You must be Elspeth. I met your father earlier today. He told me the two of you were close friends with my mother." Those weren't Gabriel's exact words. He never said "friends," but I want to observe Elspeth's reaction to see what she really was to Mom.

She smiles. "Yes, I knew your mother very well. She meant a great deal to me. And to Gabriel. To a lot of . . . people." Elspeth's voice is clear and slightly accented. The latter adds to the puzzle that is Elspeth: Her father speaks in a perfect

Midwestern brogue, so maybe Elspeth acquired her accent while living overseas? Or inherited it from her mother? I search for an explanation on her face, in the bold twist of her eyebrows, in the knowing turn of her lips, but she reveals no secrets. As a side note, I find it slightly odd when people refer to their parents by their first names, but that's the least of my concerns here.

"I'm Del, by the way." Disturbing our moment, Del offers Elspeth her hand. The woman shakes it slowly.

"Hello, Delphine Chauvet. I'm pleased to welcome you to our forgotten kingdom. We're thrilled you decided to join Hayden on her little homecoming tour." Elspeth sniggers at her own words before letting go of Del's hand. "By the way, did you enjoy your reading at Angie's? Have you met your tall dark stranger already?"

Del stares at her blankly. "How do you know about that?"

Elspeth's eyes practically twinkle with joy. "News travels fast. It's a small place and, you know, us small-town folk get bored out of our minds. Besides, we don't get new blood very often around here, so your arrival has been noticed."

Time for me to intervene before Del retaliates—I can tell she's freaked out at last (and rightly so), biting her lower lip and hiding her hands in her pockets. It's only a matter of time before she makes some smartass comment that'll get us both in trouble. Normally I wouldn't care, but a faint feeling lodged at the back of my skull tells me this Elspeth person's not to be antagonized, that behind her cool facade hides a rattlesnake danger.

"Is it a family thing—the talking in riddles, I mean—or is it a Promise thing?" I ask Elspeth, drawing her attention back to me.

"Both, I think!" She laughs softly. "I brought you girls some food." Elspeth walks to her car and extracts a handful of aluminium containers. She's about to hand the food over to us when a lone raven caws overhead. Clutching the containers, Elspeth stands tall, abnormally still, and stares upward to where a white dot, luminous against the dark skies, is circling us.

"So many birds out here," I blurt out. "We don't get to see much wildlife in New York. I've never seen one, let alone *two*, white ravens over the course of two days before." I might just be tired, but Elspeth's presence makes my brain fuzzy, disoriented. I think of whales that lose themselves and get beached.

Snapping out of her reverie, Elspeth shoves the food into my hands. When Elspeth's eyes fall on my face again, the skin on my back goes all pins-and-needles. When she speaks, her voice is heavier, more accented than before. "Those eyes of yours . . . In the days of old, folks would burn you at the stake, you know. Just for having eyes like that, they would. Hmm-hmm." *Spoken like she knows from experience.* A memory of Mom saying the exact same thing to me—about my eyes and witch hunts, though not so creepily—makes my pulse spike.

I take a breath. Calm down. "Ah, thanks for the food?"

A pleasant smile forms on Elspeth's lips. "I hope you like lasagna and potato bake. The only things I know how to cook." A short laugh. When she smiles again, it's the disembodied smile of the Cheshire cat, not connected to the rest of her face. "Why don't you hand this over to your friend so we can have a little chat?"

Obedient, I nod and entrust the food to Del, both of us moving like marionettes, our limbs in the complete control of our puppeteer. When Del disappears into the house, I shake off my trance and meet Elspeth's eyes. "Was that hypnosis?"

"Hypnosis? Don't be ridiculous." She shakes her head as if the mere suggestion of her hypnotizing us is offensive. "Just good old Niflheim compulsion. You have it, too, you know, you've just never used it on purpose, so it lies dormant, coming up to the surface when you least expect it."

"*Niflheim?*" I repeat, the word settling nicely on my tongue, provoking a sensation of heat traveling through my body. *Like that foreign tongue from my dreams.* Vaguely, an audial memory resurfaces of my horseback army screaming their battle cry. *For Niflheim! We'll rise again!*

Elspeth says, "Your mom and I, we went a long way back . . . since before you were born. Did she ever mention Niflheim to you? Did she talk to you about your duty to your people?"

"And by 'my people,' you mean what exactly?"

Her face stretching in disappointed ways, Elspeth says, "Just as I thought. You know nothing. It was dangerous and reckless on Ella's part. . . . Hayden, I'll be blunt with you. Your mom and I didn't always see eye to eye, but we did agree on one thing: that we'd combine our resources and our powers and keep trying until the day we succeed. That we'd keep at it for as long as it takes."

"I don't follow."

I doubt she hears me at all; she's too caught up in the importance of her cryptic message. "There's something you have in the house," she says, "something your mother left for me. Something she stole from me, actually. I want it back."

As she speaks, I see the three vials of blood flash before my eyes. Elspeth must read it off my face, because her eyes ignite with mad fire. "You know what I'm talking about. You found it. Can I see it?"

Again there's that pull, that enraging hold on my mind, signaling that I'm about to lose control and walk into the house so I can deliver the vials to Elspeth. I slow down my breathing and tense up, fighting Elspeth's compulsion. If her intent taints my mind with tendrils of black smoke, I push back with the coils of my own fire, sparking like chromed steel under the sun. Compulsion, hypnosis—whatever this is, there are ways to resist it. "Why should I trust you?" I say when I regain control of my mind, earning only a slightly arched brow from Elspeth, like she's not particularly surprised I've put up resistance. "If you two were as close as you claim, how come I don't remember you at all?"

"Are you sure you don't?" So quickly I don't see her coming, Elspeth cups my chin with her left hand while her other hand's ice-cold fingers touch my forehead. I'm being hurtled into deep space in a flimsy spacecraft. My heart rate accelerates. . . .

They say people who get struck by lightning describe the experience as being stung by a million wasps from the inside out; as being punched in the head with a heavy, blunt metal object; as burning inside out.

If Elspeth is lightning, I've become a tree split in half. When the first shock of contact begins to lift, I see it through the wall of pain that surrounds me: a series of unconnected images fleeting before my eyes, coalescing into a complete picture, a puzzle coming together piece by piece. I see Elspeth and Mom as two little girls, playing with wooden swords and shields in a field of rye. Then I see the older versions of Elspeth and Mom, riding battle horses side by side, grim determination painting their faces. Then it's Elspeth and Mom tearing their way through a fog till they emerge on the other end of a vortex. They are weak but not beaten down. They wait, wait at the edge of a clearing in the woods. But the vortex is gone now. No one else is coming. Gabriel appears at their sides and the three of them leave the woods, swearing to return every night, together.

An angry caw sounds from above. Followed by another, the noise disturbing the images racing through my mind, distorting the completeness of my memory, or vision, or whatever it is.

With a jerk, Elspeth lets go of my chin as a bird collides with her head. Like in a dream, the world slows down as I watch Elspeth fight off the crazy bird's attack. Elspeth's regal stature is replaced by comical awkwardness, and I can't help but (internally) laugh at the view. The bird—a white raven—loses interest as suddenly as it launched its assault, taking off in a flurry of wings and claws. Elspeth swears at it, but the bird's already high up in the skies, moving fast.

Turning her attention back at me, Elspeth's shaking her head, full of impatience and disapproval. "Gabriel gave you the amulet. Use it. We'll talk again once you hear its message."

After imparting her instructions, Elspeth gives one last glare to the skies, then gets into her car and leaves.

ᚠᚷᚠ

"Well, that was odd," Del concludes once I join her inside the Manor. The containers full of Elspeth's food offerings are piled on the kitchen table. While I was outside, Del brewed some fresh coffee. Now, nursing a large mug, Del studies me from her seat at the kitchen table. "That woman is something else."

"Yeah. She is." My tone echoes Del's uncertainty. "I think I know her from before, from the time when I lived here. At least, it feels like I *should* know her. . . . She looks so familiar, but when I try to recall anything specific about her, my memory turns blank."

Once again since coming to Promise, I'm not being completely truthful with Del. After all, I did have that disturbing dream-memory of Elspeth waiting for Mom by the Manor's porch, both of their faces becoming way too intense for their encounter to be meaningless. And then there's the tiny little detail of Elspeth touching my face just moments ago and . . . what? Transmitting something directly into my mind? Was it meant to be a memory? I flinch internally as I replay the deranged white bird swooping down and going for Elspeth's face, as if to prevent the woman from touching me. What the hell is happening? And am I seriously going to entertain the idea that Elspeth has some otherworldly power? Doing that would be embracing everything I've spent my life avoiding.

Despite some intensifying queasiness following my weird standoff with Elspeth, I go through what happened, piece by piece: the visceral imagery of Elspeth and my mother as kids, then as teens riding those beastly horses I keep seeing in my dreams . . . and then the grand finale of the two women tearing their way through . . . what?

I must be going nuts. Del's presence in the kitchen is the

only thing stopping me from grabbing the blood vials and the amulet right now and running into the woods to test a certain out-of-this-world hypothesis.

"Maybe Elspeth's a witch and she put a spell on you," Del offers, her tone teasing. I look up at her sharply, but her shrugging shoulders tell me she's joking. Whatever happened to us seems to have worn off by now, and she's back to her nonchalant ways. Too quickly, if you ask me.

"Maybe you're right," I admit, studying her face for any signs of a freakout but finding none. "Though she did know your name and that you went to Angie's."

"Yeah, right." Del takes a large sip of her coffee. "Like Elspeth said herself, this town is small and everyone's superbored and they talk."

"I hope you're right," I say.

"What's the alternative?" Del shrugs. "I mean, you come to this town that used to be your home and find that almost everyone here is pretty much a weirdo. Some chick who says she was your mom's friend stalks you while her dad gives you some trinket that may or may not have belonged to your mom. Fine, but you know what? They can't actually force you to do anything you don't want to do, so I say just relax and take these things at face value. You can write a book about it when we go back to New York."

I stare at her in mild shock. "Who are you? And what did you do to my friend?"

She laughs it off. "Let's eat. I'm starving."

I pull the metal foil off one of the containers to reveal red sauce and pasta goodness, while Del discovers something resembling a potato bake in the other container. I pick up two plates and fill them up. My disturbing physical reaction to Elspeth's presence has mostly subsided by now, but I still quiver at the sight of the food. Even so, despite all my suspicions about Elspeth, I really don't think she'd try to poison us.

Or would she?

. . . When, exactly, did I become this paranoid person?

We remain silent as we pick through our food.

Del's first to speak. "So about tomorrow. I'm pretty sure Santiago will come by the Manor, maybe even with your broody boyfriend in tow. In any case, we should both be ready, but not, like, sitting-around-the-house-waiting-for-them-to-come ready—casually ready, you know. Also, I need to know if you've got anything nice to wear. If not, we should probably go check out some of those local shops, because my clothes won't fit you."

"Come again?" I set down my fork in quiet alarm. It doesn't even reach my mind straightaway what she's talking about. With everything that happened to us today, the question of whether Shannon likes me has suddenly become the least of my concerns. Well, at least I'd like to think so. I say, "This better not be another attempt at a makeover."

"All I'm asking is if you brought some nice things with you. You know, not the usual practical stuff you like so much." She makes *practical* sound like an insult.

"You want me to wear nice things tomorrow evening *in case* Santiago comes by the house and brings Shannon with him?"

"Oh, honey, no, not *in case* Santiago comes. I *know* he's coming here. That's a guarantee. I'm just saying this so you're ready *in case* Shannon gets over whatever Hayden-related chip he's got on his shoulder and comes along, too."

"You think Shannon's got something against me? Like a grudge?"

"That much is obvious. Or it's just sexual frustration. Or both. Probably both."

"How would you even know? You were barely there in the tent long enough to—Ah, never mind! Doesn't matter. I really don't care what Shannon thinks of me. And whether or not he's coming over tomorrow, or the next day, or . . ."

"Keep saying that and maybe—*maybe*—you'll believe it." Del sniggers, much to my annoyance. Our casual banter works like magic to exorcise most of the suspicions from my head, but still, a thin, dark shadow remains.

I say, "To show you how little I care, I won't wash my hair tomorrow and I'll wear my running gear all day."

"Now that's just nasty." Del starts to laugh harder, and I can't help but laugh, too, and together we're so loud, it feels like the Manor is shaking on its foundation, laughing with us.

24
THE UFO CRASH MOMENT

After Del disappears upstairs to work on her group project, I retrieve the raven amulet from my pocket and let it swing before my eyes in a hypnotic pendulum motion. Gabriel's instructions are clear in my head, while the memory of Elspeth's cold fingers gripping my face gives me shivers. And then, of course, there are the blood vials.

I stare at the amulet. What do I expect to happen? The surface of the necklace remains cold, inanimate.

And then there's the big question: Should I do as I was advised and take the amulet into the woods?

Coming as a surprising revelation, I find that a growing part of me feeds on a meager hope that something extraordinary *will* happen when I give in to this mystery that is my mom and follow the instructions, achieving some kind of personal apotheosis in the process. But the rational part of me insists that it is highly unlikely that anything unusual will occur and in the end I'll just look and feel stupid. Standing alone in the woods, clutching this New Agey piece of jewelry in my hand.

But so what? What have I got to lose? Besides, taking the amulet into the woods seems like a *rational* thing to do compared to the bloodletting Mom's second clue demands. If anything, I should try with the amulet first, try and hear its message—or whatever—before I attempt anything else more drastic.

I shake my head as the realization hits: Somewhere along the way, I changed, recognizing that it's time I deal with a possibility that maybe—just maybe—my mother was involved in something otherworldly. And so it's my newly found openness that's telling me it's worth a try with the necklace. Worth a try with Mom's legacy. Besides, do I even have the luxury of being a skeptic anymore? I doubt it; doubt that I can go on lying to myself that I knew my mother. Because I clearly didn't. And now, knowing that my father's borderline-obsessive protectiveness of me was just a cover-up for his enduring secret relationship with Promise and, I suspect, with the ghost of my mother, I decide that I can let my inner believer run wild. For what it's worth, I'm going to take the raven necklace into the woods and beg it to reveal its secret, no matter how stupid I'll look in the process.

Just as I make up my mind and head out the Manor's door, the day succumbs to rain. And what a rain it is. The storm attacks the Manor from all angles with punishing force. Even driven by my suddenly acquired sense of purpose, I only manage a few steps before I change my mind. Lightning scars the dark skies as a boom of thunder rushes to catch up with its flash.

I'll have to wait it out.

Spooked by the sudden weather change, Del joins me downstairs. With no Internet or television, our attention turns to the only book available: the weighty tome I've taken to thinking of as *The Adventures of Eydís*. But the problem with the Eydís book is that it's written in what I suspect is an old Germanic language, making it unreadable to us. Still, I nurse this half-baked hope that somehow the book will just reveal its secrets to me the same way I instinctively seem to understand the foreign language my shadow army speaks in my dreams. But no matter how long or how intently I stare at the lines of gorgeous medieval print (and despite the fact that I spot an occasional runic symbol), I feel nothing in the way of recognition.

And then there's the book's creepy illustrations. If you think the creations of Hieronymus Bosch are disturbing, the book of Eydís is in its own league of spooky art. As I leaf through the volume, some of its particularly nasty images burn into my mind in the way the most outrageously bad horror movies do: by entering my psyche under the guise of laughable, WTF-were-they-thinking moments and then staying there, embedded into my soft gray matter only to resurface when I'm alone in my bed and the room is dark.

There's Eydís tearing off her human face to reveal a beam of alien white light underneath. (The poster for Carpenter's *The Thing* comes to mind.) Or here's Eydís going all Lady Godiva, riding naked atop a demonic horse-dragon hybrid, leading an army of skeletons, their eyes and swords ablaze, toward an unsuspecting settlement nestled in a valley. And, of course, my personal favorite: Eydís hanging from a tree, naked and blissing out in a trance.

"I like this one." Del points at a particularly obscene image of a naked couple, their limbs entwined suggestively, eager bodies splayed in a forest clearing. Standing out against the pale moonlight, the trees' long shadows stretch across the lovers, as if trapping them in a cage.

I study Del's suddenly dreamy face. She appears serious. "Why?" I ask.

"It's romantic, I think," she says.

ᚠ ᚷ ᚠ

We spend what's left of the day keeping each other company. A few times I feel an urge to tell Del about the blood vials, but then I recall Del's earlier dismissal of my suspicions about Elspeth and change my mind.

As night falls and we sit down to eat some more of Elspeth's food for dinner, Del gets into a rare maudlin mood and decides to recite some crappy poetry her ex-boyfriend's been texting her along with his smirking selfies ever since we left New York and up until the moment we entered Promise's apparent reception-blocking field. I keep it civil at first, but each new "poem" is more ridiculous than the last, so after a short while I can't hold off my evil laughter anymore. My timing is horrid, as Del's eyes are wet with tears—she's reading out some particularly twisted lines professing Bolin's undying love for her (ingeniously, he rhymes *love* with *broth*). I laugh so hard, I can barely hear Del's accusations of insensitivity, but then she gives up and joins me, both of us wailing with laughter as we repeat some of Bolin's best/worst lines.

We part for the night early and, as I fall into the dark hole of sleep, my mind offers a visual of how my taking the amulet into the woods is going to unfold: A beam of light slices the ground under my feet to reveal an opening to another world, its bowels clouded with sentient fog. Through the opening, my mother walks out of her supernatural prison cell, her face shining with unrestrained *otherness*, her humanity completely stripped away. Her eager arms open in anticipation of an embrace. I don't notice her hands curling around me until she's too close, and I look up to find her eyes are missing from their sockets and her lips are rotted away, revealing two rows of razor-sharp, dirt-stained teeth.

ᚠᚷᚠ

I don't know the time, but the sun's barely up, its fragmented light bathing the insides of my old childhood room in a way that makes me think of those carefree days when my main concern was how to carve out more time from homework to spend playing with Shannon in the woods. Those days are gone, and Shannon looks at me funny now—and not in a good way. The silent demeanor of the Manor accents my mind's heaviness. The best way to clear my foggy brain is to go for a run. After I exchange my pj's for some tights and a well-worn sweatshirt, I pick up Mom's amulet and hold it by the chain, making the shiny disk swirl in the air and catch random rays of light. After a moment's thought, I put the necklace on and fasten the chain's clasp. The round silver disk hangs low, hidden underneath my hoodie.

Once outside, I scan the skies and the ground for birds, acknowledging my disappointment at not finding a white raven anywhere nearby, watching me.

Then I run without stopping till I reach the line of trees. This time I rush headlong into the woods without giving myself any time to think, to doubt.

The powerful bodies of firs, pines, and spruces shimmer over me, around me, as I race through the sea of dark green. The too-loud noises of brushwood crunching underfoot make my skin crawl. Gabriel said I should take the amulet to where the earth's burned black. I know exactly the place he means, even though I've never seen the Black Clearing with my own eyes.

My skin tingles as I delve deeper into the thickening forest. I count the seven turns my path takes through the dense woods before, in a rather dramatic fashion, the trees give way to . . . *nothing*.

I remember the way this trail used to end: It used to take me to a wild spring that cut the forest in half before continuing north, culminating in a waterfall that crashes into Edmunds' Gorge. I should be able to hear the water's roar, but instead it's quiet—which is odd, since I don't recall reading that the decade-old blast destroyed the waterfall. It's like this place is stripped of all life: Without moisture, the air tastes sour.

I cast my eyes over the wasteland before me. Blanketed by thick fog, its paleness is crisscrossed with shifting shadows. In the years following Mom's disappearance, I agonized over what the infamous Black Clearing might actually look like. There were the evocative newspaper descriptions, of course— all nature burned to the ground, soil solidified into glass, trees stomped down. . . .

But nothing could've really prepared me to see it for myself— my mother's last known location on this Earth. The impact of the visual before me is so powerful that silent tears escape my eyes while my mouth twists up in an unrealized sob. There's no way Mom could've experienced whatever happened here and come out of it alive. No wonder they found no human remains—aside from that creepy severed pinkie that didn't belong to my mother.

Pushing back tears, I take in the complete desolation of this dark place that exists in the middle of the lush forest and try to feel Mom's presence. But there's nothing here. No life. No memories.

A barb of irrational fear pokes at the boundaries of my perception, urging me to pull the amulet out from underneath my hoodie. To my fingers, cold and slippery with sweat, the metal's almost hot to the touch.

I sense it before I feel it: a slight push, a big cat's paw landing against my back, its subtle force compelling me to take a step forward. As my feet land in the ankle-deep fog, the ground vibrates, sharp tremors reverberating through me.

I bring the amulet to eye level. "Okay, if you have anything to show me, *now* would be a good time."

My words provoke no reaction, not even after I rub a finger over the disc's smooth surface, as if it's a magical genie-keeping lamp and my touch will release its secrets. I even bring it to my mouth and exhale on it, to no avail.

Just as I start to feel *very* stupid, the Black Clearing shifts and shivers in my peripheral vision, like a desert mirage rearranging itself. Next comes a ringing in my ears.

My numb fingers release the amulet, and, freed from my grip, it hits my chest. Once more the ground tremors beneath me, making me sway on my feet. *This is happening—this really is happening. My dream from the other night.* I focus my eyes on the middle of the Black Clearing, bracing myself for what the tremors are about to release from the earth. As the shaking intensifies, I close my eyes for a long blink and, when I open them again, I'm in the middle of the clearing. I have no memory of walking there, so either I just had a minor blackout or I've mastered the art of teleportation.

The fog thickens around me, quickly rising to my chest, and my breathing becomes strained. Pulling air into my lungs is a struggle.

Is this what harmed my mom? Is this what my father's been trying to protect me from?

The aftertaste of my recent anger at Dad acquires a hint of guilt. What if my father isn't a crackpot? What if all this time I was busy being angry with him, he was actually trying to shield me from whatever this place is, from whatever these woods are hiding? What if his theories are . . . real?

But I have more important concerns right now: When I take a step away from the clearing's center, heading back the way I came, the ringing in my ears turns into high-pitched buzzing, growing louder and louder till it transforms into the familiar clanging of metal against metal, the soundtrack of my recurring dream.

My heart's beating too fast for me to think clearly. The air turns dark, whipping up into a spiral, locking me at the center of a maelstrom.

I'm pulled in all directions and then I'm in two places at once: There's me in the eye of a storm and there's another me outside it, at the edge of the clearing, clutching the amulet in my hand. But it's not until I register long hair beating around me in a crazed blond halo while my right hand clutches a weirdly curved knife that I know . . . I'm inhabiting my mother's body.

I scream at the sudden pain of the cut, as the knife runs down the length of my left arm. As if of its own accord, my bleeding hand lifts—an offering to the vortex. This experience is too intense; I try and shake off the possession. In my mind, two realities fight for domination: Logically, I know that what I'm seeing now is a message from long ago, a *memory* of my mother's last deed in this world, and that it's somehow trapped in the amulet but replaying now for my eyes only. But the part of my mind that's melded with Mom's psyche in this final moment of her life translates Mom's thoughts into my head: *My army will rise again! I sacrifice myself to release you! Rise, my warriors, and conquer this world!*

I'm thrown back into my own body, stranded at the periphery of the clearing. From my new vantage spot, I get one last glimpse of my mother as she's sucked into a foggy vortex, its unstable shape collapsing on itself and erupting into a mighty blast.

25
THE RAVEN PARADOX:
PART 1

In the 1940s, philosopher Carl Gustav Hempel described the *raven paradox*.

What we call the "scientific method" relies heavily on the logic of induction—our understanding of current events based on our observation of previous events. For example, we assume that the laws of physics governing our universe will always be as they have been simply because we have never observed otherwise. Our observations constitute our sole evidence for our induction. But here's where Hempel's raven paradox comes in: *All* ravens we have seen are black, and, therefore, we may presuppose that all ravens *are* black. But the paradox hits us square in the head when we discover that, though rare, there are indeed white ravens. What we didn't see is still true—and it means that everything we know might be wrong.

After coming back to Promise, I've seen my actual white ravens. Dead and bleeding at my feet and alive and watching my every step. I've also now seen the wider application of

Hempel's paradox—my metaphorical white raven—right now, right here in the Promise woods. It wasn't pretty; my hands turned sweaty and my throat closed up with an unrealized scream.

I've now seen what happened to my mother. I've seen her grisly fate. The worst part? She brought it on herself. Willingly. But then why did Mom leave the blood for me along with instructions to use it to close some kind of doorway—when she so clearly was trying to open it? Was that a trick? If I do what she asks, will I die like she did? Or something worse?

All my conscious post-Promise life, I've trained myself to believe that even though Mom's disappearance *seemed* mysterious, it was still located within the realm of logic. I told myself over and over again that everything can be explained with science.

Well, science, explain this: a clear-as-day experience of me being stuffed into my mother's burning skin, the horror of being torn apart and, at the same time, consumed by an otherworldly vortex as Mom's last thoughts thundered through my brain: *Rise, my warriors, and conquer this world!*

I wouldn't peg Mom as an apocalypse-welcoming, destroy-the-world kind of gal, but how can we say we know someone if we barely even know ourselves or what we're capable of? I rub at my wet eyes with the back of my hand. Why would Mom want to end the world? She had a family, people who loved her. . . . Did none of that matter to her? I wonder if this is what the family members of murderers feel like: devastated, powerless, deflated.

As I reel on my feet, my brain's chemical composition rearranging itself manifests as a numbing pain at the base of my skull.

The fog dissipates, revealing a large circle of black soil encased by the vibrant woods, an awkward patch of death surrounded by life. In the light of day, the amulet is back to being a lifeless piece of metal, the drawing of ravens on its surface crude, unsophisticated.

The amulet served its purpose, I suppose. Now that I've seen Mom's horrifying message, there's no way in hell I'm going to do as she asks—take the blood vials into the woods. And I'm not going to give the vials to Elspeth, either. Maybe I can destroy them.

My headache is the only reminder of the whirlpool of sensations that entrapped me seconds earlier. I'm still shaky and disoriented; my primal instinct is to put some serious distance between me and the Black Clearing, and fast. So I run.

26
THE RAVEN PARADOX:
PART 2

Racing back into the woods, I almost immediately trip over a low-sitting branch and slip on the wet moss. I flail my hands in an attempt to stay upright, hitting the rough tree bark in the process and, despite my best efforts, I end up on the ground, my hands barely stopping my face from meeting the dirt.

Kneeling in the mud, I stare dumbly at the mess that is my injured palm. Shit! A deep scratch with oozing blood. Its rusty smell makes my stomach turn. I need to disinfect my hand.

Also: *I've just spilled my blood in the woods.* Kind of. Unintentionally. Does it count? Despite clearly remembering Mom's instructions that I spill my blood *in addition* to releasing what's trapped in the vials, I'm still shaking all over.

Wouldn't want to unleash the apocalypse because of my clumsiness.

When I stand up, something brushes against my shoulder, making me jerk back in response. Another brush follows, its force pushing against my back. My ears pop. All sound multiplies tenfold. I look around in fear. No wind out here, but the air's disturbed nonetheless, swirling in constant movement. The hair rising on the back of my neck matches one clear signal in my brain: *Run*. But . . . if I run, wouldn't that be acknowledging for real that my mother was entangled in something supernatural? There's still a pretty good chance, after all, that Mom was nuts—and that I'm losing my mind also. There is no otherworldly army. Just some kind of scientific anomaly that sucked Mom up into nothingness. I must be imagining the whole thing!

As if on cue, a horse neighs nearby. Laughing at my attempt at rationalization. The beating of hooves announces the beast's approach.

I've got no better explanation of what happens next but that an unseen army on horseback is passing by me. *Through me.* Their chatter is the roar of a seashore multiplied to a planetary proportion; the thunder of the beastly hooves accompanies the words of the heart-wrenching language from my dreams. Whispering, singing a call to battle, giving commands to the powerful creatures carrying them. I hold my breath until my numb feet regain sensation.

Then I run at breakneck speed.

As I put the clearing behind me, the woods become so quiet I can make out the noisy clatter of my heart's beating, my sharp and shallow breathing. I slow down, catch my breath. My adrenaline-induced shivers subside, but the cold sweat remains, covering my skin. I hear a branch snapping behind me and sprint again, jumping over fallen trees and spiraling roots. . . .

When I collide with something—*someone*—I yelp as I fall on my back. Whoever I just smashed into swears in surprise. I know this voice. *Please, anyone but him.*

But, of course, it *is* him.

I stare up at Shannon as he pushes back his sweatshirt's hood and leans over me. His towering shape casts a shadow over my face. I expect him to say something snarky or look annoyed, like he did at the blood collection point, but he's just offering me his hand. I have a moment's thought to reject it, but I accept.

He pulls me to my feet, but we both underestimate the inertia and I end up chest to chest with him. Caught off guard by our proximity, I'm reminded of Shannon as the boy next door, the way he's been preserved in my memory: sweet and eager to please, his lips full and eyes innocent. But that picture wavers in my mind, the grown-up version of Shannon eclipsing the young boy from the past.

I take a small step back, but not too far. With only our combined breathing for a soundtrack, we stand facing each other, a too-small space trapped between us. The subtle heat of his breath is on my face. A crazy thought occurs: If I stand on tiptoe, I can *kiss him.* Maybe I'll be the kind of girl who kisses a boy first. Though, with Shannon's earlier hostility, I'm also likely to be the kind of girl who sends the boy running right afterward. My thoughts take me by surprise. What is wrong with me? After my Black Clearing experience, how can I even think about kissing?

I take in Shannon's appearance. There's a thin sheen of sweat on his face; his hair is ruffled. *He ran here.* But why? My question retreats to the back of my mind as I register that

Shannon's still holding my hand. The moment I realize it, I have to make an effort to keep cool. Shannon's presence makes my earlier encounter in the forest take a dreamlike shape of something incorporeal, something imagined, not experienced.

"What are you doing here?" I ask huskily as Shannon lets go of my hand—a slow movement, our fingers brushing, hesitant to let go.

"I live here. Remember? In the house across the field from yours." There's a smile in his voice, but his lips are serious. He doesn't look unhappy, just curious.

"With Abigail." I say his mom's name and immediately wish I hadn't, because Shannon's expression turns grave.

"No. Mom doesn't live there anymore. Just me."

His tone is a warning: *Do not go there.* I wonder if I should take another step back, but Shannon doesn't seem to mind standing so close, and I don't want to appear intimidated by him. Instead I say, "Sorry I smashed into you."

"Why were you running like that? It looked like something was chasing you, but there're no animals in these woods that are going to hurt you. Unless you're scared of chipmunks."

"Ha-ha. There are bears around here, you know."

"Nope. Not this close to town. Not anymore. All big and scary things retreated deeper into the woods a long time ago."

"Maybe I just wanted to see how fast I could go. Or maybe dashing through the woods like that is the only time I really feel alive. You know how big-city people can get all weird when they're so close to nature," I joke, but Shannon looks serious.

"I wouldn't know," he says. "Not a big-city person. And it's unlikely I'll ever leave this place. You know how small-town people can be. If you don't leave by the time you're eighteen, you don't leave at all."

"True. And once you do get out, you better stay out. What's there to go back for, anyway?" I can hear exactly how bad it sounds the moment I say it. I can tell that Shannon hears it, too. "I didn't mean it like that . . ." I start.

He interrupts, "I'll walk you out of here, if that's okay. So you don't get spooked by a squirrel and crash into someone else."

I nod, quickly falling into step with him as we move through the woods. Our silence is tense. Even lost in our own thoughts, we're acutely aware of each other. I wonder if Shannon saw or heard anything weird in the woods today, but I don't know how to ask without having to explain my experience earlier. What does he know about Promise, anyway? He's been here his whole life while I've been mostly kept prisoner in Dr. Erich's office by my overbearing father.

And yet, with all the possibilities, the question I want to ask him has nothing to do with Promise.

I'm rather impressed with the ability of the human mind to compartmentalize: While a part of me is still reeling from watching my mother disappear into the fog, another part re-members Del's flirting with Santiago and her full-of-it assur-ance that Santiago's so hooked on her charm, he'll be coming to see her tonight *and* (possibly, maybe) bringing Shannon along with him.

I give Shannon a long, sideways glance. "What?" He meets my eyes, almost making me trip over another stupid root.

"Just wondering . . . by any chance, were you thinking of dropping by the Manor tonight?"

"Why? Do you want me to?"

"Can you just answer the question, please? I'm testing a theory here."

"If I answer your question, will you answer mine?"

"Sure, I guess."

"Okay then. No, I wasn't planning on coming by the Manor tonight. Or any night. As a matter of fact, I'm planning to stay away from you and your Manor as much as I can till you leave Promise."

Mud squelching underfoot, I stop in my tracks. Shannon's rude words, delivered in a pleasant, polite voice, get the cognitive dissonance neurons firing in my brain, sending me down the rabbit hole.

Shannon doesn't pause, his steps remaining wide and certain, leaving me no choice but to catch up with him. When I do, my confusion gives way to a kind of self-righteous anger. "What was *that* about?" My voice is fake-calm, as pleasant as his was just seconds ago.

"That's your second question, and our deal was for one. Now it's my turn."

I don't spare him a glance. I'm starting to really dislike this grown-up Shannon. "Fine. What do you want to know?"

"Why are you really here, Hayden? What are you looking for?"

"Hmm, that's two questions. Which one do I answer?"

We step out of the woods then. From here I see the path that will take me all the way to the Manor's porch.

When I face Shannon again, I hope I look as indifferent as I sound when I say, "I inherited the Manor. I'm here to check it out and see if I should sell it. You're right, though—there are other reasons for me to be here. *You* are one of the reasons

I've always wanted to come back, but since it doesn't feel like you want me around, I'll leave you alone. Del's waiting for me anyway. Have a nice day, Shannon."

I take a step, eager to move away, but Shannon places a hand on my elbow, sending a shiver over my skin. "What happened to your hand?"

In all the commotion of smashing into Shannon and having my mind shaken up by his rudeness, I forgot about my injury.

"Nothing. I fell." Calmly, I wrestle my arm out of his grasp.

"You're bleeding, Hayden. Let me help you." He searches his pockets, but I shake my head, and, keeping my back ballerina-straight, start on the path toward the Manor. I have to fight the immediate urge to turn around and see Shannon's reaction.

To my deep-seated disappointment, he doesn't come after me, doesn't say anything. When I give up and sneak a look over my shoulder, the space where I left Shannon by the edge of the woods is empty.

ᚠᚷᚠ

A certain fairy tale tells a story of a girl who is entrusted with a set of keys to a castle upon one condition: not to unlock one special door. *Just one.*

It is, of course, a test, and the girl fails it. The price of failure? Her life.

This bugs me to no end. Why give the girl the key to a forbidden door and then instruct her *not* to open it?

Is it to ensure she obsesses about what she cannot have, to the point that it kills her?

Or is it to guarantee the girl dies in the end?

Another question I have: Was the girl's life worth it? Or was her death only a stepping-stone toward a higher plan?

At least the girl died after having solved the mystery.

Let's see if I make it that far.

ᚠᚷᚠ

I study my face in the bathroom mirror. Do I look any different now that I had my UFO Crash Moment? Does my experience with the amulet vision in the woods mean I'm now willing to entertain a possibility that strange phenomena can have other-than-normal explanations? Regardless, I know that something enormous took place in the woods today and I'll never be the same. I might've seen Mom's final moments on Earth, and those moments were rough. Like the menacing statement on Elspeth's old bumper sticker—WE WILL NOT GO SILENTLY INTO THE NIGHT—Mom's passing wasn't gentle. I recall my vision again, hoping to commit its sequence of events to memory: Mom cut her arm and opened some kind of portal (in hopes of what? Bringing some mysterious army into this world?), and that's where things went immediately wrong. Instead of releasing the army, the portal sucked Mom in and blasted the clearing. Okay, so if that solves the mystery of what happened to Mom, it still doesn't explain the rest of the bizarre puzzle. What about the blood vials? And the finger they found in the woods when searching for Mom? All these questions leave me more confused than ever.

I clean and bandage my hand with some first-aid kit gauze before making my way to the kitchen.

Considering my next steps, the way I see it, I have two choices: I either experiment with this bloodletting business in the woods and then move on with my life when (*if?*) nothing happens, or I stay the hell away from the woods, return to New York, and somehow try to put Promise behind me.

Once more, the curious scientist in me wins out. I decide to gather more information about my mother's extracurricular activities before I make up my mind.

ᚠᚷᚠ

Del's rumbling stomach demands breakfast. We settle on an omelette and coffee. The latter turns out unusually bitter, but I can't find any sugar and I used up our last reserves of milk making the omelette. While I'm busy cooking, I consider coming clean and telling Del everything, including my experience with the amulet and finding the blood vials in the basement on our first night here. But as I sneak glances at my friend, I change my mind. Hearing me mumble about experiencing a blast from the past and seeing Mom try to open some interdimensional portal will most likely get Del all freaked out. She'll think I'm losing it and worry about me. I even wonder if her sudden turn toward a rational perception of the world has anything to do with my abrupt descent into supernatural belief. Maybe Del thinks I'm on the verge of getting my mental wires burned and is trying to counterbalance my nutcase behavior with her aloofness.

Del wrinkles her nose as she tastes my nuclear caffeine concoction, then puts down her cup and suggests we go borrow milk from our neighbors. The way she says it, it's clear she expects *me* to do the borrowing. Keeping a straight face, I explain to her that our closest (and only) neighbor is Shannon, and that there's *no way* I'm going anywhere near his house, not after my earlier conversation with him in the woods.

With eerie intent, Del listens to a heavily edited account of my meeting Shannon in the woods earlier and shakes her head in disapproval when I tell her about Shannon's "I'm planning to stay away from you" declaration.

"He's totally bluffing," Del concludes, all sagelike as she gulps down her coffee. "You wanna hear what I think?" Clearly not needing my confirmation, she goes on, "He probably spotted you leaving the Manor this morning and went after you so he could *accidentally* run into you. You know, kind of like when Bolin kept *accidentally* showing up in my six a.m. yoga class every other day."

"I dunno. . . . He sounded pretty certain with his whole I-don't-like-you vibe. But then there were moments when I could swear he was looking at me with . . . whatever. What is it with these hot-and-cold guys? Why can't they just say what's on their minds? Save us all a lot of guessing."

Del gives me an incredulous look before breaking into a short laugh. "Wow, Hayden. I think with your recently gained great insight into the intricacies of the male mind and the fact that you've read way too many psychology books for someone your age, you're totally ready to pen the next edition of *Men Are from Mars*."

"Seriously? That's your advice? You're making fun of me?"

"Didn't realize you were after advice. Okay. Let me give you a prediction instead: Shannon is *totally* going to show up here tonight, tagging along with Santiago. I'd bet money on it if I had any to spare."

I roll my eyes at her cocky certainty, but my head's already buzzing at the possibility.

"What's with the arctic winter in here?" Abruptly changing the topic, Del rubs her arms and shoulders. Too busy alternating between thinking about my mother and Shannon, I haven't noticed what Del's wearing till now: way too many layers and, for good measure, a blanket spread over her knees. Just looking at her now makes me sweat. The Manor feels toasty to me: I'm certain I left the central heating blasting last night, set on *tropical*.

"Are you sure you're not sick?"

"I'm fine," she says.

I reach out to touch her forehead, but she wiggles out of my reach. "I said I'm fine."

"Okay. Don't bite my hand off."

She stares at me, her eyes unblinking, suddenly unfocused. "Sorry. Had bad dreams last night. Still feeling weird. And really cold."

"After breakfast I'll look at the central air. Maybe something's off with it." I doubt that's the case, but I can't think of another explanation for Del's discomfort except for her coming down with a fever.

Del rubs her arms some more, and I pick up on a few other telltale signs of her being unwell: Her skin's lost some of its glow and reddish, dark half-moons have formed under her eyes.

When we sit down to eat our modest breakfast, Del mechanically consumes her share. I wonder if she even senses the food's flavor. After she finishes and washes her plate, she tells me she's going to work on her group project in her bedroom.

ᚠᚷᚠ

Whenever my mind's about to go into overload, I have two choices: Recite Mom's lullaby till I calm down, or busy myself with some menial task. At this point, after everything I learned about the weird happenings of Promise and after having *seen* (Felt? Experienced? Was it *real* in any sense?) the amulet's dark message, I find the lullaby too spooky to use as a calm-me-down technique. So I distract myself with the task of fixing the possible heating problem, grabbing the ring of house keys just in case.

I look at the controls, which are on the wall in the living room. They seem fine, but I bring the temperature a few degrees higher and shut the thing closed.

While I'm on handywoman duties, I take a walk along the perimeter of the Manor's first floor, wondering what other surprises lie dormant in the building. Not quite sure what I'm looking for, I feel the keys dangle from my hand as I move. I count them, memorizing their shape and features in my mind. Anything not to think about Mom and her riddles.

Key number one is a cylinder, its cuts sharp like shark's teeth. *One* unlocks the Manor's front door.

Two is for the Manor's back door. To an untrained eye, *two* is *one*'s twin, but if you look closer, its cuts are smaller, less pronounced.

Three looks like something you'd dig up at an archaeological site. A voided key is the proper term for it, because a key like this is designed to open a pre–Industrial Revolution pin lock. My educated guess is that *three* opens the cellar door outside.

Four is for the basement. Though unlocked now, I remember the times when that door was always shut tight.

And here's *five*, so mundane in my hand but maybe the

most important. *Five* opens the chest containing the vials of blood. Blood Mom wants me to spill in the woods along with my own.

And *six*? It has an uneven surface roughed up by rust. Where do you fit, little key? What door do you open?

My aimless stroll through the Manor becomes a search for the sixth lock. Once I finish circling the Manor's first floor and finding nothing, I head upstairs. My legs carry me toward the master bedroom. Six keys sing melodically, in sync with my hurried pace.

The master bedroom is empty, expect for a bare mattress on the floor and what looks like a desk hiding under a dust-covered white sheet.

Besides the entrance, there are two other doors: a built-in closet and a bathroom. The latter reveals nothing of interest. The former seems oddly sinister to my inflamed mind.

In anticipation of a Narnia moment, I slide the closet door open, exposing the dark interior to the weak light. The bandaged cut on my palm tingles, and without thinking about what I'm doing, I begin reciting Mom's lullaby in my head. *No! Stop that.* I don't need to calm down right now. I need to focus, to be fully present.

I step into the closet. Its claustrophobic space is scarcely lit. It smells of old wood, dust, and something else . . . paper? Like a whiff of a library. Hmm . . . My hands explore the closet's paneling. I don't know what I'm looking for till my fingers sense a pulsing ping: The back wall's surface feels like it vibrates in response to my touch.

Something's in there, behind the thin layer of wood. I slide my hands in a wide arc, going down, until . . . *Bingo!* My fingers land on a . . . keyhole? Painted, inside and out, the same gray as the rest of the closet's back wall, the keyhole is virtually undetectable unless someone's looking for it.

Keys on the ring clacking against one another, I slip the sixth key in and turn it. A hesitant click.

Bluebeard's room is unlocked, ready to reveal its ghastly secrets.

27
UNLOCKING

We can find patterns in a series of (seemingly) random events. If you roll dice once, the result's considered a random event. But if you keep on rolling, random events will begin exhibiting patterns. And those patterns can be analyzed and, based on what the analysis reveals, future patterns can be predicted. I guess that makes physicists a sort of soothsayer.

Ever since my visit to Doreen's office, I've been experiencing a series of seemingly random events. The bizarre conditions of my inheritance, the moody town of Promise, Elspeth's sinister presence, Gabriel's amulet that either makes me trip or is actually imbued with supernatural power, and, of course, Mom's call for bloodletting. But even with all the information I have now, I'm still not sure what patterns are emerging. Maybe my analytical method is all wrong and I need to change my perspective completely.

For the first time in a while, I wish Dad was here with me

so I could ask what the hell he thinks is happening. But can I ever trust him again, after a decade of lies? That's another question.

When I open the secret door and step through it, my wish is partly fulfilled—I feel Dad's presence as I see the physical evidence of him living and working in the Manor all these years. The walk-in closet in my parents' old bedroom doesn't lead me into Narnia. What it reveals instead is a very cramped and dusty room full of Dad's research.

And here's that anger I've been waiting for. A wave of fury comes over me. So yeah, Shannon didn't make this up—my father's been coming to Promise a lot all these years. And every time Dad looked me in the eye and said we both had to put Promise behind us, in his mind he was probably already planning his next trip. I wish there was cell reception in this town. I wish I could call Dad and tell him where I am right now and what I think of him and his lies.

I suppress the impulse to scream. To throw things around. To break stuff. To build a bonfire of research journals in the backyard.

Taking deep breaths, I look around me. *Focus, Hayden.*

A wall made entirely of shelves is bursting with books, most of which, by the look of it, are home-printed manuscripts. A simple wooden desk is overloaded with papers and leather-bound journals. A lot of journals. There's a serious-looking computer—bulky and military. Its screen is lit up and showing a weird moving chart, where one axis is a timeline of dates and the other carries what I'm pretty certain is a Latin symbol, but my memory draws a blank when I try to identify it. Dead languages have never been my forte. The best I can make of the symbol is that it looks like an armchair turned upside down.

I forget about the mystery symbol the moment I focus on the contents of the chart flaring up on the computer screen, the digits are speeding toward . . . something. Mesmerized, I study the frenetic movement of numbers. The counter is at 570,240 when I start watching. In less than a minute, it dips below 570,000, and it's specifically at 569,970 the moment I turn away. The numbers are large, but they're dropping fast. In my book, anything counting backward to an unnamed event is never good.

My heart heavy with premonition, I turn toward the sheets of continually printing data slowly coming from the nearby printer. The printout looks like historical numbers showing a steady, low count of something, its presence going back months, with small but periodic fluctuations occurring roughly once a quarter. But it looks like there was a recent huge spike in numbers, right about the time Del and I arrived in Promise. I flip through the printouts some more until my eyes register something sticking out from the dry columns of numbers. One word: *muon*. Suddenly the Latin symbol I couldn't identify makes sense: it stands for *mu* and is used to signify the muon, an elementary particle that's frequently found in so-called *air showers*, when Earth is bombarded with cosmic rays.

I look back at the screen, at the steadily dropping numbers, and connect the dots: Dad's monitoring the muon count in Promise.

If tripping on the amulet's message in the woods scared me into a primeval fight-or-flight response, seeing the muon count going up to the stratosphere makes my brain freeze. My guess is the counter is linked to some kind of muon count detector. But what's going to happen when the chart reaches phenomenal heights? The data is confusing—a counter counting down to something, and a chart tracking muons spiking—but they both seem to be converging on some kind of event, and it is happening soon.

Of course, I can always do nothing and hope that what I'm seeing is just an unfounded doomsday prediction. Or I can grab Del and get us the hell out of Promise, just in case. Or I can try to do something to prevent the event the numbers are counting down to. But that last option seems like the stuff of action movies. Besides, how do you stop a swarm of elementary particles?

Flicking between the computer screen and Dad's bursting bookshelves, I decide to do what I do best: research.

I turn my back to the monitor and study the bookshelves. The topics range from theoretical physics to metaphysical works to myths and the paranormal. The latter mostly center on one topic I'm rather familiar with: Nibelungs.

I hate the Nibelungs.

The Nibelung legends may have inspired Tolkien's *Lord of the Rings*, but the *real* Nibelung stories are scarce. All we know is that the Nibelungs were a half-legendary Germanic tribe. Also, they possessed or wanted to possess some kind of treasure.

By far the most embarrassing part of all this mess is that Dad believes the Nibelungs are very much real, as in, they exist, trapped somewhere, biding their time before their release.

By the looks of it, Dad is also certain that the key to releasing the Nibelungs is hidden right here in Promise. My fingertips turn cold and I feel as if I'm floating through space, weightless and small. Suddenly, everything clicks, forming that pattern I was so eager to see all along, only instead of triumph, I sense the beginning of a panic attack. For the first time I truly wonder if all of it—my recurring dream about the shadowy army, Mom's clues, and Dad's crackpot science—point toward an impossible truth. Like an obnoxious neon sign, an all-consuming question flashes through my mind: Are Nibelungs real?

My brain foggy and breathing shallow, I scan through Dad's binders on the desk. Numbers, unfinished calculations, formulae, graphs. Data reports going back some twenty years. *From before he even met Mom.* Twenty years' worth of obsession.

The longer I stare at the data reports, running my eyes over Dad's spidery handwriting, the more I understand what my father's been up to. He's trying to model something. The starting point in his calculations is a tectonic shift that occurred centuries ago in this area, forming Edmunds' Gorge. Dad's hypothetical model claims this shift wasn't a single occurrence and is likely to happen again, when the muon count spikes to a certain, rather high number. As it is about to do again, and very soon, by the looks of it.

Ignoring the sense of dread flooding me, I remind myself that Dad is obsessed. *Delusional.* He's never been okay, not since Mom didn't come back from the woods and possibly even before that. But what if he's right? What if Dad's some kind of scientific equivalent of a seer no one believes until it's too late?

I set Dad's reports aside and pick up a journal from the top of the pile. A handwritten diary. One of many, judging from the shelves busting with similar-looking volumes. The first entry dates to the year I turned eight. I catch my breath and leaf through the diary, all the way to the last pages.

Abigail Reaser has grown more distant. Her sleepwalking condition has worsened. She constantly complains of being cold. Her hands shake and her lips are perpetually dry and cracked, though no official medical ailment has been diagnosed.

I think Ella might be responsible for Abigail's decline somehow, though, of course, there is no proof. As always, Ella keeps her secrets close to heart.

I worry about Shannon the most. His close friendship with Hayden has been the anchor of normalcy for both of them. In the past months, to escape his tense home environment, Shannon's been spending more and more time in the Manor. His arrival each time signals that Abigail's having an episode. I've seen scratches and minor cuts on his skin, but he denies any wrongdoing on his mother's part and grows distant and standoffish if I pry.

Shannon's relationship with my daughter is intense; they are connected like two old souls who've found each other and won't let go. If a day comes when I have to take Hayden away, I fear what will happen to that boy.

Ella is changing—physically, emotionally. Her body is weak. Or rather, less material somehow, like the very force that holds her atoms together is dissipating, relinquishing its hold on her.

Yesterday, once more, I saw her standing at the edge of the woods. Frozen in her spot, she was staring at a wall of unusually thick fog. As a primeval sort of fear rolled up and down my spine, I had trouble telling where the fog ended and Ella began. I fear I'm losing her. I hope I'm wrong.

Our lawyer, Doreen Arimoff, came over to the Manor last night when Ella was out for a walk. Doreen hinted there is some trouble brewing. She told me to watch over Ella more than usual in these coming days.

But I know my wife. I know she's just going through one of her dark phases and that she'll snap out of it eventually. I know Ella will be fine. If not for me, then for Hayden.

My priority is Hayden. I'll do whatever it takes to shield her from Ella's troubled mind. My main concern is that Hayden will have to deal with Ella's legacy as she grows up. After all, it is in Hayden's blood.

My mind is at odds with what I have just witnessed. As a physicist, I theorize about possibilities, about what might be when certain conditions are met. But when a theory actually tests itself out before your very eyes and you have nothing in the way of coping, nothing to help you deal with this new version of reality... what is left of you then? What's left of your beliefs?

I have no doubt anymore that Ella, the woman I love, the one I married and the mother of my only child, is not a being of this world.

Her heart may have a beat and her blood may flow red when her skin is cut, but she is not human. Not in the biological sense of the word.

Ella goes into the woods every day, and until now, I've never spied on her, allowing her privacy. But last night I followed her.

Now I can confirm that those never-healing cuts on her arms are indeed from self-mutilation. However, her bloodletting serves a different purpose from what I imagined.

Ella inserts her bleeding hands into the fog, as if to "feed" it.

There were others in the woods with her.

I recognized Abigail, her face pale, her hands bleeding, but the identities of two others were concealed behind hooded black robes, falling all the way to their feet.

A minor earthquake occurred when Ella first touched the fog with her bleeding hands. I felt a change in the air, an electric discharge. But nothing else happened after that, nothing tangible that could be seen or measured.

I watched Ella as she left the forest, disappointment written on her face. The others followed her. Abigail was so weak that she had to be carried by one of the unidentified others. Whatever Ella was hoping to achieve didn't work, I presume. Not this time.

28
ESCAPE

A *compelling natural force* is the perfect term for a phenom-enon that can't really be explained. Stand in front of a skeptical audience and say some catastrophe happened because of a "compelling natural force," and you will sound credible without really explaining anything. The secret is in the word-ing. *Natural* implies the phenomenon is located within the boundaries of normal human experience. *Compelling* means it is unlikely the phenomenon can be controlled, which shifts blame away from the authorities. And *force* can mean anything you want it to mean.

In the mid-twentieth century, a group of Russian skiers met their disquieting end in a snow-covered wasteland deep in the Ural Mountains. Led by Igor Dyatlov, a group of nine—all experienced athletes and survivalists—perished in the freez-ing tundra. Their camp's remains showed that the skiers were awakened by something at night and, spooked into a frenzy, cut their way out of their tents and dashed half-undressed for the nearby forest. There were no survivors. The official cause of death was recorded as hypothermia. But some of the unlucky travelers were missing eyes and tongues. One had traces of radiation on his body.

By the end of the investigation, Soviet officials blamed the skiers' demise on a compelling natural force. This indescribable but very lethal force, it was concluded, was what drove Dyatlov and his group to temporary insanity and, consequently, their deaths.

Compelling natural force was just an abstract concept for me until the day I returned to Promise. This town, I am now convinced, has a mind of its own. From the start, Promise had a plan for me, and everyone and everything else around me are just bolts and cogs in its doomsday machine. Its heart is hidden in the woods.

ᚠᚷᚠ

My hands holding Dad's journal are shaking. These things he wrote about Mom . . . It sounds like he really meant it. Another, uglier thought crosses my mind: How much did Dad really know about Mom's past? What did his obsession with the Nibelungs mean in the context of his marriage to a woman who, for all I know, opened some kind of portal in the woods with her blood? I don't need to be a genius to put two and two together: Mom was (or thought she was) a Nibelung, whatever that is. And maybe, if what I saw in the woods is real . . . maybe she *was* a Nibelung. Something other than human. And what does that make me?

"What the hell is this place?" Del's voice behind my back jolts me out of my trance. With a soft bang, the journal falls out of my hands and meets the floor.

I open my mouth but can't think of appropriate words. My best option feels like, *I'm a hybrid between human and some alien species, and I think you and I are in terrible danger.*

"What's this place?" Del asks again, absently crossing her arms over her chest.

"My father's lair," I reply flatly.

Del's glare tells me she knows I'm not telling her everything and that she is not happy about it.

She pushes past me, deeper into the secret office, and comes to the wall of books. She glances at the computer and then swiftly picks up the journal I dropped on the floor. My cool runs out right about now, and I grab the journal out of her hands. "My dad's diary," I explain when Del gives me a half–pissed off, half-questioning look. "Just some ramblings and stuff."

"I'd *really* like to know what's going on here." Despite Del's attempt at controlling her voice, her exasperation spills over, mirroring the whirlpool building up inside me. "Don't you think I have a right to know why there's this big mystery about your father's research? You know, since I came out here with you and this whole town's freaking me out and no one knows or tells us what's going on, and now there's a computer counting down . . . What is it counting down to?"

"The second coming of the Nibelungs, I presume."

Maybe it's my half-Nibelungen blood rising. A wave of shivers rushes over me and my stomach twists as raindrops hit the secret room's only window: a skylight above our heads. The skies turn gunmetal gray, readying for the onslaught.

How can this be? Is all this one long Alice-like dream, where I followed a white rabbit into a hole and fell in way too deep? Even if I try to leave, will that be giving in to my family's insanity? Will that be acknowledging that my mother and father really were implicated in something out of this world, something that can't be explained with science and rationalized away? But more important, if I'm indeed half Nibelung—can I ever run away from my own nature? Will my volatile, semi-alien blood ever let me be?

I dare a glance at Del. She's watching the changing skies through the skylight. Her eyes are stern and her hands are tight by her sides. When she speaks, the words are a loud whisper. "This morning while you were out, I had the worst headache ever. And I almost never get headaches. But this one, it just hit me so bad and wouldn't let up until I was on the floor, moaning in pain. I was so scared. Really scared for the first time in my life. But when it was gone, I had a clear memory of what happened that night when I sleepwalked into the Manor's basement."

I avoid her eyes, avoid the finality of having to accept her words, focusing on the motion of her fingers instead. Curling and releasing. Curling and releasing. Del continues, "I remember everything about the crawl space now. And I never have any recollection of what I do during my sleepwalking episodes. But this time, I remember waking up and hearing this weird humming, like the buzzing of an electric razor. Coming from the basement. And then this creepy booming voice in my head kept saying, over and over, *dig deep, dig deep, dig deep*. What does all of this mean, Hayden?"

I place my father's diary on the desk and reach out to hug Del. She's shivering. As I drown in her scent—a bittersweet perfume and something that's unmistakably Del—I feel my tongue grow heavier with the weight of the words I'm about to spill. Mom's vials, the amulet, the forest vision, Elspeth's dark compulsion, and, of course, the latest: the extent of my dad's research into the Nibelungs and the world-altering conclusions he's reached as a result. But as I consider all of it now, I don't even know where to begin. All these things just add up to a bunch of deeper mysteries. The bottom line, I realize, is that I don't really have any answers to give Del.

"Del, I think we should get out of here," I tell her as I let her go. The certainty I hear in my voice comes as a surprise to me. "I wish I knew what was happening, but I don't. Not really. I just feel that we need to go. To leave Promise. Now."

ᚠᚷᚠ

We quietly pack our bags and brave the pelting raindrops to load our luggage into the rental car's trunk. I read the agreement off Del's face; she believes we're doing the right thing by leaving.

I leave the box of blood vials in my bedroom's closet. Let this be someone else's mystery. I don't care. I'm choosing *normal*.

I lock the Manor and hide the ring with six keys above the front door, exactly where I first found it. Elspeth can go in and do whatever she wants for all I care. I'm done. I'll sell the Manor, like Doreen recommended, and my father will never need to know I came here at all. He can keep Promise all to himself.

"Leaving so soon?" In our flurry of packing up the car, I don't notice Elspeth sitting on the hood of Silverfish and watching me. Upon meeting her eyes, a shiver goes through me. In this moment I'm my mother, coming out of the woods to find this unwanted guest waiting for her on the Manor's porch.

"Get in the car and wait for me," I hiss at Del. She opens her mouth in protest, but after she takes one look at Elspeth, I know Del's alarm bells are ringing as loud as mine. In the drizzle, Elspeth's black-clad figure has the menacing halo of a cursed saint. Del backs away from Silverfish and into our Kia, moving like someone would around a wild bear.

With Del out of earshot, Elspeth slides off Silverfish's hood and comes—or more like *flows*—toward me. Gone is her simple red dress, replaced with a tailored, sharp-shouldered black tunic, its back trailing after her. Add a pair of twisted horns and Elspeth could audition for the next *Maleficent* movie.

With a sexy kind of smirk playing on her flawless face, Elspeth nods toward the Manor and says, "Why the rush?"

As I fight the urge to follow Del into the car, a weird kind of defiance raises its head, and I give in to the hot anger flowing through my veins. "Something came up and we need to go back home earlier than planned."

She snorts, the crude sound contrasting with her regal composure. "Hmm . . . I don't think that's it. Let me make an educated guess. You were curious, so you took the amulet into the woods, but its message proved too much for you to handle, probably because your half-human brain can't even comprehend what you truly are, so you're doing what a human would do—you're running away. Am I close?"

She is right on the money, but I won't admit it to her. "What would you do in my place? Go cut yourself in the woods so you can *maybe* release a supernatural army that will . . . what? Destroy the world? Yeah, maybe my half-human brain finds it difficult to believe that would actually happen, but I'm not going to take the chance."

"You know you can't escape this," Elspeth says quietly. "It's as much a part of you as your mother's eyes or your father's human heart."

"Good-bye, Elspeth. I'd say that I wish we had more time to get to know each other, but I don't like to lie." The drizzle turns into a rain, drops sliding down my face and clouding my vision.

When I move toward the Kia, I hear Elspeth's words clear and close, as if she's right next to me, whispering into my ear. "Can I at least have the blood vials? I know you found them."

"They're in the Manor. You're welcome to them." I turn and watch, waiting for her to move, but she stays in her spot. Her eyes trained on the Manor, Elspeth looks wistful and frustrated. I recall the runes running in lines around the Manor's entrance and walls and more runes crudely cut into the outer surface of the box containing the vials. Runes that made my fingers tingle on contact. "You can't enter."

"A little inconvenience, that's all."

"Good-bye, Elspeth," I say again. I leave her by the Manor just as the rain hits full-force.

By the time we drive off, the downpour reaches Biblical proportions, making me doubt our chances of getting out before the roads flood.

Del lets me drive, and after she says of Elspeth, "I don't

like her. She's tense like a coiled snake, ready to strike," we don't talk till the Manor's distorted silhouette is gone from the rearview mirror. Even then, we limit our communication to an occasional conferral on directions. When we enter the forested section of the road, the rain intensifies and the view through the car's windows becomes opaque.

Blinded and panicked, I slow down, straining my eyes to see the condition of the road ahead through the frantic movement of the windshield wipers. A flash of lightning illuminates trees under assault by the slashing rain. Another lightning bolt. Then another. And another. No thunder. Just endless sparks of light hitting seemingly the same spot, over and over again. A tree falls with a thud, making me jump in my seat. Del lets out a squeak. I hit the brakes. "Crap! That was close." The car jerks to a stop.

A fallen blue spruce, not fully grown but still large enough to block the road entirely, has missed us by a few feet.

I meet Del's eyes, red-rimmed and wide, and I see in them what goes through my mind, too: We are trapped.

29
EVENT HORIZON

Black holes are created when a large star grows so old it begins to collapse into itself. With star matter getting packed tighter and tighter, the gravitational pull grows stronger and stronger—until it packs so tightly that the ordinary rules of physics break and everything starts getting dragged in. The dead star collapses into a black hole. Once trapped in a black hole's gravitational pull, not even light can get out. What happens in a black hole stays in a black hole.

The *event horizon* marks the boundary where escape is impossible. Put simply, an event horizon is the point of no return.

I have a feeling that the fallen spruce that nearly crushed our car was our event horizon.

ᚠᚷᚠ

All but deafened and blinded by the sky's angry deluge, I reverse on the narrow, slick road. I slow down whenever the car threatens to swerve and, once we're out of the woods, I turn onto another road that runs parallel to the trees, hoping to get to the highway via the town's center. Hallelujah! I can see the spire of the clock tower and the outline of the church next to it, both coming up on the left. We're almost in Promise's downtown.

I step on it and don't slow down until the car rolls onto Promise's sleepy main street. From there I aim for the town's heart. The rain is slamming down like mad. Not a soul on the streets. I know on a rational level that this town isn't abandoned, but it sure feels like it.

"Take a left here, I think," Del says, pointing through the rain.

Going left gets us just off the town's center, not far from Angie's Shop of Curiosities. From here I take course for the clock tower up ahead. When the tower grows nearer, a wave of relief washes over me, clearing my head like a doubleshot of espresso.

My euphoria doesn't last. The road takes an unexpected turn, making me lose view of the spire for a second. I blink away the sudden fuzziness veiling my eyes and swear. Following the turn, our Kia has somehow ended up going the opposite way, the clock tower now haunting the rearview mirror. We pass Angie's Shop of Curiosities again, heading back the way we came.

"This makes no sense!" Del whispers. "It was just one turn. We couldn't have made a one-eighty!"

Shaking my head, I spin the steering wheel and make a U-turn, going for the spire again only to lose it once more and end up on the street leading back to the Manor.

"I don't know what to do, Del!" I whimper, not recognizing the sound of my own voice.

"Just go back."

"No."

"Just go back to the Manor, Hayden. We need to regroup." The note of defeat in Del's voice takes me off guard. "Something's wrong with our sense of direction. Or we're both having some kind of episode. The end result is the same: We can't leave. Or at least, we can't leave right now. So let's just go back to the Manor and think this through."

She doesn't mention the possibility that must've crossed her mind in the last few minutes: Promise is blocking our way, doing all it can to redirect us back to the Manor.

And it's winning.

Despite my subconscious knowing that we can't leave, I still want to argue with Del, but her words sound so much like something I would say—stone-cold logical—that I have no choice but to nod my reluctant agreement.

Satisfied, Promise reshapes the space-time continuum once more and spits us out of the town proper and into the woods. Our Kia heads down the road all the way back to the Manor without incident.

I'm relieved that Elspeth isn't here to gloat when I step out of the car and take in the familiar landscape. The Manor's gothic-novel-worthy outline shimmers meaningfully in the gloom. Defeat tastes like rainwater, plain but poignant.

We haul our luggage back into the house, getting drenched to the bone in the process. The Manor creaks and murmurs, either welcoming us back or ridiculing our failed escape attempt.

After changing into dry clothes, I can't help but sigh in relief, letting out some of the pressure that's built up in me during our drive to nowhere. I appreciate the soft and dry cotton of clean clothes, pure happiness against my skin.

I go down to the kitchen, eager to reconvene or, as Del called it, regroup. We have a lot to talk about, and, as usual, I don't know where to start.

I take a seat at the kitchen table and watch Del as she extracts an aluminium container of cocoa from Dad's stash in the storage closet and makes hot chocolate. I'm grateful for Del's presence now more than ever, thankful for her calm bravery in the face of this highly unusual spring break trip, but I'm still unsure of what to say, how to express my gratitude, and how to explain all the things I've just discovered and the even crazier things I suspect. A large part of me feels guilty for dragging her out here and getting her mixed up in my family's mess, but I also remember that she volunteered to come along. Still, I owe her the truth about what's been happening to me since we arrived in Promise. The need to tell her everything burns inside me, an all-consuming fire. I savor the moment as I pass over my own event horizon and let the words flow.

"Here's the deal," I start, and Del, sensing that this is important, meets my eyes. Grasping my mug of hot chocolate with both hands, I seek courage in its warmth. "My mom wasn't mentally stable, and my dad was . . . *is* obsessed with her. His obsession extends to this town and this mythic warrior race called the Nibelungs. There are legends telling of the

Nibelungs' treasure, but Dad used to tell me—back when I was still willing to listen to his ramblings—that it's supposed to be a metaphorical treasure, something abstract, like power or knowledge, not diamonds and gold."

Del doesn't interrupt, so I continue, wondering how much she already suspects after sharing a roof with me for many months and having had a chance to observe my family's comings and goings. "After Mom disappeared, Dad and I moved to New York. In school, I've always struggled being around other kids. Or maybe it was *they* who struggled being around me. I used to have these anxiety attacks caused by recurring dreams— I was either haunted by Mom or leading an army through the night, or both. Whenever I had those dreams, in my head I could feel the warriors' intent—to raze this world to the ground so they could build one of their own on its ashes. I thought these supernatural army nightmares were a courtesy of Dad's Nibelung tales, but now I don't know anymore. Then one day in school, someone got hurt. I don't remember what happened. Not exactly. But a teacher claimed that we were arguing and I pushed this girl, Jen. Her face was a mess. . . ." I shudder at the memory.

I wait for Del's features to twist into disgust or pity, but she just nods, a curt move of her chin, beckoning me to go on.

"You know the rest, I guess. I was pulled out of school. Dad hired tutors to homeschool me. I was in therapy, taking antianxiety meds for a while. It was only a few months ago that I was allowed to come off my meds completely. It was decided that I was adjusting fine."

I tell Del about Doreen, my mother's "conditions" and "clues" in the codicil to her will, and then the big one: what happened when I took Gabriel's amulet into the woods.

After a moment of alarming silence, Del takes a long sip of her hot chocolate before saying, "You actually *saw* your mother open a portal in the woods and then get sucked into it?"

I consider her emphasis on *saw* and say carefully, "It was as if I was in two places at once. In that moment I *was* my mother, opening the portal and welcoming the army into this world, and at the same time I was *me*, watching my mother . . . perish. Whether it was all in my head or not, it was horrifying. I mean, at that moment, Mom really wanted to destroy the world. . . ." I pause. "You probably think I've finally lost it."

Del becomes quiet again. This time the silence drags on for what feels like ages, though it must be barely a minute. Deliberately, she finishes her drink and places the empty mug on the table. I know her well enough to recognize the mannerism as her attempt to stretch out her response time, so she can gather her thoughts and formulate her words properly. "I haven't told you this before, but I have a sister who's in a cult. They call themselves the 'Watchers' Disciples.' They believe they can develop superpowers by cultivating silence and abstinence. There was this BBC documentary about them. . . ."

"You never mentioned you had a sister." I think of Del's family, her proud parents, her gorgeous brother, the way they are so happy and radiant every time they video chat with Del.

"That's because we don't talk about Alice. My family's way of dealing with a problem, *any problem*, is to distance ourselves from it and never *ever* talk about it. Alice must've been eighteen, straight out of high school, when she met the cult's leader. Weeks before her nineteenth birthday, she announced her move out of my parents' home to live in a compound on the outskirts of Paris. Our parents didn't fight for her. Mom and Dad just watched as she packed up her things and left. I know it sounds unrealistic, but my parents are like that. Their pride was hurt. They took her decision to leave as if she made it to personally wound them, as if they weren't good enough for her. And maybe there was an element of resentment on her part, but that's not the point. The morning my sister left, my mother removed all photos of her from the walls. Alice got *erased* from our life, completely cut out."

"Del, that's really screwed up and I'm so sorry . . . but why are you telling me this? Why now?"

"I'm going somewhere with this. You see, I visited Alice regularly after she moved into the compound. I had to keep our meetings secret from our parents—they would be mad if they found out—but I had to see Alice. She was always the cool-headed one, the logical one. Actually, now that I think about it, you remind me of her a lot. So when logical Alice got involved in this cult stuff, it just didn't make sense to me. Brainwashing wouldn't work on her, I knew that, so I thought it had to be something else. My sister would have to *believe* that this cult and its leader were the real deal, otherwise she would've never left her family like that."

"So what happened?" I ask, captivated by the story as much as I'm numbed by the revelations about Del's family. "What did you find out?"

"The compound turned out to be a lot less sinister than it sounds. Not the creepy Manson stuff at all, but more like a happy hippie commune, you know, everyone's content and real quiet. When I went there to see Alice, she told me that she decided to join the commune after she saw the cult's leader levitate and move objects with her mind."

I can't help the freaked-out expression forming on my face, but Del misinterprets it as skepticism and shakes her head, saying, "I know what you're going to say, Hayden. This supernatural ability stuff can be faked, etcetera, etcetera. I've watched those Uri Geller videos with you, so yeah, I know where you're coming from, but hear this: It doesn't matter if it was fake or not. My sister really *believed* she saw the leader do all these things. And that belief shaped her reality, no matter whether the leader could really levitate or not."

"So I'm a victim of trickery?"

Absently Del rubs her head, once more careful to choose her words. "I didn't say *that*. Remember that I *do* believe in the paranormal and you don't—unless you've changed your mind at last. What I'm saying is that this Elspeth chick is superscary, and I wouldn't put it past her trying to pull some crazy stunt to—"

Del stops midsentence and gives me a suspicious look. "She wants something." When I don't confirm or deny her words, she says, "And you know what it is. You have it."

I'm about to tell her about the blood vials, but then I decide showing is better than telling. So I run upstairs. The rune-decorated box is where I left it.

Back downstairs, when I open the box for Del after explaining how I found it in the crawl space, I watch her face, fascinated by the way her expression tightens in confusion. "What the hell?" she asks.

"Blood that doesn't go bad," I say. I extract one of the vials from its keeping place and shake it to demonstrate; there's a ghoulish beauty to its waves. "This one's got Mom's initials." I run my finger over the *ET-H* printed with permanent marker on the vial's side. I cast my eyes over the other two vials (*ED* and *GD*) and make a realization. "The other two must be from Elspeth and her father. Elspeth Diamond and Gabriel Diamond. The three of them were connected somehow, and they felt their blood was important enough to preserve."

"Like the relics of a saint," Del says.

I nod. "Right. Pieces of a saint, a preserved hand or a finger that supposedly doesn't rot. But I've never heard about blood staying fresh like this. It's supposed to coagulate. Unless, maybe, the person is sick, but haemophilia is hereditary, and I know Mom didn't have it."

"Maybe something's been added to the blood to preserve it. Besides, you don't know *for sure* this is your mom's blood. Or even blood at all."

"I wish there was a way we could test it."

If lab analysis revealed something unexplained, something definitively nonhuman about this blood, then it would be proof—finally, proof!—that my mother wasn't human.

I know we're thinking the same thing, I'm just the first to articulate it. "And, of course, conveniently, there's a high-tech lab dedicated to blood research in Promise."

Del nods.

I just need to convince Shannon to help me get the blood from the vials analyzed without attracting too much attention from anyone else.

30
RESTLESS

I contemplate grabbing the blood vials and going to the Blue Haven research facility in the woods *now*, but like all the best-laid plans made in Promise, this one gets put on hold because of weather. The rainstorm raging outside is a howling, elemental beast, leaving us no choice but to wait it out.

So we stay in for the rest of the afternoon, talking about anything *but* Promise and its creepiness. As we lounge about, sticking to the less-dusty parts of the Manor, Del tricks me into giving her a pedicure. While I buff her nails to shiny perfection, she tamely suggests giving me a makeover. As I always do, I laugh it off. She waits until I'm done with her nails to start pushing my buttons. It's like we're back in Fort Greene. I realize I miss our home.

I do a double take when Del says, "Don't you even have, like, the slightest desire to impress Shannon with your understated beauty?"

"You'll pay for that understated beauty comment, you beast." I make a grab for her feet, intending to smudge her freshly painted nails, but she wiggles out of the path of destruction and slides off the couch to the floor, chortling.

"You are the beast, Hayden. Scaring boys, sometimes before they even get to see you." She stops when she notices my changed expression at her reference to my fiasco of a blind date with Ross. "I'm sorry. That was uncalled for."

"It doesn't matter."

"It does matter. To me, that is. I mean, it was my idea to organize that stupid blind date. But please, why won't you let me be a good friend to you and fix that god-awful wavy hair of yours? Just so Shannon doesn't break his fingers when he runs his hands through it."

"I'm not letting you anywhere near my hair. But fine, I will wash it and style it. Because I was going to do it anyway, not because I share your deranged belief that Santiago and Shannon are going to make their way to the Manor through this storm. Besides, once the weather calms down, I'm going to the blood collection point, so you can deal with Santiago on your own."

I drag my feet upstairs and draw a hot bath. The change from cool to hot is shocking, and it takes three deep breaths and some mental cajoling for me to stay in the bath. But soon my body starts to melt into the water. I close my eyes and allow a light smile to play over my lips as I submerge into twilight.

Twilight.

Mom's blond ponytail flickers as it vanishes into the mass of dusky trees. Mom wants me to follow her, but the forest has another idea; trees shift, moving or popping up out of nowhere, blocking my path, snapping branches at my face. My feet keep tripping over the wild underbrush. Driven by the blood in my veins, I push on. Electric buzzing—a swarm of angry, iron butterflies flapping their wings—rules the space around me, evolving into that now-familiar noise of metal clanging against metal. Dream logic keeps my emotions at bay when I realize I am the source of the clanging; head to toe, I'm encased in leather and metal. The leather is tight, its touch sensual, reminding me of Shannon's fingers running the length of my arm. Elaborate metal plates protecting my chest and back make me feel an infinite strength from within. Strength the likes of which I've never felt before.

But without a horse, I'm vulnerable out here, a voice says in my mind. As if it's totally normal to be wearing medieval gear in the middle of Colorado and bemoan the absence of a horse to carry me.

Then a horse neighs. Not far away. *My beast is searching for me. My army is waiting. Restless.*

My fingers curl and uncurl in anticipation of folding over the leathery reins of my battle horse. I can smell him, his powerful, musky scent. There's a heat building in the bottom of my belly that's both uncomfortable and liberating.

The forest tightens around me. The branches are demanding, searching as they wrap around and slide against my body. But the cold feel of something metal in my fist gives me power. I raise my hand to see the wicked shine of a curved blade, black runes running its entire length. I slash and hack, tearing through the woods, attacking the tightly woven wall of firs and spruces. Under my onslaught, the trees give in and release me into a small clearing, where a giant of a horse stands facing me, a challenge written all over his face. Only his black mane is free; the rest of him is hidden under armor, twinkling in the night.

The sudden drop in temperature sends shivers over the exposed skin of my neck and face, but I barely register it because I'm mesmerized by the steed. A cloud of white escapes his nostrils.

I take a step closer. All the light seeps from the air. Darkness, matching the steed's mane, claims the day. "I won't hurt you," I promise. "Don't be afraid." The beast shifts his weight and flicks his head impatiently. *What are you waiting for?*

"Grane. It's you," I whisper, covering the distance between us. I reach out to his powerful neck. Tight cords of muscle bulge under his hot skin.

He leans in and smells my hair. I know him. He knows me. And he's not afraid of me at all. With dreamlike ease, I fly up and settle into the saddle on Grane's back. It fits me like it's custom-made. I spread myself over Grane and murmur a command in a foreign tongue into his ear. He takes off, flowing above the ground, his knowing legs moving with almost no sound.

We ride. Bursting through the forest, through the thickening fog growing higher and higher and reaching the tips of my boots. We're swimming in a white river of haze. My mother's nowhere in sight, but I know where she's headed. Toward that vast space of burnt ground, a clearing where nothing grows, where fog rules day and night and all the unbound time in between.

Without as much as a pause or a second thought, Grane rushes straight into the heart of that cursed place. There's a sensation of my lungs shrinking and my heart screaming *no*, akin to jumping into a freezing pond.

Grane comes to a standstill. Before us, my mother's figure is twisted by a wild vortex made of fog and darkness. A white raven caws, a sound of desperate need. I watch as Mom's body loses its shape, shedding particles. As I open my mouth to scream, I'm thrown into my mom's head. The final moment nears, and I hear her thoughts: *I forbid your entry into this world. I will this gateway closed.*

Hayden . . . The forest coughs up my name and I look around. Mom is gone, and the fog keeps on rising. Myriad voices join together, forming a choir of inhuman whispers, their buzzing increasing in volume until they are the deafening roar of a jet engine.

Hayden . . . Release us. . . . It's time.

Only the tips of Grane's ears are still visible in the tight cloud of whiteness consuming us both. The fog reaches my neck, my chin, snaking its way up my nose, into my lungs. I thrash in the saddle, fighting for breath.

As the fog consumes me, Del's face, eyes open but unseeing, materializes out of the wall of white. She stares at me in silent accusation and I scream, pulling at Grane's reins.

ᚠᚷᚠ

I'm floating in the bath, lukewarm water reaching just above my half-open mouth. Shivering, I jolt upright and spit out water. I must've bitten my tongue, because I taste blood. Teeth chattering, I climb out of the tub and pat my body down with a towel. A bitter aftertaste of blood lingers even after I wash out my mouth.

My mind goes over every minuscule detail of my nightmare as I towel-dry my hair with shaky hands and then blow-dry it straight. A scratching sound at the window snaps me out of my reverie. I approach the steam-smeared glass and come face-to-face with a white raven. *Hello, old friend.* I come closer to the window, expecting the bird to take off, but it stays put, eyeing me with curiosity. I fiddle with the window's lock, but it's stuck. The raven and I exchange stares until the bird takes off into the rain, leaving my questions unanswered.

ᚠᚷᚠ

The rain doesn't ease all afternoon, so I never go to the blood collection point. Just as I grow restless enough to try my luck on the muddy roads, the Manor's doorbell sings its old-fashioned tune. I'm caught wearing black jeans and a ruffle-neck green sleeveless top. My heartbeat's going nuts, and it has nothing to do with Promise and Mom's secrets. This is it—*Del was right*—Santiago is here and I'm about to eat my piece of humble pie. Despite my determination not to care, I glance at myself in the mirror, wondering whether Del would approve. On the way down, I grab my leather jacket.

I don't really expect Shannon to show up, not after our borderline-hostile exchange earlier. But a part of me (yes, *the stupid part*) hopes he's here.

Glowing with confidence, our misadventures today clearly pushed to the back of her mind, Del is gorgeous in a tight pink woollen dress. A shiny black belt emphasizes her perfect waist and her vintage tan suede boots (a rare find, according to Del) reach over her knees, accentuating the shapeliness of her long legs.

Del opens the door. I can't quite hear what she's saying, but her intonation is of the flirty variety. Santiago swaggers into the house, dragging wet air in with him. I observe his reaction to Del's goddesslike appearance—his eyes widening in appreciation.

Santiago's not bad looking himself, I guess. Out of his camo garb, he looks less commando and more Abercrombie & Fitch. Together, Del and Santiago are like gorgeous, fluffed-up birds in the beginning of a courting cycle. Del steps aside as if to let him pass, but Santiago pulls her into a brief hug, almost too intimate. His face brushes against her hair, his mouth sliding down to find her waiting cheek while his lips spread in a knowing smile. I'm blushing but can't look away. Watching them charge the space around them with thick sexuality makes me wonder if I missed the memo and they've actually been going out for some time now.

My fingers curled tight around the staircase rail, I wait. My speeding heartbeat is a soundtrack to my anxiety. When no one follows Santiago into the Manor, I can almost taste my disappointment, sour on my tongue.

I ponder which escape path to take after I do the mandatory *hello* and *how are you*. I know Del's going to insist I come out with them, but I have no interest in being the third wheel.

And then my brain goes into overdrive, because Shannon follows Santiago into the Manor. Shaking water off his jacket, Shannon smiles awkwardly and scans the room, his face tense, cheekbones sharp in the uneven light. When his eyes meet mine, his heavy expression softens and my stomach flips. All's dizzy in my world for a frustrated moment. Catching me in my most uncontrolled moment, Del turns to look at me, her face saying, *Told ya.*

I come down to the living room and join them. His arms crossed over his broad chest, Shannon says, "Hayden." A simple nod. No intimate hugs or kisses-on-the-cheek being given out by him.

Dressed in simple dark jeans, a white tee, and a rain jacket, Shannon seems younger and slightly vulnerable, like that serious boy who still haunts my childhood memories. He says to me, "Hope you don't mind I came along, especially after . . ."

"I don't mind," I say too fast, and Shannon's lips almost smile but not quite. How long have we been staring at each other? I realize we're being watched by Santiago and Del, both looking amused and proud, as if they have accomplished some prize-worthy feat.

The spell broken, Santiago says, "We wanted to show you girls the town. We can start at Tea Salon, and then I thought we'd do something special. Tonight is a good night to get a taste of some local flavor. Thursdays are the most entertainment-filled days of the week around here." Santiago and Shannon exchange a glance, giving me the impression Shannon's not a fan of whatever "local flavor" Santiago's got in mind.

But all my follow-up questions are skillfully dodged by Santiago and shrugged off by Shannon. Del doesn't fare much better; all she gets out of Santiago is that the "show" is free and guaranteed to elicit shock and awe.

Outside, we are under attack by wind and water. The weather calmed down a little since the freaky afternoon, but the sleeting rain maintains its razor-sharp intensity. Del and I make a dash for the car—a dark-red jeep parked next to our modest rental. Del takes the passenger's seat next to Santiago, while Shannon holds the door to the back open for me. As I climb in, our hands touch, igniting embers under my skin. I'd like to interpret the look Shannon gives me as full of restless longing—but it's likely camouflaged annoyance that Santiago dragged him along tonight. I break eye contact with him and ignore the shivers rolling over my body.

I wait for Shannon to settle next to me so I can ask him what happened to his staying-away-from-Hayden plan, but when he does get close—even with the middle seat empty between us—I tense up and retreat into my personal space. I hope he doesn't notice the physical effect he has on me. Note to self: *Get a grip, weirdo.*

I remember I need to ask him about the blood vials and my hope to have them analyzed, but I decide to wait for a better moment, when we're alone.

ᚠᚷᚠ

"We got lost in the city today," Del says while taking in the night views of Promise through the car window. "It was such a weird experience. Like the town didn't want us to leave."

"Were you trying to leave?" Santiago doesn't take his eyes off the road.

"Yeah, kind of," Del says.

I stay quiet, but it's not easy when Shannon's intense eyes turn on me.

Del goes on, "We had a weird feeling in the Manor and

it triggered a moment of panic. It was this primeval fright, almost. Like when you wake up from a nightmare and your blood's still pumping." From her measured tone, I know she's fishing for information.

Shannon stares at me. "You sensed something in the Manor and decided to leave town? What did you feel?"

Santiago laughs. "You girls must've been tripping on something."

"Nope. We've just had . . . a lot of strange things happening." Del's about to say more, but I divert the focus back to Shannon and Santiago.

"Is that so surprising?" I ask them. "You two are part of a research station studying weird phenomena here in Promise, aren't you?"

"Yes and no," Shannon starts to say.

"Dude, that's classified!" Santiago shouts.

Shannon goes quiet. I shift closer to him, going as far as the seatbelt allows, and whisper, "Okay, you don't have to tell me anything that's *classified*. I'll just find out on my own. But the reason we wanted to leave . . . it's not just a feeling. There was some stuff I found in the house that upset me."

Shannon waits for a moment when Del is laughing in response to Santiago, then says, "You broke into your father's office." In contrast to my nervous heartbeat, his voice is calm.

"The Manor is legally mine," I say. "I didn't break into anything."

He shrugs. "Your father's been using the Manor as his personal headquarters for years, so maybe he's got more rights to be there than you do."

"Thanks for reminding me that my father's been secretly

coming to Promise for years. I believe I have a right to know what he's been doing here while he's been telling me to forget about this place and move on."

"What are you two fighting about?" Stuck at a red light, Santiago turns to look at us, suspicious.

"Nothing!" we say in unison.

ᚠᚷᚠ

At night, Tea Salon transforms from a bakery and café into a nightlife hot spot of Promise. Possibly, *the* hot spot. The aloof staff starts to serve mulled wine and fortified Irish coffee alongside freshly baked scones and muffins, still warm from the oven, all while Lana Del Rey serenades the dark.

As our group gorges on tea and scones, Del proclaims Tea Salon has an identity crisis. Is it a teahouse that also serves liquor, or is it a bohemian bar that masquerades as a café? Either way, the Salon bustles with life. I can't shake off a feeling that our little group at a corner table gets too many stares, though no one makes direct eye contact with me when I look back.

As the evening unfurls, I swear Santiago's one step away from dropping all civilized pretences at making a conversation. If it were up to him, he'd just gaze longingly into Del's eyes for the rest of the night. But Del's extra cool, taking her I'm-hot-but-detached thing to the master level. Santiago swallows it up. Every time he whispers something to her (which is 90 percent of the time), he leans a little farther into her space, as if her gravitational pull's too hard for him to resist.

When Santiago and Del do pay attention to me and Shannon, the four of us talk about mundane things like the horrors of bad reality television, the good and the bad of living independently from our families, the latest book-to-movie hype. It's so pedestrian and I love it. This is what normal must feel like.

We learn that both Santiago and Shannon are saving for college, which makes Del and me feel like a pair of privileged brats, since we won't really have to work to afford tuition. We also learn that they both had paramilitary training before being hired by Blue Haven Research Institute. When I ask more about the Institute, Shannon and Santiago exchange looks and abruptly change the topic, putting up barbed-wire fences and drawing demarcation lines around their secrets, just like we do around ours.

A light buzzing makes Shannon search for what turns out to be a pager. *A pager.* I've only seen those in decades-old movies. Frowning, Shannon reads the message, then excuses himself to the depths of the café.

Suddenly edgy, Santiago shifts in his seat. Before I can ask what's wrong, he starts talking about Promise's freaky weather patterns. He even swears you can see the aurora borealis out here. I find that hard to believe. Watching for Shannon's return, I say, "Is this freak weather business what your team is here to study?"

"Nice try, Ms. Holland." Santiago gives me a crooked smile. "We're not supposed to talk to civilians about what we do in Blue Haven."

"But I'm not really a civilian," I say while Del stays oddly quiet, studying Santiago. "I'm Tom Holland's daughter. And he's important around here, right?"

"Not going to get into that." Santiago shakes his head.

"Being related to Professor Holland doesn't guarantee you high-level clearance. Besides, sounds to me like he didn't want you to get involved in any of this Promise stuff. And it's probably for a reason."

"And what reason would that be?"

"How should I know?" His voice turns soft, playful, but I can still hear his message underneath the layers of nice: *Back Off.*

"Can you at least speculate?"

Del clears her throat and gives me a pointed look. "This is the sound of me getting tired of this pointless conversation." She rests her elbows on the table and puts her chin on her hands, looking between Santiago and me. "Can we just agree that Santiago knows something but can't—or *won't*—share it with us? We've reached an impasse. Let's have coffee!"

Coffee quickly arrives, but without Shannon, our table's out of balance. I'm infringing on Del and Santiago's love-charged space, so I say I need some air and go outside.

The night's extra brittle, its sharp chill snapping me out of my comfort zone and turning up my senses. Even from here, the Promise lowlands' very bottom, I hear the whispering of the woods. My blood responds, and a sharp memory of riding Grane and brandishing my rune-decorated sword hits me strongly. I heat up despite the chilly wind, and suddenly my skin feels constricting, ill-fitting.

I push away the feeling and hug myself tight. To be whole. To be *me*. I concentrate on my memories of the night so far, on my humanity. I may never know what my mother truly was, but I know very well what it means to be human. The uncertainty of it, the expectations, the sweet moments of having

Del as my friend, the embers of an unfamiliar, thirsty spark whenever Shannon is near . . . In this moment, I know that regardless of what my mother wanted me to do—whether it's to release some force for chaos or lock it away forever—*I* don't want the human world, my world, harmed. It's not perfect, but humans do enough harm to one another as it is. We definitely don't need to face whatever Promise is hiding in addition to all our other troubles.

31
SOMETHING YOU NEED TO KNOW ABOUT PROMISE

"You look like you're solving complex math problems in your head."

I turn to find Shannon standing so close to me, I can feel the heat of his skin. He studies my face. I can feel a hint of a blush threatening to paint me embarrassed, so I snap out a response before Shannon notices. "Not really. I have enough problems of my own to be solving right now. Do you really want to talk about math?"

"I wanted to apologize, actually. I wasn't very friendly earlier, and now I feel bad about it. That's partly the reason I came with Santiago tonight."

"Good to know. I was wondering if your frosty demeanor was just my imagination."

"No. You didn't imagine it. I wasn't nice to you."

"Why?"

"Because I was . . . angry. Yesterday, when you showed up at the research base, I couldn't believe it was really you at first. After all these years, you know. You were my only friend, and I missed you when you left Promise. So when I saw you, all I could think was, *What took you so long?* I mean, we grew up together and then you just disappeared."

"You know why I left Promise. It wasn't by choice."

"True. You were a kid then, but later on you could've tried to find me or reached out. I tried finding out about you from your father, but he wasn't forthcoming. When years passed and I still hadn't heard from you, I started to wonder if it was your choice not to come back here at all."

"After Mom . . . things were complicated at home. I wasn't exactly in a position to reach out. . . . How was it growing up here, anyway? After I left, that is."

Shannon looks away but not for long. Our eyes keep seeking each other out. "Quiet, I guess. Not many kids to be friends with around here, as you might recall. I had to go to a boarding school out of state after junior high because they didn't have enough students my age here to bring in teachers from outside."

"At least you got to go to school," I blurt out. "I was homeschooled." He's waiting for more, while I focus on keeping my eyes down, making a point of studying his hands. He has tough knuckles, and a few scar lines stand out against his skin. I take a long breath and give him a heavily edited, CliffsNotes version of my post-Promise life—how I was briefly at Stonebrook, then under Dr. Erich's care, and finally in Brooklyn. When I finish, Shannon stares at me. The moment lasts and lasts and *lasts.* It should make me feel uncomfortable, but it doesn't. I meet his eyes straight-on while fighting off a memory of Mom. She used to joke that my eyes drove people and animals mad. But Shannon's eyes are strange like mine, so maybe our mutual bad mojo just cancels itself out.

"There's something you need to know about Promise, Hayden." The urgency in Shannon's tone snaps me out of dreamland. "All of us who were born here, me and Santiago included—we all had it rough growing up, in the sense of strange accidents happening, some small and maybe insignificant on their own, but when you consider them within a larger picture, they're not so small. . . . Santiago likes to tell this story about how when he was a kid, his dog broke its leash and threw itself into the river. It drowned. Santiago thinks the dog did it because it was spooked and wanted to get away from someone or something in the woods."

"That's insane," I say. *But is it, really?* I want to tell him everything else, about Jen, about that poor seal throwing itself against the glass in the New York Aquarium, about the dead white raven. But I hold back. I wish I could trust Shannon, but I have to admit—I don't really know him. Instead, I ask, "What about you? Any spooky stories to tell?"

"Well . . . you know about my mom, right?"

"What happened to her?" I ask carefully.

"You know how close she was to your mom. The things they were involved in . . . whatever they did in the woods, it affected her. Badly. Ever since your mother's been gone, mine's been living in a health-care facility. It's been almost ten years now." He wants to say more but doesn't, hesitation painted across his face.

"I'm so sorry. I'm sorry for what my mother did. I—"

"Stop apologizing, Hayden. It's not your fault. None of this is your fault. I visit Mom every other month. She gets anxious easily and her caretakers don't recommend frequent visits. The weird thing is that for the past year or so, she's been mentioning you. A lot."

"Me? What's she been saying?"

"That you must do what your mother failed to do. That you have a duty to your people and you must fulfill it. Do you know what that means?"

I grow very cold. "No idea."

A bell rings as the Salon's main door opens, spilling out Del and Santiago. They're holding hands, eyes glowing with that fervor of new love you read about in young adult novels. *Is that what people falling for each other actually look like?* When he manages to tear his eyes away from Del, Santiago says, "I hope you girls are wearing appropriate shoes. Because what we have in store for you tonight requires some serious footwork."

Shannon shakes his head. "I'm not sure anymore if it's a good idea, Santi."

"Why not? It's the most fun thing to do around here, and you know it."

"It's that . . ." Shannon looks uncomfortable.

"What are you two mumbling about?" Del asks. "And does it have anything to do with that taste of local flavor we were promised?"

Santiago says, "There's something peculiar to see in these woods, and it just so happens that this . . . let's call it an *occurrence*, happens once a month. *Tonight*. To say more would ruin the surprise. Just believe me, this is something you don't get to see in New York."

"I've heard enough to be hooked." Del shrugs in her nonchalant way, revealing to me that she's truly intrigued.

It appears the final vote to cast is mine. I find three pairs of eyes on me, expecting me to either ruin the fun or join in. "This *occurrence* is occurring in the woods?" I ask, noticing how Shannon's eyes flick from me to Santiago. I wonder how much Santiago knows of my family's tale of woe and its connection to the forest.

"It's not too deep into the woods," Santiago reassures me. The way he says it gives me my answer: He doesn't know the real reason I'm uncomfortable.

But Shannon knows. He keeps his eyes on mine as he says, "It's close to the clearing, but not too close." The emphasis is on *not too close*.

"Oh yes, the infamous Black Clearing." Totally unaware of my unease, Santiago continues, "You girls are going to *love* this. About ten years ago this crazy chick wandered off into the woods and set the forest on fire—"

"Shut up," Shannon snaps at him, the animosity in his voice giving me whiplash.

Santiago's mouth drops in surprise, while Del's face twists with sudden understanding. She lets go of Santiago's hand. "You shouldn't joke about these things, Santi," she says.

"We don't have to go if you don't want to," Shannon says to me while glaring at a befuddled Santiago.

I shake my head. Tired of being treated like I'll break if life handles me roughly, I say, "Let's go. I want to go."

ᚠᚷᚠ

The four of us get back into the car. Del and *Santi* take the backseat this time, most likely so they can make out. As we get on the road, I have to try hard to avoid a compromising rearview mirror reveal of them entangled. I can still hear them, though, whispering, giggling. . . . I settle deeper into my seat and distract myself by taking sneaky glimpses at Shannon, his hands firm on the wheel.

As we leave Promise's main street and enter the muddy-road wilderness, we pass by a monument I remember clearly from my childhood. I always thought it was a statue commemorating Promise's three founding fathers—the western European explorers who mapped this part of the States. But as we circle the gray monolith, I count not three but *many* shapes. It's a weird mass of armored bodies, manes of long hair and muscled arms sticking out amidst the fragments of horses, swords, and shields. A ferocious army.

"I never noticed the detail on this thing." I motion at the monolith. "It's pretty weird."

Shannon takes a quick look as we're passing by. "You're telling me you've never noticed the monument to the Nibelungs that's been here since Promise was founded?"

I sit up in my seat. "The Nibelungs? Why would they commemorate a statue to the *Nibelungs* in the Southern Rockies?"

He gives me a puzzled look before switching his attention back to the road. Again, I get the feeling he's weighing whether to tell me something, and, if yes, how much. "This town was founded by German immigrants. I guess they brought their myths with them."

"Shannon, what do you really know about the Nibelungs? And I don't mean the myths and stuff."

"You really don't know anything about your father's work." Shannon sighs. Before Santi can yell out *"It's classified!"* from the back of the car, Shannon blurts out one long breathless sentence. "Professor Holland found an anomalous compound in the blood of some Promise residents, Hayden. He's calling it the *Nibelung strain*. It's groundbreaking. He only needs more samples before he can make a proper scientific claim."

He only needs more samples. I give Shannon a long, meaningful look before I ask, "What does this compound do exactly?"

Shannon sneaks a look in the rearview mirror, making sure Santi's too busy to protest. "No one knows for sure, but people whose blood carries this compound . . . they emit this rare type of radiation. It's very similar to black-body radiation but also linked to these elementary particles called muons. Have you heard of them?"

32
LOCAL FLAVORS TASTE BITTER(SWEET)

Shannon's words are ringing in my ears and my mouth burns with follow-up questions, but then Santiago manages to let go of Del's lips for long enough to start a conversation about our plans post–spring break, making it impossible for me to learn more. I file the information away for now, wondering if Shannon knows about my father's muon counter hidden in the Manor.

As Shannon directs the jeep toward an unfamiliar road following the edge of the forest, I study his profile. Here is the boy I knew, hiding in the straightness of Shannon's nose, in the stubborn line of his lips. Yet there's a new harshness to his cheekbones and chin, a severity I don't recognize—but that I like. And there's something else, too—that long thin scar that runs from behind Shannon's right ear down his neck, not quite reaching his shoulder. It looks like a deliberate, precise cut. I glance away before Shannon can catch me looking.

He announces, "We're here," and parks the car off the road.

Santi tells us we have to walk up a slight incline, hence his earlier remark about footwork.

Every gust of wind feeds on my body heat, burrowing deep, all the way to my bones. When I run my hands over my shoulders to keep warm, Shannon sways my way. If I didn't know any better, I'd think he wants to give me a hug. Ultimately he chooses to keep his distance as we begin our silent ascent to the tree line. Drizzling rain and howling wind combine their efforts to drain all nocturnal magic from this experience. Whatever it is Santi's determined to show us, it had better be out-of-this-world good. I do need a break from Mom's puzzles, weird blood trapped in vials, and Elspeth's thinly veiled threats. I'm betting Del feels the same way.

Breaking his stride, Shannon leans close to me. When he speaks, his breath tickles my skin. "Whatever happens, don't freak out. I've got your back."

"What's that supposed to mean?" I demand, but Santiago and Del catch up to us and Shannon steps back, not answering.

Our collective mood grows serious as we near the forest. With a heavy heart, I step into the woods. The wind stops, but the drizzle lingers.

As we walk on, I focus on Shannon's broad back in front of me. Despite my suspicions about the amulet, I find its weight around my neck reassuring.

In the near-total darkness, I hear whatever we're searching for before I see it: a slow rhythmic buzzing amidst the forest's subtle symphony of noise. A disturbed owl, awakened too early, hoots in annoyance at the growing buzz of . . . hushed voices? Chanting?

Shannon stops suddenly, causing me to collide with his

back. I start to laugh off my clumsiness, but he turns around and leans in again, as if for a kiss, making me shiver. He whispers into my hair, just above my ear, "Don't spook them. Keep it quiet, Hay." Flushed, I take a step back, leaving Shannon's warm orbit, careful not to break a twig underfoot.

"Step where I step," Shannon murmurs.

As soon as the forest thins out, our path dead-ends with a cluster of chest-high briar rose shrubs. Kneeling behind the bushes, Santi gestures for us to follow suit. The four of us crouch behind the natural hedge, shoes slipping on the ground. Just as I'm beginning to feel stupid, Shannon takes hold of my hand and pulls me close. I immediately see why—a small opening in the hedge provides a clear view to the other side. Shannon doesn't let go of my hand, making it hard for me to focus my attention on anything else. But that changes when I catch a glimpse of what's happening right ahead.

A woman is hanging upside down from a tree, her short, shiny black hair forming a spiky crown around her head, her skin glinting in the dark. I know the woman is naked, but her nakedness is muted by the night, subdued by the sound of otherworldly chanting. Hands crossed over her face conceal the woman's identity, but there's really only one suspect here.

As if feeling the four pairs of curious eyes on her, Elspeth lets her hands hang free and opens her eyes. I hear Del giggle, but I'm only partially here right now, with her and Shannon and Santiago. The rest of me is atop Grane, galloping toward the pulsating core of the woods, where my army awaits.

I loosen my fingers and let go of Shannon's hand. Pulled by Elspeth's electrifying presence, I feel the urge to move toward her, to join her, to let my blood rejoice in our likeness.

"Hayden!" Shannon hisses. He grasps my wrist, anchoring me by his side.

"Let go of me," I whisper loudly, my shoes slipping on the wet moss. Our little struggle ends when someone joins Elspeth—a man, judging from his height and size, covered from head to toe in a black robe.

The man drops the robe's low-sitting hood away from his face. *Gabriel.* Should I be surprised? He helps Elspeth untangle herself from the tree and gingerly covers her with a robe like his own. Mesmerized, the four of us watch as Gabriel pulls a knife from his robe's folds and takes Elspeth's hand into his. In quick, practiced movements, Elspeth rolls up her sleeve as Gabriel swings the blade, slicing at her skin to draw blood.

Right above my head, a raven cries out so loudly that everyone here must have heard it. And, sure as hell, Gabriel lets go of his daughter's hand and stands up straight. Elspeth hides her bleeding hand in her sleeve and stares at the shrubs where we're hiding.

She takes a step in our direction, walking into a patch of moonlight. She's a vision from a horror movie—her face twisted with the mad triumph of a ghoul. Her eyes meet mine through the hole in the hedge. "Care to join us?"

Santi barks, "Run for it!" But we're already dashing away. Shannon's at my back, urging me on, and though every cell in my body is screaming at me to turn around and join Elspeth and Gabriel in their grisly ritual, I run, and I don't stumble.

But I know I can never outrun the Nibelungen blood thundering through my human veins.

33
WARPED LOGIC

Out of the woods, the rain's power is absolute. It assaults all my senses, cooling my blood. The four of us cover the distance from the forest to the car at a brisk pace, balancing on the muddy path and waving our hands like flightless birds whenever we take a particularly slippery turn. The entire episode in the woods imprints on my memory as a series of snapshot moments, half-developed Polaroid pictures—Elspeth hanging upside down on a tree; Gabriel wielding a knife; me running away.

I propel myself into the jeep next to Shannon. He doesn't waste time, sending the car rushing into the night.

"What the hell was that?" Del yells, fighting off hysterical laughter.

"Some of Promise's more eccentric locals," Santiago says, mirroring her incredulous tone. "But don't worry. We wouldn't take you girls to see this if we weren't sure it was completely harmless."

"But what exactly *was* it?" Del insists.

Santiago tells her something ridiculous about a local Wiccan coven that makes me wonder whether he really has no clue or if he's placating Del on purpose.

I stay quiet, lacking the energy to pretend what I just saw in the woods was nothing but a harmless obsession of bored small-town residents. My darkening mood spreads to the rest of our group, and we drive the rest of the way to the Manor in loaded silence.

ᚠᚷᚠ

Del whispers into Santi's ear and flutters out of the car, heading decisively for the Manor. Santi jumps out of the jeep after her, disappearing into the house. That leaves me alone in the car with Shannon. His eyes glow a gentle green from the car's digital displays. I need to get on with my plan before I become all blushing and stuff. "The lab at the research base, it's equipped to run blood tests?" I ask.

A cautious nod. "Correct. State-of-the-art tech."

"And you said my father needs more blood samples to test his . . . hypothesis?" That earns me another nod. "So if I donate some blood samples for Dad's lab, will you promise to tell me if there's anything off about them?" *Like that compound, the Nibelung strain, for instance.*

"Is this a sample of *your* blood we're talking about? Because we already have yours. It's still being processed."

"No, it's not my blood."

"Whose blood is it then?"

We're just a couple of regular vampires, talking casually about blood.

I pause and consider how much I should tell him, but he saves me by saying, "Doesn't matter. I'll do it for you anyway. When can I have these mystery blood samples?"

"Come with me."

ᚠᚷᚠ

When Shannon lingers on the Manor's threshold, I make some half-baked joke about having to invite him in and then rescind my invitation just to keep things interesting between us. He runs his fingers over the line of runic carvings decorating the doorframe, his face scrunching up in distaste. A faint alarm bell begins to ring in my head. But then Shannon steps over the threshold and enters the house.

I continue watching him as he studies his surroundings; he takes long looks, zeroing in on this and that. His inspection doesn't miss the antique candelabra hanging from the ceiling or an oil painting of a raging ocean so wild that it's more black than blue. *Mom painted that. Dad left it here, reluctant to bring any unnecessary memories of her with us to New York.*

I beckon Shannon to follow me upstairs. Passing by Del's bedroom and hearing hushed voices and laughter add a certain awkwardness to inviting a boy into my room. I wish I had Del's unbending confidence as well as her no-bullshit attitude toward romance, but I guess I have to make do with what I've got. Before I let Shannon in, I warn him, "My room as it is now is *not* representative of my personality. I thought I'd mention that."

"You mean you took down your *Labyrinth* posters and pink wallpaper?"

"Oh God, you remember *that*?"

"Well, yeah. I did spend a lot of time in this house."

I open the door and walk inside, Shannon behind me. A nostalgic expression lingers on his face when I sneak a look. "Keep an open mind." I extract the metal box from the closet and set it on my bed.

Arms crossed tight over his chest, Shannon eyes the box like it's a rattlesnake ready to bite while I fish the keys out of my bag and locate the smallest, simplest one. My fingers keep slipping until I steady myself and insert the key into the lock. When the box clicks open, revealing the vials, Shannon's face twists in distaste, mirroring his expression at entering the Manor. "Where did you get that?"

"Found it in the basement."

"Can I have a closer look?"

"Knock yourself out."

Shannon sits on the edge of my bed and picks up one of the vials, exposing it to the light. "Your mom's initials. And the rest?"

"Elspeth and Gabriel Diamond. I think." I sit next to him, the box wedged between us, and pretend like I'm not all buzzing with anticipation. I wait for Shannon's face to reveal something—anything—after hearing me mention the father-daughter team, the very same one we just had the pleasure of seeing in the woods, but he remains stoic.

"Hayden, what do you think this means?" He looks at me in that serious way he used to.

"I don't have any proof, but I think their blood carries that compound my father discovered."

"And how on Earth are you so calm about it? You do know that if your mom had it, you could have it, too?"

"I haven't seen any direct evidence of my blood's radiation-making qualities. Therefore—for now—I'm calm."

"Somehow I doubt that." He looks at me funny, barely containing a smile. "Anyway . . ."

"What?" I demand.

"It's just . . . You're just as you were, just as I remember you from ten years ago, and yet you're a different person. It's fascinating, that's all. I keep seeing signs of the old Hayden in the way you wrinkle your forehead when choosing your words or how you use your *logical* voice. But then you turn your head and it's like a different slant of light. You're this completely grown-up version of you that's so . . ."

"So what?" I murmur, leaning just slightly into his space.

"Never mind." He shrugs, but I catch a blush painting his cheeks a faint shade of pink. I'm about to tease him, but the deliberate, careful way his hands move when replacing the vial of Mom's blood in the box makes me wonder what's suddenly made him so tense.

When unexpectedly he leans in and his lips touch mine, I freeze like a terrified bunny. To say I'm caught off guard is an understatement. In this moment, my world realigns, everything's changing, but all I know is that Shannon's kissing me and his lips are soft but persistent. Different from his strong, rough fingers that ran the length of my arm up and down at the blood collection point.

Right now, we stay very still—all except our lips, barely touching but burning. Delicately, he pulls at my lower lip before covering my mouth whole. When our kiss deepens, I shudder. Shannon lands one last short kiss on my lips and retreats, looking amused but hesitant.

"Hayden, you're like a deer in headlights." He lets out an uncertain laugh. When I can't produce any words, his tone becomes even less certain. "Okay, I think you have to say something. At least tell me if this is . . . good or bad?"

"Good. Definitely good. Just unexpected."

"I know you have a lot on your mind and a kiss from a long-forgotten friend is perhaps the last thing you need . . . and besides, you probably have a boyfriend."

"I don't have a boyfriend, and I do have a lot on my mind, but a kiss from you has been on my need list since I saw your broody face at the blood collection spot. I've been having dreams about you, you know."

"Tell me."

"You and me at the head of a supernatural army, riding side by side, ready to raze humanity to the ground. That kind of stuff."

"Oh, apocalyptic end-of-the-world dreams. I thought you meant something else."

"I've been having those dreams for as long as I can remember. You're a new addition, though." I look away, no longer blushing but feeling slightly embarrassed at having told him about the dreams. But I keep talking. "Shannon, I've been in Promise only a few days, and already I've heard some pretty outlandish things about my family! And I have a strong suspicion that there might be something very odd in my blood, and . . . other strange stuff happened, and everyone talks in riddles! Plus my own father's been obsessing about this town for years, and my guess is that he knows even more now about what Mom was—and what I am."

"We all have to deal with family secrets at some stage of our lives, I guess," Shannon says calmly. "It's just that yours are weirder than most."

"Is that all you have to say?" I look up at him, waiting for more.

He nods at the blood vials. "Let me take these to the lab tonight. Someone'll be there during the night shift, so they can get started straightaway. Once we have the results, we'll know for sure. If the blood is ordinary, it's likely you are, too."

When I fail to appear enthusiastic, Shannon says with a laugh, "What? You'd rather be a supernatural half-human hybrid with magical blood?"

"Honestly, I don't even know anymore."

And I mean it.

34
I'M *NOT* MY MOTHER

From the porch, I watch the jeep reverse out of the Manor's driveway. Shannon is a silhouette inside the car, his outline dark against the bleak moonlight.

My lips are burning from our kiss. Mindlessly I want *more*, while the logical part of me can't help but wonder what our kiss meant. Is Shannon genuinely into me, or is he driven by the emotions of our shared past? Worse, is he using me as part of some weird plot with the Institute? Or with my dad? Did I just make a huge mistake by handing the blood over to him? The night volunteers no answer, and when Shannon's car disappears into the fog, I'm left edgy in my own skin.

The rain thickens. I'm about to walk back inside when I notice a lone figure moving toward me across the field. Dressed in a long black robe, the visitor seems bathed in a weak glow. My legs refuse to move, so I remain on the porch, watching

Elspeth approach. Her short hair is wet and flattened against her head, her mouth twisted in an odd smile.

When she stops just below the Manor's porch, only the steps between us, a wave of surreal panic crashes over me. On instinct, my hands scramble to open the Manor's door. Once I'm over the rune-protected threshold, the relief washing over me is absolute. The urge to slam the door in Elspeth's face is so strong, I'm shaking. But I can't bring myself to do it. All the Shannon-induced dizziness is erased from my head, replaced by the discomfort I feel whenever I'm in Elspeth's proximity.

And yet with all her creepiness, I can't help but admire her. The slashing rain doesn't seem to bother her: An amused expression is playing on her face as she observes my clumsy rush off the porch. Her long, straight nose and delicate lips make her look like an elf from a folktale.

But when she speaks, her voice, low and husky, has almost the same dizzying effect on me as Shannon's kiss. *What. The. Hell?*

"Your mother's always been private and secretive. Even with those closest to her. When she bought the Manor, it was meant to be *our* safe house. But later . . . she decided to have it all for herself and her offspring, so she twisted the runes a little, added a few of her own, and voilà: I can't enter and neither can Gabriel."

On cue, a silver-gray raven materializes out of the night and lands on Elspeth's shoulder with a bewildered cry. Elspeth, goddesslike in her eerie serenity, turns to meet the bird's eyes before zeroing in on me again. When our eyes lock, a flash of lightning breaks through the thick clouds, illuminating everything around me. That includes Elspeth's face, all strong angles and odd shapes. She's looking even less human than before.

"Your perception changes the longer you stay here, close to your own kind," she says.

I wonder if she's reading my body language the way mentalists do when they claim to have telepathy.

"Do you feel my pull? Like calls to like." She's whispering, but I can hear her clearly all the same.

Yes, I do feel your pull. I want to come closer—every cell of my body *screams* that I need to—but I manage to stay where I am.

Instead I ask, "Who are you, Elspeth? And how exactly did you know my mother?"

"You don't need to fear me, Hayden. I have your best interests at heart. Just like I had your mother's best interests at heart." She doesn't answer either of my questions.

"And now my mother's gone."

"That wasn't my doing."

"What do you want from me?"

"Will you come and have a walk with me? I want to show you something."

"It's raining like crazy. I'd rather not." Not to mention the alarm bell buzzing in my brain, competing for attention with the urge to accept Elspeth's invitation that's setting my body on fire.

"Don't tell me you're afraid of a little rain!" she says. "Ella danced in the rain! She celebrated every storm, every flash of lightning. She especially loved nights like this one—a perfect night to be outside, to feel the water on your skin, like kisses from our gods. She'd never miss a chance to let her blood flow in the woods, if not to release her army, then at least to feed their hungry souls with her intent."

I shiver at the picture of Mom cutting herself, blood flowing, weakening her, feeding the insatiable earth while a supernatural army howls closer.

I can hear them, too, now.

In fact, I could always hear them, the voices in my head whispering in that language that makes me want to cry and scream in euphoria at once—the tongue of the Nibelungs. But I push it away and say, "I'm *not* my mother."

"No, of course not. You're something she created for a special purpose. Let me guess . . . Ella left you some instructions and they seem important. You come here and learn your daddy's been lying to you for years and your mommy had a plan for this world that entailed human extinction. And now you're all confused and haunted by these woods and what they've been keeping for a long, long time. But guess what? The choice is yours. Not your mother's. *Yours.* And you'll be a liar if you tell me you haven't considered the real implications here, your role in all this. You were born into this, yes, but you can make this into something of your own. You can be the leader your people need. . . ."

I rest against the doorframe as Elspeth's blunt words hit me hard. Everything I've learned in the past few days all appears to align with what Elspeth is telling me now: My own mother wanted to end this world. And for what? So that her dying people could have another beginning? I force the words to come, sounding like I'm announcing my own death sentence: "What you're *really* talking about is some kind of supernatural apocalypse unleashed on this planet, and I *definitely* don't want that. If that's my birthright, I refuse it."

For a second, Elspeth's face twists and ripples. "I tried to be nice, Hayden, but if you don't cooperate, I won't let you ruin it for us. If you don't want your birthright, then give me the blood Ella squirreled away in the Manor. The blood doesn't belong to you, and Ella never should've taken it. Then you can leave town and take your friend with you. Think before you deny me again. This is a one-time offer."

The steely finality of her words doesn't escape me. But I don't feel I've got much of a choice. The blood's gone now, entrusted to Shannon in a bid to find proof of my otherworldly heritage. But even if I had it, would I give it to Elspeth? The woman's goal is pretty clearly an apocalyptic vision of the human world burning.

I tell her, "I don't have what you want. I wish I could say I'm sorry, but I'm not. Also, I'm not scared of you."

She shakes her head in a gesture of impatience, as if pacifying an unruly child. "Too bad. Keep in mind, Hayden, that whatever happens from this moment on, you brought it upon yourself. And upon your friends."

I'm beginning to shake all over, but I stand my ground. "Fair enough. Thanks for the warning."

From my safe spot beyond the Manor's threshold, I watch Elspeth's black-clad shape disappear into the night.

ᚠᚷᚠ

Later, as I snuggle into my cotton pajamas and climb under the covers, I expect my busy mind to keep me awake, but I fall asleep with ease. I plummet into a soothing abyss. The sensation doesn't last long. I wake up to the sound of raucous laughter, which in my post-sleep wooziness seems to be shaking the Manor to its foundation. As I blink my eyes awake, I hear doors flying open and thumping closed, followed by the loud patter of running feet slapping against wooden floors.

Perching on the edge of my bed, I rub my numb feet till they regain sensation. Then I put on a pair of Docs, tightening the laces hard before grabbing my Hunter hoodie from the floor and putting the amulet in my pocket. My movements are mechanical; my body knows what to do and how to do it, but my brain's playing catch-up. This feels like a repeat of our first night here, and I'm already wondering what other surprises Del's going to dig up for me in the basement.

In the hallway, I look around. The door to Del's room stands open. Inside: no sign of Del or Santiago. I do a quick run around the Manor, even remembering to check Dad's secret office (dark, aside from the glowing numbers on the computer) and the basement. Nothing. I call out for Del before heading outside, garnering no response.

I'm on the porch again, half expecting to see Elspeth standing on the grass, waiting for me. But the lawn is windswept and empty. I pull the hoodie on and stare into the night. The skies are black and clear, and the moon's shining full blast. In its light, I catch the outline of a slender figure crossing the field, moving away from the Manor, in the direction of the forest.

All I'm thinking right now is that Del's having a sleepwalking episode and she needs my help. So I forget everything else and dash after her across the field and into the forest.

I come to a point where the forest path I've been following

diverges. My heart beats a little faster when I'm facing left. I'm sure this path will eventually take me to the Black Clearing. As if in response to my thought, the amulet pings in my pocket. When I rub it with my fingers, it sends electrical sparks through my skin. It's as if the Black Clearing knows I'm approaching.

I take the path to the left. Already heightened, my senses tense up and tune in as I listen and watch for any sign of Del. My choice of path pays off when the sounds of hushed crying reach my ears. Blood pounding in my head, I set my feet down more softly, thankful my eyes have now adjusted to the dark.

The part of me that feels a presence in the fog, that hears Mom's voice in my dreams, the part Elspeth wants unleashed— *that* part lifts its head in anticipation.

The Black Clearing. There's definitely something ungodly about this place. Unnatural. Being near it, let alone setting foot on its sooty ground, is like coming face-to-face with the void. I have to tiptoe carefully around it to keep the void from consuming me.

The soft cries I heard seconds ago do not subside. Instead, they're growing louder, more defined. I listen and, as I approach, my mind zeroes in on the telltale noises of a struggle. *Del's being attacked!*

I move ahead without thinking or planning my next steps. Considering my modest size and only basic knowledge of self-defense, my best chance is to surprise-attack whoever is hurting Del. In my dash for the Black Clearing, I only stop twice—first to pick up a rock and then to exchange the rock for a large branch. I figure I've got a better chance of surprise-attacking someone with a branch—I'm too squeamish to actually hit someone on the head with a rock, and my rock-throwing aim is shit.

A massive tree blocks my path, its width concealing me from whatever lies beyond. When I peek from behind the tree, my jaw drops a little at the sight of Del and Santiago getting it on in the middle of the Black Clearing, their naked bodies bathed in moonlight. Just like one of the images from the weird Eydís book.

My perspective changes; those cries I took for the sounds of a struggle take on a different meaning. The ridiculousness of this moment hits me like a sledgehammer. What I'm seeing cuts me raw and deep. Out of all places in the woods to have sex, why choose this one? My awkwardness evaporates, replaced by a sense of utter wrongness.

I avert my eyes, then retreat back into the depths of the woods, back the way I came.

35
RANDY AND THE SPACE-TIME GAPS

When I return home after my unnecessary rescue attempt, the moment I step over the Manor's threshold and take off my jacket I know it: Something's different. *Something's not right.* The air doesn't sit well in my lungs. A little voice in my head—the one I used to hear growing up that told me I'm some kind of abomination and that's why other kids were scared of me—says the vacation's over and Promise demands its payment now.

I hear it: *distant buzzing.* Vibrations in the air. I touch the wall and feel it shake. An earthquake? No, more like the humming of electrical wiring when the current's too much for cables to handle. There were times I heard this noise in Dad's lab, back when he still took me there, back when he still had a lab.

I listen, holding my breath as I go around the Manor, trying to isolate the source of the strange noise. I end up in Dad's secret office.

The computer on Dad's desk is all lit up; the screen showing the muon count chart is spiking out of control. Next to the chart, the countdown is also going nuts. Watching the numbers and timing how fast they're going down, I quickly figure out that the event it's counting down to is set to occur in less than twelve hours. *Crap.* This is it. I'm taking Del out of here. I'm going by Shannon's house to ask him to come with me. Nothing, no fallen trees or streets rearranging themselves before my eyes will stop me from leaving now.

In my agitated state, I forget that Del's not here. *Double crap.* And Shannon might still be at the blood collection point, trying to get someone to analyze the blood from the vials. Does it matter what the analysis will reveal? I've already made my peace with Mom's nonhuman nature, and it's clear to me now that Elspeth, at least, wants to end the world.

But I can't leave Del here. I have no choice but to wait for her return.

My restless fingers leaf through the pages of one of Dad's many leather-bound journals. The skylight above glows with the dawn. The light's rising fast. I can't remember the last time I had a good night's sleep. No good decisions are made when the decider's tired and agitated. To calm down, I start reading a random journal entry where Dad talks about cases of space-time anomalies and interdimensional gaps.

1907, Paris.

A woman named Clara Neff disappears from her bedroom. Her servant, the only eyewitness to this event, claims Clara was just "poof and gone." About two years later, Clara reappears, walks into the house, and resumes her chores, as if nothing happened. She has no memory of where she spent the past two years. Clara is slightly anemic, but otherwise in good health.

1986, Vienna.

A child is gone from its crib. The family is well-off, so the baby's disappearance is a suspected kidnapping. The child—a boy named Gunther—has a distinctive birthmark on his left cheek. Years later, Gunther, now six, is found playing alone in the woods not far from his parents' estate. The birthmark is unmistakable; it is Gunther. He claims he was a visitor to a court of faeries over the course of two days. Gunther is missing a pinkie on his left hand.

2007, Detroit.

On an unusually foggy day, a man named Dietrich Romm is last seen walking his dog in Palmer Park. Seven years later the dog finds its way home, but Mr. Romm remains missing, proclaimed dead in absentia by his wife.

The list goes on. I set the journal aside and flip through a couple other volumes. I start to zone out when my bleary eyes pick up on an entry in Dad's journal entitled "Randy, the White Raven." All sleep's gone from my mind now, erased by a spike of adrenaline.

Randy, the White Raven

I carry on with my series of experiments focusing on the spot in the woods that, following Ella's disappearance, became known as the Black Clearing. To date, all indicators point toward this place as the epicenter of anomalous space-time disruptions. Replicating results recorded by Serebrov's group and by Berezhiani and Nesti show that significantly large amounts of free neutrons and black-body radiation appear to be increasing (suggesting reverse direction tunneling?). Their count in and around the Black Clearing grows drastically once a month with a mathematical precision. I'm developing a formula to explain this cycle and identify the next high-count day. I've yet to learn what this means in terms of my goal of locating Ella and bringing her back.

As a separate note, animal behavior in and around this special spot in the woods is fascinating. The Black Clearing is largely avoided by animal and plant life, with one notable exception: Randy.

White ravens are rare in nature. Rare to the point that they have become a metaphor for a virtually nonexistent object. Hence, Randy is special.

I first noticed Randy when I was out in the woods collecting soil samples for Arista. Randy is a common raven, <u>Corvus corax</u>, with a heart-shaped distribution of black pigment on his wing. The rest of Randy's plumage is white. What a striking creature! Randy is inquisitive and exhibits no fear or anxiety around me, suggesting he is either a runaway pet or just a product of growing up in close proximity to humans.

Later that same day, I returned from the woods to find Randy hopping around the Manor's backyard. I stepped out to feed him some bread, but he took off, only to land a few feet away. On my approach, Randy repeated the same behavior, going on like this until we reached the border of the woods. Once under the cover of the trees, Randy flew off toward the Black Clearing. I followed only to watch the bird disappear into the quickly thickening fog. I stuck around long enough for the fog to begin clearing out. That's when I found Randy, unmoving and lifeless, in the middle of the clearing. I covered the bird's body with leaves and went home.

Three days later, I noticed there was a white raven sticking around outside the Manor. The bird looked remarkably like Randy, down to the black, heart-shaped blur on his wing. Has Randy returned to the land of the living? Or is this another version of Randy, visiting here from a parallel reality where Randy hasn't died yet?

36
FAMILIAR

Predictability is preferable to change for the human mind; psychologists call this the *mere-exposure effect*. The tendency to use certain words and expressions repeatedly, a preference for particular types of faces and voices. Even similar book and movie plots become more attractive to one's brain than others through exposure and repetition. In my case, over the years I've developed a deep-seated preference for rational explanations of strange occurrences over supernatural ones. So that's what I've been doing my entire conscious life—insisting on explaining things that made no sense to me, things that scared me a great deal. I strived to justify the weird and the odd, normalizing it all with my scientific reasoning.

Now, as I'm sitting in my father's secret office, hidden away in the house my Nibelung mother willed to me, as I'm reading my father's diaries, seeing the evidence of years and years of his observations and scientific research, I conclude that I am a fraud. Possibly, the best liar that ever was.

Research-backed studies show that strict parenting makes good liars. Still in doubt? Have a nice long look at my life: the years of Dad fussing over me alongside a near decade of homeschooling, therapy, and isolation created *me*, a girl who'd rather live in self-denial la-la land than accept that her mother is not human and that the blood of a mythical and apparently world-destroying race runs through her veins.

My scientific mind has always been my best (and perhaps only) defense, but when this exoskeleton grew so elaborate, hard, and thick that it covered me whole, it devoured me to the point where I could no longer tell where the real Hayden ended and the made-up one began. Now, with all my natural defenses stripped away by a new reality, I insist on applying my familiar old principles to make sense of this brave new world. Simultaneously, I fear the moment in the near future when this will no longer be enough and I'll be forced to evolve into something new and scary.

ᚠᚷᚠ

I keep my nose buried in Dad's journals till words begin meshing together and my eyes water. I rest my arms on the desk, forming a cushion for my head. I allow sleep to drag me into its dark, spidery lair. My last thoughts as I drift off are about the anomalous Black Clearing, bathing in free neutrons and black-body radiation. Dad's computer counting down . . . Mom wanting me to do something bad . . . Maybe all of this is a fever-induced dream. Maybe I'll wake up tomorrow and find

Del, Dad, Nadia, and Riley crowding my hospital bed, telling me how worried they were.

"Hayden, are you upstairs?" Del calls out from somewhere far away. *No, I want to stay asleep. I want to pretend for a little longer that my trip to Promise turned out to be something simple, uneventful.* But Del's voice insists on being heard, bringing me back to my current, Promise-shaped reality.

I stand and listen for Del's approaching footsteps. But she's not coming up here. I hear her moving downstairs, the fridge door opening and closing. More of those impatient footsteps. She must be ravenous after her midnight liaison.

Should I behave like I didn't follow her into the woods last night? Like I'm not concerned about Santiago's strange location choice for a hookup session? I've got no reason except, I realize with absolute certainty, that I don't like Santiago. Worse even, I suspect he's dragging Del into something strange and not entirely safe.

"Coming!" I lock the door to Dad's office and rush downstairs.

Del's munching on toast. Her hair's out of control, two tiny twigs and a miniature chunk of moss stuck in her curls. She's wearing jeans and boots and what looks like Santiago's jacket over her pajama tank top. The jacket is way too big on her, and she's pulling it tighter around her, looking mildly self-conscious. That reminds me, I still have Shannon's Windbreaker, and he probably wants it back.

"So, um, did you have a good night's sleep?" I ask her.

She gives me a funny look. "I need caffeine before we do this." She finishes her toast and starts to boil some coffee in a pot, the space filling with that undeniable smell of new mornings.

285

Once the coffee's done brewing, Del opens the fridge door and slams it, the most annoyed I've seen her in a while. "Right, no milk." Clearly still determined to caffeinate herself, Del pours a cup and takes a long sip. "I'm meeting Santi for brunch."

"He doesn't have to work?"

"Nope." She gives me another weird, long look. "He's taking some time off to spend the day with me."

"That's one fast-blooming romance."

"What's that supposed to mean?"

If I could take back my words, I would. But they're out, and now I have to face Del, who's twitching with quiet fury. When you fall in love, it affects your cells' chemical composition: Your blood gets pumped with hormones, the type your body wouldn't normally produce in such huge quantities. This change clouds your mind; it can make you dizzy with heart palpitations at the mere thought of the object of your obsession. The crazy hormones ease off with time, and the love-provoked madness thins out. In other words, falling in love's a lot like having the flu. You just have to wait it out. And that's what I should've done—waited till the fog clouding Del's head settled in a little before I started my anti-Santiago campaign. But time's something we do not have. So I take a breath and push on. "You're moving so fast, Del. I don't want you to get hurt. But Santiago aside, there's something important we need to talk about—"

She interrupts, "I'm *not* going to try and leave Promise again because you had another bad dream and got spooked. . . . I'm staying here for the rest of my spring break. I want to spend as much time as I can with Santi before I have to go home."

"I 'had another bad dream and got spooked'? You know there's a lot more than that going on here, Del!" The venom coating my words must show on my face, too, because Del steps back, her body tensing.

Our eyes locked, I go on, "This is not some nightmare I dreamt up. This is *real*, Del! I've been reading Dad's journals all night and . . . I've *seen* things, *felt* things in these woods. And I get this odd vibe from Santiago—I think he's up to something!"

I brace for her reaction, but Del is silent. I wait. Then a wave of disgust floods my stomach. Del's eyes have that dreamy expression I've now seen too many times to discard as a fluke. Her pupils have shrunk in size. The skin of her face is completely relaxed, no lines around her mouth, no frowns of disapproval on her forehead. Crap. I might've used my Niflheim compulsion on my best friend just now.

"Del?" I grab her shoulders and give her a light shake. Her head bobs in a weird, doll-like manner, unblinking eyes locked with mine. Her skin is clammy to the touch. This is so not good.

However . . . maybe this is the only way I can get Del out of Promise? Maybe I can *compel* her to come with me? No, I can't do this. Can I? Should I at least try? I mean, she's already halfway there. . . . Besides, this is evidence. I know for sure now that I do have a power to compel others, one that comes with the rest of my birthright, according to Elspeth. Without breaking eye contact, I say, "Del, I *need* you to listen. Santiago's bad news. We need to leave Promise."

A scraping sound from the nearby window makes me turn around fast, and I lose Del's attention in the process.

She snaps out of it, eyes regaining normalcy. "Cut it out, Hayden!" With an angry thump, she sets her coffee mug on the table. I expect fury, but her expression is instead disappointed in a way I haven't seen since her now-ex-boyfriend Bolin revealed which party he voted for in the last elections.

I try a different approach. "Del, I thought you were missing last night, so I . . . I went after you, into the woods."

"Oh God."

"Yeah. Look, I wish I didn't see you there, but I did. Whatever it is you want to do, it's none of my business, but, Del, why in the entire forest would Santiago choose the one spot that has such a sinister, morbid history? Why would he take you to the place where my mom disappeared, where she . . . *died*?"

Pursing her lips, Del shakes her head slowly. When she speaks, her voice is steel. "Look, I'm sorry you had to see us like that, Hayden, but honestly, your fixation on these woods . . . it's starting to wear a bit thin."

Stunned by her one-eighty, I stay quiet while she goes on, "We didn't choose that particular spot, okay? It just happened."

"Right. You had to walk quite a ways into the forest for it to *just happen* to be that spot. I'm sure that Santiago—"

"Enough."

"I'm just looking out for you, Del!"

"If that's really the case, I need you to stop. I can look out for myself, and I definitely don't need you judging me for my guy choices. You're not one to judge, anyway."

"What's that supposed to mean?"

"You haven't dated anyone for longer than a week. You got stood up by a guy who never even *saw* you. You're just a naïve, homeschooled girl who'll fall for the first guy who pays attention to you."

She might as well have dumped a bucket of ice water over my head.

"Why are you being like this? *What happened to you?*" I feel that too-familiar pressure of tears building behind my eyes, but I refuse to cry in front of Del right now. Nothing she said just now is a lie, but I wasn't expecting to hear it from my best friend.

"I need some air." Del leaves the kitchen, keeping her eyes down. I let her go.

Something's just shattered to pieces between us, and it's partly my fault. I want to go after her. I know I should. But instead I turn away and walk upstairs to my room.

I switch into autopilot mode: shower, change of clothes (my favorite jeans—skinny, black, shiny—and a clean tee). *Whatever routine it takes to feel as close to normal as I can right now.* I dust off my green Docs, an extra pair of bulky footwear I lugged here all the way from New York. Shoes that give me such an immense boost of confidence should be illegal. When I go down the stairs again, Del's gone and so is our car. Damn it.

I put my jacket on, grab my bag, and open the Manor's door, determined to walk to the research base if I have to. I step over the threshold and run smack into Shannon just before he rings the Manor's bell.

37
IN THE FLESH

His hands prevent me from falling on the slippery porch. Even through my clothes, his fingers burn my skin. I had clouds in my mind, but now a ray of strange light is making its way through the haze. I look up, and when my eyes meet his I experience an intense moment of heart-fluttering. Shannon's doing that almost-smile thing. He leans in and presses his lips against mine. A simple, fast, but firm move that leaves me weak in my knees.

"You keep smacking into me like that. What's chasing you this time?" he asks.

"I was going to the base. To find you."

His face turns serious. His hands release me, and I hesitantly step out of his personal space. "Are you okay?" he asks.

"Yes. No. I really don't know anymore! I found some more of my dad's files in the house and then Del . . . Shannon, what do you really know about Santiago?"

"Santiago? What's this have to do with him?"

"He and Del . . ." I give Shannon an edited version of Del's nocturnal rendezvous with Santiago in the woods.

"I don't think he's dangerous," Shannon says. "I've known him for almost a year. This is the first time I've seen him interested in someone."

His face changes, becoming more serious, as if he just remembered something important. He nods toward the car parked by the porch, an oldish Jetta I haven't seen before. In his research base paramilitary uniform, Shannon is a mismatch with it. "Come with me. There's something in the lab for you to see."

I lock the Manor's door and follow Shannon. While I fasten my seatbelt, Shannon asks, "So what did you find in your father's files that got you all edgy this morning? That is, edgier than usual."

The car begins to move, but before I have a chance to tell him about Dad's research notes, an earsplitting siren goes off, its high-pitched screech coming from everywhere at once.

I turn to Shannon for an explanation, but his face tells me what I already know: Something's wrong.

"That would be an evac order," he says.

I let the words sink in. Evac. As in *evacuation*. "Has this happened before?"

"No. But we thought it might one day. We trained for it. I guess I just didn't think it'd happen so quick after . . ."

"After what?"

"After your arrival, Hayden."

ᚠᚷᚠ

So it's happening. Today. Now. The event that my father's counter is counting down to. It's coming and coming quick.

The question is: Should I run from it or toward it?

Then I remember the horrible morning I was having before Shannon showed up on my porch. "Del's out there somewhere!" My voice wavers. My fingertips grow cold. "She said she had a brunch date with Santiago. Where would he take her?"

"Santiago checked in with the base about twenty minutes ago. He said Del was with him. It's okay, Hayden, he's trained to act in situations like this one. We know that Del's with him, so she's safe. The official procedure is to meet at the base and evacuate from there, but if he's unable to make it, we'll rendezvous with him at a specified location just outside of Promise. Besides, his house is equipped with a storm cellar and a panic room. If they don't make it out of Promise, they can lie low till it's safe to come out."

The cool calm in Shannon's voice soothes me a little, and I tell myself to trust him, but a nugget of worry makes its permanent home in my head.

ᚠᚷᚠ

When we roll up to the research base, we find it being stripped to bare bones. A small army of staff, some dressed like Shannon, others in white lab coats, are swarming over the equipment, disassembling it piece by piece, and loading it into small trucks parked just off the forest road. Human chatter combined with woodland noises and the clatter of boxes filling the trucks backs the scene with a soundtrack of anxiety.

"Come." Shannon takes my hand and leads me toward the white tent I remember well from the day after my arrival in Promise. The sensations from having his hand entangled with mine tinge my reality, making my focus falter.

We find a temporary reprieve from the evac madness inside the tent. A bespectacled young woman, raven-haired and sultry in the way only those 100-percent confident in themselves can be, emerges from behind a curtain. A genuine smile fills her face when she sees me. "Hayden! We've never met officially, but I'm your father's former assistant. My name's Arista."

"I've heard a lot about you," I say, my voice wooden with distrust. I can't help it.

"Surely it was only good things you heard?" Arista lets out a short laugh, having to raise her voice to be heard over the siren blaring outside. Done with the introductions, she switches into serious mode, losing the smile. "Hayden, there's someone here you need to see."

As if timed for maximum impact, the curtain hiding the back of the tent from view slides to the side, revealing my father. Part of me suspects I might be having one of those lucid dreams again. I wait for the world to waver around me, but all stays still.

My fingers curl into loose fists. The rush of blood to my head leaves me stunned, struggling to pick up my scattered thoughts and words. "You've been here all along, haven't you?"

"Did you really think I was going to let you come back all on your own?" he says. "That would make me a terrible parent. And with your mother already holding the top prize in the worst-parent-of-the-decade contest, I couldn't fail you, too."

"How did you even know where I was?" I ask.

"Your phone's got a bug."

"Oh my God, Dad!" I grab my cell out of my bag and throw it to the ground, stepping on it for good measure. The screen cracks, and I'm already sorry for doing it. My poor phone. It didn't deserve this. I push back furious tears. In my moment of phone-destroying madness, I pick up that Arista and Shannon have wisely left me alone with my father. The siren outside has transformed from a nonstop wail to a spaced-out Morse code, slightly less annoying but just as serious.

"You could've just taken out the chip." Dad shakes his head, a slightly amused expression playing up on his face. "Or you could've thanked me."

"*Thanked* you? For what? Hiding the truth from me for years? Locking me away in a shrink's office when there was nothing wrong with me?"

"Nothing wrong with you?" He looks at me like I'm an alien, my skin green with slime, eyes too many to count. He's about to say more, but instead he moves the curtain aside and invites me to follow him past it. Hesitantly, I do.

Behind the curtain is a minilab with a pair of powerful-looking microscopes sitting on a desk and, wedged between them, a plastic box containing a single test tube. I come closer, recognizing Shannon's neat writing on the tube. My blood sample.

"Hayden, you've read my journals, I take it?" Dad picks up the tube and gives it three rigorous shakes. The blood inside lights up like it's radioactive.

"Some of them. Not all," I reply, unable to look away from the blood glowing eerily in the tube. My father nods, like he knew the answer already, then opens the test tube and invites me to approach him. I watch as he drops a bit of my blood on a little glass tray, then inserts it under one of the microscope's lenses.

"I don't have enough time to explain everything right now. Your mother loved to say that showing is better than telling. I agree with that. So why don't you come here and have a look."

His face lit up with encouragement, he points at the microscope. Wary, I come closer. What I see through the lens shakes my mind into a temporarily blank state of WTF.

Multiplied by the microscope, at first my blood appears normal, but as Dad increases the strength of the lens, the view changes. The substance loses its red tint so that, instead of a sea of red cells moving in lavalike movement, I behold a truly alien cocktail of blue and purple. The longer I stare, the more the sample turns to chaos, starting to emit light and move frenetically—a storm brewing on a glass tray.

"What is this?" I ask my father when I tear myself away from the microscope. Before he responds, Dad fishes out the glass tray from its slot underneath the microscope lens and scrapes its contents off into an empty test tube.

"You already know what this is, Hayden. The real question is, why is it doing *that*?"

"It's never happened before?"

"Not like this. I mean, the composition of your blood has never been . . . completely human, but something seems to be affecting it right now on an unprecedented scale."

His casual admission that he's analyzed my blood before doesn't escape me. What makes it even worse is that I don't even remember him collecting my blood. Did he do it when I was too dazed to protest, to question his motives? Either way, it's another lie to add to my pile under Dad's name. I feel my alien blood boil in my veins. "All this time you've been telling me to forget about Promise, about our home. . . . How could you keep it all from me? Why?" I skip the transition period and go into full fight mode in one breath. Dad starts to say something, but I interrupt, "And don't tell me it was all to protect me!"

Taken aback by my anger, Dad steps back, but in the lab's tight confines there's no place to maneuver. I flinch at the wave of fear passing through his face, but then his expression softens. I have more accusations ready to be fired, but Dad looks so sad, I can't bring myself to let them out. Instead, I just say, "I miss Mom."

His eyes light up. "I miss her, too, Hayden. I love your mother. So much. . . ." He runs his fingers through his hair, a familiar, absentminded gesture that makes my heart shrink painfully. "I'm so sorry I couldn't protect her. I know you don't want to hear it, but I hid things from you because I failed your mother, and I wanted to make sure I didn't put you in danger as well. I knew there were risks in removing you from Promise, but the alternative was even scarier."

His admission turns what's left of my fury into comprehension. I realize with a start that I came to think of my dad as a one-dimensional character—a mad scientist obsessed with his pointless quest—and not a real person with complex motivations and emotions. And now, hearing the simple truth that my dad loved my mom comes as a world-shattering revelation. "It must've been tough for you," I squeeze out. "I-I'm also sorry. I wasn't exactly easy on you."

He smiles sadly. "It's not like I was father of the year, either. But, you know, every time I screwed up, I kept thinking, *All of this will be worth it if I find Ella. If I bring her back . . .*"

My breath catches at his words, but before I can ask anything, Arista stumbles into the lab, an open plastic container the size of a shoe box in her hands. "They're gone!" she cries out. "The blood vials are gone!"

Swearing, Dad runs after Arista. Left alone, my first impulse is to grab the test tube with my blood and smash it against the floor, the way I've done with my cell phone. But the danger of unleashing some unknown calamity in the tent stops me. While I debate whether I should go after them, my eyes land on a thin binder sitting open behind the microscopes.

I leaf through it, past pages and pages of Dad's familiar writing as he describes his countless experiments with my blood. Growing restless, I compulsively flip to the end—and I'm rewarded with a one-page dossier on Shannon.

As I skim through his file, I lose all feeling in my hands. Probably because all my blood is rushing into my head, hitting my brain hard.

Blue Haven Research Institute:
Shannon T. Reaser Report

Name: Shannon Theodore Reaser

Age: 20

Mother: Abigail Reaser (human/augmented)

Father: unknown (suspected Nibelung, possibly a hybrid)

Strengths: mild-to-medium compulsion; preternatural sense of direction, particularly within the bounds of the Promise woods

Weaknesses: medium-strength blood anomaly; might be susceptible to being controlled by his father due to their shared Nibelungen heritage/blood

38
THE LAST DAY OF "NORMAL"

The binder falls out of my hands.

I need to get the hell out of here. I need to find Del and go. *Just go.* Drive through these woods till we break through their barrier and leave Promise behind.

And what about Shannon? Did he know about all of this? The Nibelungs? He's one of them? Has he been lying to me from the moment I first saw him here at the base? I rush to leave but come to a halt at the sight of Shannon standing where the curtain used to be. He's blocking the way, looking bigger than before.

"What happened?" He sounds genuinely concerned, his voice lulling me into a false state of quiet.

"I really need the truth now," I say, my plea leaving me even more breathless. To my utter shock, I choke up on some stupid tears.

He steps closer and tentatively puts his hands around my shoulders. I take a step back, bumping into the table holding the microscopes. *Strengths: mild-to-medium compulsion . . .*

I spit the words out. "You and I, we're hybrids. Only half human."

A dark wave goes over his face. *He knows.*

The siren outside switches back to its full-on howling mode and the noise of running feet intensifies. Shannon finds my eyes. "It's time to go, Hayden."

"Where is it we're going exactly?"

"Your father doesn't think you should be anywhere near these woods today. Something's making our equipment go haywire, and it's getting worse. Professor Holland's instructions are clear: I need to take you out of Promise and keep you out till further notice."

"I'm not going anywhere without Del."

"Don't be stubborn, Hayden. This isn't just about you anymore—if it ever was just about you. There are terrible forces hiding in this town, in these woods, that we don't understand and that are dangerous. Honestly, I don't want to stick around long enough to find out what happens."

"You know what, Shannon?" I enunciate slowly, as the clarity of what I have to do lights a freaking lightbulb in my head. "I've been obsessing over you for years, wondering what kind of person you've become and whether you would like me. But honestly, now that I know the answers to my questions, I'm rather disappointed."

He's still processing that when I lunge at him, hoping for the benefit of a surprise attack. He yells out in surprise, but I spin past him and I'm already out the door.

In the commotion outside, I see Dad standing by one of the packed Humvees. He's talking to some bulky military guy and doesn't see me sneak out. I decide not to wait around for Shannon to emerge from the tent and make my way to another Humvee parked to the tent's right. A quick look around and then I'm inside, sinking deep into the driver's seat.

The universe was kind enough to leave this monster of a car unlocked for me, but my luck runs out where the keys are concerned. Okay, here comes the end of my attempt at being heroic and rescuing Del. I sit still, listening to the siren scream its warning. Is it as easy to hot-wire a car as they make it look in the movies? Is a Humvee like a regular car in that regard? Does it even require a key?

"Looking for these?"

Shannon throws the keys onto my lap and takes the passenger seat. He shuts the door with so much force, the car shakes. In the brief moment between the door opening and closing, I hear the wind howling something scary. Through the car's reinforced windshield, I see giant trees bending under the pressure of a monstrous wind.

"What are you waiting for? I'll explain everything I know later, but once your dad realizes you've gone rogue and taken me with you, he'll send his little army after us. Go!"

I don't need to be told twice. Blushing at the thrill, I shove the key into the ignition and send the Humvee roaring.

I wish I could see Dad's face as he waches me steal a military car and escape from the research base, but as we leave the base behind, no one runs screaming after us.

"Where are we going exactly?" Shannon asks once we're on the road back to the Manor. "I think I deserve to know what the plan is, since I'm risking my career to help you."

"Risking your career? Weren't you the one telling me just

minutes earlier how all of this is bigger than selfish me?"

"Point taken. Watch out!"

The hit comes from the left. But I don't even see what it is that hit us. Must be the wind, because there's nothing out there. Just wind and dust. Right? Another push sends me flying into Shannon, but I manage to keep one hand on the wheel. I get a lungful of Shannon's scent. The woods in the morning, after rain. Disorienting.

"Hold on!" I scream as the car gets another shove, this time from below. The force of the last push must have cracked a window, because I can hear it now, the roaring of the wind, the incessant rattle of rain. Whatever's hiding in the woods of Promise is either trying to prevent us from leaving or is eager to kill us. Either way, this is a full-on elemental assault.

When the car more or less stabilizes, I say, "Can you get in touch with Santiago? I need to know where Del is so I can go get her."

I keep the car steady on the road while Shannon pulls a satellite phone off his belt. "It doesn't always work," he warns. "Depending on the muon count, the signal can be blocked. But sometimes we get lucky." He brings the radio to his mouth. "Santiago? This is Shannon. Come in. Over." No response. Shannon tries again. I feel his eyes on me. He tries one more time. My hopes of finding Del fade.

Shannon brings me some calm when he says, "We had to evacuate quicker than planned. Last time he got in touch was to say he was safe and Del was with him, but they didn't have enough time to drive up to the research base. I'm sure he'll get her out."

I can see the Manor from here. Its walls glow with a weird

light, and it takes me a moment to figure out why. It's the runes etched into the Manor, making it a safe haven for me. "What the hell?" Shannon asks as he notices the eerie light of the runes.

"My mother's magic."

He's about to say something else, but the wind turns into a minihurricane outside, shaking the Humvee like it doesn't weigh almost eight thousand pounds. "Come on!" I shout as I wrestle the door open. Shannon joins me outside, and together we dash for the Manor.

Once the front door is closed behind us, I look around. The lights in the Manor are flickering on and off, and the window shutters are going nuts outside. At every other moment, the house shakes, as if a bunch of rocks are attacking it from all angles.

I feel weak all of a sudden and reach for the wall to steady myself.

"When was the last time you had anything to eat?" Shannon asks. I hear the genuine concern in his voice.

"It doesn't matter." I struggle out of my jacket. I consider taking off my mud-encrusted jeans and throwing them in the corner but change my mind. I'm not there yet with Shannon.

"I'm serious, Hayden," he goes on calmly. "You look like you're going to drop any moment now." Without waiting for my response, he proceeds to the kitchen, leaving me alone with my tired thoughts.

39
A DIFFERENT SLANT
OF LIGHT

I can hear Shannon going through the cupboards, looking through Dad's meager trove of supplies. I hate to admit it, but he's right: I am starving. I can't even remember the last time I had a real meal, and the exhaustion's making me see stars.

What's going on outside the Manor is another story altogether. It's pitch-black and, when I poke my head out the front door, my jaw wants to drop in shock and awe; chunks of hail are coming down. I jump back inside as a particularly nasty piece lands next to my feet. I slam the door closed, shuddering in disbelief.

I run up to my room and clean up as much as I can, changing into practical and sturdy jeans and my beloved Hunter hoodie. I keep my green Docs on in case I need to crush some Nibelungen feet in the near future.

I come back downstairs to find Shannon in the kitchen, making spaghetti. He's wearing a set of clean clothes. When he notices me staring, he explains, "Your father keeps some spare uniforms in his panic room. We're welcome to use them whenever we need."

"I don't know what's more disturbing, that my father has a panic room or that he welcomed his staff to use it as their personal closet." I try to hide my surprise at learning Dad has a panic room built in the Manor, but Shannon must feel my confusion.

"So you found his secret office but not the panic room." He has his back to me as he stirs the pasta, but I still hear a teasing smile in his voice.

"What's the panic room for, anyway?"

"For a night like this. That's why we're eating. This might be our last chance to have warm food before we hole up in there and wait this out. Promise . . . it has a mind of its own. Haven't you noticed by now?"

"Oh, I've noticed a great deal. For example, I noticed how you lied to me about your alien origin."

"I *helped* you. Doesn't that redeem me?"

"I guess," I admit hesitantly, and we both become quiet. I find that I enjoy watching him cook. Shannon's hands move with the precision of someone who knows what he's doing.

To be useful, I scavenge through the fridge for fresh produce. There's not much (an avocado and some packaged greens), but I get enough for something that resembles a salad.

"Try not to cut yourself," Shannon says over his shoulder. "I don't think anything monumentally bad will happen if you do it in here, far from the woods, but with this place you never know. Even after all these years of observation and research, we know very little about the Promise anomaly. We also don't know enough about the creepy miracle that is your blood."

Once my "salad" is ready, I begin setting the table, but I can't find matching plates or cutlery. Shannon gets a plate decorated with washed-out green leaves while I end up with a kiddie plate commemorating the Moomin characters in all their Scandinavian glory. I don't even remember being into Moomins as a kid.

"Dibs on the Moomins," Shannon calls out. A memory: *Shannon was into Moomins*. The reason we have this plate is because Shannon used to spend so much time in the Manor, he was practically living here.

"My memories are still patchy," I say. "I remembered just now that you liked Moomins and I didn't care for them that much."

"You were more of a *Labyrinth* girl."

I snort softly but stop when I notice he's staring at me. I run my fingers over my hair, then make an effort to keep my hands calm. I wait for him to look away, but he doesn't. To make matters worse, he says, "I'm making you nervous."

"Nope."

"I do. I like it."

"Well, *I* don't. And no, you're *not* making me nervous."

He looks away, smiling like he knows better, and for a brief moment I forget that these woods are (possibly) trying to kill me.

Our simple meal's ready and the pasta is served onto our mismatched plates. Shannon sits down within arm's length, facing me. To distract him from the blush building on my face, I ask, "Where did you learn to cook?"

He shrugs. "It's just pasta. All I did was drop it into a pot of boiling water."

"Well, thanks for feeding me."

"You're welcome." He looks down, avoiding my eyes. *Who's making whom uncomfortable now?* I make a point of staring at him until he looks back up and smiles. An uneasy feeling passes over me; the shape of his lips reminds me so much of Gabriel Diamond. I get a cold shiver all over my body.

"What are you thinking about?" Shannon asks.

"I don't really know how to answer that without scaring you," I say in between bites of spaghetti.

"Try me."

"I'm thinking about our bloodlines. And about that whole nature versus nurture debate. And about a certain man named Gabriel Diamond who's the only male Nibelung I know of. You see where I'm going with this?" *And if I'm right about this, it makes Elspeth Shannon's half sister.*

"The lunatic from the bookshop. Yeah, I always suspected as much, but there's no proof. Your father's been keeping Gabriel and his daughter under surveillance, but it's no use. They're here one moment, gone the next—like they can turn invisible at will or are capable of tricking our equipment."

"It's compulsion. I have it, I'm told. Your file said you have it."

Oops.

"My file?" He puts his fork aside. I've got his undivided attention now. "What else did my file say?"

Double oops.

"I take it you didn't know you had a file."

"Not the kind of file you're talking about, no."

"I saw it by accident. In my father's lab at the research station. It said your compulsion ability was mild. Or something along those lines."

"Anything else?"

"That you have a preternatural ability to find your way around these woods."

"Okay. That sounds useful, I guess."

I sigh. "One last thing . . . It said that you could be controlled by your Nibelungen father, because of the blood you share."

"The same goes for your mother and yourself, then."

"My mother's dead."

"Not according to your dad."

I turn the focus back to Shannon. "How does that make you feel, though? That this nonhuman is your father and he's been living in this town all this time and hasn't . . . approached you?"

Shannon's voice is flat. "He's the one who drove my mother to insanity. He's the reason I'm a freak. I grew up thinking I was a changeling. Like those old fairy tales, where a goblin leaves its own baby in place of a human kid? When your dad returned here and I joined the Institute, I learned that I wasn't that far off in thinking that."

"That makes me a freak, too."

"You're not a freak, Hayden. You're just different. We both are. But you had a normal childhood. You had a chance to get out of this place. I still had to live with my mother *after* she got messed up and tried to cut me once a month to see if *my* blood could bring upon the second coming of the Nibelungs."

"I wouldn't call my childhood normal. But I get your point."

Hearing the bitterness in my tone, Shannon pins me with a long look that sends goose bumps all over my skin. "I'm sorry. I didn't mean to diminish what you had to go through. But now do you at least have some kind of closure? You know, with this place?"

"Well, I grew up convinced my mom suffered from psychological issues and one night wandered into the woods and couldn't find her way back. A part of me believed that perhaps she left us. Left *me*. Now, I'm told she wasn't human but was instead a Nibelung—whatever that means—and that I'm supposed to finish what she started. Which apparently means cutting myself in the woods so that my blood will either open a portal or close it."

"Whoa, who told you *that*?"

"Elspeth. And then Gabriel gave me this." I find the amulet in my pocket and place it on the table. "It showed me what happened to my mother the night she disappeared. She was trying to open the portal with her blood to release . . . something. Maybe the army I keep seeing in my dreams?" I watch Shannon's face twist in recognition.

"This . . . this thing has nothing to do with your mother, Hayden." He reaches out as if to touch the amulet but then he moves his hand back in disgust.

"You've seen this before."

He looks up at me. "My mother used to have it. She wore it every day. And whenever she'd put it on, she'd get this weird, remote look on her face. She'd often trash the house, break stuff, harm herself . . . and me. One day I took it from her jewelry box and threw it in the fireplace. It didn't burn. The thing is indestructible. When Mom discovered what I did, she went nuts. She told me my father gave it to her, as a symbol of his love and devotion."

"Oh, Shannon." Bile rises in my throat. *I wore this amulet around my neck. I invited it to show me its message.*

"What do you think it really is?"

"Some kind of compulsion vessel. Gabriel probably cooked it up for you, to show you what he wanted you to see."

And I ate it up.

And then the real implication of the amulet's true origin slaps me in the face. Mom wasn't trying to open the portal and unleash the Nibelungs on this world. How could I have ever believed that? I have a horrible sinking feeling as I mentally scream at myself for not trusting Mom, for not doing as she asked. And now the blood vials are lost, and my chance at fixing things is lost with them. And yet I have a fuzzy warmth inside of me: Mom wasn't some supernatural supervillain. She was . . . good.

Outside, the wind howls, and I hear hail smashing into the house, apparently from every direction.

"What now?" I ask, knowing full well we're trapped in the house till Promise decides to calm down and let us out.

"Come on," Shannon says. "I'll show you the panic room. We'll be safe there."

40
(DON'T?) PANIC

The air pressure's changing, the temperature dropping. I feel it with my bones. Promise is bracing itself, as if readying to be torn apart.

Thunder explodes again and again, raging over the Manor's roof.

Together, we navigate the Manor's stairwell and the corridor to my parents' old bedroom. Despite my worry for Del—I hope Shannon's right to be so confident that she's safe—I can't help the excitement that's filling me. Having Shannon by my side changes everything. I know I could do this alone if I had to, but it's much better to do it with him.

Once in the bedroom, we enter the closet, its tight space bringing us so close I feel tension rolling off Shannon in waves. I'm about to extract the key to Dad's office from my bag, but Shannon produces one of his own from his back pocket. Makes sense, if Dad was sharing the panic room with his staff.

The concealed door slides inward. We're in.

Dad's office is the same as I left it—a surprising isle of stability amidst the chaos. I look around. "So where's this panic room?"

Straight ahead lies an L-shaped desk holding the computer and piles of Dad's journals. Behind it, the unpainted brick wall follows the shape of the Manor's outer edge. To my left, there's a ceiling-high construction of bookshelves. Above us is the lone skylight. This house must have some hidden dimensions, bending reality to its will to accommodate this panic room.

Shannon nods in the direction of the bookshelves.

"Seriously?" I watch him locate Dad's magnum opus, his self-published manuscript explaining the true meaning behind the Nibelungen myths: *The Space-Time Anomaly and the Nibelung Warriors.*

Even now that I know Dad wasn't a nutcase, I still snort at his research into the Nibelungs. Must be a defense mechanism embedded in my bones and joints. Despite everything I've been through, it's going to take some time getting used to a reality in which Dad was right and Mom wasn't (completely) mad.

Shannon pulls the book partially out of its place and, hidden mechanisms creaking and moaning, the wall slides aside. The small space of the panic room is lit up by a single lightbulb. I take in the symbols covering the walls, the ceiling, even the floor. I can't read the runes, but I feel a pinch of familiarity wash over me in that unsettling way déjà vu makes your brain tremble as it digs up a false memory from its secret trove. Like the runes encircling the Manor's outer walls, the ones in here are all lit up, glowing in a spooky will-o'-the-wisp way.

Shannon steps in after me, letting the door slide back into its frame, cutting us off from the rest of the Manor. On the inside, the door is also lined with bookshelves. *Nice touch, Dad. At least we won't get bored if we have to stay in here for a while.*

Complete with a bare mattress, a pillow, and some blankets folded on top, a single bed haunts the panic room's far corner. And that's it as far as the room's furnishings are concerned. I guess Dad didn't imagine there'd ever be more than one person hiding out in here.

Shannon grabs a book from the shelf and opens it to the middle. He sits on the floor, resting his back against the bed.

I sit on the bed and throw off my shoes. Not sure what to do with myself, I lie on my back and stare at the ceiling. My limbs fill with the familiar restlessness this town seems to provoke in me.

Every time my brain attempts to think about Del, I shut it down. It won't help and will only leave me biting my nails and worrying endlessly. I know I won't feel totally at ease until I have her safe by my side.

The panic room's got no windows, so our only way of knowing when it's safe to go out is sound. And we get plenty of that in here. The roof shakes from the thunder and whenever it takes a hit from a particularly nasty chunk of ice. I'm wondering whether the rest of the town is safe, whether Dad and Arista and the rest of the Institute staff got out of the base on time.

And my eyes keep returning to Shannon. He's trying to look busy with his book and almost succeeding. *Almost.* I know he's not actually reading from the tense angle of his shoulders, from the way the skin of his neck appears to be blushing.

The longer I stare at him, the more his presence seems to expand, filling the space, dominating all my senses.

"Didn't know you could read Old Norse," I comment when the pressure becomes too thick to handle.

He sets the book down quickly and turns around. His eyes appear more pronounced in here, more green than gray, one much darker than the other. My breath catches and I sit up, coming close to the edge of the bed, closer to Shannon, pulled in by his gravity. Where this particular celestial object is concerned, I crossed the event horizon a long, long time ago.

He takes a tentative seat on the side of the bed, facing me. I struggle to conceal my shallow breathing. But instead of kissing me, he says, "I was just thinking about something you said."

"What's that?" I lean back, away from him.

"Back at the base, before you tried to Krav Maga your way out of the lab tent. You said you've been obsessing over me for years, that you wanted to know me, the grown-up version of me."

"First of all," I start slowly, "I didn't *try* to Krav Maga my way out. I *succeeded*. And second . . . Yes, I've thought about you. *A lot.* I guess you really made an impression on me as a kid." I make it sound breezy and casual.

In response, Shannon's tone is teasing, but there's a note of seriousness underneath when he asks, "And do I measure up to your expectations?"

"What do you think?" I rest my back against the cold wall and hug a pillow to my chest. "Don't my awkward-girl impressions constitute enough evidence of . . . my crushing on you hard? Or do you require a verbal confirmation, too?" Right about when I say *crushing*, blood rushes into my head, sending a wave of dizziness through my body.

But my honesty-provoked embarrassment is short-lived when I see Shannon change expression. Do I imagine it, or does the gleam in his eyes turn hungry, feral? When he speaks, his voice is rough. "I've been thinking about you a lot, too, Hayden. When you left Promise . . . it's like a part of me went with you. I've been having these dreams of us as kids playing in these woods and then . . . we'd be these grown-up versions of us, and I didn't want to wake up from those dreams."

"But you don't know *me*. I mean, you *knew* me as a kid, but you don't know me as I am now. How can you feel this way about someone you barely know?"

He laughs, an incredulous, beautiful sound. "Of course I *know* you. I've always known you. Before you left and now—you're the same. I mean, you're totally different now, but you're still my Hayden."

My Hayden.

Shannon covers the distance between us in one seamless movement, a gliding bird of prey going in for the kill. He takes my hands into his. His fingers burn my cool skin.

I lean in, but he doesn't move. He waits for me to cross what's left of the space between us. Pulled into him like charged iron to a magnet, I move forward, bringing my lips to his mouth.

Our kiss deepens and the remaining distance disappears. I shift my weight and we slide on top of the bed, our arms and legs tangling.

I shudder. In the pit of my stomach an ember grows warm, hot. My mind's in shambles. I forget everything except Shannon's mouth moving against mine, parting my lips. Our breaths mingling, I circle my hands around the back of Shannon's neck, drawing him in. He presses his body against mine and kisses me back, pausing only when we have to come up for air.

The doorbell rings. Unwelcome, its sound comes from far away and forces its way into our endorphin-filled reality. Shannon pulls back and I'm about to protest, but . . .

"Do you hear it?" he asks, and I know he's not referring to the doorbell. The shattering noise of hail falling down outside is gone, replaced by a faint whispering of rain.

We sit up, disoriented and wide-eyed, staring at each other in the dim light. The bell rings again. Shannon answers my unvoiced question. "Someone human. No Nibelung would be able to come close enough to this house to ring the doorbell. That doesn't mean we're not in danger, though."

Oh, I know that.

The bell rings once more, demanding our attention. I think I hear pounding on the door, too. Someone's impatient.

I lace up my Docs. My clothes feel clammy and ill-fitting.

"Not sure it's wise to answer that door," Shannon says. "But I guess you're doing it anyway."

"That's right," I say. "Maybe it's Del out there."

He looks at me seriously. "I hope so."

41

INTO THE NIGHT

In medieval Europe, the aurora borealis was feared. The colorful lights in the sky were thought to herald an approaching war or famine. Meanwhile, some American Indian tribes—Menominee and Inuit among them—believed that the lights were the ascended spirits of great hunters and fishermen.

But now the auroras can be explained by science. The sun's charged particles enter the Earth's atmosphere, colliding with its gaseous particles and producing ethereal beauty in the process.

What cannot be explained by science, though, is what the hell auroras are doing shining their light all over Promise, Colorado.

Out of the safety of the panic room, my eyes struggle under the assault of the blinding light streaming through the skylight in Dad's lab. As my vision adjusts, I see all the colors of the rainbow gleaming through the glass. Enthralled, I watch the hues morph, transforming from neon red to green to yellow to silver blue. Can this really be? I guess I shouldn't be surprised—everything's possible in Promise, but still . . .

The doorbell rings again and again, followed by three knocks. Shannon and I dash along the length of the corridor, down the stairwell, and into the living room. From here I can see the outline of the Manor's main door.

The rumble of raindrops is more audible out here—unforgiving, unapologetic.

Someone's yelling outside, struggling to be heard against the growing roar of the rainstorm. "Anyone there? Hayden? Shannon? I need help!"

Santiago.

Shit.

With Shannon right behind me, I rush to unlock the door, but a nugget of suspicion makes me keep the door's small chain in place. When I look outside, I see it's indeed Santiago. And he looks terrible. Soaking wet, trembling, his short hair slapped down with rain. His lips are nearing the bad kind of blue, and there's blood on the side of his face, dripping from a shallow cut. Maybe from a tree branch snapping at him during a mad dash through the woods? My heart heavy in anticipation of bad news, I close the door and undo the chain.

I meet Shannon's eyes and, once he takes a strategic position to my right, I let Santiago in.

Shaking, Santiago collapses at our feet. I kneel down to face him. He just sits there, staring at me, expression blank. I ask, straining to keep my voice calm, "What are you doing here? Aren't you supposed to be with Del, halfway to Denver by now?"

Santiago starts to speak but is shivering so hard, all I hear is his teeth rattling. I leave him with Shannon while I run upstairs to grab a towel and a blanket, along with my first-aid kit. By the time I return, Santiago's on the couch, Shannon hovering over him.

I sit next to Santiago and attempt to clean his cut, but he keeps shivering and rubbing his eyes. "Del's . . . in t-trouble," Santiago finally squeezes out.

He takes the towel from me and starts to dry his hair, but his hands tremble so bad, he gives up, setting it aside. With effort, he stands from the couch. "You have to come help me. She's in the woods. Alone."

"What the hell?" Shannon glares at his friend, disbelief in his voice. "You were supposed to be with her. You were supposed to get her out of here the moment the siren first sounded!"

"I *was* getting her out of here!" Santiago cries out, slurring the words. A flash of light outside is followed by a ricochet of raindrops against the Manor's walls, an urgent reminder of what's going on out there.

Del is outside. Alone.

My breath becomes short and the room dances before my eyes. Dumbfounded by Santiago's words, Shannon and I stare at him until he finds the strength to talk again. "We were in her car, driving out of this hellhole, making good time to reach Denver, when Del has a freakout and makes me turn around. She was worried about Hayden. . . . We almost made it back to Promise, but I had to slow down in the woods to go around a fallen tree when there was this weird crackling sound followed by a flash of light. The car swerved off the road. I blacked out for a bit, and when I came to, Del was gone. But I think I saw her go deeper into the forest."

"Why would she go into the woods?" Shannon demands.

"I don't know. Maybe she got a concussion when the car crashed? She's been acting strange ever since I picked her up this morning. She said she had a huge fight with Hayden. She was so upset, she cried. I don't know why she ran off on me like that, but we need to go out there and find her before something bad happens."

Shannon shakes his head. "Out of the question. We shouldn't go anywhere near these woods tonight."

"But it's Del we're talking about," I say quietly.

A boom of explosive thunder outside is followed by a flash of light. It illuminates the entire living room like it's daytime. At least there's some normalcy to the weather now: lightning and thunder come together. I run to the window and peer into the night. As I watch, another lightning bolt strikes, landing somewhere in the woods.

And then I imagine Del, alone and lost, dodging lightning bolts and freaking out. Or maybe she's unconscious or about to sleepwalk into Edmunds' Gorge . . .

"I have to go out there," I say. "I brought Del to Promise and if anything happens to her . . ."

Before Shannon starts to argue, I run into the basement to grab a couple of flashlights. I refuse to rely on the unnatural northern lights outside to illuminate my way through the dense forest. Santiago catches up with me downstairs. In the weak light, I note that his face has regained some of its normal coloring. I hand one of the flashlights to him.

"Thank you for doing this," he says.

I shake my head. "Don't thank me. Del's my friend. I'm not doing anything she wouldn't do for me. Now let's go bring her back."

We return to the living room to find Shannon pacing the length of it like a caged lion. When he speaks, his words sound like a growl. "Are you really going to risk it? Even after everything you've learned?"

"Wouldn't you risk it for me?"

"It's not the same."

"How so?"

I let my question linger in the air while I head for the main door.

I hear Shannon's steps as he follows me and Santiago out of the Manor and into the night.

42
MURPHY'S LAW, REDEFINED

Anything that can go wrong, will go wrong—so-called *Murphy's law*.

Our early human ancestors thought the physical world was governed by vengeful, jealous gods who created storms and rained fireballs from the sky. Now our suspicions that the universe is out to hurt us are less obvious, but they're still there, hidden away in the remnants of our myths and superstitions. They resurface from the dark, primordial swamps of our minds and make us think our toaster burned our breakfast on purpose, that misfortune attracts more misfortune, and that all it takes is one misstep to trigger a Rube Goldberg–style series of unfortunate events that will see us sliding on a banana peel straight into an open Dumpster that's rolling off a cliff.

Despite all my love for logic and science, I'm starting to think there's something to Murphy's law. Based on my experience in Promise, I can even say I've redefined this unofficial law of the universe: Whatever you *think* the worst-case scenario is, multiply that by ten and brace for the storm of the century. Because it's going to hit you and hit you hard.

Then add Nibelungs into the mix and you're totally screwed.

ᚠᚷᚠ

I step outside the Manor and into a dark fairy tale, the world changing its color palette with every blink. The heavy rain all but ceases, turning into a light drizzle. The air carries a fragrance of exotic flowers and sandalwood, as if a giant incense stick's been burning for hours and hours. Every shape is sharply outlined in the dark. The night's crispness soothes my flushed skin. The woods beckon me into their living, breathing realm.

I keep reminding myself why I'm here. *To find Del.* But the darkest corners of my soul sing another reason. This reason has nothing to do with my lost friend.

We follow Santiago's directions. He locates the spot where Del entered the woods, a natural archway created by two firs bent toward each other, branches meeting overhead. In more ordinary times, Del would likely want to take a photo of this spot to add to her collection of portals.

Behind me, Santiago flicks on a flashlight. I follow the light, searching for any sign of Del. For a moment I turn on my own flashlight, but I quickly realize, to my surprise, that my eyes see better in the dark unaided.

I look for any spots where grass appears flattened or a patch of moss carries an imprint of a shoe—anything that doesn't look like the natural way of the forest. We're getting close to the Black Clearing; I can sense the cursed place on my skin.

Fog crawls from behind the trees, licking the edges of our path. Up above, the alien lights of the auroras begin to weaken, blocked by the tightly woven canopy of trees. The untamed song of the storm rattles the skies, rain and wind working together to ruffle the tree branches and my nerves.

Upon reaching the Black Clearing's edge, we fall back, concealed by the patchy cover of trees. From my hiding spot, I see a lone figure standing in the middle of the clearing, unmoving, her back to me.

It's Del, clothes stained with mud and covered with leaves. And there's blood. Del is dotted with blood, like red sprinkles on a sundae. My stomach turns.

Shannon tries to hold me back, but I shake him off and leave our hiding place, covering the space between Del and me in one fast dash. I sense Shannon and Santiago keeping close just behind me.

Putting a hand on Del's shoulder, I immediately know something's wrong. Slowly, she turns around, and I catch a glimpse of her left hand, cradled against her chest. Dark red with drying blood, the hand seems oddly incomplete, smaller than normal, maybe. My breath hitches when I see why. Del's missing a pinkie. *Oh no.*

Frantic sound forms on my lips when I see it a moment too late: the glint of a curved blade in Del's other hand as she slices at me.

Even with her eyes glazed over, Del's aim is true. With an eerie sense of disbelief, I see blood oozing through the sleeve of my hoodie and feel the burn of the cut.

Growing dizzy from the surprise attack, I tackle Del, trying to keep her knife-wielding hand turned away from me, but she's no longer dangerous—a lifeless marionette abandoned by her puppeteer. Having achieved its purpose, the knife leaves her hand and hits the forest floor without a sound.

"We need to get her out of here—" I start to say, but a blast of thunder devours my words. I take Del's undamaged hand and pull, barely making my friend move an inch. I see them then: two figures, covered in hooded black robes from head to toe. They glide toward us across the Black Clearing. Elspeth and Gabriel.

"We need to move!" Pulling Del along, I head back the direction we came, but Santiago blocks my way.

"I'm sorry, Hayden." His voice makes my skin prickle. "I wish it didn't have to be this way, but there wasn't enough time and my lords are out of patience."

"Your *lords*?" I ask in an angry whisper. "What have you done?"

Santiago's response is drowned out by a now-familiar clanging of metal followed by a chorus of subdued, guttural voices. I whirl around, looking for the source of noise, but, aside from Elspeth and Gabriel still about thirty feet away, the clearing's empty. Yet . . . I know they're here. Watching me through the thinning veil between the worlds. The Nibelungen army from my dreams. My mother's darkest secret. Her burden. The cursed amulet in my pocket pings. Like calls to like.

I hear their presence: invisible horses letting out impatient huffs, digging their hooves into the wet soil.

I *know* we need to move, but my feet refuse to follow my brain's orders.

A ghostly hand sweeps against my cheek and I spin around, bumping into Shannon and coming face-to-face with a stunned Santiago. His lips are tight, drained of blood, his eyes glued to something behind me.

A horse neighs so close, I feel hot air ruffling my hair. A loud racket makes me shut my eyes tight in a moment of blind panic. Whatever's coming, it's making the forest vibrate with its sheer, terrible power.

A ghostly rider swishes past me, grabbing Santiago and disappearing into the woods.

"Watch out!" Shannon brings me close to him as another rider passes by, swinging an iron mace. I bury my face into Shannon's chest.

"What's happening, Hayden?" Del's shaky voice makes me regain focus. Her eyes are clear and she's looking around, spooked. Any moment now, she'll feel the pain of her mutilated left hand.

"You've been compelled," I say. In a blink of an eye, Elspeth and Gabriel are here, their robes swirling behind them like menacing wings. We're out of time. Before I can react, Shannon makes a rapid move toward Gabriel, but he's thrown back by some invisible force.

"Don't hurt him!" I scream. I want to run toward Shannon, but my legs feel like they're glued to the ground and sinking. When I look down, nothing's out of ordinary, but the sinking sensation doesn't go away. It spreads up to my knees, leaving me paralyzed.

"You could've freed yourself easily just now, you know," Elspeth says while Gabriel produces the three vials of blood out of his robe's hidden pockets. "You could've sensed my magic on Santiago from a mile away, and you could've succeeded in your half-baked attempt at compelling Del to leave town this morning. If only you embraced your true nature. But alas."

"You tried to compel me?" Del's quiet words make me shiver on the inside. I avoid her eyes. Shannon stands up and shuffles closer to me. I exhale in relief that he's unharmed. When he addresses Elspeth, his voice is shaking with anger. "What do you have on Santiago to make him do this?"

"Nothing." Elspeth grins at Shannon, showing white and pointy teeth. "He *wanted* to serve us, just like Abigail did. There'll always be willing humans. Their minds are so easy to corrupt."

"What do you want from us?" I try to keep her occupied while I shift in my spot, attempting to separate my feet from the ground but failing.

"Not much now." Elspeth shrugs, then gives her father a nod. At her command, Gabriel opens the blood vials one by one and shakes their contents out, the droplets of blood falling to the ground, glowing as they disappear into the restless soil. With unnatural clarity, I recall the wording of Mom's instructions, urging me to spill the blood from the vials in the Promise woods and then will an entrance closed as I draw my own blood. The words of Mom's lullaby hit me hard: *The blood of the first three, it'll break down the walls.* As a strange fever builds in my mind, I picture a doorway closing. But it's not enough. I have to dig deeper.

Meanwhile, Elspeth nods at Del. "She served her purpose. Just like the amulet Gabriel enchanted with false memories served its purpose, I suppose. Just like you're about to serve yours." Her speed unnatural, Elspeth makes a rapid move into my personal space and grabs my injured arm at the same time that Gabriel lunges at Shannon. The two men crumple to the ground, each landing punches on the other.

I focus my will on what's about to happen and call on whatever ancient power resides inside me. I think of a door closing, a vortex collapsing on itself, while Elspeth tears my sleeve to shreds, revealing the long cut Del's knife left on my skin. "Did you really think I was going to let you ruin it for me? Your mother tried to close the gateway; she was willing to let her people wither and die. I won't let you finish what she started." My wound opens further, oozing so much blood that my vision wavers and my knees buckle. I swear in pain and watch my blood seep to the ground.

The earth shivers under my feet. I scramble to find my footing, but the ground cracks opens and the clearing breaks in half. The growing chasm separates me and Del from Elspeth, Gabriel, and Shannon. I squeeze my eyes shut and concentrate all my intent on the task of closing the portal that Elspeth's so eager to open.

"I RELEASE YOU!" Elspeth's scream is the roar of an otherworldly creature unleashed on this world from the bowels of hell.

Elspeth is winning. The world is changing, the interdimensional portal is opening, rearranging space-time into a new—*scarier*—version of reality. Somewhere beyond the forest trees, a demonic horse lets out an impatient cry.

From her side of the chasm, Elspeth screams, "Watch this, Hayden! Watch as I claim what could've been yours by birthright, what your mother discarded so she could live a life with humans!"

The portal opens, its vortex spinning fast, fueled by an energy that human physics could not even begin to comprehend. I take a step away from the growing portal, but Del stays immobile, pinned to her spot, so close to the spiral that its expanding reach is almost touching her feet.

"Del, move away!" I yell, but Del, still stunned from her compulsion, takes a wrong step and staggers closer to the spinning vortex.

"Control your human!" Elspeth's words are lost in the rumble of the passage opening between worlds.

It happens fast, leaving me with only a second to react. When Del is sucked into the spiral of the vortex, I go after her.

"Hayden, don't!" Shannon calls after me, but I'm already diving into the vortex.

The last thing I hear is Elspeth's scream. Through the smoke of the portal I see her running toward me, jumping across the chasm, her black robe swirling around her like a disembodied dark shadow. She looks beautiful.

43
I DON'T THINK WE'RE IN PROMISE ANYMORE

My body loses shape and importance. Only my consciousness remains as I wade through the fog that seems to fuel the portal. I absorb the fog, welcoming it into my bloodstream, where it attaches itself to my cells, forever altering me and filling me with a power that can destroy planets and send galaxies spinning and colliding into one another.

In this moment I cease being, and I don't feel particularly sad about it.

ᚠᚷᚠ

When I regain my physical shape, I see the rain and hear the thunder.

I float through space in a bubble that gleams and shivers but does not break, the downpour bouncing off its transparent walls, leaving me dry and warm inside.

ᚠᚷᚠ

There's no *time* to speak of in here. No *space*, either. I can't see the world beyond the wall of rain. I can no longer tell the difference between up and down, left and right. I'm suspended in nothingness.

But the longer I stare into the space outside the bubble, the more I see it's not as empty as I originally thought. On the contrary, it's full of incorporeal shapes—beings roaming just outside my reach.

ᚠᚷᚠ

My bubble bursts.

My stomach contracts as I rocket down (or is it *up?*), wind making my hair flap around my head. I scream, but the cotton-like fog and ravenous wind eat up all sound.

ᚠᚷᚠ

As far as my perception of reality goes, there are only three things I'm absolutely certain of in this moment: my wildly beating heart, the impenetrable whiteness around me, and the swishing sound my body makes as it falls with ever-increasing speed.

My thoughts as I plummet are of Shannon and quantum physics.

ᚠᚷᚠ

When I first register a glimmer of light beneath my feet (*or above them*), I could've been falling for seconds, or hours, or days. Like a drowning woman holding on to a piece of driftwood, I cling to this first ray of hope, a break in the monotony of my strange new existence.

As the light approaches, I brace for impact, readying myself for bones breaking, anticipating pain and death. Every question I've ever had about the afterlife is about to be answered.

But when I hit the ground, I land on my feet with an unfamiliar yet natural grace.

The fog clears and I find myself in a small grotto, moss-covered walls glittering and the ground squishy to the touch. An opening several feet above my head is the source of the vague light I saw as I was traveling through the vortex.

With the protective warmth of the bubble gone, the temperature drop is dramatic. Each exhale releases a visible cloud from my mouth. Shivering and frantic, I search for something to use to climb out.

The walls around me are wet and slippery. I doubt I can climb my way out of here. So I jump, reaching out high with my hands, aiming for the overhead ledge.

A surprised gasp escapes my lips when my body lifts off the ground. I hover in the air, international-space-station style. Without much effort, I pull myself through the gap and float out of the cave.

In this state of weakened gravity, I bring myself into a vertical position and eventually find my footing. The cut on my arm has opened up again, leaking fresh blood. I wipe it against my torn jeans and shove the dull pain to the back of my mind.

I look around me. The grotto I just floated out of is nestled in a cliffside at the foot of a giant, silver-gray monolith that stretches up high, disappearing into the bloated clouds. Down below, opaque fog carpets the ground for as far as the eye can see. And far ahead, where the horizon meets the rose-tinted skies, clusters of spiral aurora borealis rule space. This world, alien yet familiar, takes my breath away.

I focus on what lies right before me. From my elevated platform and through the mantle of fog, I can make out uneven ground about ten feet below. Moving carefully, I come to sit on the edge of the slippery rock. Then I take a leap of faith and slide off, legs first, till I land on the rubbery terrain. Jellylike, it wiggles under my feet.

Surrounded by the fog, I extend my hands, feeling my way forward. When I yank my hands back, a ghostly shimmer is left as a residue on my skin. Like fairy dust. Mesmerized, I blow on it and watch the glittery powder scatter, becoming absorbed back into the fog.

I detect a distant chatter of voices. They're approaching fast. I knew this world was inhabited, but I've yet to see its denizens in the flesh. The anticipation of that encounter makes my toes tremble.

The thought of Del—alone, vulnerable, thrust into this foreign world—is the only thing that keeps me from turning back and crawling into the cave where I entered this dimension.

From above, a raven caws. Once. Twice. I look up. A splash of pure white is circling me. *Randy?*

The white raven's presence warms me in an unexpected way, and I face the inevitability of meeting this land's inhabitants with renewed courage. When the voices draw close enough for me to distinguish words, I recognize the language from my dreams. "Who's there?" I ask, but the fog remains silent. "I'm only here to get my friend."

My words are met with hushed whispers, which are followed by a tense silence. Whoever's out there in the fog may not speak English, or any other human language for that matter. Seconds stretch into minutes and nothing happens. *They're* waiting. *I'm* waiting. The fog listens.

I decide to try something different and begin singing Mom's lullaby. I hum it at first, hoping that the uneven tune will travel through the fog, reaching the ears and minds of my silent observers. The fact that I'm still alive makes me bolder, so I add the lyrics. "*The first one was a warrior, the second a hand-maiden; their queen who led the army was third. They'll save their people! The blood of the first three, it'll break down the walls—it'll set their people free, and the new world will emerge. . . .*"

A single voice picks up the melody, singing Mom's lullaby in that ancient language—the language of the Nibelungs. Another voice joins in and then another and another, till I lose count and the song seems to come at me from everywhere.

Their tall, distorted shapes appear out of the fog. I make out the silhouettes of warriors. Most sit atop horses though a few move on their feet, but they do so in a sliding motion, as if not touching the ground. The foot soldiers as well as the riders and their beasts are clad in silver armor decorated with dark runes.

My eyes search for Grane, the battle horse from my dream. But he's not with this group. Instinctively, I focus on his name and let my mind conjure up Grane's image the way I keep seeing him in my dreams and visions. I reach out to the beast and, from a distance, he answers.

He's on his way.

My little experiment with telepathy appears to have agitated the shadow knights. The whispering intensifies, and I can feel their attention; it's making me break into a cold sweat. But when I focus on the knights' faces—or, more correctly, on what lies beyond their open-visor helmets—I shiver.

Nothing.

The knights have no faces, just slight elevations indicating where a nose and lips should be. The runic symbols etched on their helmets give off a neon light, casting shadows over their empty eye sockets.

My army is faceless.

44
NECK-DEEP IN FOG
AND TROUBLE

Mom's lullaby radiates back at me, off the knights. It's an uncanny experience given that the knights have no mouths, yet the music is clearly coming from them. The song ends, but a few chords, spiky and rough as lizard skin, linger. One of the front-row horses shakes its head and digs a hoof into the fog-shrouded ground.

We have waited long for you.

All is now in place for you to lead us out of the fog-cursed space between Niflheim and Miðgarðr.

Spoken in the style of a Greek chorus, the words flutter through my mind. I guess telepathic communication makes perfect sense around here, in this land populated by mouthless and earless beings.

We can hear you and you can hear us because Niflheim blood runs through your veins. It is stronger than your human blood— just as the Telling predicted. Your blood calls for us, and ours calls for yours. It has taken you ten years to hear our call, but now that you are here, you will take your rightful place and lead your people out of the eternal fog, into Miðgarðr, as it was sung in the Telling.

"Who are you exactly and what is . . . Miðgarðr?" I shift my eyes from one empty face to the next. I can only count twelve of them in the first row, but I suspect their number is much higher.

We are many.

In time, you'll learn our names.

Gylfi, Jafnhárr, Alin, and Helga. Also Aurgelmir and Ulfran, his son . . . All two hundred and six of us. Yours to command.

Miðgarðr is our home to be. You are to lead us there before the rest of our kind can follow.

Based on my rusty knowledge of Germanic mythology and Norse folklore, combined with what I've learned of the Nibelungs in the past few days, I'm guessing Miðgarðr must be the human domain, since it also sounds a lot like *Midgard*. And these strange faceless creatures believe I'm going to lead them there . . . to conquer it?

I don't know if they can only hear what I choose to trans-mit or everything that goes through my head, but regardless, it'll be superawkward when I break the news that I don't have any immediate plans to lead them anywhere. But, for now, I have to focus on Del's retrieval. That's all that matters.

"I came here to save my friend." My words are met with cemetery-at-night–grade silence. Even the horses stop their fretting and just stare straight ahead, unblinking. I notice that whatever plague wiped the faces of these warriors clean of eyes and mouths didn't affect the horses.

I continue, "I'm looking for a girl. A human girl. Black

hair, dark skin, hazel eyes, has a bit of an attitude? Delphine Chauvet? Goes by Del? She must have come through here just seconds before I showed up. Do you know where she is?"

Their already-long silence stretches into an *uncomfortably* long one. These creatures must have all the time in the world. Well, *I* don't. I'm on a deadline to locate Del and take her back to the human world before . . . before what? A thunder clap echoing far away is the only sound disturbing the tense stillness.

The human child you seek is now forfeit.

My skin grows cold despite the humidity of this place. "What do you mean 'forfeit'?"

Her sacrifice was not expected, but it is welcome.

There are times when humans enter this world by mistake or design . . . but to leave . . .

I shake my head, unwilling to believe what they imply. Besides, I remember reading those snippets from Dad's scientific journals—the instances of people disappearing, then returning unharmed. Before the knights can detect my mental protests, a raven calls from above. I can't see the culprit in the fog, but the sound elicits a reaction among the knights. Their heads move side to side, as if looking at their fellow riders. Do they *know* they have no faces?

She is here.

The bird's powerful wings cut through the fog, disturbing the air above and around me. My hands fly up on impulse to protect my head as a giant white raven materializes out of the fog.

The bird lands on the outstretched arm of one of the knights.

Everything's in place for our release.

Except for Grane. But he is on his way.

A wave of excitement runs over me at the mention of Grane. *My battle horse.*

The Telling sings of Grane carrying you to Miðgarðr on his mighty back. He was created to be our leader's battle horse. Ella was once Grane's rider. It is now your turn.

The earth trembles with the staccato of powerful hooves.

I want to see Grane. My need for his presence is almost primal. But . . . accepting Grane as mine would be akin to giving in to my Nibelungen nature. And I can't do it now. Not when Del needs me.

As much as it breaks my heart, I push Grane away, my telepathic rejection stopping him midstride somewhere in the fog. His despair paints my world dark, but I send my sadness away, exiling it to the back of my mind.

I shake my head. "I'm here for Del, and I'm not leading anyone anywhere until you give her back to me. She doesn't belong here. There must be something that can be done for her!"

Nothing can be done. Not if you treasure the balance of the universe. . . .

Supressing my murderous impulse to rage and threaten, I decide I need to find another way to convince them to lead me to Del. "How about this: You release Del, and I'll lead you out of here."

When they remain silent, I wonder if they're about to turn on me. After all, my proposed bargain implies that I'm less than willing to perform my duty.

When they do respond, their chorus is weaker, less defined. *If we do as you wish, there will be consequences.*

"Whatever I have to do to get Del out of here, I'll do it."

If that is your wish, we shall take you to where the human child slumbers.

They retreat deeper into the fog, leaving me alone and fighting against the panic that threatens to freeze me in my spot. Do I follow them into the unknown? Can I really trust them?

But if I turn around and try to get back into my world, leaving Del here, will I ever be able to look at myself in the mirror again?

I realize my mind has been made up all along. I'm ready to follow my eerie sentinels deeper into the land of fog. As I take my first steps, the ground underneath my feet trembles, moving in rough waves. I struggle to stay upright.

"Hayden!" Shannon jumps down nearby, having come from the higher ground, like I did earlier.

"What are you doing here?" My heart's doing crazy leaps. I'm not sure if I'm happy that he came after me or frustrated with him for putting himself in danger. I decide that regardless of how I feel, he's here now and I no longer have to do this alone. I fling my arms around him, and he gives me a short but meaningful hug.

When he releases me and takes a long look around, I watch him accept this alien world and see it all again with him, through his eyes. What does he make of it? When he pauses to stare at the faceless knights, his eyes grow bigger. "Just roll with it," I whisper in his ear.

"Okay. . . . Just an FYI, but I now know the true meaning of the expression *all hell broke loose*, because that's what happened after you jumped into the vortex. Elspeth went after you, but the vortex spat her back out. Then Gabriel tried, but the same thing happened. Then they turned on me, but I followed you, fell through an opening in the fog, and now I'm here."

"They're going to take me to Del." I nod at the silent army. "But I may have promised them something in return. Something they want."

"What is it?"

"Their freedom."

45
THE TELLING TELLS MANY THINGS

The horseback riders encase me and Shannon in a semi-oval formation, ushering us into the depths of this foggy alien world. The white raven follows us, its form barely visible through the milky haze. But I know the bird's there; I can sense its calming presence and the workings of its powerful wings, and I can hear its occasional cackle.

I shove my hands deeper into the fog, then show Shannon the residue of the fairy-dust powder coating my skin. He takes my hand and gives my fingers a light squeeze. Despite the fog clogging my view, I see the familiar dark gray of his eyes and feel a tiny bit safer. Leaning into him, I whisper, "The moment we get Del, I want you to take her and run back to that cave, and hopefully go home, okay?"

"Actually, I was going to ask you to do the same thing."

"Shannon."

"Do you honestly think I'm going to leave you here?"

I let the conversation drop. I've caused enough trouble for

Del. I'm not going to endanger her or anyone else anymore. If getting her out of here while preventing the Nibelungen army from entering the human world means I have to stay, so be it. For now, I can pretend like I don't have to make these decisions in the near future.

Holding on to each other, Shannon and I begin our hike through the fog. Every rise and fall of the unstable terrain beneath my feet reverberates through my body. Soon the fog begins to lift, thinning out enough to allow a glimpse of a large edifice looming up ahead.

We continue toward this construction till a tall iron gate emerges from the fog. The gate is cut into a crumbling, stone-laid wall and stands half-open, periodically releasing thick puffs of dark smoke from whatever lies beyond.

You are expected. Come inside, the faceless crowd informs me.

Not letting go of Shannon's hand, I step over the threshold of the building. The moment we cross over, the fog all but disappears. It makes no sense—the ruined walls surrounding the building would, in theory, be useless at keeping fog out.

A musical voice rolls over me, making my stomach lurch with odd pleasure. "For lack of a better word, I'd call it *magic*."

This voice I'm hearing is real. As in nontelepathically transmitted.

I stare into the corner where (I think) the voice came from. The space is shrouded in shadows. But the longer I stare, the more I see it: a twitch of a movement followed by the physical act of air reshuffling as a humanoid figure assembles itself out of the shadows, growing taller and taller until it towers over me and even Shannon.

Shannon wants to step forward, to position himself between me and the shadowy being, but I hold him back.

"Magic is what's keeping the fog out of this place?" I ask the vaguely defined creature.

"Yes." The speaker's tone is mocking but not hostile. "And as the Telling informs us, hybrids such as yourself possess roughly as much magical ability as the rest of us magi of Niflheim. But you might already know that."

I want to ask him about this Telling I keep hearing about, but Shannon speaks first. "Look, whoever you are, we're only here to get the girl that came through the vortex earlier. She's human. Her name is Del. Have you got her?"

Shannon's words provoke a series of odd movements in the darkened corner—shadows pulling and twisting as if to fill in the gaps where the being's shape lacks physical matter.

At last the owner of the voice steps out of the corner and into the light that streams from an unidentifiable source above.

The being's lovely, androgynous face is stunning. It reminds me of those charming angels that grace old-fashioned Christmas postcards. But if his face is angelic, the rest of him is all fey from folktales: pointed ears, high cheekbones, mischievous look. His short hair is platinum white, contrasting with eyes so deep blue, they could compete with those dark patches of water where the ocean floor plunges into an abyss.

"Call me Hel," the being says. "I'm the last oracle of the Niflheim realm. And I shall get to the matter of Delphine's fate shortly, but first, I understand you'd like to know more about the Telling?" He grins, locking his magnificent nonhuman eyes on me.

I want to know him, I realize. To keep hearing him talk.

But most important, I desperately want to trust him. The need is almost visceral.

With catlike fluidity in his long limbs, Hel lowers his lean frame to the ground and crosses his slender legs underneath his flowing black robe. He's barefoot. Elongated toes with pale-aquamarine nails peek from beneath the folds of his clothing.

"Don't touch anything!" Startled by Hel's warning, Shannon steps away from some shelves overflowing with murky glass jars, hourglasses, broken clocks, doll parts, and who knows what else. A sheepish smile on his face, Shannon comes to my side, his arms crossed over his broad chest.

"Why don't you two restless kids take a seat?" Hel chuckles, and, as if on command, my legs fold down, taking my body with them. Dizzy from Hel's blunt compulsion, I land on the warm, stony ground. Shannon's next to me, our knees touching.

I don't like that Hel has this power over me. Not one bit. So I push back. Most of my resistance comes from pure instinct, but the rest is my building rage. *He's got Del*, I remind myself. *He's got Del, and for all I know, she's hurting while he's distracting us.* I don't know what I'm doing exactly, but everything that led me to this moment tells me I have an innate power inside me that I should be able to access on command. In fact, I've already seen the effect of this power on those around me—in Del's hypnotized response when I voiced my unease about Santiago, and also even earlier, when I spoke to the red-haired guy at the airport car rental in Denver. And I can even recall similar experiences from further back in time. Jen Rickman. Probably Dr. Erich. Even Dad. I know at some stage I must've compelled my father to do something he didn't want to do, like let me go to school with all the other kids when he knew for sure it must've been a very bad idea.

I pull at that invisible thread inside me, focusing all of my intent on Hel. As if he can feel what I'm trying to accomplish, Shannon places his hand on top of mine. The warmth of his skin gives me strength. Still, my mental attack on Hel is clumsy, all over the place. I don't think it's working at all. But then a shiver goes over Hel's body, like a mild seizure. *He's fighting me off*, I realize. Whatever I'm doing, it's working. But before I can try again, Hel claps his hands—one powerful clap that deafens me for a second, breaking my concentration.

"Not bad for a rookie, my dear. Not bad at all."

I study his face. His relaxed tone doesn't match the shadow of surprise that darkened his features for a quick moment before disappearing. I realize with a start: He's afraid of me. Good to know. I file that knowledge away. For now.

Looking between Shannon and me, Hel's stunning eyes assume a vulturelike intensity, the scrutiny making me feel like he knows everything, can see right through me, down to the deepest recesses of my mind. I push back, and his presence recedes from my head slowly.

"What's this place?" I ask, hoping to break Hel's concentration the way he broke mine moments ago. "And how come you have a face and they don't?" I look around, expecting to find our silent escort nearby, keeping guard at the perimeter. But they're gone. "Where's Del?"

"So. Many. Questions." Hel laughs, looking at me like I'm a talking monkey and everything I say is hilarious. "But I guess that's to be expected, since you've been cut off from Niflheim your entire life. If you must know, this is a place between places—

a *no-place* at all. My theory is that it used to be a universe of its own until it shrank and shifted out of balance, forced to dwell on the periphery of space-time. If the clearing in the Promise woods is a doorway, then this place is a corridor connecting Niflheim and Miðgarðr. As to why I have a face . . . you see, being stuck in this no-place for so very long has had a terrible effect on our kind. The emptiness here slowly deletes us from existence, chipping away at our bodies and souls like water eroding rock—slowly but surely. But I'm no ordinary Niflheim dweller. I was strong when I crossed over here. Obviously I was not strong enough to follow Ella into Miðgarðr, but I was strong enough to retain my identity, unlike those poor faceless creatures you've met." He takes a breath, holds it, and lets it out. "Any other questions before we get to business?"

"Sure," I retort. "I'd like to see Del now. Where is she?"

Hel lets out an exasperated chuckle, like someone who's quickly losing his patience. But guess who's also losing patience? Me.

"It's not as easy as you might think, Hayden," Hel explains. "Delphine's been sacrificed—"

"She shouldn't have been sacrificed in the first place! It was an accident. She clearly doesn't belong here."

"You know who else *clearly* doesn't belong here?" Hel's mocking gaze turns serious. "Me. And the rest of your people. Your mother and her allies worked so hard to reopen the portal and set us free. Your mother had quite a vision for the world you call home."

"And then my mother changed her mind," I protest, remembering Mom's clear instructions on closing the portal once and for all. If only I'd trusted her and done as she willed me to do, then we wouldn't be in this mess now. Del wouldn't have been compelled and mutilated. She wouldn't have been sucked into a vortex in the woods and trapped in this foggy wasteland. To Hel, I reiterate, "My mother wanted to close the portal, not reopen it." *Mom wasn't a monster. She loved me. She loved my dad.*

"But it is not a matter of love, my dear Hayden," Hel replies, apparently having read my unguarded mind. "It is a matter of blood and duty. Your mother may have had a moment of weakness, but in the end her blood would have prevailed. She would have always chosen her people. Always."

"I don't believe you!" I spit out the words. "You didn't know her after she left this world. But I knew her."

"Did you? Really?" Hel scowls. "Did you also know how badly she wanted to conquer the human world, to rule over it? But then she realized that in Miðgarðr, away from her homeland, her power was diminished, and she had to think of another way to make her vision a reality. That's why she created you! Because she's been listening to what the Telling sang to her, to what it's been singing to our kind for eternities."

I'm shaking my head, refusing to let Hel's words snake their way too deep into my mind.

"And what does this Telling tell exactly?" Shannon asks, not without a hint of sarcasm. I envy him for being able to retain the ability to be sardonic, given the circumstances.

After giving Shannon a dismissive look, Hel turns to meet my eyes. I hold his gaze. "The Telling tells us many things. You know some parts of it, don't you, Hayden? After all, you grew up with the Telling's first verses as your lullaby." He starts to hum the melody I know too well. Mom's lullaby. Of course. How fitting.

"It means nothing to me," I lie, my voice threatening to shake. "No matter what you say, I don't believe for a second Mom would've really destroyed an entire world just to fulfill some ancient prophecy. Regardless, I won't be some tool you can use to set yourself free."

Shannon says something to me then, but I can't hear him through all the blood pounding in my head. I feel Hel's presence in my mind again—the intoxicating, dark pull of oblivion. He yearns to control me, and it's my human half that allows him to do so; it even welcomes him in. *Humans ... Their minds are so easy to corrupt*, Elspeth said. Santiago's terrified face flashes through my mind. I pool all my rage into one task: refusing Hel's entry into my head and blocking his path before he can burrow in too deep.

But Hel doesn't retreat this time. Instead, he doubles his efforts. I gasp, only partially feeling Shannon squeeze my hand in response to my shallow breathing. I lock eyes with Hel and concentrate all my intent on getting him out of my head. With perfect clarity, I remember the day of my eighteenth birthday and one of Del's gifts, the Blu-ray of that creepy old movie we wanted to watch together. *Scanners.* Its ghoulish cover—a screaming man, his head about to explode—becomes my inspiration. I see sweat coating Hel's skin. Mirroring his intensifying power, his body also appears to grow in size, turning more otherworldly with each second in our standoff.

I attempt to come off the floor but only manage to rise to my haunches, unable to stand up.

"Why are you fighting this?" I hear genuine surprise in Hel's question. "Your mother has left you this amazing gift! Why won't you accept it?"

"I already told you. I don't want it!" I press on and, with an almost audible snap, Hel relinquishes his hold on my mind. Released from his compulsion, I stand up, my legs shaking. Shannon joins me. I wonder how much he knows about what just happened between me and Hel, about our mental tug-of-war. Judging from his furious expression, I bet he could feel at least some of it.

I lock eyes with Hel again. His expression guarded, he says, "And what if I told you your mother is still alive but trapped someplace and that I might know how to release her?"

His words slap me in the face.

Hel gives me a winning grin.

"My mother's still alive somewhere?" A tiny shiver grows at the center of my heart, like a wildflower opening its petals. My mother might still be alive. The possibility fills me with hope. *I can fix this*, I assure myself. *I can find Mom. I can put my family back together.* Of course, it's never going to be the way it was, but it's worth trying, anyway.

Hel whispers, but I hear his words like thunder in my head. "Nibelungs are capable of compulsion, as you know. That extends to wielding control over animals—birds, in particular. Their minds are weaker than a human's, making it possible for one of our kind to completely take over the creature's body."

It takes a gigantic mental effort on my part not to do something impulsive right now, like tackle Hel. He'd probably just send me flying and smack me against some hard surface, like I did with Jen Rickman in school. Shannon must feel my murderous vibe, because he comes closer to me, tense, ready to stop me. Or help me.

I keep my voice low when I ask Hel, "Where is my mother?"

"She's been with you all along, Hayden. Ever since you returned to Promise, she's been keeping an eye on you. As much as her limited new form allows, anyway. In fact, I can sense her nearby now. Do you feel Ella's presence, Hayden? Like calls to like, you know."

Somewhere outside, a raven lets out a desperate cry. I've heard it before, its cadence peculiar enough to burn itself into my memory. It's the white bird that kept popping up wherever I went in Promise. The very same raven that first got my father's attention years ago. *Randy.*

I watch Hel's alien face change from dreamy to sad. As my hearts speeds up in terror at my mother's fate, I sense a rapid movement of air around me. It's all happening so fast, I'm only half aware of Hel's bony, long fingers wrapping around my arms, his razor-sharp nails digging into my skin, and I pass out.

46
THE BALANCE

I'm back in the vortex, its nothingness pulling and pushing at the matter that makes up my body while I drift through space-time. A soft, melodic voice soothes my rapid heartbeat. "It's okay, Hayden, my love." The voice is so familiar, it makes me want to give in to the tears building in my eyes. Even ten years on, I recognize my mother's voice. "Do not feel sad," she goes on. "I haven't done anything I didn't want to do." Mom's voice is the only thing that keeps me aware, that reminds me I am real. "But, Hayden, you need to listen to me now." Mom's voice rises, fighting its way in through the fog around me. I struggle to focus my eyes. To regain control. I can't see him, but I become viscerally aware of Shannon close by. The way his body heat makes my blood sing whenever he's near . . . its influence can't be ignored.

"Where am I?" I ask. "Mom?"

All is quiet until a flash of lightning illuminates my dreary world. I wait for the roar of thunder, but it never comes. Abnormal. Defying the rules of the natural world. Another lightning bolt strikes, then another, the flashes of blinding light morphing into the flapping wings of a white bird. A raven.

Hovering over me. Watching me.

I open my eyes wider and focus on this blur of white before me. The bird is moving in slow motion, as if suspended in thickened air and having to fight for each movement with its powerful wings. "We haven't got much time, Hayden." I hear Mom's voice in my head. "Hel's in your mind right now. He thinks he's overpowered you, but you have to fight it. Fight it! You need to get out of here before Elspeth breaks in. She's strong—very strong—but you're strong also. Fight!" Another flash of light burns my retinas, and I cry out in pain. I feel the burn under my skin. It'll consume me if I don't take control.

I hear the raven's cackle as I open my mouth to scream. But instead of my voice, I hear a thunderous roar that's as otherworldly as they come. My body changes, rearranges itself, and something shifts inside my head, allowing me to see what's going on in my own mind: It's a forest on fire, and Hel's the one controlling the blaze. I see Hel's presence everywhere, his pollution. But now that I know he's here, *I* can burn *him* out.

I regain my focus, drawing on Mom's lingering presence around me, and raise a wall of fire so tall, it dwarfs the trees. Too certain of his victory, Hel doesn't see me coming. I use that to my advantage and sneak up on him, hitting him with everything I've got, Nibelung and human.

He senses me then, feels my growing presence. I can hear him chant in the rapid guttural words of the ancient language from my dreams. Dark words that fling curses my way, but bounce off me on contact with my power. I block Hel's path when he attempts to retreat. There's nowhere to hide. He's trapped in my head, all exits cut off. I'm the puppetmaster now. I prepare for the final assault, my will gathering around me like a mantle. "Go to hell, Hel!" I hit him with everything I have, but he's already weak, and my tsunami wave of compulsion is overkill. I blast him out of my head and in the next moment find myself back in his lair. Shannon, who also passed out, comes to his senses next to me.

I hear a raven's cry outside. For whatever reason, my mother can't enter here, but she could transmit her thoughts into my head. "I'm coming, Mom, I promise," I murmur, catching an odd glance from Shannon.

I scan the space around me and see Hel's tall frame crumpled on the floor. His shape wavers, but he stays corporeal. His chest is rising and falling, but otherwise he's totally out of it. "What did you do?" Shannon sounds impressed as he regards me with a new kind of admiration.

"Hel used his Niflheim compulsion on us," I say, "but I turned it right back on him."

Shannon hovers over Hel's immobile body. "I don't think we've got a lot of time. He can wake up at any moment."

"Let's go find Del," I say.

Together, we search Hel's headquarters, and it's Shannon who first notices the silver-thread curtain billowing in the wind. Maybe it wasn't even here a blink ago and only revealed itself to us now that Hel's been knocked unconscious.

We head straight into the opening. When I touch the ethereal fabric of the curtain, the material dissipates, turning into swirls of fog. It smells of an empty place, of staleness. The walls around us seem to vibrate as they go transparent in places. "This place is dying," Shannon comments, touching the shelf running the length of the wall, his fingers coming back smudged with gooey blackness. "We must've tipped off the balance by coming here. We need to hurry."

I see Del. In the short time that she's been trapped here, she's uncannily become a part of this place. She's still beautiful but muted and deathly bluish. She lies atop a high rock slab made of white marble. Her arms are folded on her chest, her eyes closed, lips bent in a haunting twist. She's breathing, but the movement of her chest is erratic, and she's whimpering in her sleep, like she's having a nightmare. I notice that her mutilated hand, the one that will forever miss a pinkie, is wrapped in a bandage.

I go to her, grabbing her uninjured hand. "Del! Wake up!" She stirs, but her eyes remain shut.

Working together with Shannon, we manage to slide Del from her altarlike pedestal. Shannon weaves his hands around her shoulders to keep her up while I gently slap her cheeks. Del's eyelashes tremble, eyelids opening halfway. I exhale in relief when I glimpse the familiar dark hazel of her eyes. Turning her head sluggishly, she glances around before meeting my eyes. She cries out and then fights against Shannon's hold.

I keep saying her name until she stops her frenetic movement and zeroes in on the sound of my voice. "Where am I?" she asks, her voice hoarse.

"In a place that's about to collapse in on itself," I reply, seeing the motion of space all around me as this world between worlds begins to self-destruct. "And we really need to get going!"

"Can you walk?" Shannon asks her when she stops shaking. Del nods. My heart shrinks at the sight of silent tears traveling down her smooth skin.

"She cut off my finger," Del lets out in disbelief. "That crazy woman!"

"I know," I say, feeling terrible. "But we'll deal with her later, I promise. Right now, we're alive and we need to go." Del nods at my words, her lips assuming the stubborn expression I know and love. With caution, Shannon lets go of Del, leaving her swaying on her feet.

The three of us leave Hel's lair and dive into the shimmering fog without looking back. Our faceless escort is nowhere to be seen. Something becomes obvious: Without the Nibelungs, we can't find our way back through the fog. "Are you there?" I call out to the warriors who led us here earlier. My question meets poignant silence. I can swear they are nearby, their presence emitting cold. They're just choosing to ignore me. Before I try again, that familiar otherworldly chorus returns.

We have fulfilled our part of the bargain. Now it is your turn.

"What's the point of you taking me to Del if I can't send her back to the human world?"

The fate of the human no longer concerns us.

I exchange a pointed look with Shannon, while Del remains slack in his grip. "Well, it concerns *me*," I say, while thinking through my options. I suspect the Nibelungs trapped in here know I have no intention of saving them, but I also bet they are too weak to actually do *anything* to me. Of course, they can just leave us stranded. The air becomes thinner, and soon the three of us are gasping for breath. "We can go back and you can compel Hel to tell us how to get out of here," Shannon proposes, but judging from his voice and expression, he doubts it'll work.

Desperate, I study the fog around me, trying to see the outlines of the warriors, but the thickening matter is absolute. Before I can offer the Nibelungs more false promises, I hear a flutter of wings above. I tip my head up and stare into the fog, looking for movement. "Mom?" I whisper.

And she descends, slowly, like a ghost of a bird. White against white.

"Is that a white raven?" Del asks weakly.

The bird doesn't come close, but from its movement in the air above us, I can detect the direction it's telling us to go. "Come on," I say. "I think I know the way."

"We're following a bird now?" Shannon deadpans.

"Can you think of a better option?" I ask him, unable to share the heartbreaking revelation that Randy's mind is being hijacked by my mother's will. To make this reality even sadder, something tells me the bird's time is limited, too. Even the way the creature holds itself in the air is erratic, like it's a chore to flap its wings. It's running on the empty fumes of determination.

Randy leads us back to the cliffside where we entered this world. When we attempt to climb the rocky formation leading to the cave, that weak gravity effect I experienced earlier takes place, and we half float, half walk up the rocky wall, our feet barely touching the surface. After carefully helping Del through the cave opening, Shannon reaches for my hand, and I take it, his fingers firm on mine, like a promise.

I take a wrong step and slip on the wet rock, but Shannon's hold prevents me from falling. He pulls me close and, as we embrace, our eyes meet and don't let go. I feel the soft trace of drizzle on my face. When our lips touch briefly, the warmth of the kiss travels through me. I open my eyes and watch as the world before us becomes consumed by a faint flame, its movement slow but deliberate.

This world is ending, and I hope the Nibelungs end with it.

"Thanks for coming after me," I say to Shannon.

He smiles lightly. "I'd follow you anywhere, I think."

"Whatever happened to your I'm-going-to-keep-my-distance plan?"

"It had to be revised after all the facts were taken into consideration."

I snort at that. He sounds like me.

My mood darkens suddenly when I remember what comes next: our return to Promise, potentially to face Elspeth and Gabriel. "We better go." I step away from Shannon even though I don't want to. "Be ready to fight or run, depending on what awaits us on the other side."

Our time's almost up. The wave of destruction that's consuming this world is near. I swear I can hear the panicked mental chatter of the faceless knights that are trapped here. I feel their pain, their anger. But the alternative to their suffering is more suffering, and I can't allow that.

I ask Shannon to go first, but he lingers on the edge of the opening, looking uncertain. "I'm not going to do anything stupid. I promise," I say. Hesitant, he nods. I watch him disappear into the gaping hole underneath our feet.

My heart starts to beat faster as I stand up tall to take in the blurry landscape one last time. This bleak world is vanishing before my very eyes.

With a loud flutter, Randy lands on the ground at my feet. The bird's eyes are trained on me. I try to see beyond them, to find any evidence of my mother's presence in the bird's expression. The raven cocks its head side to side and stares back, eyes unblinking.

"Staying here, or coming with?" I ask.

In response, Randy lets out a strange noise, not quite a cackle but not human speech, either.

I find Gabriel's amulet in my pocket and send it flying in a wide arc. Once the trinket vanishes into the fog, I turn my back on this world of mist and jump into the black opening.

47
RETURN

Thunder is cracking over and over again as the wind screams murder, tearing the clouds into shreds. Spat out from the fog, I land beside the chasm in the Black Clearing. The moment my feet touch the ground, a particularly beastly burst of wind slams into me, nearly knocking me down. It's sleeting. This is nothing compared to the brick-size hailstones that bombarded the Manor earlier today, but it's still nasty enough to bite into my exposed skin. I rub my forehead where a particularly pointy ice pellet landed.

I scan the clearing and find Del seated on the ground, not far from me. Shannon's next to her, talking to her as she looks around. Aside from the two of them, the clearing looks empty.

Still sensing the aftershocks of the miniearthquake we must've caused by jumping between worlds, I approach Shannon and Del. Shannon's eyes meet mine, and he allows a brief smile to grace his lips. I return it before asking Del, "How are you doing?"

"Let's see. I've been hypnotized and kidnapped by a guy I kind of liked, then mind-controlled into attacking my best friend before getting sucked into a giant whirlpool. Oh and also, not to sound like a broken record, but . . . Elspeth cut off my finger." There are tears in her voice, but there's also defiance.

I get down on my knees and pull Del into a fierce hug, moving carefully around her bandaged hand. "I'm so sorry," I exhale into her hair.

"It's not your fault," she says.

"Of course it's my fault!" I say, my volume rising. "I brought you here. I kept things from you. I put you in danger."

She shakes her head. Stubborn Del. "I chose to come here with you, and I ignored you when you tried to tell me Santiago was bad news. . . ."

"Not to interrupt the teary reunion, but we have some unfinished business here." Elspeth's voice rings high over the sudden rush of blood in my head, even drowning out the chatter of rain. To my perception, she simply blinked into existence next to me, likely some kind of Nibelungen illusion keeping her shielded from view till now.

"Welcome back, I suppose," Elspeth hisses as she attacks my mind while Gabriel emerges from the trees and tackles Shannon. Del moves out of the way and struggles to stand up while Elspeth pins me to a nearby tree with her unleashed power. But she doesn't know me anymore, doesn't know that I overpowered Hel and that I can certainly put up a fight against her. I reach out with my will and curl it around Elspeth's throat.

The shock in her eyes is priceless. "It's too late," I tell her as I tighten my psychic noose around her neck. "Your world is dying, and your army is dying with it."

She struggles against my power. Meanwhile, Shannon is having his own standoff with Gabriel, the inhuman being who possibly helped create him. I can only guess what exchange is happening between them right now. And I can't help Shannon, as I have my hands full.

I realize a second too late that Elspeth is reaching out for my arm, the one Del cut with the knife while she was entranced. Elspeth's nails dig into my fresh wound before I can pull away, breaking my concentration. I'm bleeding again, and Elspeth is smiling. "I only need a drop," she growls.

Her hand smeared with my blood, she pushes me away and retreats, running for the chasm's edge. There, she kneels on the ground and rubs my blood against the soil before standing up in anticipation. Gabriel twists out of Shannon's grasp and sprints toward his daughter.

My eyes meet Shannon's, while, in the periphery, I catch a glimpse of Del picking something up from the ground. A familiar glint sparkles as it catches a ray of random light. "Looking for something?" I call out as Shannon, Del, and I surround the father-daughter duo. Elspeth looks up, her eyes landing on the curved blade in Del's hand while her mouth twists into a closed-lip smile.

"Why don't you keep that?" she says. "A souvenir for you to gaze at wistfully when you're drowning in regrets."

Elspeth produces a simple Swiss Army knife from the folds of her robe and swiftly cuts her arm, then Gabriel's. As their blood spills, the fog thickens in response, forming another vortex within the broken earth. Like in a bad dream that just won't end, I hear a horse neighing nearby, a plaintive sound full of sorrow and disappointment meant just for me. A chorus of demonic whispers and the chiming of armor kick in. The clearing is surrounded with ghostly shapes and forms once more. "Oh, hell no!" I hear myself shout as I run at Elspeth. My mind uncoils, ready to strike.

But it doesn't need to.

A white raven swoops from above and torpedoes into Elspeth's back. Already teetering on the edge between our world and the other, Elspeth trips and falls forward, her hands flapping uselessly around her. Gabriel shouts something in the language of the Nibelungs, but it doesn't matter. Elspeth's already gone, having succeeded this time with this unstable gateway into foggy purgatory.

Gabriel falls to his knees at the spot where his daughter stood just moments ago. His hands, folded into fists, beat at the invisible barrier before him, but then something changes and his hands go right through it. He looks surprised, then triumphant. He doesn't know about the devouring force that's about to collapse the Nibelungen prison in on itself. How much time have they got? When I left their foggy world, the wave of destruction was already near. I'm about to warn Gabriel, but before I can, he jumps into the vortex and follows after his daughter.

Having exhausted its energy, the portal closes in on itself, sucking in all sound and moisture, leaving the clearing even more lifeless than before.

"Let's get out of here," Shannon says. I find his eyes and nod. This is over. There's nothing left for us here.

I definitely got more than what I bargained for when I came to Promise four days ago, looking for closure, but on some level, I'm happy I did.

Shannon and Del head into the trees, and I'm about to follow them when I notice a tiny spot of white on the otherwise black ground. I approach, my breath already catching, because I know what it is before I see it clearly.

The white raven. Barely alive but its chest still moving, frantically fighting for breath. It must've been already weak when it got into the vortex with me and guided me out. Attacking Elspeth took what was left of its life force. I kneel on the ground before the bird and wait for it to reach out for me, to hear Mom's voice in my head again. But Randy is silent, its eyes closing. The bird stops moving. Tears running from my eyes, I take off my Hunter hoodie and wrap Randy in it like a blanket. I can't just leave it here in this place. The least I can give it is some quiet, in a spot near the Manor, as far as I can take it from these woods. I can't quite think of the raven as "her," I realize. Maybe I'm not ready to admit who the bird really is. *Was.* Maybe I never will be.

Shivering in my sports tank top, my hands busy with the little bundle that is Randy's body, I walk away from the Black Clearing. I can't see Shannon and Del yet, but hearing the sounds of their progress through the woods up ahead is reassuring. My heart slows down, my breathing returning to normal after the short but intense battle with Elspeth. I'm almost out of the woods, about to see the Manor down in the lowlands, when I hear my name.

I whirl around, almost dropping Randy. I don't see the caller at first—just trees draped in fog. I only notice him when he moves, his armor-covered body tall and willowy. Seated atop Grane's mighty back, Hel smiles at me. His bewitching gaze burns a hole in me when our eyes meet.

I blink, and he's gone.

ACKNOWLEDGMENTS

Aside from time, massive brainpower effort, and resilience, it takes a group of creative geniuses to turn a manuscript into a book. As a writer, I was lucky to have such a group to guide me through the complicated terrain that is book publishing toward what eventually became the final version of *What the Woods Keep*.

Words cannot adequately express my gratitude, but I'll try. I thank:

Amy Tipton, my agent extraordinaire. Your immense knowledge, enviable skill set, and "we will emerge victorious" attitude are my shield and sword. It's a privilege to be working with you.

Erin Stein, for taking a chance on me. You cannot be thanked enough. I will never forget the sheer joy of our first conversation—and all the awesomeness that followed!

John Morgan, for quickly stepping up to the task of making my debut-to-be better and better and better after joining my editorial team. I'm so psyched to keep working with you!

Rhoda Belleza, for your thoughtful editorial ideas and support. You rock!

Hayley Jozwiak and Kayla Overbey, for their excellent copy edit. (Reading your reactions to my quirky jokes was the best!)

Ellen Peppus and Signature Literary Agency, for always being so supportive, friendly, and a paragon of professionalism.

Jeff Miller at Faceout Studios, for the mind-blowing cover art design. Wow.

Nicole Otto and everyone at Imprint, for being splendid and always going above and beyond on all counts. Dawn Ryan, for her managing editorial excellence; Raymond Ernesto Colón for his work on the production of the book; and Natalie C. Sousa and Heather Palisi for art directing the cover and designing the book's interior.

Preeti Arora, Jessica Smith, and Stephanie Makin, for being my first readers and for your unceasing enthusiasm for Hayden and her offbeat personality. Sorry I edited out the tree hollow—hope you like the vortex that came to replace it.

To all my fellow Electric Eighteens debuts! Thank you so much for all the support and your general awesomeness.

Last but not least, I thank my family across two continents and three countries (Olga and Vitaly; Angela, Paola, Roberto and Miguel; and Augusto—we miss you every day), but most of all I thank Jorge, my partner in mischief, travel, and everything.

Smoke and Mirrors
Author's Note

Thank you for picking up this paperback edition of *What the Woods Keep*. It has some extra content: a short story called "Smoke and Mirrors," set in the *What the Woods Keep* universe before the events involving Hayden and Promise. I originally wrote it to support my debut's preorder campaign. I'm beyond excited that it's now being included in this edition of the book.

So what's "Smoke and Mirrors" about? It focuses on Del Chauvet, Hayden's best friend. I love Del. She's bright and clever and a counterweight to Hayden's (at times) rigid and rather dark outlook on reality. I wanted to explore more of Del's character and give a deeper perspective into her life before she came to the US and before she met Hayden. We do learn bits and pieces about Del and her family in *What the Woods Keep*, but all of it is seen through Hayden's perspective. While writing my debut, I felt more than a few times that Del is too big of a character to be only seen through that lens. Therefore, I give you "Smoke and Mirrors," which takes us back to Del's time in Paris, centering on a critical moment of her life that involves her sister, Alice. I hope you'll find it intriguing.

—Katya de Becerra

SMOKE AND MIRRORS

For Del Chauvet, it was not the day her big sister left home to join the Watchers' Disciples that shattered her. It was the day after.

Just seconds after Del woke up in her trendy bedroom over-looking the Luxembourg Gardens, all of yesterday's tension returned, twisting her belly into a knot. A reminder that her old, mostly carefree life was gone for good. Alice had taken it with her, stuffed haphazardly into her weekend bag alongside a change of clothes and her well-read collection of Watchers' Disciples books.

Last night, while their parents were busy arguing with Alice, Del had contemplated her sister's reasons for leaving. On a certain level, Del could understand why some people sought out these experiences, why they were attracted to charismatic leaders: They wanted to belong somewhere, to feel special, to be surrounded by like-minded people. But it was also about giving up control, about placing your life into the hands of someone else, someone you believed was better equipped to not drive that metaphorical car off a cliff.

And that's exactly where things stopped making sense: Why would Alice, the most cool-headed, logical, smart-to-the-point-of-scary person, want to join a cult? Because that's what the Watchers' Disciples was—a cult. They might have gotten away with using the "communal farm" definition, but still. And also, why was it this particular cult that attracted Alice? After all, the Watchers were just one among many of France's so-called new "spiritual communities," which had been springing up like mushrooms after rain thanks to loosening anti-cult regulations in recent years.

Alice must've been going through something bad. And Del had missed all the signs. In fact, she'd been completely blindsided. And so were her parents and her older brother, Bastian, who responded to Del's frantic phone call last night with a shocked silence. Annoyed at herself, Del sifted through her recent memories of Alice, trying to find something—*anything*—out of place.

One night in particular stood out. It was months ago. Del and Alice had been returning home from a party, a rare kind of party where the Chauvet sisters had enough friends-overlap to both be invited and interested in going. Del was listening to Alice wax poetic about some boy she fancied when something pulled her attention to a homemade poster taped to a lamppost. The poster in question featured a photo of a youngish woman. There was nothing interesting about her appearance aside from a strange half smile playing on her mouth.

Del's eyes lingered on the image before shifting down to read the words underneath the photo. THE WATCHERS' DISCIPLES HAVE THE ANSWERS, the poster announced, but it didn't say to what questions—which made Del laugh and make some sharp remark.

Did Alice also laugh? Del couldn't recall.

And now Alice was gone, and maybe Del was responsible somehow.

As that first dreadful morning post-Alice unfolded, Del had to force herself out of bed. The sun was streaming through the blinds, but everything around her seemed just a little bit darker, a little bit stranger. Even her latest dress renovation project, a 1970s cheerful vintage floral displayed on a headless mannequin torso in the corner of her bedroom, now looked sad and a little creepy. Ignoring the foreboding sensation that stalked her every step, Del went through her routine on autopilot. She styled her tight curls with a silken scarf and spread foundation over her already flawless dark skin. Del was bracing for a battle, expecting her parents to rage and fight over Alice's departure, but, to her shock, her mother's customary Saturday brunch feast was waiting for her in the kitchen.

All traces of Alice were erased from the apartment. Alice's portrait: gone from its spot over the fireplace, with the remaining portraits of Del and Bastian repositioned to cover up the square absence on the wallpaper. All the framed photographs featuring Alice: missing, with glaringly obvious empty spaces left in their wake. Alice had hurt their parents' pride. It was personal, and now she was being erased from their lives, one framed photo at a time. Even the round table in the kitchen had only three chairs. A deep scratch on the floor where the fourth chair used to be was the only sign that Alice once ate her meals there, too.

Del couldn't look away from that damn scratch, to the point where her eyes started to fill with tears. She brought her coffee cup to her lips to hide her weakness. When she met her mother's questioning eyes, Del gave her what she hoped was an untroubled smile.

Her mother smiled back.

Later that day, when her parents went out for an afternoon drink at their social club, Del headed to Alice's bedroom. What exactly was she looking for? *A sign*, Del decided. An explanation of Alice's motives. Something. *Anything*.

The door was locked. Of course. Their parents had likely already arranged for someone to come and take all of Alice's stuff away when Del wasn't around to protest. Del snorted at her parents' naivete. As if a locked door was going to hold her back. She went back to her room and returned with a couple of bobby pins. She used them to play with the old lock, just like Bastian taught her, until the mechanism clicked and the door flew open.

The blinds were closed, and the room smelled wrong, but Del couldn't place the scent. Wilted flowers? Something rotten? Her stomach-turning feeling from the morning returned tenfold, this time bringing with it a flashback: that Watchers woman from the poster, her smile a suggestion rather than a real thing. The memory of the poster, once laughable, made Del dizzy with fright.

Alice's things were just the way she'd left them; even her

laptop sat open on the bedside table, its screensaver photo of Del and Alice, in their preppy school uniforms, flickering in and out of existence. Del looked around, running a hand across the spines of Alice's beloved books, checking inside her sister's closet, searching the drawers for clues. But there was nothing out of the ordinary. Disappointed, Del returned to her own room. To divert her growing frustration, Del occupied herself with making her bed, pulling and tugging at the bedsheets and blankets with unnecessary force.

A white piece of paper flew up into the air and landed on the floor at Del's feet.

Alice's handwriting. Del's heart raced.

Dearest Del, meet me at 133 Rue de Arnaud this Sunday. Don't say a word to Mom and Dad. I'll try and explain everything. Love, Alice

All anger gone out of her in one exhale, Del's eyes flooded with tears.

ᚠᚷᚠ

Mindful that her father could track her movement via GPS if she took one of the family cars, Del left the house on foot and hailed a taxi. Her phone was turned off but placed safely in her pocket, along with some cash. As far as her parents were concerned, she was out for a long run, her sporty attire composed of a baggy sweatshirt, blue tights, and sneakers so white they could probably shine in the dark. While she conducted herself with confidence, Del was a ball of tension. Yesterday, when she'd searched online for the address Alice left her, the results had turned up a photo of an empty field. Granted, the image was from years ago, but still, Del worried Alice was sending her on some weird wild goose chase.

Del didn't feel like talking, and luckily her older gentleman of a taxi driver must've felt the same way. After confirming the directions, he just drove in silence, leaving Del alone with her thoughts.

But when the paved road transitioned into a dirt one, Del noticed the driver wrinkling his forehead in disapproval. "I'm visiting my sister," she volunteered.

"Does she have a house out here?" the man asked in a grumble.

"Not exactly. . . . It's a communal farm of sorts."

After a loaded pause, the driver asked suspiciously, "She wouldn't be one of those silent folks, would she?"

"Ah . . ." Del was about to say something in Alice's defense, but then the car stopped.

Del looked out the window. The dirt road dead-ended at a wooden gate, which was cut into a fence surrounding the place where the field should've been. The fence was high enough to conceal the space behind it from nosy onlookers. The gate carried no signage and no identifying marks, and there was no buzzer. The fence stretched far into the distance.

"This is your address, mademoiselle," the driver announced gravely.

Del paid and got out of the car, ignoring the man's concerned stare.

She waited for the taxi to leave before she knocked on the gate, focusing her attention on her feet while she waited. Her white sneakers were now covered in mud, and the bright blue of her tights seemed almost offensive in this gray-and-green landscape. She was all alone here and starting to get freaked out by the thickening shadows.

She knocked on the gate again. More silence followed. No one was coming. *I should call a taxi and get the hell out of here*, she thought.

Then the gate creaked open and a young white woman, likely in her twenties, peeked out. Del offered, "I'm looking for my sister, Alice Chauvet. My name is Del." She was about to say more but held her tongue. Would she get Alice in some kind of trouble if she told how she'd learned their location?

The woman nodded, pulled the gate open wider, and indicated with a hand movement that Del should follow her. Del pushed down her instinct to run and instead proceeded after the woman and into the compound.

The empty field Del found online when she searched for the address from Alice's note was empty no more. It had been turned into a compact settlement that was surprisingly nice-looking and modern in a micro-house, eco-living kind of way. Del followed the woman along what must've been the community's main street—it forked every forty meters or so, with smaller paths disappearing into clusters of low-sitting houses. There were people everywhere—walking or working on the vegetable patches that lined the paths. Some carried baskets with clothes; others pushed carts with boxes of produce. Del realized she was looking for signs of distress in their expressions, but they all seemed content. It took her another moment to realize what felt so wrong about this place: Aside from the subdued noises of shuffling feet and garden tools digging into soil, there were no sounds. No laughter, no whispers of conversations. Nothing.

"You're a really silent bunch, aren't you?" she asked her guide before she could think better of it.

The immediate disturbance her question caused was like the roar of thunder. The guide flinched, and a nearby group of workers paused what they were doing to stare at Del. Del focused on the ground below her feet, trying not to make eye contact with anyone.

Eventually they arrived at a house on the outskirts of the compound. Del's guide twisted the doorknob, then left the door open before walking off without a warning. Unsure of protocol, Del waited for someone to come out of the house and greet her, but she soon got anxious and went in uninvited.

Alice sat on the couch in the living room, feet folded comfortably underneath her and an open book in her hands.

For a painful moment, Del took her in. Her sister. It was like a million years had passed since she saw her last. Alice's eyes rose from her book and then her face lit up from within, lips stretched into a genuine smile.

"Delphine, baby!" Alice threw the book away and ran to Del. Nearly deafened by the sound of her sister's voice, so alien in this silent place, Del stood petrified as Alice hugged her. "You came!" Alice exclaimed, beckoning Del to the couch.

Despite having prepared and practiced her opening line that morning, Del was now lost for words. Her mouth opened and closed without a sound. Finally, she managed to say, "How could you leave?"

Alice's face fell but quickly regained its light. "Whether I left home or have actually *arrived* home depends on one's perspective, doesn't it?" She smiled cleverly.

Del wasn't amused. "Oh. Sorry, I didn't express myself clearly. How could you leave *me*?" She spat the words.

"I know you're angry, Delphine," Alice said in a pacifying way that irritated Del. "But . . ."

Suddenly Del realized she wasn't that interested in Alice's reasons after all. "You left me! And Bastian. And Mom and Dad. And for what? To join some compound full of weirdos who grow their own vegetables and walk around all silent and superior?" Del screamed the last bit, but Alice's face remained calm, unshakable. This only made Del angrier. She was about to throw more accusations at Alice when the front door opened and the same young woman who'd led her here walked in, holding two tall glasses filled with greenish liquid.

"Delphine, this is my housemate and fellow neophyte, Marcella," Alice offered.

The moment the door shut behind her, Marcella grinned in a mischievous way that contradicted her previous subdued behavior. She offered one glass to Del and the other to Alice. "It's nice to finally meet you, Delphine," Marcella said.

Del eyed the contents of the glass with distrust, making both Alice and Marcella laugh. "It's just some green stuff. Good for you," Alice assured Del as she proceeded to drain her glass. "We grow our own vegetables, as you've probably noticed. Eating from the land and avoiding the clamor of the city—it clears your mind and helps you hear what the universe is saying."

"And what is it saying?" Del took a tentative sip from her glass. It did taste like a green smoothie of sorts. Cucumber, spinach, maybe a dash of mint. It was plain but good.

Alice and Marcella exchanged an odd look, prompting

Marcella to quickly say her good-byes and disappear into one of the other rooms in the house.

Alice set her empty glass down. "We're allowed to speak inside our homes but not outside and definitely not in the temple. That's where we go to cultivate our hidden strengths."

"Your 'hidden strengths'? Like superpowers?" Del recalled reading something about the Watchers' core belief that various kinds of deprivation, including voluntary silence, would spark the development of extraordinary abilities, like levitation and telepathy.

"Something like that." Alice chuckled.

"And you're not allowed to see your family ever again? Is that part of your beliefs now?" Del questioned, her anger rising once more.

"What nonsense," Alice retorted. "No one's prohibiting me from seeing my family. You're here, aren't you? I chose to leave home because I don't want Dad interfering with my life anymore. Deciding everything for me—my career, my life, everything!"

"Oh no, poor Alice." Del rolled her eyes. "She doesn't want to go to the law school Dad was going to pay for. What a martyr."

"You know it's more than that. It's like . . . we go to *this* church, *this* is our church, we don't deviate. We're not allowed to think for ourselves. We follow orders. Dad may have retired from the military, but he's too used to ordering people around. And our family? It's all glossy on the outside, but it's suffocating as hell on the inside. Bastian knows it. That's why he moved out the moment he got a job. And you know it, too, even though you like to pretend it isn't so, pretend like you can tolerate it. But I just can't do that anymore. Besides, the

Watchers? Say what you will, Delphine, but they're the real deal. I've seen the proof of it."

"You've seen *what* exactly?" A bit confused and a lot nauseated, Del looked deeper into her sister's eyes, searching for answers.

"The proof of the prophet's power."

Del's hands turned cold. The image of the woman from the poster, her weird expression, all of it came back to haunt Del. *She must be the prophet.* "You've met her, then? This . . . prophet?"

Alice nodded, her expression filling with something like devotion. Zealotry? This must be the new Alice. The cult Alice. But what could she possibly have seen that shook her rational mind to its very core, making a believer out of her?

"So does this prophet . . ." Del stalled. "Does she live here?"

"In a way," Alice said evasively. "Come, I'll show you. On some days she manifests herself for us to see." Alice's choice of words sounded off to Del, but she didn't have enough time to think about it. Alice quickly led her outside, though not before bringing a finger to her lips, reminding Del to be silent.

It was now dark and cold, the temperature having dropped some serious degrees since Del's arrival. There were less people out now, making the compound look deserted, menacing. Del was grateful when Alice took her hand and led her toward a central building, the only three-story edifice around here. *This must be the central temple*, Del thought.

As they entered, Del braced herself. The temple felt and sounded empty, though it was hard to tell in this silent place. It smelled odd, too. Del still couldn't quite place it, but it was that same scent she'd discovered in Alice's abandoned bedroom the day before. Something sweet and rotten. Tense and jumpy, Del followed Alice into an inner sanctum of sorts, a small room behind a raised podium. The sanctum's walls were lined with mirrors, making endless corridors and countless reproductions of Del and Alice, still holding hands.

Alice grabbed a couple of flat pillows from just outside the room and threw them on the ground. Del followed her sister's example and crouched on the floor, eventually lowering herself into a seated position on the pillow, her movements lacking Alice's practiced grace. Del wanted to ask her sister what the point of it all was, what she hoped to achieve by bringing Del here, why she was trying to make it look like there was actually something paranormal at the core of this temple. But instead Del just sat quietly and mimicked what Alice was doing: staring at her own reflection and trying to blink as little as possible.

Some time passed, and Del found herself growing sleepy. Despite her mind's tension, her body relaxed. This little room she occupied with Alice was warm and cozy, and while she knew how bizarre and illogical her actions were, Del couldn't help curling up on the floor and resting her head on the pillow.

She must've dozed off for a while, because when she woke up, she was alone. The mirror room was freezing, and Del could see her own breath clouding against the cold. Her skin was crawling, a nightmarish sensation.

She stood, her legs shaky. Last time she'd been this frightened was when she'd sleepwalked all the way out of her family house and onto a busy road in the middle of the night. It was years ago, back when her father was stationed in Sarawak. Del couldn't remember the act of sleepwalking itself, but the sensation that came afterward, of breaking into a cold sweat, had burned itself into her mind. She recalled sitting on the side of the road and coming to her senses as her shocked parents and a scared driver hovered over her. She'd never gotten used to the idea that there was something inside her that she had absolutely no control over, some *thing* that could take control and make her do things that endangered her life—like walking out into the traffic.

The way Del felt now, alone in this bizarre mirror room, was similar. What was she even doing here? Was she endangering herself by coming to this creepy compound in an ill-advised attempt to rescue her brainwashed sister, this familiar stranger who now maybe wished her harm? She wasn't sure. Though what she knew for sure was this: She didn't want to be here, alone in this cold room, surrounded by mirrors.

Del dashed out of the mirrored room. She was just making her way across the temple's main floor when she heard a beehive-like buzzing coming from a corner. Del turned to look and froze, eyes open in shock at the marvelous sight.

In the corner was her. The woman from the poster. *The prophet.*

But something was terribly wrong: The woman's feet were hovering about a meter off the ground. At first Del thought the woman was suspended by an invisible rope, but when she looked closer, she couldn't see one.

Del approached, her feet moving as if of their own accord. The woman's eyes were closed, but somehow Del knew she was aware of her presence.

Del's insides were on fire. Where was Alice? Why did she abandon Del in here with this . . . floating aberration? This phantasm? Close enough now to see the details of the levitating woman's face, Del noticed that she was identical to the image on the Watchers' Disciples poster. But the rest of her didn't match what Del thought of as befitting a prophet of any sort—a clerical white robe? Some flowing ankle-length dress? The woman was barefoot and dressed in a simple pair of jeans and a white T-shirt. And she was silent—except for that infernal buzzing enveloping her like an electric halo. *Otherwordly* was a perfect word to describe her.

The buzzing sound increased, coming off the floating woman's body in waves. Soon the noise was deafening, hurting Del's ears, turning her arms and legs numb. But before she could run away, Del felt weightlessness creeping up her toes, climbing higher and higher. She gasped as she lifted off the ground, being pulled up and then toward the floating woman like a piece of metal to a magnet. The inevitable attraction. Del cried out, and the sound of it seemed to disturb the buzzing. Fighting to regain sensation in her numb body, Del flailed her arms and legs in the air. Sensing Del's resistance, the floating woman's shape tensed and then . . . she opened her eyes.

"Dig deep," the woman said, the movement of her mouth lagging behind the guttural sound.

Up in the air, Del was shaking all over, her body rejecting the woman's influence. She desperately wanted to blink but didn't dare break eye contact. There were tears in her eyes, but underneath all her fright and panic there was something else—almost like wonder. Del's blood was pumping, but her traitorous mouth wanted to smile in joy. Her very essence on fire, she was torn apart by conflicting sensations. The woman's words—*dig deep*—roared in Del's head like thunder. The words meant nothing to Del and yet they felt important. *Prophetic.* The woman's body shivered and Del's mirrored the motion. Del knew that what she was seeing, feeling, witnessing was completely outside the laws of physics. It was simply impossible. And yet she could sense this tangible moment with every cell of her being. This was really happening. She was floating, too.

This *right here* was the reason her sister left home. But what about Del? Would she also want to leave her Paris life in favor of this place? To be silent so she could break the laws of reality? She wasn't sure.

Del's limbs were gradually regaining sensation. The buzzing was growing stronger. The woman wavered in the air. Del strained not to blink, but the instinct overpowered her. When her eyes reopened, the woman was gone. Del was no longer floating; her feet were firmly on the ground.

Del whimpered and ran out of the temple. She didn't stop running until she reached the compound's main gate and dashed outside. She kept expecting someone to stop her, to drag her back into the temple, into its terrifying mirror room or the corner where the otherworldly woman floated.

But there was no one around. Just Del. Alone.

She looked for her phone, but before she could turn it on a taxi appeared out of the darkness. Del sprinted for it, waving to attract the driver's attention. Maybe it was the same older man who'd driven her here. Maybe he'd decided to stick around the area because he was worried about her.

But the driver turned out to be a woman. She was in her thirties, brown-skinned, talkative, friendly, and not at all surprised to find Del out here in the middle of nowhere, alone and shivering in terror.

"Such a strange place," the woman commented when Del was safely inside the car. "I half expected it to be a prank when

I got your request for a car. I mean, all the way out here. You were lucky your reception worked at all!"

"I wasn't . . ." *the one who called*. Del allowed the words to die in her mouth. "Yeah, lucky, I guess."

The driver didn't ask her about the compound, and Del was grateful for that. She wanted her memories of what she'd experienced tonight all for herself. All the bewilderment and terror she felt—as well as that odd joy—at seeing the floating woman's face as her own body was lifting off the ground. But was it all real? Or was Del's experience in the temple just smoke and mirrors? Some clever illusion created by Alice and Marcella and other disciples?

In the end, did it matter? Each person has their own perception of reality, and if Alice threw her lot in with the disciples, then she must've believed it was no hoax. While Del was yet to be fully convinced, she knew one thing for sure: Tonight had opened her mind just a little bit more to all the strangeness in the world. And now she was eager to experience more of it, all of it. Even if it was, at times, terrifying. Even if it involved things she could not fully comprehend or explain.

Even if her own sister was now one of those things.

Don't miss Katya de Becerra's follow-up to

WHAT THE WOODS KEEP:
OASIS.

The oasis saves Alif and her friends.
But who will save them from it?